PENGUIN BOOKS

Frankie

Frankie

KEVIN LEWIS

PENGUIN BOOKS

PENGUIN BOOKS

Published by the Penguin Group
Penguin Books Ltd, 80 Strand, London WC2R ORL, England
Penguin Group (USA) Inc., 375 Hudson Street, New York, New York 10014, USA
Penguin Group (Canada), 90 Eglinton Avenue East, Suite 700, Toronto, Ontario, Canada M4P 2Y3
(a division of Pearson Penguin Canada Inc.)
Penguin Ireland, 25 St Stephen's Green, Dublin 2, Ireland
(a division of Penguin Books Ltd)
Penguin Group (Australia), 250 Camberwell Road, Camberwell, Victoria 3124, Australia
(a division of Pearson Australia Group Pty Ltd)
Penguin Books India Pvt Ltd, 11 Community Centre, Panchsheel Park, New Delhi – 110 017, India
Penguin Group (NZ), 67 Apollo Drive, Rosedale, North Shore 0632, New Zealand
(a division of Pearson New Zealand Ltd)
Penguin Books (South Africa) (Pty) Ltd, 24 Sturdee Avenue, Rosebank, Johannesburg 2196, South Africa

Penguin Books Ltd, Registered Offices: 80 Strand, London WC2R ORL, England

www.penguin.com

First published 2007
2

Set in 12.5/14.75 pt Monotype Garamond
Typeset by Rowland Phototypesetting Ltd, Bury St Edmunds, Suffolk
Printed in England by Clays Ltd, St Ives plc

ISBN: 978-0-141-02131-7

The Groovy Gang
with love
Dad

'Damaged people are dangerous. They know they can survive.'

Josephine Hart

Prologue

The bottle was less than half full. She had been rationing herself carefully – the strong, sweet alcohol would have to last her the rest of the night – but it wasn't going to be enough. Not that it really mattered. The air seemed to bite her skin, and the light dusting of snow turned to water the instant it fell on her dirty, tangled hair. She was going to need more than a few mouthfuls of booze to keep her warm during the bitter night ahead.

The snow had come early this year, but she didn't let it get to her. It was just another thing to deal with if you were going to survive on the streets of London. Her boots were sodden, her hands numb. Beside her the cars churned the snow to a mushy sludge, occasionally spattering icy water from a puddle onto the pavement, soaking the lower half of her beat-up jeans. She did her best to put this from her mind as she walked purposefully down the street.

It had been a bad day. She had woken up in a shop doorway in Conduit Street, just off Regent Street, to the sound of somebody urinating not two metres away, and that was just the start. Everybody had been too cold and busy hurrying to get off the streets to pay any attention to a down-and-out nineteen-year-old woman begging for loose change outside Starbucks. Normally it was a good spot – Hamleys toy shop was just across the road, packed with excited children and shoppers preparing early for Christmas. Normally she could rely on parents wanting to instil a charitable nature in their kids by giving them a few coins to drop into the empty polystyrene coffee cup of the bedraggled homeless girl, but today it was too cold even for that. Her cup practically empty, she had just stared at the festive display in the window across the road and thought of a happier time: her father had taken her there once, promising her that she could have one toy, whatever she wanted. But it seemed like a lifetime ago.

Those thoughts had been wiped from her mind when she had been forced to move on by the shop manager. Where now? The usual Christian volunteers with their charitable handouts were nowhere to be seen because of the snow; but for the soup kitchens it was their busiest time. They meant that people like her didn't have to spend the few precious coins they had earned that day on food. But now the kitchens were closed for the night, and the hostels were full, just as she knew they would be in weather like this. They were the last place on earth she wanted to be, in any case. She still needed to find somewhere with a little warmth, though, somewhere she wouldn't be moved on every hour by the police who, she thought, had nothing better to do with their time. Shivering, she hurried on.

To her left, a derelict warehouse rose towards the sky, its brown Victorian bricks and broken windows protected by a criss-crossed wire fence; ahead of her, she knew the concrete monolith of the Elephant and Castle would still be bustling with life. But her destination was neither of these places – she was heading for a small park nestled between the two that ordinary people seldom set foot in, especially after dark. And with good reason. For the homeless unfortunates who congregated there it offered comfort of a sort, companionship even. But anyone entering into this circle did so on its terms, and those terms were fierce. After all, these people had nothing to lose.

She pushed open the iron gate and took in the scene. Half a dozen fires smouldered in bins, flames occasionally licking above the rims. They had been placed under trees, in an attempt to protect them from the snow; but the trees were bare anyway, so they did nothing to stop the silent flakes drifting in. Around each bin were small groups of ragged-looking souls, their bodies silhouetted against the flames, their faces half illuminated by the meagre light of the fires. Some of them sat hunched on old crates, others leaned against the trunks of trees, and a few just sat on the ground.

Other groups of down-and-outs huddled together away from the bins. Clearly they had not been part of this community long enough to earn themselves a coveted place by a fire. It was an unspoken rule, and they knew better than to approach without being asked. This was a vulnerable community, full of drug addicts, alcoholics and the mentally ill – frowned upon by society as the lowest of the low. But like any other community it had its ranks and power struggles. The strongest overruled the young, the weak and the elderly, and it paid to know your place.

As she walked further into the park, she could see a crowd gathering on the other side. From this distance she couldn't tell what was going on, but it was most probably just another drunken fight. Nothing unusual. Not here.

'You got anything for me, love?'

The woman turned in surprise. She hadn't seen the gnarled figure of an old man approach her from the darkness. He had a threadbare blanket wrapped around his shoulders, and wore an old woolly hat that could have been any colour once upon a time, but was now grey. His face was grizzled and lined, his eyes pale and watery. He eyed the bottle of Thunderbird in the woman's hand meaningfully. 'It's been a slow day,' he continued, before abandoning his attempts at subtlety. 'Just a couple of pulls, love. It's a cold night.'

She looked at him for a moment. He was a pitiful sight. She took one last swig, then handed him the bottle. 'Take it, old man,' she told him, her voice emotionless. He greedily snatched it, fumbled at the cap, put the bottle to his lips and drank deeply, stopping only to cough wretchedly. With difficulty he replaced the top and secreted the bottle under his blanket. There was no word of thanks.

'What's happening over there?' She nodded in the direction of the disturbance.

The old man sniffed. 'Bob Strut. Looking for new girls.'

Her eyes narrowed.

'Stay out of it, love,' the old man advised. 'At least they get a bit of money.'

She barely acknowledged him – her gaze was fixed on the scene ahead of her. The old man shrugged as he shuffled off towards one of the fires.

She'd heard of Strut, of course. They all had. And so far she had managed to ignore him, as she knew she must. He was the worst kind of scum. Strut liked it when new faces arrived in these miserable communities. Where other people saw just another wasted life, he saw an opportunity. He had a special knack for finding people's weaknesses, and he would supply them with small quantities of whatever substance – drugs usually, or sometimes alcohol – they needed to bring themselves a little piece of oblivion; but he always expected something in return. The younger men and women were more able, and would sometimes be forced to carry out acts of petty theft or drug running. But Strut was mainly interested in them because they offered a more lucrative commodity: their bodies. Pimping was his trade, abusing the fear and vulnerability of both boys and girls, and he would take the lion's share of any money they earned on the streets. And the pittance that was left to them normally went his way too – the small packets of chemicals or bottles of spirits he sold would become more important to his employees than what shred of dignity they had before he entered their lives.

The noise was becoming louder now as the crowd grew bigger and bigger. Not the old-timers – they knew better than to get involved, and Strut had no interest in them anyway. They were too elderly or too weak to be of use to him. But gradually the younger ones, high on whatever substances they could get their hands on – crack if they could afford it; more likely stolen glue – were gathering round like a pack of hyenas, jeering and screaming at the sight in front of them. They had no reason to avoid Strut. He already had them in his pocket.

As she made her way through the crowd, she saw Strut standing there in a heavy overcoat, his bald head uncovered. He was a tall, strong-looking man with two unkempt henchmen, one on either side. At his feet a girl was crouched on the ground, a look of horror in her eyes.

She knew that girl. She had met her somewhere before.

It couldn't have been more than two weeks ago. She had been walking across Westminster Bridge when she had come across the pitiful sight of a young girl staring over the side, a vacant look in her eyes. She had stopped alongside her. 'You're not thinking of doing anything stupid, are you?'

The girl didn't reply, so she tried again. 'What's your name?'

The girl hesitated before stuttering, 'M-Mary.'

'Why don't you go home, Mary?'

'I can't.' Mary answered forcefully and turned to look at her. Her face was dirty, but the grime could not hide the fact that she was young. Barely a teenager. 'I can't,' she repeated, more quietly this time, her eyes welling up.

She understood. God knows she understood better than most. 'When did you last have anything to eat?' Mary shrugged her shoulders as she turned back to look down at the fast-flowing current of the river. It was clear what she was thinking: with one jump the Thames would take her away and all her problems would be solved. 'Do you know where the soup kitchens are?'

The young girl slowly shook her head.

'Come on. I'll show you. There's no point staying hungry, and it's that or the bins.' She took Mary by the arm and marched her away. The last time she had seen her, Mary was hungrily sipping at hot soup from a polystyrene cup. It had been all she could do for her, really . . .

Tonight she looked different. Two weeks on the streets had changed her almost beyond recognition. You could tell she was young but she had lost that clear, fresh look in her face that had revealed she was a newcomer to the streets. Now she was dirtier, her face leaner and hungrier.

Around her lips and chin were the red pimples that told of a body that was undernourished and underwashed, and there was a soreness around her nose that suggested she too had been tempted by the sickly high of cheap glue.

One of the teenage boys who had congregated around the scene shouted out an obscenity, his voice high-pitched and wired. A few others laughed, and Mary turned to look at them in panic. Strut just ignored them.

'One of this lot gave you a toke on her pipe last night.' His voice was hoarse, his accent south London. 'And you haven't even thanked me.' He leaned over to meet her face to face and almost whispered, 'I've had my eye on you for a few days.'

Mary stared at him with fear in her wide-open eyes. She didn't reply.

'Better than a tube of glue, darling, and lots more where that came from. But you *are* going to come with me. I've got plenty of gentlemen clients who'll fall for *your* charms . . .'

Mary shook her head. Her body was shivering, but not from the cold. Strut breathed out heavily, impatiently. Then, with a deft movement, he put his hand in his coat pocket and removed a large flick knife. With one click, the point of the five-inch blade was resting gently on the underside of her chin. Mary gasped. 'Get on your fucking feet,' he told her in a voice that wouldn't be argued with, 'and stop pissing me about. I haven't got all night.'

Slowly she stood up, the cold blade resting on her skin as she did so. 'Good girl,' Strut muttered, his voice less menacing now, but only just. He closed the knife, put it back in his pocket and grabbed hold of her arm. 'Come on.'

Just as he was about to turn, Mary pulled away and

ran. It was a hopeless attempt, but the anger in Strut's eyes was violent nevertheless. 'Get her,' he barked at his heavies.

It didn't take long for them to catch her. She couldn't get out of the human circle that surrounded them.

As one of them grabbed her shoulder, she fell on the hard path. Her face scraped along the concrete, but she didn't have time to put her hand to her cheek and feel the wetness of the graze before her hair was grabbed once more and she was pulled, struggling, back towards Bob Strut.

The two men each held one of her arms. 'Get off me!' she screamed through her tears. 'Let me go.' But they had no intention of doing that. Strut walked up to her, his face emotionless. He stood there for what seemed like ever to Mary, and gradually she stopped struggling, exhausted and aware that it was useless.

It was not until her screams became drawn-out whimpers that he hit her. The back of his hand suddenly lashed out and thumped the side of her face that was bleeding from the fall. He looked with distaste at the blood smeared on his hand, before wiping it on the unwounded side of Mary's face. Again, he removed his flick knife from his pocket.

Mary was too scared to cry out. As Strut pointed the knife towards her she could do little more than gasp for breath, until she found the words she was trying to say. 'Please,' she wept, 'please leave me alone. Please. I want to go home to my mum.'

Her wide eyes watched the blade as Strut slowly moved it towards her, relishing her fear before he inflicted his violence on her.

'I just want my mum . . .' Her voice was quieter now, almost as if she was talking to herself.

'Well, she doesn't want you, you little fucking bitch,' Strut whispered.

Nobody else spoke. Even the group of teenage junkies had fallen silent at the violence of the scene, and the noise of the traffic on the main road seemed to fade into the background.

And then the silence was broken.

The woman couldn't watch this any longer. 'Leave her alone!' Her voice cracked as she spoke, so she repeated herself, more firmly this time but still with a faint tremor. 'Leave her alone!'

Strut's knife stopped just millimetres from Mary's face.

'She's fourteen years old,' the woman insisted. 'Just leave her alone.'

Bob Strut turned round to see who dared talk to him like this, but her features were half obscured in the dim light. As she stepped forward, however, he saw that she had long, matted hair that had once been blonde, tied back into a ponytail that was frizzy with knots. She had black jeans, ripped in places, neatly patched in others, but filthy nevertheless, and she wore a beaten-up woollen coat that was done up to the top to protect her from the cold. Her face was thin, but her piercing blue eyes were bright and alert, and she held her chin high – everything about her body language spoke of a woman doing her best to hide her fear.

'Who the fuck are you?' Strut gestured at his men to let Mary go. They threw her down and stood flanking him on either side.

The woman didn't answer.

He strode towards the woman, raising his knife hand as he did so in preparation to swipe it across her cheek; she covered her face in defence and the knife cut deeply across her palm. She gasped sharply as the pain shrieked through her body, then looked at her hand to see the blood seeping down to her wrist. Strut stood in front of her, breathing heavily. After a few seconds he put his knife in his other hand and whipped her across the face with his fist, knocking her to the ground.

Then he turned his attention back to Mary. She was frozen with horror at the scene that had unfolded before her. Strut stormed up to her and began kicking her hard in the stomach. She curled into a little ball, screaming with every kick. All of a sudden he stopped as the beam of a car's headlights swept over them all. He turned as the man who had been waiting patiently in a quiet street leading off the park drove away – scared, no doubt, that the commotion might attract the police, and unwilling in any case to pay for damaged goods. Strut swore under his breath: he'd lost his punter.

'Keep an eye out for Old Bill,' he muttered to his sidekicks. 'There's going to be a tear-up.'

'What d'you mean?' one of them asked, a bit nervously. They knew what he was capable of doing to the young girl.

'I mean, I'm going to see to these two bitches.' His voice was impatient, and the men took their cue, striding purposefully away to take up their lookout positions. Strut sniffed hard, his face determined and his upper lip displaying the ghost of a sneer. He moved his knife back into his right hand.

The woman was lying in pain, knowing that she and Mary couldn't get out of this without serious damage to themselves. Suddenly she caught a glimpse of the old man she had given the bottle of Thunderbird to earlier, standing at the front of the crowd. Their eyes met as he bent down and rolled the nearly empty bottle towards her. She clasped it firmly in her hand then struggled to her feet as Strut leaned over the terrified Mary. One of his guys called out, but it was too late: she smashed the bottle over Strut's head with all the energy she could muster, leaving the jagged glass neck in her hand. Strut fell to his knees in a daze, a horrifying mixture of alcohol and blood rushing down his face. The crowd had started up again, but it sounded as though their fickle allegiance had changed sides: Strut's men looked nervous as the crowd started to turn against them, and they edged away.

Dizzy, but spurred on by blind rage, Strut managed to jump to his feet. His face was like a wild animal's, even more terrifying for the streaks of red that dripped down from his forehead. The woman took a nervous step backwards. She had not expected him to stand up.

And now Strut was bearing down on her like a man possessed.

It happened in a split second. She didn't even give it any thought – she just knew she had to defend herself. As Strut lurched at her and raised his knife arm to attack, she struck out blindly with the stump of the bottle. It sliced through the skin of his neck like a knife through jelly, before becoming wedged in the tough knot of his Adam's apple. Strut froze, more out of shock than pain, but as the blood started to flow profusely he fell once more to his knees. The bottle was stuck deep in his neck – the woman had let go once she had realized what she had done.

Strut made a pitiful gurgling sound as the upper part of his body slumped heavily to the ground, his life oozing rapidly from him. The bottle neck quivered in time with his faltering heartbeat.

The woman stood above him, looking down aghast at what she had done. A few metres away, Mary was being comforted by two older women. They put their arms round her and made reassuring sounds, but she hardly seemed to know they were there. Her crying had stopped, replaced by short, sharp breaths as she hyperventilated with shock. Her eyes were darting everywhere, but always seemed to return to the body lying in front of her. She looked as if she was trying to say something, but the words would not come.

'Jesus, Frankie,' she managed finally, her voice a panicked, high-pitched whisper. 'What have you done?'

PART ONE

Chapter One

The same night, a mile or two away

Rosemary Gibson strode down the corridor clutching an armful of heavy files. 'Look confident,' Carter had told her, 'and nobody will suspect what you're doing. Trust me – these things only go wrong when people show how nervous they are.'

Easy for him to say, she thought as she turned the corner. Her heart was racing, and it was all she could do to stop herself from looking over her shoulder every few seconds to see if anyone was following her. There was no particular reason why she shouldn't be here – that's what made her perfect for the job – and she had her story all worked out in case she was asked what she was doing. God knows how she would react if she was actually questioned, though. Rosemary was the last person you'd expect to be doing this, but Carter thought that was her best asset.

'You've worked there for so long,' he'd told her. 'You're part of the furniture.' He was right. She had worked at Lenham, Borwick and Hargreaves, a merchant bank in Belgravia, longer than almost anyone.

'But I never normally stay as late as that.'

'Then put in a few late nights for a couple of weeks beforehand. There'll be plenty of other people working, won't there?'

'Well, yes, I suppose so. They have to be in contact with offices around the world, you see . . .'

'So there you are.'

'It's just . . .'

'What?'

'It's just that I'm not very good at this sort of thing.'

Carter had sighed with impatience. 'We've already gone through this. If you don't want to do it, just say.'

'No,' Rosemary had replied just a little too sharply. 'No. I'll do it. It'll be OK.'

She had started something and was determined not to pull out of it now.

Finally she arrived at the door she had been heading for. A shiny brass plaque bore the name 'Morgan Tunney'. The door would be locked, of course, but that wasn't a problem. For the past few evenings she had been asking the night-time receptionist for a key so that she could leave confidential financial documents on Tunney's desk. She was a senior member of the accounts team, so it was reasonable enough that she should do this, and the documents she had been delivering contained information that Tunney definitely wanted to see. As far as the receptionist was concerned, tonight was no different to any other.

She quickly unlocked the door, stepped inside, then locked it behind her, too scared to switch the light on for fear of it drawing attention to what she was doing.

It took only a few seconds for Rosemary's eyes to adjust to the lights of London illuminating the room enough for her to see her way around. Morgan Tunney's office was richly furnished, as befitted his status as chairman. The couches were made of leather, and the huge oak table was home only to a laptop computer, a lamp, a virgin blotting pad, a picture of his grandchildren in a silver frame, and a gold pen. Like almost everything else in the office, the pen was there just for show; whenever he signed anything, he used the fat Cartier that he always kept inside his jacket pocket. There were several oil paintings on the wall, behind one of which was a safe with a numeric touch pad. But Rosemary knew for a fact that it was empty: Morgan Tunney was not the sort of man to leave precious or sensitive material lying around.

The office had one of the finest views in London. The floor-to-ceiling windows looked out from the fifteenth floor over the grand buildings of Belgravia, and anyone standing there might well feel like the lord of all they surveyed. Under other circumstances, Rosemary would be captivated by the scene – it was a far cry from the view she enjoyed from her own desk, or from the little terraced house in an unfashionable part of north London that was her home. But tonight she hardly glanced out of the window. All her attention was focused on the laptop in front of her.

She put the files down on the desk. Standing in front of the computer, she removed a small silver locket hanging inside her blouse from a delicate chain round her neck. She lifted her necklace over her head, wincing slightly as the chain caught in the hair that was gathered severely into a bun. She held the locket up to her eyes and squinted at it over the top of her half-moon glasses. The letters 'RG' were engraved in immaculate copperplate, and on the side was a small clasp. She pushed it with her thumb and held it in for three seconds, just as she had practised so many times at home. The interface of a small USB storage device clicked out of the top.

Rosemary took a deep breath and mentally went through the instructions Carter had given her. 'Plug the locket into the computer *before* you turn it on, otherwise the patch won't work.' She picked up the locket and gently tried a couple of the ports at the back of the laptop before she found one that would accept it. She closed her eyes, took another deep breath, opened the computer and switched it on.

Immediately the office was bathed in the familiar blue light, and she quickly tilted the screen downwards slightly in an attempt to dull its glare. As she did so, she noticed the white light from the corridor leaking in underneath the office door, and the telltale shadow of a pair of feet standing in front of it.

She held her breath. The whirring of the computer's hard drive as it cranked itself up seemed impossibly loud; surely whoever was outside would be able to hear it.

Then, to her horror, the laptop beeped.

Even if she had wanted to, Rosemary would not have been able to move a muscle. Her eyes were glued to the bottom of that door, and the shadow that stubbornly refused to move. Suddenly, though, it disappeared, and she heard the sound of footsteps walking away. She breathed out, gently but shakily.

Lifting the screen back up slightly she saw the log-on window for the company's intranet. Carter's device was clearly working, because every fifteen seconds or so a new asterisk appeared in the password box. It took a couple of minutes for the ten asterisks to appear, indicating that the password had – with any luck – been broken.

She pressed the enter key. The log-on screen flickered

away; a few seconds later her boss's desktop was displayed. She was in.

With the speed of somebody who spends her working life at a computer, she navigated to the folder she wanted. She quickly scanned her way down the files she was used to working with all day long, until she found an unfamiliar one. That was what she was after. This document did not appear on her system. To the best of her knowledge it did not appear on *anyone's* system apart from Tunney's. That was why she needed it. She copied the file onto the USB device.

It was a big file, and took a couple of minutes to download. Rosemary counted the seconds as she watched the animated yellow folder fly repeatedly across the screen. Her palms were clammy and her blouse moist with nervous sweat – it seemed to take for ever, and all she wanted to do was get out of there. The instant the operation was completed, she shut down the computer, waiting, as she had been instructed, for the screen to go black before she removed the locket. She pushed the USB device back inside the locket with a click, and replaced the necklace over her head, before picking up her folders and taking a moment to compose herself. She moved to the door and stood there for a few tense seconds, carefully listening for footsteps outside.

When she was sure there were none, she slipped out and locked the door again. She marched quickly back down the corridor, eager to put as much distance between her and Tunney's office as possible.

Rosemary couldn't quite believe what she had just done. How had she got herself into such a dangerous position? What if she was discovered? She couldn't deny a vague feeling of excitement now that she'd done what she came to do, but she knew it wasn't over yet. All sorts of confused thoughts were firing through her head when she turned the corner and almost walked into a tall, uniformed security guard. In her surprise she dropped the folders, and papers spilled everywhere. 'Oh!' she cried, as she knelt down in a fluster to start picking them up. 'Oh dear!'

The security guard bent down to help her. 'You're working late, Mrs, er . . .' He glanced at the identity badge clipped to Rosemary's jacket. 'Mrs Gibson.'

'*Miss* Gibson,' Rosemary replied automatically. 'Yes, it is rather late, isn't it . . . delivering paperwork . . . lots to do . . .' The words were not coming out as she had practised them. She scrabbled around, stuffed the final pieces of paper inside one of the folders and the two of them stood up.

For the first time Rosemary looked at the security guard's slicked-back hair and immaculately groomed goatee beard. It wasn't the person she had expected to see. 'Where's Ray?' she asked, doing her best to take control of the situation.

'Haven't you heard?' the guard replied in his thick East End accent. 'Sick leave. Could be permanent.'

'I didn't know he was ill.' Rosemary was shocked. Ray always had a bit of banter with her as she left the office of an evening. Surely he'd have told her if something was wrong.

'Nor did he. Come on very sudden. Makes you think, doesn't it?'

'Yes,' she replied. 'Yes, it does.' Rosemary stood in silence for as long as she thought was respectful. 'Right.

Goodnight, then. Time for me to go home.' She side-stepped the guard who was still standing in front of her.

'G'night, *Miss* Gibson,' he replied without a smile.

Rosemary continued down the corridor to the lift. Once she had pressed the button, she looked nervously over her shoulder.

The security guard was still there, looking straight at her. Their eyes met for a few uncomfortable seconds. Then he turned and walked round the corner, out of sight.

Frankie wasn't afraid to do what it took to look after herself, but it had never gone this far. There was no point checking to see if Bob Strut was dead – nobody bled as much as that and lived; the main thing now was to get the hell away. Her hand was bleeding badly from the cut of Strut's knife; but more importantly the police could be on the scene any minute. They wouldn't care less that the world was a better place with Strut six feet under – if they could charge her for the killing and get one more vagrant off the street, it would be a result for them.

Behind her was chaos. Strut's cronies had fled the moment they realized what was happening, and most of the remaining down-and-outs were in a state of confusion: nobody wanted to be anywhere near the dead body, to be associated with it in any way, and yet they had no place to go. They held urgent conversations with frightened looks on their faces. In a far corner of the park, a few of the younger ones were more boisterous – happy Strut was gone, but too high to understand the seriousness of what was happening. Mary was still being comforted by the two older women as Frankie hurried up to her and crouched down. She didn't have time to console her, but she knew from the one conversation she'd had with the teenager since she arrived here that a softly-softly approach was called for. She gently put her arm around the young girl. 'Mary,' she whispered hoarsely.

The girl just carried on sobbing.

'Mary,' she said more firmly, 'you *have* to listen to me.'

Mary turned her reddened eyes towards her.

'When the police arrive, you've got to let them take you away.'

Mary shook her head in disbelief. 'They'll think it was me –' she started to say.

'No, they won't,' Frankie interrupted her. 'Everyone's seen what happened. Trust me, Mary. This guy has friends. When they find out what happened here, they'll be back. The safest place you can be is a police cell, and when they let you out, you must never come back here. If you can't go home, move to a different part of the country. And whatever you do, don't tell the police anything about me. Do you understand?'

Mary just looked at her blankly, and Frankie couldn't tell if she had taken in a word she had said. But she couldn't stick around. She gave the girl a weak smile, then she turned and left, knowing that she would never see Mary again.

As she made her way down the street along the side of the park, she walked as calmly as she could, not wanting to attract attention to herself. But she felt her pace quickening almost involuntarily as her body screamed at her to get away from that place. Soon she was running. As she hurried, her mind was working overtime. What the hell had come over her? Scumbags like Strut weren't worth the time of day, and now she had risked everything on his account. It wasn't even as if he had his eye on her – she was too streetwise to allow guys like him anywhere near her. But she'd seen too much of herself in little Mary to allow anybody to take advantage of her. It was a reflex action, a coil deep inside her that had finally snapped. Frankie couldn't change the past, but maybe if she could stop it happening again . . .

'It was him or me,' she muttered, trying to convince herself as she ran. She needed to get to the other side of the river, as far away from the scene as she could, so she headed towards Vauxhall Bridge. Her breath steamed in the cold air, and her hand throbbed with pain – she kept her fist clenched to stem the bleeding. But as soon as she stood on the bridge, she saw the heart-stopping sight of blue police lights coming from the north side. She had been on the streets long enough to know to avoid those flashing lights, and tonight she had more reason than usual.

She turned and headed away from the bridge and into the streets of south London. She knew them like the back of her hand. God knows she'd walked them often enough.

There was no knowing what Mary – or any of the others – would say about her to the police. They wouldn't go out of their way to shop her, but their first loyalty was always going to be to themselves. Suddenly Frankie realized that in her eagerness to leave the scene she had forgotten that her prints would be firmly on the bottle that killed Strut. She had been arrested enough times for her fingerprints and mugshot to be on file, but she knew she couldn't go back to collect the bottle. She needed to disguise herself, and get out of town as quickly as possible.

To do that, she needed money. And fast.

Still running, Frankie turned a corner and headed west. She kept a lookout for a shop that would be easy to break into, but most of them had metal shutters fastened tightly over their windows, and in any case she doubted their tills would be full. Had she been in a richer area, she might have taken the risk of breaking into a couple of expensive-looking cars and rooting around for the small change the owners often kept in the front for parking – that little trick had seen her out of more than one hungry evening before now. But she needed Mercedes and BMWs to earn her money that way, not the clapped-out rust-buckets parked up round here.

After thirty minutes of half-walking, half-running, she figured she was far enough away to think about crossing the river. She took a right-hand turn and started weaving her way up towards Chelsea Bridge.

It started to snow again as the lights of the bridge came into view, but she wasn't cold: the running, spurred on by the adrenaline pumping through her body, had taken care of that. The imposing towers of Battersea Power Station were lost in the flurries of snowflakes. It was pretty, but Frankie did not have time to take in the scenery. She knew that she was going to have to be driven to another act of desperation tonight if she was going to disappear. She didn't want to do it, but she couldn't think of any other way.

She ducked into a dimly lit side street and stopped to catch her breath in the arches that ran under the railway line. Her hand was still bleeding, and she knew she needed the use of it for what she had in mind. There was no way she could risk going to a hospital to get a clean bandage, so she took off her overcoat, ripped a strip of material from one of the two dirty T-shirts she was wearing, then tied it tightly around her hand. It still hurt, but at least she could use it.

As she was pulling her coat back on, she saw two police officers in their bright yellow jackets walking past the end of the street. She pressed her back against the wall of the arch and waited for them to pass. The fight had been forty-five minutes ago, and in a different part of the city, but she couldn't take any chances. The police might already have a description, in which case they would all be keeping a lookout for her. She silently gave thanks that the clothes she was wearing – the only ones she had – were black.

Frankie stayed hidden for a couple of minutes after the police officers had passed before gingerly walking back out to the main road. Chelsea Bridge was illuminated in front of her, but the snow was falling more heavily now and she couldn't see the other side. She stood watching as people occasionally appeared like ghosts out of the blizzard – couples, mostly, on their way home from an evening out, huddled together as they walked to protect themselves from the elements.

She let them pass. There was no way she could take on two people. Not in her state. Come to think of it, she didn't know if she could take on a single person – she had never done this before.

A thin layer of snow had settled on her clothes before a suitable candidate appeared. She could just make her out, standing on her own halfway across the bridge. She was not well dressed for the weather: a sensible jacket and skirt, with just a checked scarf to keep out the cold.

Her handbag was slung over her shoulder, and she was stamping her feet on the ground, trying to keep herself warm as she looked around as if waiting to meet someone.

Frankie strode up to her and walked past, peering through the snow to the other side of the bridge to check that nobody was coming. It was difficult to see, but the coast seemed clear. She doubled back. The woman was looking the other way, so she quietly approached her from behind and grabbed the handbag.

The woman slipped, fell with a scream and landed on her back. Her handbag was still hooked to her arm, so Frankie knelt down and tugged it hard, breaking the strap. As she pulled, the woman's scarf unfurled slightly, and Frankie noticed she was wearing a necklace. She grabbed the chain and yanked it off, pulling the scarf with it. Her victim cried in pain as the metal bit into her neck, but by that time Frankie was already standing up. She barely looked at the chunky silver locket at the end of the chain before stuffing it into the pocket of her jeans. It might be worth something to someone.

Suddenly she saw figures running towards her from the north side of the bridge. Shit, she thought. I've taken too long. Clutching the handbag and the scarf, she turned and ran. Have-a-go heroes – was there one or two? Or maybe more? She didn't know how the hell they had seen what she'd done – they hadn't been in sight when she grabbed the bag – but she didn't have time to worry about it. They were bearing down on her. She just had to get away.

Manslaughter and assault: the police would have a field day with her if she was caught.

As if summoned by that thought, she heard the familiar

sound of sirens, and looking over her shoulder she could make out the telltale blue glow somewhere on the other side of the bridge. There were two options: run across the road and scale the railings over into Battersea Park, or try to lose herself back under the arches.

It was a split-second decision. Battersea Park would be too exposed – there was nowhere to hide – and the railings were sharp; so she would have to take her chances under the arches. She ran with all her strength and turned back into the side street.

She heard footsteps running behind her. A voice shouted 'Stop!' as Frankie disappeared once more into the shadows, her eyes welling up with tears of panic.

Chapter Two

Working late wasn't something that was high on Detective Inspector Mark Taylor's agenda. Nor, for that matter, was paperwork. But it never seemed to get done during the day, so tonight was going to be a late one whether he liked it or not. He took a gulp of tea from a brightly coloured mug – a Christmas present from his daughter three years ago – then pulled a face when he realized it was stone cold. Perhaps he should go and find himself a fresh cup. Then again, maybe he should just push on through. The sooner he got all this crap out of his in-tray, the sooner he could get home and have a proper drink. The one good thing was that people left him alone at this hour – they knew they were likely to get their heads bitten off if they didn't.

Suddenly there was a knock and the duty sergeant stuck his head round the door. 'Sorry to disturb, sir.'

'What is it? I'm leaving in ten minutes.'

'Incident in Newington Park, sir. Looks like a fatality.'

Taylor sighed. That was the rest of his evening mapped out. He stood up and grabbed his coat from the back of his chair. 'What sort of incident?'

'A fight of some sort, sir. None of the witnesses are being very forthcoming.'

'I bet they're not.' Mark Taylor knew Newington Park well. It was a hang-out for the dregs of society, a place they went when they had been moved on from everywhere else. He'd lost count of the number of times he had suggested to his boss that they crack down and clean the place up, but the DCI had other plans. 'Much better to have them all in one place, where we can keep an eye on them' was his constant refrain, though Taylor suspected there was more to his line than that. Moving these people on was a nasty business, but after twenty years in the force Taylor knew there was no room in the job for bleeding hearts, and these homeless scumbags were his pet hate. 'I'll be down in a minute,' he said without much enthusiasm. 'After I've called the wife.'

He didn't speak to the constable who drove him to the scene; he just stared out of the window at the incessant snow until the car pulled up at the park. Already there were three police cars and an ambulance, their flashing lights silently illuminating the bare trees and the confused down-and-outs. A handful of officers were talking to the few people that had remained in the park, the lapels of their coats pulled up against the elements, notebooks in their hands. Slightly apart, two female officers were comforting a weeping girl.

Taylor slammed the door of the unmarked police car and strode through the park, making a beeline for the cordoned-off area where the body was still lying. The forensics team was already on the scene – four of them in white boiler suits inspecting the body, taking pictures and collecting evidence. They seemed to be interested in everything – cigarette butts that might hold a DNA clue, empty cans that carried incriminating fingerprints, footprints surrounding the body and, of course, the broken glass. Taylor recognized Dr Michael Simms, who was crouched over the body removing hair strands. He walked up to the body and took a closer look. He knew the victim immediately. It was a gruesome sight, but his face didn't flicker. Twenty years in the Met and he'd seen worse.

'Any idea who it is?' Simms asked him, still working on the body.

'Yeah,' Taylor replied casually. 'Bob Strut. Dealer, pimp, general lowlife.'

'Well, he met his match tonight.' Simms stood up to face Taylor. 'You can see that the bottle pierced the jugular here.' Both men looked at the broken bottle embedded deep in Strut's neck. 'I'd say he was smashed over the head with the bottle from behind, then had his throat cut. All fairly obvious.'

'OK, Michael. Thanks.' It was always reassuring to have Simms along – he'd been a forensic pathologist for as long as anyone could remember, and was well known for his ability to unravel the most complex crime scenes. By the look of things, this wasn't one of them.

A young sergeant approached as Taylor was taking in the scene. 'What have you got, Steve?' the DI asked him.

The sergeant shook his head. 'Not much, I'm afraid, sir. No one will give us a name. They definitely know, but I think they're just too scared to say.'

'Too scared to spend time talking to Old Bill, more like,' Taylor replied, scarcely masking the contempt in his voice. 'Don't waste your time with them. I know who he is.'

The sergeant looked at him quizzically.

'Bob Strut,' Taylor explained. 'He's been working this patch for years, on and off. Nasty fucker. Make sure his file's on my desk first thing in the morning, will you?'

'Yes, sir.' The sergeant pointed at the weeping girl being

comforted by the two women police officers. 'Looks like she was involved in some way.'

'Did she do it?'

'I don't think so, sir. She's not making much sense, but from what we can work out it seems he was giving her a hard time and someone stepped in.'

'Either brave or stupid,' Taylor muttered.

'One more thing you should know, sir.'

'What?'

'I can't be sure, but looking at her I'd say she was definitely under age.'

Taylor sighed. 'How old?'

'Thirteen. Maybe fourteen. Certainly no older.'

That was all he needed. A dead pimp and a witness who was not only as unreliable as they came, but also a minor. 'OK. You'd better call social services.'

'I've already done that, sir. They can't get anyone out until the morning.'

'Then get someone to take her to hospital, and have an officer put outside her room – I don't want her disappearing.' He gestured vaguely at the few remaining vagrants in the park. 'And take as many statements from this shower as you can. I want them on my desk first thing.'

'Yes, sir.'

'Good. Now if you lot can manage without me, I'm going home.'

Sean Carter stood on the cobbled street and looked left and right. 'For fuck's sake,' he chastised himself. He'd had her in his sights all the way from the bridge, but as soon as he had turned the corner at the far end of the side street, she had disappeared. All he could see was a long parade of dark, steel arches that supported the railway line. She could be under any – or none – of them.

Suddenly he thought he heard the sound of running footsteps, but the acoustics of the echoing arches meant that there was no way for him to tell which way they came from. And then a train rumbled past, drowning out the sound. He cursed himself for coming out alone – all his instincts had been to bring someone with him, but there really hadn't been anyone he could rely on. And in any case he hadn't expected this to happen. There was nothing for it. He could spend hours looking for her here, and she probably knew her way around much better than he did – in fact, she was probably already long gone. He'd better get back to the bridge and check Rosemary was OK. She was more important to him right now. He turned and jogged up to the main road.

'Rosemary!' Carter called her name as he ran back onto Chelsea Bridge. She was still there, not knowing quite what to do, her normally neat hair dishevelled, the low, sensible heel of her right shoe broken off. A few by-standers had surrounded her, checking she was all right and offering what assistance they could. 'It's OK,' he told them briskly as he approached. 'She's with me.'

The bystanders looked dubiously at this out-of-breath man, casually dressed in smart jeans, brown leather jacket and new white sneakers. He hardly cut the sort of figure you would expect to be acquainted with someone as tweedy as Rosemary. 'Is he your friend?' one of them asked.

Rosemary nodded her head, her lips tight, all the while looking daggers at Carter. 'Thank you for your help . . .

very kind . . .' she stuttered, before moving towards the man, hobbling slightly because of her broken shoe. 'You said you'd be here on time,' she whispered accusingly as they walked away.

'I know,' he panted, out of breath from the chase. 'But I had to check you weren't being followed.'

'You weren't checking very hard!' she hissed. 'Couldn't you bring someone with you?'

Carter seemed to ignore her outburst. 'Are you hurt?'

'No,' she replied. 'No, I don't think so. Just shaken up.' She breathed deeply to regain her composure, but couldn't help shivering from the cold.

'Did you get the information?'

'I did, but . . .'

'What?'

Rosemary stopped and turned to look at the man. 'Whoever it was that attacked me stole my locket, Sean. I'm sorry.'

Sean Carter looked blankly at her, then closed his eyes. 'Shit,' he breathed.

'I'm so sorry, Sean.' Rosemary looked worried. 'I'm sure I wasn't followed. I did everything you told me to make sure —'

'Come on,' he interrupted her. 'Let's get out of the cold. My car's just up here.' Carter took her by the arm and marched her to the south side of the bridge, where a saloon car was parked on the road, its hazard lights blinking. Carter pressed a button on his key fob and unlocked the car. He opened the door for Rosemary before taking his place at the driving seat, doing a tight U-turn and speeding over the bridge and along the Embankment.

They hardly spoke in the car, and twenty minutes later

they were pulling into Gray's Inn Road and then down Elm Street. 'What is this place?' Rosemary asked as Carter stopped the car.

'My office,' he replied. 'We can talk here, and you can get cleaned up.'

The security guard at reception clearly recognized Carter and waved him through with a friendly smile. The two of them entered a lift, got out on the fourth floor and then walked down a long corridor. There didn't seem to be anyone about, which was unsurprising given the lateness of the hour. Carter stopped outside an unmarked door. 'This is my office. The ladies' is down there on the right,' he pointed down a corridor leading off the room, 'if you want to sort yourself out.'

'Thank you,' said Rosemary, her hand involuntarily touching her ruffled hair. 'I think I will, if you'll excuse me.' Her voice was steadier now, and its primness had returned. She began to make her way out of the room.

'Hang on a minute.' Suddenly Carter was right behind her. He put his hand on her shoulder.

'What's wrong?' Rosemary moved away. She didn't like people touching her.

'Are you sure you're not hurt? You haven't cut yourself?'

'No. I don't think so.'

'Well, there's blood on your jacket.' Rosemary looked over her shoulder and saw a dark, sticky smear that made her feel slightly nauseous. 'You'd better take it off and give it to me. I'll need to get it checked.'

Rosemary frowned, but did as she was told, then hurried down the corridor to the bathroom. She returned five minutes later, putting her head nervously round the office door. Carter was sitting upright at his desk, a look of intense confusion on his face. 'Sit down,' he told Rosemary after a few moments.

Silently she took a seat opposite him.

'I'm only going to ask you this question once, and it's very important you tell me the truth. Can you do that?'

Rosemary nodded mutely.

'Did you tell anyone – and I mean *anyone* – that you were meeting me on Chelsea Bridge?'

'No.'

'A close friend? A boyfriend?'

Rosemary blushed and looked at her feet.

'It's important, Rosemary.'

'I promise I haven't told a soul.' Her voice started wavering, and she buried her face in her hands, weeping silently as the events of the last hour caught up with her. Carter looked away. He could deal with most things the job threw at him, but he never quite knew how to handle crying women. Maybe he had been a bit harsh with her – she had, after all, gone through a lot this evening. 'I just want to go home now, please,' she sobbed.

'Come on, Rosemary,' he said awkwardly. 'Don't cry on me. I just had to ask you, that's all.'

She looked directly at him, her eyes red. 'I promise you, Sean, I haven't told anyone. How on earth did they know where to find me? I'm sure I wasn't followed.'

Carter shook his head. His instinct told him she was telling the truth. 'I don't think they did. I think it was just a random attack. That girl came at you from the south side of the river. If they'd been following you, they'd have come from the north. There's no reason to believe they're on to us.'

That had always been the biggest worry. If Rosemary had been caught copying the information he needed, then he would have been able to step in and protect her. But if her bosses had any suspicion of what she was planning to do, they'd have buried the information even deeper, and it would be impossible to get hold of it.

The two of them sat in silence for a minute. Finally Rosemary spoke. 'I'm going to have to try again, aren't I?'

Carter seemed reluctant. 'I don't know. I think it's too dangerous. I might have to find someone else.'

'There isn't anybody else,' Rosemary almost snapped. They had been working on this for months now. Carter had been the first person she had dealt with when she alerted the Serious Fraud Office to the anomalies she had noticed in the bank's accounts, and they had been working hard since then to try and find out what was going on. He was hardly the kind of person she would have expected to be working for the SFO – normally she'd have thought they would be more the pen-pushing type. People like her, in fact. She felt uneasy in his company, more timid than usual, but she knew she had to stand up to him now if she wanted to remain involved in this thing that she had started. She'd gone this far. There was no way she was going to let another person take her place. 'There isn't anyone else,' she repeated. 'Not that you can trust, anyhow.'

Carter did his best to keep the emotion from his face, but he knew she was right. It could take weeks to find someone else to train up, and by that time the window of opportunity might very well be closed. This wasn't the sort of thing you could easily get a second crack at. He just hoped he hadn't screwed the whole thing up. 'I'll think about it,' he told her, a bit ungraciously. 'But don't do anything for a few days.'

'Should I go in to work?'

'Christ, yes. You've got to act normally. If they suspect you of anything, they'll be on the lookout for warning signs. Just act as if nothing has happened.'

'What are you going to do?'

'Try and find the locket. I've got some friends in the Met. With a bit of luck I'll be able to track down your mugger.' He didn't look very convinced. 'What else did she take?'

'My handbag. Oh, and my scarf.'

'What was in the bag?'

'Not much. My mobile phone. And my purse. I suppose I'll have to cancel everything.'

'Not yet,' Carter told her. 'If she tries to use the phone or your credit cards, we might be able to track her.' He handed her a piece of paper. 'You'd better write down your bank details for me.'

'I haven't got any money,' Rosemary mentioned casually as she did so.

Carter took his wallet from the inside pocket of his jacket and fished out a few notes. 'That'll keep you going for now. I'll put in a requisition order for some more tomorrow and get it over to you. Come on, it's late. I'll take you home.'

The two of them stood up. 'And Rosemary,' Carter said quietly.

'Yes?'

'You did a great job. Well done.'

*

Frankie hadn't stopped running since she left the bridge, and although she had managed to shake off her pursuer, she didn't feel any safer for it. Every street seemed to present something to make her heart stop – strangers looking at her in a suspicious way, police officers walking the beat in pairs. And everything she saw was obscured by the tears that would not leave her eyes.

With her good hand she gripped the bag she had stolen, praying it contained enough cash to help her get away; she tried not to think about the pain in her bad hand. She was moving blindly, unsure where she was, but desperately trying to find somewhere that she could gather her thoughts and look through the bag. But there seemed to be people everywhere.

As she turned a corner, she saw the yellow lights and concrete tower blocks of a housing estate. Just one look showed that it was the kind of place respectable people avoided, especially at this time of night: the children's playground had been neglected; car windows were broken and their stereos ripped out. There was nobody about, but it was not just because of the cold – it was only a certain sort of person that loitered alone after dark round here.

Frankie felt right at home.

She headed for the outside staircase of one of the towers and hurtled up it, knowing from experience that there would be a hot-air vent at the top, somewhere she could take shelter for a while. Her footsteps echoed as she stamped her way up the twenty-two graffiti-filled floors, not stopping for breath until she reached the top. The lock of the door leading on to the roof had been vandalized, and the door itself was half open, swinging slightly in the wind. She climbed up the short flight of metal steps that led to the door, tentatively opened it a little further, and was relieved to see that the roof was deserted. By now, her body was screaming out to her for rest. The material she had wrapped around her hand was saturated with blood, which was dripping down her fingers, and as she collapsed on the roof she was overcome with exhaustion; she sat there for what seemed like a lifetime before she raised her weary head and looked around.

The lights of London were spread out beneath her. She could see the bridges crossing the river – they were hazy through the snow, but distinct nevertheless, and the cars that were crossing them seemed to move more slowly than they were actually travelling. Up here there was no sound other than the low hum of the hot-air vent that had melted all the snow around it. Frankie went over and sat beside it, huddling herself up into a ball.

How long she stayed like that she didn't know, but it was long enough for her shivering to subside in the warmth. Eventually she looked up again, and breathed in deeply as she tried to focus her mind on what she needed to do next. Rosemary's bag was lying beside her; her scarf was wrapped round her neck. Using her good hand she fumbled at the clasp of the bag with difficulty and fished around inside. The first thing she touched was a mobile phone. It was an old model, unfashionable, though Frankie was not to know that: in the days when she owned a mobile phone, it would have been the height of style. She put it to one side and tipped the remaining contents of the bag on to the roof. A set of keys, some loose make-up, a purse and a packet of tissues. Quickly she rifled through the purse: a ten-pound note, a few coins and a couple of credit cards. Damn it. She shut her eyes and leaned her head back against the concrete wall. This wasn't going to be enough to get her anywhere. She flicked through the purse a second time, hoping she might have missed something; but her first search had been thorough enough.

Ten quid. It would buy her food for a couple of days, but was not nearly enough to get her out of the city. Suddenly she remembered the locket that she had tugged from her victim's neck. She pulled it out of her pocket and looked at it carefully. It was silver – or silver-plated, more like. Maybe she could hawk it for a few pounds. But not tonight – there would be nowhere open, and those places always had security cameras. She was going to have to think of another way to find some money. The credit cards seemed to be her only option, but she knew she couldn't risk using them to buy anything. Aside from the fact that there was no way she could practise the signature on the back, the state she was in was bound to arouse suspicion if she tried using them. And they'd probably been cancelled anyway . . .

Frankie felt the tears welling up in her eyes again as the hopelessness of her situation became clearer by the second. She couldn't go to the hostels or the soup kitchens – she'd be spotted in minutes – and the only safe places on the street had CCTV and a police presence. A huge sob racked her body as she realized the truth: she was totally alone. More alone than she had been these past few years, when the solitude of life on the streets had been tempered by the uneasy camaraderie that existed among the homeless. It might have been a camaraderie based on self-preservation, on lying to others about your past and to yourself about your future; but it was friendship of a sort.

Now there was nothing, no one – how could it have come to this? More than anything, she wanted her dad. In her mind's eye she saw his thin, gaunt face. In Frankie's memory it was always as pale as the last time she had seen it, never the ruddy demeanour of a man in rude health, as he had been before his body had been eaten up by cancer. And as it had so many times before, their last conversation echoed in her head. 'I love you more than anything in the world, Francesca.' He had started to weep then. 'Look after your mother for me. She needs looking after.'

Frankie had been unable to speak. Her wide-open, nine-year-old eyes just looked at him.

'And look after yourself,' he had continued, before dissolving in a fit of coughing. Frankie had been led from the room kindly but firmly by a nurse. The next time she saw her father he was dead.

She had had more conversations with her father than she knew how to count since then, in her head and under cover of night. Sometimes she had been angry with him for leaving her; at other times she pleaded with him to do the impossible and help her. And somehow, without any doubt, she knew what he would want her to do at this moment: to pick up the phone and call her mum. She gazed through her tears at the mobile phone next to her. Home was just a phone call away. But gradually, involuntarily almost, she shook her head. It didn't matter what had happened: she would disobey her father today as she had done every day since she left.

There was no way Frankie was going home.

Her mind started entertaining a more elaborate scenario. Maybe she should just use the phone to call her victim and offer to return the cards and the locket for a reward of a few extra pounds.

It was madness, of course. But fear and pain had overtaken her, and she was ready to consider anything. She picked up the phone and started flicking through the numbers stored in its memory.

ASHWORTH, DIANE

CLARKE, PETER

DAD

EDISON, GEMMA

GOLD

HOME

That was it. Her home number. Frankie's finger hovered above the call button. She knew she shouldn't do this, but she couldn't think of another option.

She paused briefly when she suddenly realized what she had just read.

GOLD

A strange entry – all the others were neatly categorized names. She flicked back to it and inexpertly located the select button: 6139. A four-digit pin. She dropped the phone, picked up the purse and hurriedly pulled out the credit cards. One of them wasn't a credit card at all, just a membership card to a video store in north London. But the other two were a bank debit card and – this was what she had remembered seeing – a Visa gold card. Maybe she had inadvertently found the number for the card. What if the woman kept the number for the other card in the phone as well? She scrolled down until she finally found the word SWITCH. Sure enough, it was another pin.

Frankie stood up immediately. She turned the phone off and stuffed it into the back pocket of her jeans, then discarded everything else apart from the credit cards, money and the locket – she found it too disabling carrying the bag when her other hand was out of action. Carefully she wrapped the scarf over her head in the manner of a shawl, wincing slightly whenever she knocked the cut on her palm. It wasn't much, but at least it disguised her features for a while. Clutching the cards she turned back to the staircase and trotted down.

It took some time to find a cash machine – even on the main streets of this part of south London there was little more than yellow-fronted kebab shops and late-night off-licences, their grilles already pulled halfway down as the owners prepared to shut up shop without losing any last-minute customers. Eventually Frankie came across an all-night minimart, apparently deserted apart from a bored-looking shopkeeper and a couple of people queuing to buy cigarettes. A sign in the window shouted out CASH MACHINE HERE. Frankie took a moment to draw breath, then stepped inside.

As she entered, she felt everyone's eyes on her. The shopkeeper allowed her to walk past the counter, then gestured to a colleague who was standing in a doorway at the back of the shop. The colleague – older, slightly fatter and with a proprietorial air – followed Frankie to the red and blue stand that housed the cash machine, making no attempt to hide the fact that he was watching her every move.

Frankie tried the gold card first. It jammed as she tried to insert it into the slot, until she realized she was holding it the wrong way round. She tried again and, reading the

43

instructions on the screen carefully, she punched in the pin number she had found on the phone. The keypad beeped slowly as she completed the unfamiliar actions, holding her breath all the while. Frankie breathed out slowly and with relief when the screen asked her how much money she would like to withdraw. She looked over her shoulder briefly – the owner was still at the end of the aisle, his arms folded and his eyes directly on her – then turned back again, typed in 5 . . . 0 . . . 0 . . . ENTER, and waited.

The cash machine beeped. MAXIMUM WITHDRAWAL AMOUNT 250. Quickly Frankie tapped at the screen again: 2 . . . 5 . . . 0 . . . ENTER. The machine started to whirr, spat out the card and then delivered a thin wad of notes. She snatched them quickly and stuffed them into a pocket. She began to insert the second card into the slot. As she did so, she felt a hand grip her shoulder firmly.

She stood absolutely rigid, her arm still outstretched. 'Come on, darling, I haven't got all night,' a voice slurred behind her. She turned round to see a gruff old man. His skin was black, his stubble curly and grey, and he leered at her before coughing and then spitting out on the floor. She instantly recognized the drunkenness in his bloodshot eyes. Normally Frankie took such people in her stride, but not tonight. 'Get off me!' she shouted hysterically, pushing the old man's hand from her shoulder and raising her arm in self-defence.

'OK, you two, get out, now!' Suddenly the shop owner was upon them, pulling at Frankie's clothes as he dragged her from the store. Frankie didn't resist; the old man did. In an instant the owner had let go of her and with his colleague was restraining the drunk's flailing arms and shoving him towards the door. They hadn't forgotten she was there, though. 'Get out, now,' the owner repeated. 'If I see you in here again, I'll call the police.'

But Frankie was already running from the shop. Once on the pavement she looked left and right, her brain a mass of confusion. She ran in the direction that seemed to be more populated, slipping occasionally on the icy pavement but managing to stay on her feet, desperately looking for a taxi. After ten minutes, she spotted a black cab driving down the opposite side of the street, its yellow FOR HIRE light glowing. Frankie waved frantically at it, shouting at the top of her voice, but it drove straight past her, stopping fifty metres down the road to pick up a more well-heeled passenger. 'Bastard!' she shouted, before collapsing on a street bench and burying her head in her arms. 'Bastard,' she wept quietly to herself.

But as quickly as she collapsed, Frankie stood up. She knew she didn't have time for this. Again she looked up the street – not so far ahead she thought she could see the illuminated sign of a minicab firm. She crossed the road and walked briskly towards it. Behind the shop window advertising the firm's phone number in big, blue lettering was a small, cramped office. A fat man with a couple of days' stubble sat behind a glass pane that made him look more like a serial killer during visiting hours than a cabbie. 'I need a cab to the station,' Frankie told him urgently.

The man's radio crackled into life, and he spoke loudly into it before turning back to Frankie and eyeing her up and down. 'Which station, sweetheart?'

Frankie looked at him blankly – she hadn't given it any thought. 'Paddington,' she said, choosing the first name that came into her head.

The man tapped lazily on the window, indicating a sign. POLITE NOTICE. CUSTOMERS MAY BE ASKED TO PAY FOR THEIR JOURNEY IN ADVANCE. Frankie was past caring. 'Fine,' she told him, pulling out the money from her pocket. 'How much?'

'Thirty,' he replied gruffly, eyeing the notes she held in her hand.

Frankie counted out the money and passed it across the counter. 'I'm in a hurry,' she told him curtly. 'Where's the car?'

Chapter Three

'Why the hell didn't you call me earlier? What do you think I pay you for?'

'I tried to, but your phone was switched off.' The man spoke with a thick Eastern European accent, but his words were clear and controlled.

'Damn it! Did you get her name?'

'Rosemary Gibson.'

The man at the other end of the phone went quiet. 'I see,' he said finally. 'Was she carrying anything?'

'Just files, according to the security guard. She dropped them when she saw him. She was nervous.'

'There was nothing else?'

'No.'

'And how long was she in my office?'

'Eight minutes.'

'Longer than it would take to deliver a few files?'

'She didn't leave any files.'

'And how did she seem when he spoke to her?'

'Nervous, flustered.'

'Did she say anything?'

'She asked about Ray.'

'And what did he tell her?'

'What we discussed.'

'Did she believe him?'

'Yes.'

A frustrated sigh. 'OK. We'd all better meet. In the meantime, you know what to do.'

'Yes, Mr Tunney. I do know what to do.'

The cab driver didn't speak to Frankie. He just kept glancing at her in the rear-view mirror, suspicion etched on his face. Frankie ignored him – she could deal with suspicion as long as it didn't come from someone that could do her harm. This guy just wanted to earn his money and get her out of his cab.

The car radio was playing classical music very softly. Frankie allowed herself a few moments to close her eyes and let it wash over her, enjoying the warm fug of the car even if it was tempered by the cabbie's coldness. Music was a rare treat these days, something she loved but seldom heard – apart from the bland strains from invisible speakers in heated shopping centres. Occasionally buskers would work the same patch as her, but she tried to avoid them as they were invariably more successful at diverting the attention of generous passers-by. You always earned less if you were near a busker. The music on the radio sounded familiar, something she recalled from her child-hood, but she couldn't put a name to it. Still, it took her back to Sunday afternoons, the radio on in the kitchen as her mother efficiently went about the business of cooking the roast. Her mother. She'd be shocked to think people like Bob Strut even existed, let alone that her only daughter had just killed one of them with a broken bottle. She hated the idea of anything encroaching on her ideal village life, and would do whatever she could to keep up the pretence that all was well with the world. Her friends called it cheerful optimism, one of her most admirable qualities; but Frankie knew better. She knew more than anyone the secrets that house held, the secrets her mother kept from the world.

The car came to a halt. Frankie opened her eyes. The snow had stopped, and they were waiting at a set of traffic lights. 'How much longer?' she asked the cab driver.

He refused to look at her. 'Couple of minutes,' he grunted as the car moved off again and turned a corner.

Soon enough, Frankie saw a long line of red buses and recognized the large arches behind the Great Western Hotel – Paddington Station. 'I'll get out here,' she said quietly, and the cab driver seemed only too happy to pull over. He didn't say a word as Frankie climbed out of the car.

She knew that before she did anything else, she needed to attend to the cut on her hand, so she headed briskly to a parade of shops just ahead. She walked for five minutes before she found a late-night pharmacy. A sticker in the window indicated that there was a CCTV camera inside, but Frankie had to take the risk. Not wanting to attract attention to her hand, or the questions that would come with it, she undid some of the buttons of her coat and rested her arm inside it before opening the door. There was only one other customer in the brightly lit chemist – a man buying cold remedies for his wife – and he left quickly once his transaction was complete. Keeping her head bowed, and her body turned away from the camera she had clocked behind the counter, Frankie browsed the shelves, trying to look nonchalant but desperately searching for what she wanted.

'Can I help you?' The pharmacist was eyeing her.

'I need a bandage.'

'Behind you,' the pharmacist replied.

Frankie turned to see a selection of cream-coloured bandages sealed in see-through polythene wrappers. She grabbed a couple without really checking what size they were and walked up to place them on the small counter, keeping her head down all the time. 'I need something to clean a cut with,' she muttered.

'How bad's the cut?'

'Pretty bad,' Frankie replied unhelpfully.

The pharmacist looked meaningfully at Frankie's arm. 'Why don't you show me?' she asked, her voice softening slightly.

Frankie hesitated a moment, then pulled out her arm.

The pharmacist screwed up her face as she took a look. The makeshift bandage Frankie had created from her T-shirt was saturated with blood, which had started to clot and congeal around the edges. There were dark stains along her fingers where it had dripped and then dried to a sticky film, and her fingernails were an unpleasant mixture of grime and coagulated blood. Once the initial shock of the sight had subsided, the pharmacist looked Frankie straight in the eye. 'You really should take this to casualty,' she told her. 'St Mary's is only two minutes away. You need stitches, and probably a tetanus injection, otherwise it will just carry on bleeding and get infected.'

'I can't,' Frankie's voice started to waver. 'Please, give me whatever you can.'

The pharmacist seemed undecided, as if she was struggling to make the right decision. 'OK,' she said. 'I don't know what you're up to, but I'll help you if you promise to go to a hospital as soon as you can.'

'I promise,' Frankie replied quickly, looking nervously over her shoulder.

The pharmacist went about collecting various bottles and packets. 'You need to clean it thoroughly. Do you have a sink somewhere you can use?'

'I'll find one.'

'Mix this with warm water and soak your hand in it – it will probably hurt, but I've given you the strongest painkillers I can. Once it's clean, dry it, then stick this gauze along the cut. It should seal the skin and stop it bleeding. Then put the bandage round your hand. *Then,*' the pharmacist sounded almost like a headmistress, 'go to hospital.'

Frankie smiled for the first time in days. 'Thank you,' she said. She handed the pharmacist some money and turned to leave, but as she did so something caught her eye. She walked up to the shelf and took a small brown box, then looked around until she found a pair of long, silver nail scissors tightly packed in near-impenetrable plastic, and a small compact of foundation make-up. She took these items back to the counter and the pharmacist clocked them up on her till.

'I don't know what you need with hair dye in your state, but just look after yourself, OK?' She gave Frankie a weary smile.

Frankie nodded. Don't worry, she thought. I can always look after myself. It's looking after other people that gets you into trouble.

Mary sat on the edge of the hospital bed and stared straight at the wall. Her eyes were still red from crying, but there was a harshness to her face that made her look older than she was. It was as if the events of the evening had robbed her of whatever scraps of childhood she had managed to cling on to.

Ordinarily she might have been revolted by the laminated posters displaying symptoms of burns and skin infections, but they didn't seem to have any effect on her at all. A female doctor washed her hands carefully at a small sink, dried them on some paper towels which she dropped into a big yellow bin, then went to open the door. 'I think I'm just about done,' she told the female police officer waiting outside.

'How is she?' the officer asked.

'In shock,' the doctor replied. 'I'd like to keep her in for a couple of days.' The two women conferred in the corridor, leaving Mary to sit motionless on the bed. 'She's going to be fine,' the doctor said in a low voice, 'but she'll need some psychiatric care to deal with the trauma of what she saw tonight. I've given her a thorough examination, though. But as well as the fresh wounds on her face and body, this girl is showing signs of repeated physical abuse.'

'What sort of signs?'

'Two fingers on her right hand seem to have been broken in the past and allowed to heal without medical attention. There's what looks like a burn mark on one of her arms, and there's the remnants of severe bruising along the right-hand side of her abdomen.'

'Could that have happened tonight?' the officer suggested.

'No. The bruising is too old. I'd say that it happened a few weeks ago.'

'Can you tell what it was?'

The doctor looked meaningfully at her and shrugged her shoulders. 'She seems to have been hit with something. Or kicked. But I can't confirm that.'

The women stood in silence for a moment, their faces grim. 'They've arranged for a social worker to come and see her in the morning,' the officer said finally. 'And then she can be questioned. But I might just go in and keep her company for a bit. To reassure her that she's safe, if nothing else.'

'Good idea. I'll be back in a moment.' The doctor walked down the corridor, her clipboard hugged to her chest, and the policewoman slipped quietly back into the hospital room. Mary watched her as she walked in, before resuming her original position and staring straight at the wall. The officer pulled up a stool and sat in front of her.

'Mary.' The policewoman, who had already told her that she was called Lizzy, spoke in a low, calming voice. 'You know you're not in trouble, don't you? All we want to do is help you. Why don't you just tell us where you live?'

It was as if Mary hadn't even heard her.

Lizzy tried again. 'We can call your mum and dad and let them know where you are.'

Suddenly Mary shook her head in short, jerky movements.

'Why not? They'll want to see you, won't they?'

Mary turned to Lizzy but kept her head low while she played nervously with her hands. 'Please,' Mary whispered – the first words she had spoken since the police had arrived, 'please, don't make me go back home.'

Immediately it made sense to Lizzy. 'The doctor said

you have bruises down your side,' she said quietly. 'Did that happen at home?'

Mutely, Mary nodded her head.

'Was it your dad?'

She looked at first as though she wasn't going to answer, but then she shook her head. 'I haven't got a dad,' her voice croaked.

'Then who did this to you?'

Mary glanced around the room, as if checking that there was nobody else there.

'Who did it to you?' Lizzy repeated. 'You can tell me.'

She looked up with wide eyes at the police officer, and suddenly all the harshness of the street urchin fell from her face, leaving no more than a little girl, alone, confused and distraught.

'It was my mum,' she whispered.

Lizzy stared at her, not knowing what to say.

'Will she be in trouble?' Mary asked, before burying her head in her hands and dissolving into tears.

The big black departure boards at Paddington Station were getting emptier by the minute as the last trains of the evening left. Frankie clutched her plastic bag of pharmaceuticals and looked up at the destinations, searching for the place name that meant something to her. The concourse was busier than she would have expected at this time of night – drink-soaked office workers rushing to get the train home, mostly, and a few people with heavy suitcases heading for Heathrow. Everyone seemed to be in a hurry, but that didn't stop Frankie feeling as though she stuck out like a beggar outside Buckingham Palace. And no matter how rushed everybody seemed, they all appeared to her to find the time to stare quizzically in her direction. Or maybe that was just her imagination.

An announcement came over the tannoy. 'Ladies and gentlemen, please be aware that pickpockets operate in this area. You are advised to keep all your personal belongings close to hand at all times.' Frankie involuntarily touched the pocket that held the remains of her money, and then she smiled ruefully to herself. She knew enough pickpockets to know that she was the last sort of person who would be their target. Still, it felt strange to have cash in her pocket.

She thought about using one of the credit cards she had to buy a ticket out of London, but soon discounted that idea – she didn't know much about these things, but surely the police would be able to trace her then, and find out where she had escaped to. So instead she headed to the ticket office where she could pay with cash, and was relieved when the bored-looking man behind the counter barely gave her a second look. 'Single or return?' he asked in a monotone voice.

'Single,' Frankie replied quietly.

Her train left in fifteen minutes. She felt nervous just hanging around, so she headed over to McDonald's, one of the few places that were still open. McDonald's washrooms were where Frankie – along with almost everyone else she knew on the street – went when they wanted to maintain some level of personal hygiene. They often got kicked out – when the poorly paid staff were enthusiastic enough about their jobs to bother with them – but at least it was somewhere they could wash in relative peace. It was hardly the height of luxury, but it served its purpose. She had no intention of washing here tonight, though – that could wait for the train. For once she had a bit of money in her pocket, and could buy herself something to eat. It was surprisingly busy as people stocked up with fast food for their journeys; Frankie ordered herself a burger and a hot drink.

She wolfed down the burger in a matter of minutes – she had forgotten how hungry she was until she took the first bite – but the coffee was too hot to gulp down, so she took it with her to the waiting train. She climbed on, found seats at an empty table and flung herself down, exhausted.

As the final whistle for the train blew the electric door of the carriage hissed open and two men in suits staggered in and took the seats opposite Frankie, dumping a four-pack of beer on the table. One of them belched as he opened his can of lager and fixed her with a stare and a grin. Frankie looked out of the window, but she could not ignore the fact that this guy was doing his best to make her feel uncomfortable. 'Fancy a beer, darling?' He slurred the words lazily.

Frankie's face hardened as she avoided his gaze, so the man brushed his foot along the length of her leg as he took a swig from his can, his eyes still on her. Instantly, violently, she kicked it away. 'Don't fucking touch me,' she hissed.

The man put his beer down slowly. He seemed shocked by Frankie's vehemence and by the wild look in her eyes, but his companion was either too drunk to see the warning signs, or he didn't care. 'Calm down,' he said as if he were talking to a small child. 'He only offered you a drink, love. What's the fucking matter with you?' They sniggered to each other.

Frankie drew a slow breath as she fought off the urge to lose it with them. That's what she would have done under different circumstances – go crazy, shriek and shout, protect herself by making them avoid the mad, maybe violent, woman they'd had the misfortune to stumble upon. But she knew she couldn't make a scene, so she bottled it up, grabbed her chemist's bag and headed for the toilet, lurching slightly as the train jerked into motion.

The toilet cubicle was cramped but clean enough, apart from the usual scratched graffiti on the mirror. Frankie locked the door, then filled the sink with water. She gave herself a long, hard look in the mirror – something she didn't have the opportunity to do very often, and which she didn't like doing even when she could. She never liked what she saw. Looking down, she slowly picked away at the knot she had made on her makeshift bandage before unwrapping it as carefully as the jostling train would allow. She winced with pain as she eased the material away from her palm – the clotted blood had stuck the bandage to the wound in places, and it started to bleed as she pulled it away.

Soon enough she had treated the cut as the pharmacist had instructed her. It still hurt, of course, but somehow the pain was less persistent. She gulped down a couple of painkillers, then took the scissors out of the pharmacist's bag. It took a while to open the plastic packet – clearly she could not use her bad hand, so she ripped at the tough packaging with her teeth, pulling the scissors out with difficulty. Removing the scarf from round her head, she gingerly held her ponytail up with her bandaged hand, then cut through it just above the dirty hairband that tied it together. The rest of her hair, greasy and matted, stayed almost in shape, so she ruffled her hair forward and did her best to chop it into some sort of fringe before wrapping all the cut hair up in the scarf. She looked awful, no doubt; but at least she had started to look different to the girl the police would be looking for. Next she opened the box of hair dye and read the back of the sachet. Seconds later she was wetting her dirty hair under the tap and massaging the thick goo into it. She had twenty minutes to wait for it to do its work, so she sat on the toilet, leaned her back against the wall and closed her eyes as her body rocked gently in time with the train.

Suddenly she jumped as there was a heavy knock on the door. Shit, she thought. The place looked like an operating theatre, with bloody bandages and red stains around the metal sink. She ignored the knock, hoping it was just someone wanting to use the toilet, but then it came again. 'What?' she shouted aggressively.

'Tickets.' A muffled voice sounded on the other side of the door.

'I can't,' she replied feebly. 'I'm being sick.'

'Sorry, madam, I have to see your ticket, please.'

'Shit,' Frankie muttered under her breath. She took her ticket from her back pocket, opened the door a couple of centimetres and squeezed it through. The ticket collector took it, punched it, then handed it back. 'You all right, love?' he asked.

'Just travel sick,' Frankie answered, not entirely untruthfully, before slamming the door shut.

Fifteen minutes later she walked out. She glanced at the two men who had been giving her trouble but they were fast asleep, with their chins resting firmly on their chests. They would hardly have recognized her anyway:

her hair was jet black, still wet and boyishly slicked back; the bruise on her face from where Strut had hit her was covered over with foundation. She walked away from them into the adjacent carriage, still feeling that all eyes were on her, but quietly confident now that, for the first time that evening, she was in control.

'Turn left here and it's about halfway down on the right.' Rosemary and Carter had hardly spoken on the journey from the office to Rosemary's house in north London. It wasn't an uncomfortable silence, it was just that there wasn't much to say. As Carter slowed down, Rosemary pointed ahead a bit redundantly. 'Just by this lamp post,' she told him. 'The one with the green door.'

'Are you going to be OK?' Carter asked.

'Yes . . . yes,' she stuttered slightly, as if she wasn't used to men asking her questions like that. 'I'll be fine. I'll just have a hot bath and go to bed. I'll be right as rain in the morning. Oh . . .' She put her hand to her mouth.

'What's wrong?'

'My keys. They were in my bag.'

'Does anyone have a spare?'

'Yes, my neighbours. But it's terribly late . . .'

Carter smiled. She was such a good woman – how the hell had she got mixed up in all of this? 'Well, it's either that,' he gave her a cheeky look, 'or sleep on my couch. And I don't think you'll find that particularly comfortable.'

Rosemary looked momentarily horrified at his in-appropriate comment before she realized he was joking. 'No . . .' she did her best to laugh, 'no, I suppose you're right.' She opened the car door.

'I'll give you a call at work tomorrow,' Carter called as she walked away from the car. 'Check you're all right.'

She walked up the stone steps leading to her neighbours' house, taking care not to trip on her broken shoe as she did so. Timidly she pressed on the bell, a short, sharp burst that she half hoped wouldn't wake anyone. She felt the bitter cold as she stood there waiting – Carter had kept her jacket, so there was only her blouse and vest to protect her from the elements. She hugged herself to keep warm. After a short time, the hall light came on, the door opened and Veronica, her neighbour, appeared at the doorway, a little bleary-eyed. 'Rosemary!' she said in surprise. 'What on earth's the matter?'

Rosemary and Veronica got on well enough, the way neighbours who must accept each other's presence even if they would never have chosen to live next to each other often do, but Rosemary always found her a little nosy for her taste. 'I'm so sorry to wake you, Veronica,' she said. 'I'm afraid I've left my keys at work. Could you let me have my spare pair?'

Veronica looked Rosemary up and down. Ruffled hair, no jacket – it was obvious what she was thinking. She looked over Rosemary's shoulder and saw Carter's car, its hazard lights blinking, then raised one eyebrow slightly as she turned inside to fetch the keys, without inviting Rosemary to step inside into the warm. As she returned, she noticed that Carter was still there. 'Friend of yours?' she asked delicately.

'Oh . . . just a work colleague,' Rosemary lied. 'He was kind enough to drive me home.'

'I see.' Veronica clearly didn't believe her.

'Thank you very much, Veronica,' she said in a

measured voice. 'I'm terribly sorry to have woken you. Good night.' She turned and walked back down the steps, not looking back at her neighbour who stood at the open doorway for a little longer than either politeness or the weather should have allowed. Rosemary waved her keys at Carter, who waited until she had opened the front gate to her house before driving off into the night.

As she walked down the pathway, an automatic light switched itself on. It seemed brighter than usual because of the way it reflected off the snow – indeed the snow itself seemed to glow like some kind of luminous blanket covering her garden, spoiled only by the footprints leading up to her door.

Rosemary stopped halfway up the path. Why were there footprints in the snow? Nobody ever called on her at this time of night. She stood still and followed them with her eyes, as if the person who had made them were walking up to the porch, knocking on the door, waiting a moment, then walking back down.

Something was not right.

She spun round, hoping that she might still be able to catch Carter's car in the street, but let out a small, almost inaudible scream as she saw a man she did not recognize standing at her gate. Without taking his eyes off Rosemary, he silently opened the gate, walked inside, then shut it behind him. 'Rosemary Gibson?' he asked quietly, in an accent that she could not quite put her finger on. Eastern European – the Baltics, maybe. Whatever it was, it was neither threatening nor comforting. He was a tall, thin man in early middle age with a drawn, gaunt face and blond hair. The yellow light from the street lamp behind him cast his face in shadow. Rosemary said nothing as he lifted his head slightly and smiled broadly at her, an action that was quite at odds with the rest of his demeanour.

She turned quickly to the house, wondering if she had time to let herself in before he came any closer, and was horrified to see what looked like the light of a torch flashing on the other side of the frosted coloured glass that decorated the top half of the door. 'Who's in my house?' she whispered desperately.

The man was now upon her. He grabbed her arm and pushed her up towards the door, then tapped a distinctive knock. The light in the house went out and the door opened almost immediately. Rosemary found herself being shoved roughly inside; she fell to the floor as the door softly clicked shut. The blond man bent down to her level and calmly pointed a gun in her face. 'Have you ever heard of an AAC Pilot silencer, Mrs Gibson?'

Terrified, Rosemary shook her head, unable to take her eyes off the gun.

'It means,' he continued in his emotionless voice, 'that if I shoot you now, the only people to hear it will be me and my friend. No one will suspect anything until the bottles of milk start piling up outside your front door. Do you understand?'

Rosemary was too scared even to nod her head. The man tapped her roughly on the cheek with the barrel of the gun. 'Do you understand?' he repeated more harshly.

'Yes,' she whimpered.

'Good. Where is it?'

'What?' In her panic she was genuinely wrong-footed by his question.

His voice remained steady. 'I'm not a man to repeat myself, Mrs Gibson,' he said calmly. 'I'm only going to ask you one more time. You have something that doesn't belong to you. I want to know where it is.'

'Please,' Rosemary cried, gasping for breath. 'I haven't got it.'

The man sighed almost regretfully, stood up and aimed the gun at her head again.

'I promise I haven't got it!' she squealed. 'I promise!'

The two men looked at each other inquiringly. The silent one gestured towards the door, and the man with the gun nodded his head in agreement.

'OK,' he said, more quietly now. 'Here's what's going to happen. Outside your gate, to the left, there's a red estate car. We're all going to walk there nice and quietly. If you so much as speak, I'll shoot you. If you make any sudden movements, I'll shoot you. If you try and run away, I'll shoot you. Have I made myself perfectly clear?'

Rosemary nodded her head.

'Once we're there, you and I will sit in the back seat and have a nice little chat. My friend here will do the driving.'

She stared at him, numb with terror.

'And Mrs Gibson,' he was practically breathing the words now, 'make no mistake. I've killed more people than I can count. One more won't make any difference.'

Chapter Four

Mark Taylor's alarm clock went off at five-thirty every morning. Even on his days off he stuck to this routine, but only because of the pleasure he derived from being able to turn the bloody thing off and go back to sleep. How long he got to listen to the gentle babble of the Radio 2 DJ before hauling himself out of bed on work days depended entirely on his wife's mood – and this morning she was clearly in the mood for sleeping. 'Turn it off,' she mumbled drowsily before turning over, taking three-quarters of the covers as she did so. Taylor sighed as his semi-naked body went from warm and cosy to chilled and exposed in a matter of seconds. He hadn't slept well – one whisky too many, as usual. His wife had been trying to stop him drinking spirits for years now, but he always had an excuse. 'It's been a long day, I'm fucking cold and I've just had to deal with a dead pimp. Now, if you don't mind, I'd like another drink,' he'd told her as he poured himself his fourth large Scotch. Now his head was bleary. Slowly he sat up on the side of the bed and switched the radio off.

Thirty minutes later he was showered, shaved and in the car, listening to the breakfast show on the radio. 'How the hell can anyone be so happy at this time of the morning?' he muttered to himself. It took him only half an hour to make the journey from his home in Croydon into the station at London Bridge before the rush hour began – leave it any later, though, and it would be a nightmare – so it was well before seven o'clock when he was walking into his office, mug of coffee in one hand and in the other a plastic bag carrying the cheese sandwiches his wife had made the night before. He sat down in his chair, took a sip, and started to browse through a report from the previous evening.

As he read, Sergeant Steve Irvin walked in and sat down opposite him. 'You're a bit keen, aren't you?' Taylor asked without looking up. 'Haven't you got a home to go to?'

'On my way, sir. Just wanted to update you on the Newington Park incident before I left.'

Taylor had grown to like Irvin in his own way since they had started working together eighteen months previously. He was a good worker, and keen to learn – a fact Taylor found hard to accept, as he privately knew Irvin was likely to go further in the force than he ever could.

'We couldn't get anyone to give a reliable statement,' the sergeant continued. 'They were all either drunk, high or not sane enough to rely on –'

'Not bloody surprised,' Taylor interrupted.

'I've just got off the phone to the hospital where the girl was taken.'

'What do we know about her?'

'Not much. Says her name is Mary. We haven't been able to confirm that, but she seems to have some history of domestic abuse. She's still in shock, but stable – medically speaking, at least. Also, these have just come through.' He pulled four pieces of paper from his file and handed them to his boss. They were A4-sized photographs, blurry and indistinct, but as Taylor flicked through them one particular image leaped out: a girl with long blonde hair running along a road with park railings on one side.

'What are these?' Taylor asked.

'There's a disused warehouse on the west side of the park . . .'

'Yeah, thanks, Steve. I've been here long enough that I know Newington Park.'

Steve brushed off the sarcasm – he was well used to it now from Taylor. 'The security company that looks after the building has CCTV watching the road because of vandalism. I managed to pull last night's security video – it's the best we have for the time of the murder.'

'Have you got the tape?'

Irvin nodded. 'Here, sir.' Taylor gestured at the TV and video recorder that stood in the corner of the office, so the sergeant walked over, inserted the tape into the machine and fast-forwarded to the relevant section.

Taylor watched closely as the blonde-haired woman ran down the road. He couldn't believe that was his killer – she was barely older than his own daughter, and there was hardly anything to her. How could she have inflicted so much damage on the tough old corpse he saw last night? 'Has anyone shown the picture to the girl?'

'No, sir, not yet. I only managed to get hold of the tape an hour ago.'

Taylor stood up. 'OK, what hospital is she at?'

'St Thomas', sir. But . . .'

'What?' Taylor turned to face Irvin, one eyebrow raised.

'Don't you think you should wait for social services to see her first, sir?'

'What, wait for them to give her a big cuddle and a

chocolate milkshake? Of course I fucking don't.' He grabbed his coat and walked out.

Mary was recovering at the state-of-the-art Evelina Children's Hospital at St Thomas'. It was the first time Taylor had been in the new building, and even he was impressed as he looked up at the seven floors of glass as he entered. It didn't feel like a hospital at all – more like a hotel especially for children. He walked in and made inquiries at reception as to her whereabouts. Because she was being watched over by the police, she had been placed in a family room on the first floor, the Arctic Level. Each floor was themed on the natural world so that children would feel relaxed and happy. This place really did have everything a sick child would need – even its own school. It was probably the most luxurious place the wretch he had seen last night had ever experienced, Taylor mused to himself as he made his way up to see her.

Lizzy, the female officer, had finished her shift and the male officer who had replaced her was sitting on a chair outside the door, reading a copy of the *Sun*, which he quickly folded up and put away when he saw Taylor approach. 'Is she awake?' the DI asked him without any greeting or formality.

'I think so, sir. A nurse took some breakfast in about half an hour ago.'

'Has she said anything?'

'No, sir.'

Taylor knocked, and when there was still no answer he opened the door and walked straight in.

Mary was sitting up in bed wearing pink pyjamas supplied by the hospital, a tray on her lap holding her breakfast things – every last scrap of food had been devoured.

Her clothes had been washed and pressed and were neatly hanging in the open wardrobe opposite the bed. Taylor looked at Mary. She seemed much more like a thirteen-year-old girl now that she had been washed and her hair combed. The girl didn't even acknowledge his presence; she just stared straight ahead, zombie-like. More than anything else she looked vulnerable.

Taylor stood by the door. 'Can you hear me, Mary?' Her eyes didn't move. 'My name's Detective Inspector Taylor. I need to ask you about the events at Newington Park last night.' He took a few steps closer to the bed. 'Do you want to tell me your surname, Mary?'

Almost imperceptibly, Mary shook her head.

Taylor was trying the softly-softly approach. Make friends with her. Make her realize that he was on her side. But experience had taught him that that way of doing things rarely bore fruit: street kids don't trust coppers, it was as simple as that. He knew they'd be far more likely to believe that he'd be willing to chuck them in a cell before handing them over to social services, who would inevitably send them back to where they came from – be it their parents, foster parents or a children's home. So they invariably responded to a rougher hand, and over the years that had become Taylor's default position. He remained silent for a few moments before speaking again. 'Do you know what will happen if you waste my time?' he asked, affecting a bored tone in his voice. 'Young offenders' institution. Nasty place. You get fucked over three times before breakfast. Think I'd rather be sniffing glue round Elephant and Castle.'

Mary turned to look at him. Her big, frightened eyes made him feel suddenly uncomfortable, and he wished he hadn't said what he'd just said. He held up the CCTV picture in front of her. 'Come on, Mary. You can help us. Do you recognize this woman?' He tried to smile at her, but it was a false smile and Mary – with the insight of a child – knew it.

She looked impassively at the picture, and then the stony-faced front she had been putting up dissolved once more, just as it had in front of the nice police officer last night. 'He had a knife,' she wept into her hands.

'Why don't you tell me what happened?'

But Mary was too distraught to speak again. Taylor stood uncomfortably as huge sobs racked the body of the waif of a girl in front of him. He'd been too heavy-handed – she was no good to him in this state. 'Look,' he said, trying to be reasonable once more. 'If this was the girl who did it, I'll find out one way or another. You might as well tell me now, and then I'll leave you alone. OK?'

'She was just trying to help me,' Mary cried. 'It wasn't her fault!'

'What's her name, Mary?'

But the girl just returned his question with a bloodshot stare. 'I don't know,' she lied unconvincingly.

Suddenly the door opened and a young woman carrying a briefcase walked in. She was dressed in an inexpensive black two-piece suit and her hair was tied tightly back. She took in the scene before turning to Taylor with an angry look. 'What's going on?' she asked. 'Who are you?'

'Detective Inspector Mark Taylor, CID,' he replied abruptly. 'And who the hell are you?'

The woman fished an ID card out of her pocket. 'Susan Williamson, social services. This girl is a minor. What are you doing interviewing her without me present?'

'I wasn't interviewing her, we were just having a little chat. Weren't we, Mary?'

Mary didn't answer.

The social worker pursed her lips at him. 'May I have a word outside, Detective?'

'Sure,' Taylor shrugged. Mary's eyes followed him as he left the room. 'We'll continue this later, Mary.'

Once they were both outside and the door was shut, the social worker turned to Taylor with a fierce look in her eyes. 'I don't have to tell you that you've broken just about every regulation in the book, Detective,' she fumed.

Taylor raised an eyebrow at her. 'And I'm sure I don't have to tell you that somewhere out there I've got an unhinged vagrant on the loose with a penchant for sticking bottles into people's necks. This girl knows who she is.'

'Do you intend to arrest her?'

'Of course I don't intend to arrest her. She hasn't done anything.'

They stared at each other for a few seconds before the social worker let out an explosive breath of air. 'This is outrageous,' she muttered, then turned on her heel and walked back into the room.

As the door shut, Taylor turned to the officer outside. 'You could have told me she was coming,' he grumbled, before walking away and leaving the officer behind him shaking his head in confusion.

Andrew Meeken was director of the Investigations and Prosecutions Department at the SFO. He was a mild-mannered man who shunned the spotlight and was favourite to replace the current director of the SFO when he stepped down in two years' time. His head was buried in his morning briefings when there was a knock on the door. 'Come in,' he called.

Sean Carter put his head round the door. 'Sir, can I have a word, please?'

Meeken raised his head as Carter walked into the office. 'Of course, Sean. Have a seat.' He always believed in calling people by their first name – respect for your fellow man and all that. 'How are you settling in?'

'Fine, sir. I have a request on a case I'm dealing with. I need the assistance of the Met.'

'Anything particular?'

'I need help tracking someone down.'

'OK, Sean, I'll have a word with the director. He'll be speaking with the commissioner soon – I'll come back to you.'

Meeken was not the kind of man to hold his officers up. Forty-five minutes later, as Carter was sitting at his desk finishing a bacon roll, he got the call: Carter had the authority from the director of the SFO and the police commissioner himself. He dialled a number immediately.

'New Scotland Yard, good morning.'

'Put me through to DCI Jameson, please,' he asked.

'One minute, please.'

Carter knew he was going to have to do a bit of fast talking here. Jameson hadn't been at all pleased when he had been transferred to the SFO, but the order had gone above his head. They needed a good DI to help them bring criminal convictions, and Carter had been an obvious choice. He'd jumped at the chance, of course – more money, and an opportunity to climb a different greasy pole to his colleagues. 'Change is as good as a rest,' he'd told his friends at the time. Jameson had complained that he was understaffed enough as it was, but the powers on high had overruled him. With typical police bureaucracy, though, he had orders to go through Jameson if he needed to use any of the Met's resources, and he knew the DCI would make him jump through hoops to get what he wanted.

'Jameson.' His rough voice came abruptly on the line.

'Morning, sir,' Carter said, trying to keep his voice as level as possible. 'It's Sean Carter.'

Jameson sighed. 'What is it, Sean? I'm very busy.'

'I'm sure you are, sir,' he replied. 'It won't take long. I need your approval to get something checked with forensics, and to put a trace on a mobile phone.'

'Yes, so I've been told. Authorized by the commissioner himself. We *are* going places, aren't we, Sean?'

'It's important, sir.' Carter tried to deflect his sarcasm.

'Why? Someone embezzling paper clips from the Home Office?'

Carter stayed silent. He was used to wisecracks like that.

'Come on, Sean. What is it?'

'I'm afraid I can't tell you, sir. Are you going to authorize what I need?' He knew he didn't really have to ask, but he also knew that the worst way to piss off a DCI was to threaten to go above his head.

Now it was Jameson's turn to be silent. 'All right, Sean,' he said finally. 'Bring it in and we'll see what we can do.'

'I'll be there within the hour,' Carter replied. The line went dead.

Walking back into Scotland Yard always felt to Carter a bit like going back to school to see his old teachers – it gave him that same sensation in his stomach, a mixture of dread and strange excitement. 'Hi, Sean,' a former colleague called to him as they passed in a corridor. 'Still trying to nail the Swiss wankers – I mean, bankers?' Carter smiled weakly. He'd worked there for several years, and didn't feel that he missed it when he was away, but was never so sure when he came back – there was something about the buzz around the place that appealed to him, something that was missing at the SFO. Jameson's snipe about the paper clips wasn't that far from the mark sometimes, and Carter had often found himself wishing he had something a bit meatier to sink his teeth into.

This job was different, though. Important. Probably the most important case he'd ever been assigned to – and certainly more important than Rosemary thought when she first contacted him. Suddenly the sight of everyone scurrying around the Yard like worker bees didn't seem so impressive after all.

Jameson was too busy to see Carter himself – not that Sean had expected him to make himself available – but he smiled when he saw the DS who was waiting for him. 'Hello, Yvonne.' He grinned. 'Haven't they made you chief inspector yet?'

'Babies, Sean.' The dark-haired officer smiled back. 'They get in the way of a girl's career. Not that you'd know much about that – unless you've decided to break the heart of every WPC in London and find yourself a girlfriend.'

Carter's eyes flickered towards the floor. It always wrong-footed him when people referred to his personal life – or lack of it. He could flirt with the best of them, but something stopped him from ever taking anything further. Not enough time, he would tell himself. Maybe when I've left the job. But in the dark honesty of the small hours, he wondered if that would ever really happen.

'Don't they make you shave at the SFO?' Yvonne asked breezily, changing the subject as if aware that she had said something she shouldn't have.

Carter's hand automatically touched his face. 'Designer stubble – it's considered very fashionable when you work with accountants all day long. Did old misery-guts tell you what I need?'

'He's not in a very talkative mood, I'm afraid. Said something to do with forensics?'

Carter handed her the black bin liner he was holding. 'There's a woman's jacket in here with a bloodstain on it. It's a long shot, but I need to know if there's a DNA match with anyone on the system.'

'Whose jacket is it?'

'Just someone who's helping us with our inquiries.'

'Ooh, you're so mysterious these days, DI Carter.'

'Perhaps – but I still outrank you, even if I'm with the SFO.' He flashed her a smile, then took a pencil and notepad from his jacket pocket and scribbled down a number. 'I also need a trace on this mobile. As soon as anyone switches it on and uses it, I need to know exactly where they are. Call me immediately.'

'Right.'

'And just one more thing.' He handed her the scrap of paper on which Rosemary had written her bank details. 'If any cards from these accounts get used, I need to know where and when.'

'Yes, sir!' Yvonne answered mockingly. 'Anything else?'

'That will be all, Detective Sergeant.' He gave her a

quick peck on the cheek. 'Buzz me when you've got anything.'

The snow was thawing, dripping heavily from the trees in the garden of The Stables. The pond was still frozen, and a solitary blackbird was standing on the ice. Harriet Johnson watched the scene through the kitchen window, which was misted slightly by the condensation. It was warm inside – the central heating had been on constantly for the past two months, much to her husband's annoyance – and there was a pot of something slow-cooking in the oven that made the whole house smell good. Harriet loved her kitchen almost as much as her garden, and she ruled it like a benevolent queen, producing lovely meals for her husband and herself, and an endless succession of cakes, biscuits and other goodies, as well as making sure it was always clean and tidy. 'A good cook always works in a tidy kitchen,' she would tell anyone who would listen. It was certainly a kitchen to be proud of, one that wouldn't look out of place in a glossy magazine about country living, with its large oak dining table that was far too big for the two of them, the Aga and the large butler's sink. The kettle finished boiling and Harriet filled a cafetière before placing it on a chunky, wooden tray with a couple of mugs and a jug of warm milk, and carrying it through to the sitting room where Sally, her closest friend, was sitting.

Harriet was in her early fifties, one of those women to whom age lent dignity, and she dressed the part of the well-to-do Surrey housewife to perfection. Her clothes were stylish – the sort of style that needed a bit of money to maintain. Her once naturally blonde hair had been dyed to hide the grey, and it was well tended by weekly trips to the hairdresser. She was a beautiful woman who looked after herself.

She poured out the coffee and then sank comfortably into the sofa. Tuesday mornings were often spent like this – William was at work, and Sally invariably had the morning off from her part-time job at the charity shop, so they would grab the opportunity to take time out and gossip for England. No one in the village was safe from their wagging tongues. It was all harmless enough stuff – rarely did anything truly gossip-worthy happen in the village, but to hear these two during their weekly chats, anyone could be mistaken into thinking that they lived on the set of a soap opera, not in the sleepy commuter village of Limpsfield in Surrey, which lay just on the outskirts of London. This week a group of youths had had to be removed from the local pub – William had an idea about who they were. He wouldn't have wanted to be in their shoes, Harriet confided to her friend: he had his doubts about the landlord's past history, but then anyone with an East End accent was likely to be thought of as practically a Kray twin round here.

They chatted for at least a couple of hours before Sally looked at her watch. 'Is that the time?' she exclaimed, as she always did. 'I must get to work. Thanks for the coffee.'

'OK,' Harriet replied. 'I'll call you during the week.'

Once Sally had left, Harriet pottered around in the kitchen, rinsing out mugs, wiping down work surfaces and generally filling in time until she needed to get ready for her yoga class at the local gym. Almost without think-ing, she switched on the small television that sat on the corner of the kitchen work surface and went to make herself a coffee – instant this time. She stood with her back against the sink watching the lunchtime news. She was waiting for the weather forecast more than anything else – tomorrow was William's day off, and they had planned to take a drive out to a pub they both liked, but if this incessant snow was going to keep on falling, she knew he wouldn't want to move from his chair in front of the fire. She didn't really blame him. He spent half the week in an office, the other half tramping around outside, so it was fair enough that he should enjoy their home when he wasn't at work.

The news was the usual round of tube strikes that she didn't approve of – it always seemed they wanted more and everyone else had to suffer for their grievances – and foreign affairs that she didn't understand but felt she had to listen to. Another bomb in Baghdad, and security alerts around the world that seemed to be the usual thing these days. It all tended to melt into one as far as she was concerned. But she always enjoyed watching the last item, which inevitably focused on a star out of one of the many glossy magazines she read. Then the newsreader handed over to the local newsrooms. 'A man was found dead in central London last night. Police believe he was the victim of a violent attack. He has not yet been formally identified, and police have issued this picture of a young woman seen leaving the scene of the crime, who it is thought might be able to help them with their inquiries.' A blurred picture of a blonde woman running alongside some park railings came onto the screen. 'The public are being warned not to approach the woman if they see her, but to get in touch with Crimestoppers immediately.' The telephone numbers appeared underneath the picture.

Suddenly Harriet felt light-headed. She gasped as she looked at the screen and dropped her cup of coffee.

Surely she had got all this out of her system – the impossible moments when she thought she saw her in the supermarket, or in a cafe, or standing in a queue outside the cinema. The girl in the crowd who, from behind, she was sure was her daughter, but who turned out – when she rushed up to grab her – to be a total stranger.

Surely she had come to terms with the fact that she had gone.

And then the picture disappeared from the screen, just as her daughter used to disappear into the crowd every time she thought she had seen her.

Maybe she was mistaken. Maybe it was all starting again. But she didn't think so.

'Dear God,' she whispered to herself. 'Francesca.'

Back at the station, Taylor was doing his best to get his wife off the phone. He knew it was a running joke that, since his daughter had left home recently, Annabelle couldn't get through the day without speaking to him at least five times, and that all the officers took the piss behind his back; but he had no idea that the speculations for her almost obsessive need to speak to her husband ran from her inability to change a light bulb to her hourly need for passionate phone sex. The reality, of course, was much more mundane: 'When will you be home?' 'What would you like for tea?' 'Have you spoken to Samantha?' 'Do you think I should call her?' 'Can we go out tonight?' 'You're not going to the pub after work again, are you?' The list was endless.

'Look, love, if you don't let me get on, I won't be home before midnight,' he told her rather impatiently. He sighed as he put down the phone. Almost immediately Steve Irvin entered. 'I thought you were going home,' Taylor said irritably.

'I had a quick nap,' he said. 'Looks like you were right about the Newington Park body. We've got a fingerprint ID. Robert Alexander Strut. Sounds like a real nasty piece of work.' He dropped a file on Taylor's desk.

Taylor flicked through Strut's record. Drugs, pimping, GBH – a string of convictions longer than your arm and half his adult life behind bars. 'Nice,' he said almost to himself, before turning back to Irvin. 'At least our run-away beauty has been doing her bit to keep the prison population down.'

'Not sure I'd call her a beauty, sir.'

'You're too fussy, that's your problem.' The phone rang. 'Now make yourself useful and find me another cup of tea. Hello, Mark Taylor.'

'I've got a Sergeant Johnson from Surrey Police,' the receptionist told him.

'OK, Lynn, put him through.'

There was a beep as he was put on hold, and then a voice he didn't recognize came on the line. 'Detective Inspector Taylor?'

'Yes.'

'This is Sergeant William Johnson. Surrey Police.' The man's voice sounded tremulous, unsure of itself.

'What can I do for you, sergeant?'

'I understand it was you who released the picture this morning of a girl running from a fatality in central London.'

'That's right.'

'My wife caught a glimpse of it on television an hour ago. She's convinced it's her daughter – my stepdaughter – who ran away from home four years ago.'

Christ, thought Taylor, looking at his watch. 'How sure is your wife?'

There was a brief silence. 'May I speak in confidence?'

'Go ahead.'

'When Francesca left home, it hit my wife very hard. She had a nervous breakdown – believed she kept seeing her in the street and refused to accept she was gone. She's over that now, and to be honest I thought we'd seen an end to this. But I've got hold of a copy of the picture myself now, and I have to say it looks very much like Francesca.'

'Why did she leave home?'

'We don't know.'

'Has she tried to contact you since?'

'No. Not once. But maybe if she's in trouble she'll think of coming to us. I have to tell you, DI Taylor, that this is totally uncharacteristic. I'm sure you've got your reasons for thinking she was involved, but she was always a very gentle girl. I'd be amazed if there wasn't some other explanation. My wife didn't want me to get in touch with you in case it got her into any more trouble . . .' His voice trailed off.

'We're waiting for fingerprints and DNA results,' Taylor told him honestly, 'but we have CCTV footage that shows her leaving the crime scene. Can you give us any pictures of your stepdaughter so that we can do an ID?'

'Yes, yes of course . . .' Johnson's voice went quiet once

more. 'Look,' he said eventually, 'I'll do whatever I can to help. So will my wife. We just want to know that Francesca is safe. But can you keep me informed?'

Taylor thought about it. Police etiquette dictated that you didn't keep another officer in the dark if you knew something they had a personal interest in, and frankly he didn't care enough about the whole incident in any case to start coming on all mysterious. 'The guy she killed was no loss to society,' he said finally. 'Pimp, dealer.'

'What was Francesca doing involved with someone like that?'

Suddenly Taylor felt almost sorry for him. 'Look, I don't know your stepdaughter. I'm sure she's a lovely girl, but there're not many ways for girls on the street to earn a living round here.'

'But I know Francesca –'

'I don't know the full story yet. As I get more information, I'm sure we'll talk further. Give me your address and I'll send someone round to talk to your wife now and collect some photographs. If your stepdaughter gets in touch, let me know.'

'Yes, of course,' Johnson replied, his voice still shocked. 'We'll help in any way we can. I'm going home now – I'll be there when your officer arrives.'

Francesca's bedroom, with its pastel lilac walls, bookshelves filled with books, CDs and photos, and the serene view over the garden pond, had not altered since the day she left home. Harriet seldom went in there, only unlocking the door once a week so that the cleaning lady could dust and vacuum. Now, as she sat on the single bed with its colourful, patchwork bedspread, her face white with horror, she saw things as she had done hundreds of times before. The hairbrush. Harriet had loved brushing Francesca's hair when she had been small, but she had not been allowed to when her daughter developed the self-consciousness of a teenager.

The small pile of compact discs. They had done their best to persuade her to turn the music down almost every day. Harriet was never successful; William only when he raised his voice. She'd give anything to sit downstairs now and hear that God-awful racket.

The little pewter jewellery box in which she kept all her necklaces and trinkets. She had loved those things. The fact that she had left them there kept coming back to haunt Harriet – she had wanted to leave so much that she hadn't even bothered to take her most treasured possessions, and so they had stayed in their box for the last four years, untouched.

She looked at the wooden-framed picture of Francesca's father. The one taken in France the summer before he became ill. Francesca had missed him so much. They both had. But life had to go on. A year after her husband's death she had started dating, even though she believed her daughter was too young to understand. Francesca had wanted her mother to herself, and believed she was betraying her father. It had hurt Harriet a great deal, so she tried to keep her relationships secret from her daughter. That was until she fell in love with William, a forty-four-year-old sergeant at Reigate police station who had just come through a messy divorce. The relationship blossomed, but Francesca had found it hard, and hadn't understood why her mother needed to marry only two years after her father's death. Harriet had tried to make her understand that all she wanted to do was keep things normal for her, to give her a family to grow up in; and William had tried so hard to be friends with her, but she had never accepted him, always treated him with suspicion. She was a bright girl, but her schoolwork had started to go downhill. Teachers would ask Harriet if anything was wrong at home. She always said no.

Whenever she'd tried to talk to her husband about her concerns for her daughter, he just became cross. 'She's fine, Harriet,' he would snap at her. 'Just a teenager.' But her mother's instinct had known it was more serious than that. Then, one evening when Francesca and her mother were alone, the problem had come out. She hadn't believed what she was hearing from her own daughter's mouth. She *couldn't* believe it.

And then, just short of her fifteenth birthday, she was gone. No warning, no note, just an empty bed and an open window. Paranoia got the better of Harriet in those awful months after the disappearance, and she kept thinking that perhaps her daughter had been telling the truth. She couldn't sleep and became heavily dependent on the benzodiazepines her GP gave her – little tablets that offered her some short release from her torment. As the months went by she grew to accept that she had just been trying to rationalize her daughter's disappearance in some way, to find a reason for something that seemed to make no sense, but it had taken years of counselling before she could finally accept that, and she was determined not to take a step backwards.

Suddenly she heard the gravelly sound of her husband's Mondeo coming up the driveway, and by the time he had started to climb out of the car she had run down the stairs and was standing at the doorway, her cardigan wrapped tightly around her shoulders. He was a small man, slightly paunchy, but with bright eyes that often seemed to be full of suppressed mirth, though today they were steely and serious. His greying hair was curly and a little unruly, and he wore a small, neatly trimmed moustache that Harriet had never really liked but in which he took great pride. She broke down in a sea of tears as he approached, and he held her firmly in his arms as they stood together at the entrance of their house. 'It was her,' Harriet sobbed. 'I know you think I'm making it up, but I'm not. It was her.'

'I know,' William replied quietly, reassuringly. 'I know.'

'Is she in terrible trouble?'

'It's hard to say.' He lifted her head up from his shoulder. 'Listen, Harriet, you need to know something. I've spoken to the officer in charge of the case.'

William felt her body stiffen. She pulled away. 'What do you mean?' she whispered. 'I told you not to.'

'I had to, love. For her own sake. I'm sure it's all a big misunderstanding, but the longer she avoids the police, the worse it will be for her.'

'What do you *mean*?' Harriet repeated her question but more forcefully now, and more tearfully. She turned and stormed inside, her husband following swiftly. 'She'll end up in prison,' Harriet wailed as she collapsed on the sofa in the front room.

'You don't know that.' William said the words firmly as he put his arms around his sobbing wife. 'But she must speak to the police. We must help them find her.'

'How can I help them find her? I thought she was dead.'

'I know,' replied William, gazing momentarily at the only picture of the three of them. In its sparkling silver frame it took pride of place above the fireplace. 'So did I.' They remained silent for a few moments, as if contemplating the magnitude of what they had just admitted. 'They're sending someone round to talk to us,' William said, breaking the silence. 'We have to help them as much as we can. I can't be seen to be obstructing them – I'm a serving police officer.'

Harriet flared up. 'This isn't about you, William! The police think my daughter has just killed someone.'

'I know, I know,' he said apologetically. 'I'm sorry, I didn't mean that to sound like it did. But they have CCTV footage, fingerprints and DNA. We have to help the police, for her safety as much as anything else.'

She nodded weakly. He was right. 'I'm sorry,' she apologized quietly. 'I just miss my baby so much.'

'Come on, love,' William said calmly. 'We just have to make sure we do the right thing – for all of us. You know I want to find her as much as you do.'

He held her again as the sobs shook through her body, and gazed once more at the picture of his stepdaughter. The eyes in the photograph seemed to gaze straight back at him.

Chapter Five

Carter was slurping noodles out of a takeaway box, his feet on his desk, when his phone rang. He totted it up in his brain: this was his fifth takeaway in a row. He really ought to get some vegetables down himself, but he knew he wouldn't be able to face the prospect of cooking when he got back to his flat – not that he ever would anyway.

It had been a frustrating morning since he arrived back at the office from Scotland Yard, one of those times when he knew he should be working in his assigned team, but couldn't. He was just thinking about Rosemary's evidence and what it held, and about the girl who took it. No leads, no nothing – he just had to hope Yvonne managed to come up with something, but he wasn't optimistic. Until she did, he simply had to wait, sitting there shuffling piles of paper around his desk. It wasn't something he was very good at. He let the mobile ring a few times as he shovelled another forkful of food into his mouth, then picked up.

'Sean Carter.'

'Sean, it's Yvonne. Are you eating?'

Carter swallowed his food quickly, and clumsily wiped his mouth with the back of his hand. 'No, no, it's OK. That was quick – have you come up with anything?'

'Certainly have. Forensics have come up with a match for the blood on that coat.'

'Go on.'

'There was a fatality last night. Two separate blood samples were taken from the scene, victim and suspect. Looks like whoever was wearing this coat had a lucky escape – the sample matches that of the suspect.'

'What else do you know about them?'

'Female. Probably a vagrant, maybe a prostitute. That's all we have at the moment.'

'Where did the fatality take place?'

'Newington Park – just by Elephant and Castle.'

Carter looked puzzled – that was quite a distance from Chelsea Bridge. He'd have to look at the timings. 'Who's in charge of the case?'

'A DI Mark Taylor. Do you want his number?'

Carter went a bit quiet. 'No, it's OK,' he muttered finally. 'I know Mark. I'll call him now. What about the credit cards?'

'One of them was used to withdraw a sum of money from a cash machine in south London last night. We're trying to get hold of any camera evidence from the shop.'

'Good. Anything on the phone?'

'Nothing, I'm afraid. It obviously hasn't been turned on yet. I'll keep on it, but Jameson's been piling stuff on me today – he'd go bananas if he knew I was prioritizing you over him. He really hates it when you ask him for a favour, doesn't he?'

''Fraid so.'

'Any idea why?'

'He's jealous of my good looks and charm, Yvonne. Keep on that phone trace – it's really important.'

'Don't worry, Sean. I'm more than happy to sacrifice my family's livelihood on your account.'

Carter smiled at her sarcasm. 'Good girl.' He hung up.

He pushed the carton of half-eaten food to one side and drummed his fingers absent-mindedly on the desk, contemplating his next move. One of the best things about leaving the force had been that he wouldn't have to speak to Mark Taylor again, and he had no doubt that the feeling was mutual. They hadn't spoken for two years, and even then it had been on pretty unfriendly terms.

It hadn't always been that way. He and Mark had come up the ranks together – even shared digs in Aylesbury when they had been training – and had been good friends. But his career had blossomed more obviously than Taylor's, and his friend had found it difficult to be left behind. Mark had always set his sights high, but now it looked unlikely that he would ever make it past DI, and Carter's promotion to the SFO had been the final nail in the coffin of their relationship. There was no way round it, though. He was going to have to pick up the phone, call his former friend and ask for help.

This, thought Carter, is turning into a really shitty day.

He picked up the phone and dialled London Bridge CID. 'Put me through to DI Taylor, please.'

'One minute.'

He continued to drum on the table while he waited. Finally he heard the voice he recognized so well. 'Taylor.'

'Hello, Mark,' he said quietly. 'It's Sean.' Taylor didn't respond for a moment. 'Sean Carter,' he clarified.

'Yeah, I know who it is,' Taylor conceded abruptly. 'What can I do for you, Sean?' His voice was level, emotionless. Carter knew him well enough to know that he was waiting to take offence at something, anything, no matter how small.

'I need your help, Mark.'

'I'm very busy.' It was the second time someone had said that to him today.

'I know, Mark. Look, it won't take long. It's about the incident in Newington Park last night. Can I come and see you? I'm just round the corner.' A silence. 'Please, it's important.'

'OK. But you'll have to make it quick.'

Twenty minutes later Carter was being escorted to his old friend. It had been a while since he had seen him, but it took only one glance for the features to crystallize in his mind once more. He looked older; his brown eyes were as sharp as ever, only masked now with a glassiness that spoke of a little too much fondness for drink. He's not a stupid man, Carter reminded himself. Cynical, maybe; jaded, certainly; but don't underestimate him. And remember: he used to be your friend.

Neither man proffered a hand – they knew it would be an empty gesture. Taylor merely indicated that Carter should pull up a chair and sit down beside his desk.

'Long time,' Carter said warmly. The fact that the relationship had cooled over the years gave him no pleasure. 'Family well?'

Taylor shrugged, but he couldn't stop himself making a few proud comments. 'Annabelle's fine. Still making my life hell, but that's her job. Samantha wants to be a teacher, more fool her.'

'I remember when she was a little girl and wanted to be a police officer like her dad.'

'Yeah, well, we soon talked that out of her. Look, Sean, much as I'd love to sit here and reminisce about the good old days, us proper policemen actually have a bit of work to do, and I'm bloody busy.'

Carter smiled ruefully to himself. 'Then I won't take up any more of your time than I have to. I need everything you've got on the Newington Park killing last night.'

'Why?'

'Because I think your suspect is involved with a case I'm investigating.'

'Don't be stupid,' Taylor scoffed. 'She was a bum. Homeless. Probably a junkie. Why would the SFO be interested in her?'

'Do you have a name?'

'Yes,' Taylor replied unhelpfully.

'Well, what is it, Mark?'

'Why do you need to know?' Taylor folded his arms and looked stubbornly across the table.

Carter pinched between his eyes in frustration. 'I can't tell you, Mark. I'm sorry.'

'Oh for fuck's sake, Sean,' Taylor burst out. 'Why do you always have to be so cloak and dagger?'

'I'm not being cloak and dagger, Mark. I just can't tell you at the moment. Now do you want to give me the information I need, or am I going to have to go above your head?' He hadn't wanted to make that threat, but Mark was being childish.

Taylor looked at his former friend with undisguised dislike. 'You'd love that, wouldn't you?'

'No, Mark,' Carter told him wearily. 'I wouldn't. I just need to know what you've got.'

Reluctantly Taylor rummaged through a pile of papers, pulled out a copy of the photograph of Frankie and handed it to Carter. 'Francesca Mills,' he told him. 'Nineteen years old. Ran away from home four years ago, hasn't been heard of since. Mother and stepfather live in Surrey.

She's a housewife, he's a local sergeant. There's no other close family that we think she could have gone to, and she hasn't been in touch with anyone since she disappeared. The stepfather told us they thought she'd gone the same way as her dad.'

Carter looked quizzically at him.

'Dead,' Taylor explained shortly. 'And frankly it would make my job a lot easier if she was.'

'Does she have any criminal record?'

'She's been pulled in for vagrancy and petty theft a couple of times and cautioned, but that's it.'

'What are you going to do to find her?'

'Not much.'

Carter looked quizzically at him again. 'What do you mean? She's a suspect in a murder case.'

'Oh give me a break, Sean. The bloke she topped was a pimp and a dealer, and we think it was self-defence anyway. I can't imagine the CPS showering me with gratitude for bringing her in. I'll do all the usual, and if we nail her, fine; but if it's not going to end in a conviction I'm not going to throw everything I've got at it. Knowing who she hangs out with, I wouldn't be surprised if she was drugged up to her eyeballs, and she probably still is. She's a waster, Sean. She'll be dead in a year.'

Carter hated to admit it, but Taylor was probably right. 'Just do me a favour,' he replied, 'and let me know if you get any leads.'

'Yeah, OK, Sean, whatever you say. But you know as well as I do how hard it is to find these people if they don't want to be found.'

'Something always comes up,' Carter said optimistically. 'You've got a photo of her already; I might have another on the way. Surely she'll have been caught on CCTV somewhere else.'

'Come off it, Sean.' Taylor didn't even bother to hide his derision. 'God knows how many thousands of cameras there are in London – where do you suggest we start? We don't have the resources to trawl through every camera in London.'

Carter's mobile rang. 'Excuse me,' he muttered automatically to Taylor before accepting the call. 'Sean Carter.'

'Sean, it's Yvonne. We've located the phone.'

'Where?'

'Surrey.'

Carter looked sharply at Taylor, who returned the look blankly. 'How close can you get it?'

'I can give you an address. The only house in the area is on its own down a private road. Have you got a pen?'

He jotted down the address Yvonne gave him. 'I'm going to need some back-up,' he told her. 'What are my chances of getting Jameson onside?' He glanced over at Taylor, who was making no pretence that his ears were not glued to the conversation.

'Very slim, Sean. You've got a real knack of upsetting him, did you know that?'

But Carter's mind was elsewhere. If he found Rosemary's phone, the chances were the locket wouldn't be far away, but he had to move quickly. He could make some calls, go in above Jameson, but it was all going to take time, and that was the one thing he couldn't risk. 'OK, Yvonne. Thanks. I'll call you back soon.'

He turned to Taylor, realizing he was going to have to talk fast. 'Mark, this may sound unlikely to you, but I've got good reason to believe that this girl is in a house in Surrey. I've got the address. Can you arrange for some officers to get round there and pick her up?'

Taylor eyed him sceptically. 'How the hell could you possibly know where she is? You didn't even know her name until two minutes ago.'

'Mark, I'm right about this. Think how good it will look for you if you bring her in less than twenty-four hours after the killing.' He'd known him long enough to understand which buttons to press.

But Taylor seemed to dither. 'I'm not sure, Sean. Sounds to me like you're clutching at straws.'

'Come on, Mark, you know we have to check out this lead. We've had our differences, but I'm not in the business of wasting your time. Please?'

The question seemed to hang in the air. Finally Taylor spoke as he glanced at the photographs on his desk. 'You're going to have to give me more than that – you know I can't just raise a team to go onto someone else's patch like I'm ordering a pizza. It's going to be my arse on the line, so you'd better tell me where you're getting your miraculous hunch from.'

Carter bowed his head. 'OK, Mark,' he gave in. 'Last night, I think your suspect stole some personal belongings from a contact of mine.'

'Why?'

'I don't know. But one of those items was a mobile phone. It's been traced to an address in Surrey.'

'And why do you give a fuck that some bum off the street has nicked a mobile phone? Or is that the sort of thing the SFO are investigating these days?'

'I'm sorry, Mark.' Sean was beginning to lose patience now. 'That's as much as I can tell you. Are you going to do this or not?'

Taylor stood up and walked to the window, looking out at the suits crossing over London Bridge. 'OK,' he said at last. 'I'll send some people down there now. But it's my arrest, and my suspect, do you understand?'

'Just give me twenty minutes with her when you bring her in, Mark,' Carter replied. 'That's all I'll need. I promise.'

Carter walked down the street towards his car with misgivings firing through his mind. He didn't like leaving things to Taylor, but there hadn't been much choice in the matter: if he wanted the elusive Francesca Mills brought in, he was going to have to trust his former colleague. He had known not to bother asking if he could go along – this was too good an empire-building opportunity for Taylor for him to allow anyone else on the scene to take the credit. He was just going to have to sit tight and wait.

As his car pulled out into the traffic, he decided to check on Rosemary. She had been pretty shaken up last night, and with good reason. But she was tougher than her prissy exterior suggested, and he reckoned she'd recover pretty quickly. He was still in two minds as to whether to ask her to repeat her night-time tiptoeing round the corridors of the bank, but with any luck it wasn't going to be necessary. By this evening he'd have the information he needed.

He punched Rosemary's office number into his mobile. It was answered immediately by a sprightly sounding receptionist. 'Lenham, Borwick and Hargreaves, good afternoon.'

'Could you put me through to Rosemary Gibson, please?'

'Who may I say is calling?'

'It's her brother.'

'One moment, please.'

Carter whistled along tunelessly to the familiar holding music as he waited for Rosemary to come on the line. He was suddenly caught off guard when a man's voice answered, a deep Eastern European voice that spoke slowly and precisely. 'I understand you wish to speak to Miss Gibson.'

'That's right.'

'May I ask who this is?'

'As I told your receptionist, I'm her brother.'

'I wasn't aware that she had a brother.'

Carter began to feel uneasy. 'No,' he replied quickly, 'I don't suppose she discusses her family much at work.' He cursed himself for sounding like a smart-arse.

'Quite,' the voice said impassively. 'Quite.'

'May I ask who I'm talking to?'

'I'm afraid Miss Gibson called in sick this morning.'

'Shit,' Carter muttered silently to himself as he forced the car into an emergency stop to prevent himself from driving into the line of traffic in front of him. He coughed slightly to clear his voice. 'I see. OK, well . . . I'll try her at home.' Carter wanted to end this conversation as quickly as possible. 'Thanks for your help.' He hung up.

Something was wrong. He had specifically told Rosemary to go into work this morning, and she wouldn't have ignored his instruction without checking with him first. Carter quickly did a U-turn and screamed north over

95

the river, before dialling Rosemary's home number. He had to speak to her immediately.

Her phone rang four or five times, then the answering machine kicked in. 'Hello, this is Rosemary.' She spoke the message precisely and, it seemed to Carter, interminably slowly. 'I am unable to take your call at the moment, but do please leave me a message after the tone.'

'Rosemary!' he said urgently after the beep had finished. 'Are you there? Pick up, Rosemary. It's me. Answer the phone!'

But there was no reply. 'Fuck!' Carter shouted as he desperately tried to negotiate his way around the jumble of cars clogging up the street. He dialled the number again, but there was still no answer.

It took him an hour to reach Rosemary's street, but it felt like half a day. Every light was red, every road seemed to have some sort of obstruction. He was sweating uncomfortably by the time he had pulled the car up outside the house for the second time in twenty-four hours. He jumped out and splashed his way up the slushy front path. He pounded his fist on the front door several times before crouching down and shouting through the letter box. 'Rosemary!' he called. 'Rosemary, are you there? It's Sean, come to the door.'

But the only reply was an uneasy silence.

'Can I help?'

Carter turned, startled, to see a middle-aged woman peering at him from over the hedge. Her face was a picture of barely concealed curiosity. 'I'm looking for Rosemary,' he told her abruptly. 'Have you seen her this morning?'

'Well, now –' the woman made a pretence of thinking

back – 'I saw her last night, of course, when she forgot her keys and needed me to let her in . . .' She looked at him knowingly, one eyebrow raised.

Carter snapped. 'I didn't bloody ask you if you saw her last night,' he shouted at her. 'I asked you if you'd seen her this morning.'

The woman's lips tightened. 'There's really no need to swear at me. No, as it happens I haven't seen her this morning. And might I ask who you are, in any case?'

But Carter had already turned his back on her and was trampling over the winter-flowering pansies as he approached the front window. The curtains were closed, but there was a small gap at the top, so he climbed up onto the window sill and looked through into the front room.

Inside was chaos. Drawers were overturned, papers sprawled all over the carpet. Carter felt a chill run through his body as he jumped down and looked again through the letter box. The corridor looked as empty and neat as he would have expected it to, with one exception. Alone in the middle of the floor was Rosemary's shoe that had been broken in the attack the night before.

Carter closed his eyes and breathed in deeply as he tried to calm himself. Then he stood up, breathed out, and kicked the front door with all the fury and frustration he felt bottled up inside him.

It was a futile gesture, and it didn't make him feel any better.

A succession of images flashed through Mary's head. Normally they came to her at night as she slept, but as she sat bolt upright in her hospital bed in the half-light

97

of the wintry dusk, she saw those scenes as clearly as if she was living them.

She saw herself under her bedclothes. They were coarse and uncomfortable, and they smelled – the stench of months without washing, although she had long since ceased to notice it. If she could cover herself completely, she told herself, and stop any light from getting in, maybe she could blank out the noise of the screaming in the next room. It was the closest she ever got to a game. And at least while her mum was shouting down the phone she wasn't shouting at her.

She heard the sound of footsteps in the corridor. Mary froze, praying that those footsteps would not lead into her bedroom; but her prayers were not to be answered this time. 'Where the fuck are you?' She heard the gravelly, cigarette-parched voice of her mother in the doorway rise an octave when she realized her daughter was hiding in bed. 'Get out of there, you stupid little bitch,' she screamed, pulling the blanket away and hurling it to the floor. Her mother clutched her hair and pulled her up. Mary knew better than to scream, but she couldn't help letting a sob escape. Her big eyes looked up at the furious woman in front of her, and she recognized the hungry, desperate look in her face that she found so terrifying. 'What were you doing under there?' Her voice was quieter now. More threatening.

Mary lowered her head and looked at the floor. 'Nothing,' she mumbled.

Suddenly she felt a blow across the side of her face and she fell to the ground. 'You don't fucking get it, do you?' her mother started screaming again as she kicked her hard in the ribs. Then she stormed out, leaving Mary alone and in dreadful pain in that tiny room, with not a toy, book or object from which she could derive the slightest piece of comfort.

And then, as it so often did, the image in Mary's mind faded, and she saw the other side of her mother. She was still in that lonely bedroom, gazing out of the window at a series of featureless tower blocks, but when her mother entered this time there was a softness to her features. There had clearly been some money today – a giro cheque or cash from one of the other infrequent sources that Mary knew nothing about – which always meant a bottle. A bottle to stay her trembling hands and calm her frayed nerves. She sat beside Mary on the bed and took her in her arms, locking her in a long embrace that stung the bruising along her ribs. She heard her mother crying, and pathetically whispering, 'I love you,' almost to herself. It was affection of a sort, and Mary clung desperately to it.

But a bottle and its effects would not last longer than a few hours, leaving behind it only the memory of Mary's momentary reprieve, and confusion in her young mind.

Mary was suddenly snapped back to reality by the sound of the officer who was guarding the room scraping his chair as he got up and walked down the corridor. She slipped out of bed and opened the door. Looking down the corridor she saw the door of the Gents slam shut; she started walking in the opposite direction.

She was a strange sight, barefoot in her hospital pyjamas, with her wild eyes and wild hair, but the hospital staff she passed were too busy to pay her much attention. She walked almost in a trance, not really knowing where she was going, but vaguely aware that she was heading for the exit.

'Are you OK, dear?' A voice from behind stopped her in her tracks. She turned round to see an elderly porter looking at her with kindly eyes.

Mary nodded. 'I'm just going to find my mum,' she said, before turning back and continuing on her way. Ahead of her was a fire exit. She knew there was no other way out – you needed a pass to get in and out of the wards as security was tight in a children's hospital. She opened the door and the shrill ring of the fire alarm going off made her jump. She ran down the escape route and away from the hospital.

Five minutes later she was on Westminster Bridge. Her feet were numb, but she didn't notice, and the hospital pyjamas offered her hardly any protection from the biting cold. Her teeth chattered, but she was barely aware of where she was, still less of being freezing. Even now no one approached her, too scared, embarrassed or busy to help. They just stared as she went past.

She gazed over the side, just as she had done only a few weeks before when Frankie had taken her under her wing. Frankie. She thought of what she had said to her last night: 'Trust me, Mary. This guy has friends. When they find out what happened here, they'll be back. The safest place you can be is a police cell, and when they let you out, you must never come back here. If you can't go home, move to a different part of the country . . .'

She thought of Strut – the image of his horrifically broken body came into her head, not for the first time that day – and of what he had said to her last night when she had called for her mum: 'Well, she doesn't want you, you little fucking bitch . . .' She knew he was right.

She thought of the policeman who interviewed her

earlier today. He didn't care what happened to her. His words echoed in her head: 'Young offenders' institution. Nasty place. You get fucked over three times before breakfast. Think I'd rather be sniffing glue round Elephant and Castle . . .'

And she thought of her mother. She thought of her mother most of all. She wondered if she cared where her daughter was now, or were her worries swimming at the bottom of a vodka bottle? She heard her mother's voice too: 'You don't fucking get it, do you? You just don't fucking get it.'

No, Mary thought, her mind suddenly clear. I don't get it.

Frankie had asked her when they had met on the bridge if she was going to do anything stupid. But now she knew with absolute clarity that what she had in mind was far from that. She had nowhere else to go. No other options. If she had done it weeks ago, Bob Strut would still be alive and Frankie would not have had to risk her freedom on account of such a useless little girl.

The swirling water below was inky – the tide was running fast. The lights of London glittered on its surface hypnotically. She climbed onto the deep wall and teetered on its edge. Suddenly she was vaguely aware of a crowd of people around her, calling out, imploring her not to jump. She looked over her shoulder. Thirty metres away she saw hospital security staff running up to her, closely followed by a couple of nurses she recognized, with panicked looks on their faces. She gazed back down at the Thames.

'I'm sorry, Frankie,' she muttered to herself.

She looked down again and felt dizzy from the height.

'I'm sorry, Mum,' she whispered, leaning forward.

And as she fell, she heard the scream of a woman on the bridge.

It was strangely fitting that it was the last sound she ever heard.

Mark Taylor was quiet as he sat in the back of the police van with Irvin and four members of the armed response unit he had requested. He couldn't shake off the feeling that he should have been party to Carter's information – what was he hiding? But Taylor was sensible enough to admit to himself that Carter's hunches often paid off. This woman *had* killed someone in the last twenty-four hours – even if that someone was a scumbag like Strut – and clearly there was more to her predicament than he knew about if Carter and the SFO were taking such a close interest in her. The gruesome image of Strut's dead body rose freshly in his mind, and he did his best to suppress a shudder. Even if she wasn't armed, she was willing to do whatever it took, and she was a violent little bitch. Truth was, he didn't know what the hell he was going to find – and if his time in the job had taught him one thing, it was that it was better to be over-prepared for the situation ahead. So in the circumstances, armed response seemed a reasonable course of action. He felt unprotected sitting beside the four men in their black jump suits, helmets and body armour.

The light was fading outside, which was making them all nervous. At times like this you wanted to see what you were doing, not fumble around in the dark; but he knew that the Mills girl would be unlikely to stay long in one place, so they couldn't risk waiting till tomorrow. Chances were she'd have seen the newspapers or the TV, and would want to get as far away as possible from London where her picture was on every local news report. The mother had sworn her daughter hadn't been in touch with anybody in the area, but he thought that was unlikely to be true. People always go back to their roots at times of trauma – basic psychology, rookie stuff.

Their destination was the outskirts of a small village about three-quarters of an hour outside London. Taylor glanced at his watch – they should be there any minute. Why the hell was he so on edge? It had been only yesterday that he'd been stomping around the office complaining that all he ever seemed to do these days was paperwork. Now he was out and about, doing real police work like the old days. So why did he keep licking his lips nervously? Why was his stomach churning? He was only after some kid who'd gone off the rails. More than likely they would find her with a belt strapped round the top of her arm and a needle stuck into a protruding vein, too spaced out even to speak, let alone pull a gun on them. And even if she did, the armed officers would be there in front of him. All he had to do was bring her in.

The van slowed down as it turned a sharp corner into a private road that was in need of resurfacing, but the two squad cars that had been following them pulled up on the main road, keeping out of sight. The van shook as it bumped down the road before coming to a halt. The armed officers started tightening their straps and checking their weapons. 'Right, lads.' Taylor felt that it was up to him to say something. 'Remember, our suspect is unlikely to be armed and is *very* likely to be fucking frightened. We don't want to find ourselves explaining our way out of an unarmed stiff, so take it easy, will you?'

The men looked at him almost contemptuously. 'Tell you what, Detective Inspector,' the squad leader said gently but meaningfully, 'why don't you take the lead, and if she looks like she's pulling a gun, you can read out her rights? How does that sound?' There was no laughter from his grim-faced colleagues as they piled out of the van.

'I mean it!' he whispered hoarsely after them, before jumping out of the van himself. 'Wait here,' he redundantly told the officer driving the van.

Without speaking they continued down the driveway on foot. The ground was covered in frozen snow and crunched beneath them, even though they tried to be as light-footed as possible. As they turned a corner, the house came into view.

Taylor had expected it to be something rather grand, sitting there in its solitary splendour, but when he saw it he realized it was in fact a pretty poor-looking place, ramshackle and run-down. The front of the house had once been rendered white, but the render was now greying and breaking away; an old black Transit van was parked at the front; the garden showed no sign of having been cared for, and resembled a scrap yard more than anything else. It was fully dark now, except for the shine of the snow, and most of the lights on the upper floor of the house seemed to be switched off. On the ground floor, however, a few were switched on, and the light from one of the rooms illuminated a small heap of rubble that was piled up against the wall. The gentle babble of a television was vaguely discernible in the background. Taylor felt himself become a bit less edgy when he realized that his target was probably just watching TV.

Silently the team took up its positions: two at the front door, one at the back and the fourth member covering the driveway they had just come down. Taylor stood in the shadow of the Transit van, watching everything from his vantage point but hidden out of harm's way in case anything went wrong. He watched in the darkness as one of the armed officers at the front door gently tried to open it – it swung open without difficulty. Taylor began to move towards the house, trying his best to be as skilful as his colleagues but looking more like a target himself. With care, the two armed officers gingerly entered, then one of them reappeared at the doorway a few moments later, giving a thumbs-up sign to Taylor: the first room was secured and empty. Taylor approached the door and peered inside.

The kitchen was sparse: an old Formica table, a sink and a stand-alone oven that had seen better days. The whole place looked as though it could do with knocking down. On the back of a chair a beaten-up jacket had been flung carelessly, and from behind a door on the other side of the room the noise of the television was even more distinct. The two armed officers took their positions on either side of the door, lightly gripping their MP5K semi-automatic machine guns. One of them raised three fingers of his right hand and started a silent countdown.

Three.

Two.

One.

They burst through the door and suddenly started

screaming: 'Armed police! Get onto the floor! Get onto the floor now!' There was a pause, and then a desperate clattering as their target fell to the ground. 'Put your hands behind your back!'

Taylor stayed in the kitchen, listening as the officers restrained the suspect with handcuffs. Then he took a deep breath and walked in. 'Are you Francesca Mills?' he asked as he entered the room.

And then he stopped still.

Sprawled on the floor, his hands cuffed behind his back, was a man. He was tallish, but fat, and he wore nothing but a pair of boxer shorts and a greying white vest. There was an awkward silence as the armed officers, their brows sweating, looked to Taylor for instructions; but Taylor didn't know what to say. 'Who the hell are you?' he managed finally, spitting out the words with genuine venom.

The man didn't answer. He couldn't – he was lying on the floor trembling with the fear that can only be inspired by two grim-faced gunmen brandishing machine guns. Taylor looked around: an old-fashioned mobile phone lay on the coffee table. 'Is that your phone?' he shouted at the man.

Again, no reply.

'I said, is that your phone?'

'No!' For such a big man his voice was surprisingly high-pitched.

'Who gave it to you? Where is she?'

'I found it,' the man gasped. 'Last night. In a taxi.'

Taylor stared at him blankly for a few seconds, then turned on his heel and strode out of the room. 'Let him go,' he said curtly as he left, putting his hand in his pocket to take out his own phone. He wanted to call Carter – Sean *fucking* Carter – and explain to him in very minute detail what an idiot he thought he was.

PART TWO

Chapter Six

Bob Strut was as alive as he ever was.

Frankie saw his sneer, and the coldness of his eyes. She saw his burly fist gripping the wicked-looking knife with which he had attacked her.

And then she saw him lying on the ground, the bottle embedded deeply in his neck. The blood that poured from the wound was more copious now — it seemed to run out like water from a hose. It swamped her boots and stuck her feet to the ground. She tried to run, but found she couldn't move. Suddenly Strut opened his eyes and looked straight at her. He grinned, a horrible grin but one that seemed to suit his face, and then he started whispering. Frankie strained her ears, desperately trying to hear what he was saying, but the rasping sound was being drowned out by a scream. She turned her head, expecting to see Mary in a state of hysterics, but Mary was nowhere to be seen. Instead, dressed in a smart woollen skirt and a matching cardigan, her hands covering her ears as if to drown out her screams, was Frankie's mother. Again she tried to run, but the blood swimming around her feet was stronger than any glue, and she found herself rooted to the spot. She turned round again to see Strut standing up. He walked towards her, oblivious to the screaming, and hit her round the side of the face. Frankie felt herself falling to the ground, and braced herself for the whack on the hard concrete.

But instead of concrete she felt herself lying against something soft. It was a mattress, and she found herself at home, as she so often did. The duvet that covered her was warm, the pillow plump, and by her side was a small white teddy bear, her constant companion since before she could remember. She lay there wide awake, as though she was waiting for something, before she heard the door to her bedroom creak open. She closed her eyes and held her teddy a little tighter, lying with the improbable stillness that only a child pretending to be asleep can achieve, as she listened to the footsteps entering her room. Gradually, as slowly as she could manage, she untightened her eyes so that they were still closed but she could half see through her long eyelashes. A figure stood there, silhouetted in front of the curtains. He knew she was awake. And she knew she couldn't fool him. 'No one will believe you, Francesca,' he whispered as he walked towards the bed and bent down to her . . .

Frankie awoke with a start, damp from sweating even though it was still cold. Her face was protected from the concrete of the shop doorstep by a dirty tea towel that she had managed to pilfer from a cafe the day before; her body was protected from the elements by a thin, ragged blanket – holey in places – that she had found discarded by some waste bins near the station when she had arrived two nights previously. For a few moments she didn't move, disorientated by the unfamiliar surroundings and the uncomfortable feeling the dream had left her with.

It was still dark as she sat up, but the steely tinge to the sky told her that morning was not far away. Almost involuntarily Frankie reached up and touched her crudely cut hair. It felt strange still, as if she was somehow naked, but at the same time it gave her comfort to know that she must look so different to how she appeared two days ago. She knew she had to move before the owner of the shop – a newsagent's – arrived to find her blocking his entrance. The last thing she needed was an irate member of the public calling the police to get her moved on. Her blanket wrapped around her, she fumbled in the pocket of her jeans and pulled out the remainder of the money. In her half-awake state she thought she could feel a chunky two-pound coin, but her eyes narrowed in annoyance when she discovered it was just the locket she had taken from the woman on Chelsea Bridge. It was pretty enough, but useless to her at the moment – she'd convert it to money when the time was right – so she stuffed it back in her pocket and counted out her real money. Just a few pounds – barely enough to buy herself something to eat for breakfast. She was well used to surviving on one meal a day, however meagre it was, but she knew she had to think about how she was going to manage when the money ran out. She had been on the streets of Bath for thirty-six hours now, but she had been wandering around in a daze, keeping out of people's way. She had noticed other vagrants, of course, but had been too distracted to follow them, to find out where they stayed and, more importantly, where they begged. Today, all that would have to change. She couldn't afford to be distracted any more.

Slowly she pushed herself to her feet, picking up the plastic bag that held the remains of her bandages. All of a sudden she felt dizzy – the cold had clearly got to her more than she thought – and she put her hand against the wall to steady herself. 'Shit!' she muttered, wincing as a shock of pain stung through her hand. She staggered down the road, the blanket still wrapped tightly around her shoulders, looking for a cafe. She wanted somewhere that wasn't too full, as she was paranoid people would recognize her, and she wanted to make sure they were desperate enough for customers that she wouldn't be asked to leave the moment she walked through the door. She decided to head away from the centre of town, towards the run-down areas on the outskirts where she felt more at home.

As she walked, she came across a pretty bed and breakfast that was just beyond Bath Abbey and opposite the Roman Baths. She stood staring at the ashlar stone facade, and welled up inside: it was the place she used to visit as a child, where she spent long weekends with her mother and father. The last time she had been here was just after her father had died, and they had come to get away from it all. Frankie remembered being impressed by the grand architecture and the quaint shops surrounding it. They always stayed on the second floor. It had great views of the busy town, and as night fell she would always sit by the window and watch the people below: some would be dressed for dinner or the theatre, while others just strolled around watching the street entertainment. She remembered the twin double beds with their soft, white sheets and warm quilts, the floral design on the curtains, the television that hung excitingly on the wall and which her mum had allowed her to watch in bed, and the tea tray with its stash of chocolate biscuits wrapped in cellophane. How different her previous trips to the city had been from this one. Now the buildings looked colder, the streets dirtier – but then she hadn't been paying much attention to the streets any other time.

As dawn started to break, she found herself outside a cafe opposite a building site. Part of a small parade of shops on the west side of town that led to the countryside and the motorway beyond, its front windows were steamed up enough for her to find it difficult to see inside. She peered through the glass as best she could – just making out a few plastic tables and brightly coloured seats that were secured to the floor. Four or five people were in there – all of them builders filling up on big plates of food before the day ahead, happily gossiping as their cigarettes smouldered in tinfoil ashtrays. The woman at the counter was smoking too, standing guard over her enormous metal urn. It was as unappealing as a place could be; but it would be warm, and the food would be hot and cheap. Frankie pushed the door open and walked inside.

She could feel all eyes on her as she walked up to the counter. The woman looked her up and down, her face a picture of mistrust that bordered on contempt. She didn't speak to Frankie as she stood there reading the menu scrawled in chalk on a blackboard behind the counter; she just stared meaningfully as she prepared to take her order. 'I'll have the full breakfast,' Frankie spoke quickly, 'and some tea.'

'Three eighty-five.' The woman stated the price almost as if it was a challenge. Frankie pulled a handful of coins out of her pocket and counted it out to the nearest penny. As she did so, the woman continued to stare at her, her expression making her feelings perfectly plain: I don't like tramps, she seemed to say. If you'd come here an hour later, during the breakfast rush, you'd have been turfed out, for sure. Frankie laid the money on the counter, then went to find herself a seat, ignoring the stares of the builders who turned and continued their conversations as Frankie went to sit down.

'Oi!' The woman shouted at her above the noise of the radio in the background.

Frankie turned quickly, shocked by the note of accusation in her voice. 'Yes?' she replied as mildly as she could.

'It's not the Ritz.' The woman scowled as she filled a mug with hot water from the urn. 'You can take your tea now.' She held out the mug full of hot, white water, a teabag floating insipidly on the top.

By the time her food arrived, Frankie had already finished the tea. Hot and sweet, it had revived her and brought some feeling back into her numb fingers. Before she left home she had never been able to stomach sugar in her tea, but now she liked her hot drinks as treacly as she could make them – she found it comforting, almost nannying, and it gave her a burst of energy that she imagined helped her through the day. She was counting out her last few coins to determine if she had enough for another cup when her plate of food arrived. Eggs and bacon were swimming in a sweat of grease, surrounded by a puddle of beans and halves of hot toast. Frankie fell upon it hungrily, devouring it as though it would be her last. It was gone in a matter of minutes. She walked to the counter and ordered more tea.

As she was returning to her seat with her drink, she noticed a tabloid newspaper lying unread on one of the tables. She picked it up and sat down to read it. She flicked through the pages, uninterested in the seedy revelations of celebrities whose names meant nothing to her, or the self-important pronouncements of politicians whose policies were next to meaningless to someone in her position. Frankie liked to look through a newspaper when she found one, even if it was a few days old. She always saw them as a way of keeping in touch with that side of her life that had long since passed; but if she was honest with herself, the very act of reading stories about people who had homes to go to made her feel increasingly detached from them. She had got through the first four pages when her eyes were instantly drawn to an article at the top of the next page. She took a sharp intake of breath, and suddenly it didn't seem so warm in the cafe after all.

The girl in the picture was her.

She looked around. The people in the cafe were ignoring her now, and the stern-faced woman behind the counter was serving someone else – a regular, by the way she was talking to him. Frankie tried to read the article, but her eyes simply jumped from word to word, not taking in much of what it said – though she read it closely enough to establish that at least her name was not mentioned. She gazed at the image of herself, unnerved by the look of impassive determination that marked her face as she ran. Thank God I changed my hair, she thought to herself.

As she read, her paranoia was combined with a wave of panic that made her whole body shudder. She looked at the picture more closely – her features might have changed, but it was perfectly clear what she was wearing. Don't be stupid, she told herself. Plenty of people wear clothes similar to that, if not the same. But none of them were on the run. None of them had killed a man. She had to find herself some new clothes.

As calmly as she could, she folded up the newspaper, put it under her arm and stood up, leaving her tea on the table. As she headed for the door, she heard the serving woman's voice again, just as harsh. 'Hey, you can't take that.'

'What?' she asked, genuinely confused.

'The paper! Go on, put it down and get out.'

Everyone was looking at her again. She returned their stares with nervous defiance, slung the paper down on a table and left.

Frankie had been wanting to find herself a new set of clothes ever since she arrived. She might have known Bath as a child, but she certainly didn't know where to go to find hostels to shelter from the night-time cold, even though it was a lot smaller than London, or if the homeless people congregated in special places where they burned fires in old metal dustbins to ward off the chill. Now she had even more reason to change what she was wearing. But clothes were hard to come by on the street. They were cheap enough in charity shops, but even the few pounds needed to buy a warm jumper were more likely to be spent on food or booze – or something stronger to dull the pain. Sometimes the charitable organizations that dished out hot meals also had bags of second-hand clothing, but not often. And in any case, Frankie was new to town and did not know where – or even if – such places existed. She was going to have to find another way to change her appearance even further.

She crossed the road and sat on a low wall opposite the parade of shops. She didn't know what time it was but the other shops were preparing to open up so, at a guess, it would be about eight o'clock. There was a newsagent's, a dry-cleaner's next to a laundrette with a gaudy orange front, and a Cancer Research charity shop. Frankie sat there wondering what she could do, her blanket once more wrapped around her as she watched the customers come and go in their dribs and drabs. She knew that, usually, the bags left outside charity shops were a good source of used clothes, but today there were none; and although she had heard people say that laundrettes could offer rich pickings, it required guts to steal right from under people's noses. But the panic she had felt in London was rising again, and she could think of nothing except how to continue her transformation.

From her vantage point she could see that there were five or six people sitting in the laundrette. On one side of the room were the washing machines, on the other side the huge tumble-dryers. The punters sat reading magazines, or staring into space, oblivious of the time passing or of each other. Frankie eyed them closely, her face stony: she knew what she was waiting for. Eventually a middle-aged woman fished her wet laundry from a washing machine and carried it across the room to the dryer. She was a big woman, her skin black and her clothes brightly coloured – hardly the sort of thing that Frankie would choose in order to melt into the background, but she was not in a position to be picky. The woman slipped a few coins into the machine, then waddled out of the door and into the cafe.

Frankie had no way of telling the time – the watch she had received for her thirteenth birthday had broken – but she estimated that she would have to wait about twenty minutes. That would be long enough for the clothes to get reasonably dry and for the other customers to forget the half-noticed face of their true owner, but not so long that she would risk the woman coming back and catching her red-handed. So she sat there, keeping her head down and doing her best not to be noticed, estimating how much time had passed.

Finally she decided to make her move. She walked to the end of the parade of shops, where there was a small alleyway, and carefully placed her blanket by a rubbish bin – she knew nothing shouted out that she was homeless louder than that item. Then, taking a deep breath, she walked as confidently as she could into the laundrette. For once nobody paid her any attention as she entered. It was warm inside and smelled of heated washing powder – a comforting fragrance that Frankie had almost forgotten. Only two of the dryers were in use: one of them had a customer sitting in front of it, the other just a colourful plastic laundry bag. She walked straight up to it, opened the dryer and started to stuff the still slightly damp clothes into the bag. Nobody spoke as she tried to squeeze in all the crumpled laundry, but as she struggled with the zip she felt everyone's eyes burning through her. She immediately knew, instinctively, that they were suspicious – they were just being timid about confronting her. It would need only one of them to take the plunge, though. Frankie had to get out.

She picked up the laundry bag, ignoring the fact that a pair of tights was still trailing from it, and went straight back to the door. 'Excuse me . . .' someone said falteringly behind her, but she did not turn to see who it was – she just opened the door and ran. She heard the voice behind her once again – 'Hey, that's not yours!' – so she didn't stop to pick up the blanket she had stashed in the alleyway. She just ran and ran until her lungs hurt and her legs would not physically take her any further. Only then did she look behind her.

There was no one. She had got away with it.

She slipped down a deserted side street and took shelter

in the shadow of a big yellow skip full of rubbish. Rummaging through the clothes she found very little that was of use to her – large underwear and colourful headdresses, mostly – but there were two jumpers, one far too small and one far too big, that would at least disguise her a little, and keep her warm. Taking off her coat, she ripped the seams of the smaller jumper so that she could pull it on, then covered it with the larger one. It was a chunky polo neck with pink and white stripes – not that Frankie was looking at the colour – and still damp. If I walk around, it will soon dry off, she thought. She pulled her coat back over the jumpers, and then a small headdress caught her eye. It was plain, just a square of pale blue material. She picked it out of the bag and tentatively, as if remembering something she had done many times before but had half forgotten, she placed the material over her hair and tied two opposite corners together. Her newly black hair peeked out from under the front of the headscarf, and the colour of the material made her already blue eyes seem more piercing. She stood up with an air of delicate confidence, and walked back out into the street.

Had anyone paid her any attention as she walked serenely across the road, they might even have thought she was pretty.

It was ten-thirty, and Harriet Johnson was sitting at the kitchen table, still in her dressing gown having not slept all night. An untouched cup of coffee sat on the table in front of her, but it had gone cold long ago. Her eyes were red from crying, and they stared ahead of her. The soft murmur of the radio played in the background, but Harriet barely heard it.

The phone rang; she didn't acknowledge it. It had been ringing on and off all morning, but she didn't want to speak to anyone. Not even William. Especially not William, in fact. She knew it was illogical, but somewhere in her confused mind she couldn't help blaming him for all this. Why had he told his colleagues? Why couldn't he just do this one thing for her? She knew his motives were for the best; deep down she knew he was right. But that didn't change how she felt.

The attitude of DI Mark Taylor, who had come round to question her, had said it all. He had tried his best to be polite, of course, but there was no way that Harriet could persuade him that Francesca was anything more than a street bum. But although she'd seen with her own eyes the picture taken from the CCTV, she still couldn't believe that her daughter was a killer. The most haunting thing was the look in her eyes. Desperate. Hunted. Harriet remembered when Francesca was a small child, toddling around on sturdy little legs – her eyes had been the most appealing thing about her. Soft and beautiful. Eyes to fall in love with. Eyes like that should never be filled with such fear. Harriet felt her own eyes welling up again as the phone stopped ringing.

How long she sat there gazing into space she couldn't say. Suddenly, though, there was a tap at the window that made Harriet jump. She looked up to see her friend Sally standing there, waving at her with a cheery smile that turned into a quizzical look when she saw the blank, unsmiling expression on Harriet's face as she stood up slowly and went to open the door.

'Harriet, I . . .' Sally was flustered to see her friend in

her dressing gown so late in the morning. 'I'm sorry, I didn't realize you were still . . .'

But Harriet had turned her back on her and was heading back to the table.

Sally closed the door quietly and followed her. 'Harrie,' she asked, her voice unable to mask her concern, 'is everything all right?'

Harriet put her face in her palms and started to weep.

'What on earth's the matter?' Sally persisted, putting her arm tenderly around her crying companion.

Between sobs, Harriet pointed to the work surface where a photograph lay. Sally picked it up. 'Oh my . . .' she whispered. 'Harriet, is this Francesca?'

Harriet nodded.

'Where did you get this? Is she all right?'

'The police gave it to me,' Harriet managed to gasp. 'They think she's killed someone.'

Sally looked incredulously at her. '*Killed* someone? They can't think that.'

'Do I look like I'm making it up?' Harriet snapped.

'No, no,' Sally tried to mollify her. 'I'm sorry, I didn't mean that. I just meant . . . well . . . Francesca. There must be some mistake.'

'I don't know. I just don't know.' Harriet's crying started to subside now, as if she hardly had the energy to summon up the tears.

'Can't William do something? Speak to people . . .' Sally asked vaguely.

Harriet shook her head. 'It was he who told the police that I recognized her on TV. He says we can't keep it a secret, that we'll only make more trouble for her if we do.'

'Yes, of course.' Sally nodded her head. 'Is there anything I can do? Anything you need?'

Harriet pulled a tissue from up her sleeve and dabbed at her face. 'No,' she replied. 'No, thank you. Just . . .'

'What is it?'

'Just keep this to yourself, won't you? I don't want the whole village knowing about it.'

'Of course I will.' Her eyes flickered back down to the picture. 'Call me if you want anything, won't you?'

'I will,' Harriet replied, watching her friend let herself out. 'I will.'

In central London, the clouds had cleared. It was still sharply cold, but the sky above was a clear blue, and the sun was casting shadows from the trees surrounding the small patch of park in St James's Square, just south of Piccadilly. The snow resting on the railings of the park area had turned overnight from soft powder to hard, crunchy ice; but it looked picturesque, adorning the metal spikes with a gentle, pleasing regularity. In the background was the hum of traffic making its way along Pall Mall, but this square was a respite from all that, a small haven of tranquillity in the crazy bustle of the city. There weren't even that many people here – just the occasional office workers in heavy overcoats on their way to a meeting or nipping out early to buy themselves a sandwich for lunch.

A large black Bentley turned left into the square and slowly drove almost an entire circuit of the one-way road before coming to a halt outside the unmarked door of a rather grand-looking townhouse. The uniformed driver stepped out and opened the rear door nearest the pavement, allowing his passenger to step out. He was a large man, not in height but in build, and his round face was unsmiling as he spoke to his driver. 'I shouldn't be more than half an hour,' he told him as he rearranged his scarf.

'Yes, Mr Tunney,' the driver nodded, before closing the door and stepping back into the warmth of the front seat.

Tunney stood at the bottom of the stone steps that led up to the pretty Georgian townhouse next to the London Library. Unlike all the other buildings in the square it had no sign or plaque to say what it was. He pulled a small mobile phone from his coat pocket and switched it off before walking up the steps and ringing the bell. There was a short pause, then a woman's voice spoke in friendly, patrician tones. 'Good morning.'

'Morgan Tunney for Sir Ainsley Cooper,' Tunney grunted.

'One moment, Mr Tunney,' the voice said politely. There was another pause – clearly she was checking that he was expected – before she spoke again. 'Do come in, Mr Tunney.' There was a long buzz, and Tunney pushed the door open.

Inside could not have been more different to the austere exterior of the house. As Tunney stamped the snow off his shoes, somebody appeared seemingly out of nowhere to take his coat and scarf. Ahead of him was a long corridor with a plush red carpet, high ceiling and small but elaborate chandeliers; to his right was a reception desk with an immaculately dressed, extremely pretty young receptionist. 'Good morning, Mr Tunney.' She smiled at him, forcing a grudging smile back from the middle-aged banker. 'Sir Ainsley is already here. He's waiting for you in the Montgomery Room. Turn left at the top of the stairs and it's the second room on your right.'

'Thank you,' Tunney muttered almost under his breath as he walked quickly past the reception desk. To his left was a small dining room, already exquisitely laid out for lunch with creamy starched napkins and bright silver cutlery. If the meeting were to be more congenial, he knew he would have been invited to take lunch there; but today's business was too serious to be discussed over three courses and several bottles of Pomerol. No one was going to be entertaining anyone today. He'd even had to cancel lunch with his daughter – a monthly treat that neither of them would ever consider missing. Tunney headed straight up the stairs, clutching the banisters with his fat, clammy hand.

The door to the Montgomery Room, like all the other doors in this very private club, was a dark mahogany colour. Tunney stood in front of it for a few moments, dusting down the lapels of his expensive, single-breasted, pinstripe suit and needlessly straightening his tie, took a deep breath then knocked firmly on the door. 'Come,' a voice on the other side sounded. He turned the brass door handle, opened the door and walked in.

The room in which he found himself was richly appointed. A long table stood in the centre, surrounded by comfortable-looking chairs. A tray with a large pot of coffee and a plate of freshly baked biscuits and cakes sat at one end. There was a merry fire blazing in the fireplace at the far end of the room, and the walls were lined with leather-bound books. Looking out onto a deserted courtyard from a floor-to-ceiling window framed by thick velvet curtains was a tall, thin man. He didn't turn round as Tunney entered the room, but stayed standing there, immobile and unmoved by the awkward silence. 'Do help yourself to a cup of coffee, Morgan,' the man said in a quiet but deep voice.

'I won't, thank you,' Tunney replied, out of breath slightly from the exertion of climbing the stairs. 'Jeanette tells me I drink too much,' he gabbled a bit nervously. 'Makes for a much quieter life if I just cut down.' He walked the length of the room and stood by the fire. 'Are the others not here yet?'

The man turned slowly and smiled at him – the sort of smile that betrayed no friendliness. His grey hair was brushed back to disguise his encroaching baldness, his face tanned from a recent family holiday, and healthy-looking despite its reptilian thinness. He spread his arms to indicate that the room was empty apart from the two of them. 'It would appear not,' he said lightly. 'Why don't you have a seat, Morgan?'

'Thank you.' Tunney collapsed into a chair at the head of the table.

'You don't mind if I stand, I suppose,' Sir Ainsley purred. 'I find it clarifies my thoughts and helps me think straight. And we need to think straight just at the moment, don't we, Morgan?' He gazed into Tunney's eyes in a way that always made the banker feel uncomfortable.

'Yes,' he replied, his voice cracking slightly. 'Yes, we do.'

'Good. I'm glad we agree on that. It will make our little chat so much more straightforward.'

Tunney didn't answer – he just avoided Sir Ainsley's gaze.

Suddenly Cooper slapped his hand forcefully down on

the table. The coffee cups jangled slightly. 'What in *heaven's* name were you thinking?' he spat, his bright green eyes glaring with fury. 'What idiocy possessed you to leave that information at the bank?'

'Security!' Tunney spoke the word louder than he had intended, then quickly looked nervously at the door. 'Security,' he repeated himself more quietly.

Cooper stood up straight and regained his composure. 'How could it possibly ensure the security of our venture, Morgan? If this information falls into the wrong hands . . .'

'Not *your* security!' Tunney was less deferential now, angry that Cooper had spoken to him in such a way and contemptuous that he was taking him for an idiot; but he still seemed unsure of himself. 'Mine. Those documents can put me in prison for a very long time, as well as you. Do you really think I'm going to let someone else be the only person to have a copy?'

Sir Ainsley remained silent.

'You might do this sort of thing every day of the week, but before I met you I never had so much as a parking ticket. And I don't trust you, *Sir Ainsley*. I don't trust any of you – any more than you trust me. You might have convinced your precious electorate that you are a man of moral fibre, but let's not forget what it is we're doing here. And please don't try and tell me you don't have a copy of these documents yourself.'

Cooper's eyes narrowed slightly, momentarily, before he smiled once more, seemingly ignoring everything Tunney had said. 'I'm sure we'll be able to sort everything out,' he said calmly. 'Might I presume that nobody at the bank can access this information any more?'

'They never could.' Tunney's voice was quieter now too, though he could not hide the waver of nervousness that had found its way into his speech. 'It was only on my system and nobody had the passwords. She may not even have found anything – all I know is that my computer was broken into. I could have just kept quiet, but I thought it best to get our, er –' he never knew quite what words to use to describe the men they were waiting for – 'our *friends* to find out exactly what happened.'

'I'm sure they will have done,' Cooper answered, his face expressionless and his voice implacable. 'They're exceedingly efficient.' There was a knock at the door. 'Ah, speaking of efficiency . . . Come!'

The door opened and two men walked in – both tall, but one slightly taller than the other. They looked so similar they could almost be brothers. One had ruffled blond hair and strikingly blue eyes, while the other one, taller than his companion, had army-style short hair and brown eyes. His face was drawn and pale. They were both dressed in tailored suits with open-collar shirts and no tie. 'Gentlemen,' the blond one said shortly in greeting, his voice deep and with a thick Eastern European accent. 'A cold day.' He removed his gloves and flung them nonchalantly on the table.

'I would have thought you would be perfectly used to such weather in your part of the world,' Cooper replied blandly, clearly making small talk for the sake of it.

The man shrugged. His companion was standing by the closed door, his hands clasped gently together. The blond man looked around the room. 'Can we talk freely?'

Cooper nodded. 'It's perfectly secure. Have you spoken to the woman?'

The man allowed a whisper of a smile to pass across his lips. 'Yes,' he replied quietly. 'We have had a conversation. She was most forthcoming.' He enunciated his words with the strange precision of a man whose first language was not English.

'And?' Morgan Tunney's brow had beads of sweat on it.

'You appear warm, Mr Tunney. Perhaps you should not sit so close to the fire.'

The two men glared at each other. 'Gentlemen,' Cooper interjected sharply. 'Enough.' He turned to the blond man. 'Andreas, what was she doing in Morgan's office?'

'Downloading information.'

Tunney and Cooper glanced at each other uneasily. 'Why?' Cooper asked.

'She noticed some irregularity in the accounting,' the man replied, 'and alerted the Serious Fraud Office. They persuaded her to break into Mr Tunney's system and locate certain documents.'

The blood seemed to drain from the faces of the two men. 'Does this sound likely, Morgan?' Cooper asked quietly. 'Would this woman know what she was looking for?'

Tunney shrugged non-committally. 'She might. She's quite senior and would notice irregularities that are not normally on the system and not compliant with the FSA. But she wouldn't know how to get into my machine – I'm the only person who has the password –'

'I could hack into your computer in less than two minutes,' Andreas interrupted starkly. 'And if I can, so can anybody else. Especially the SFO. They gave her a device hidden in a silver locket that contained a patch to crack your password. She then loaded the information she wanted onto it.'

'And gave it to the SFO?' Sir Ainsley breathed the question as though he could not bear to hear the answer.

'No.'

Tunney's eyes widened, and Cooper turned his back to look out of the window again, as if he was unwilling to let anyone read the emotions on his face.

'Why not?'

'She was attacked in the street. Her bag was taken, and so was the necklace holding the device.'

'Do we know who it was?'

'No. It was just a random attack. A young girl. The woman couldn't tell us what she looked like.'

Sir Ainsley turned round again. 'I think, my friend, that you ought to press her a little harder for a description.'

The blond man smiled once more. 'I can assure you, Sir Ainsley, that if she could have given us any more information, she would have done. We can be very persuasive when we need to be.'

A silence fell upon the room as the four men seemed deep in thought. It was broken by Cooper. 'It appears you have been fairly lucky, Morgan.'

'We've all been lucky, Sir Ainsley. You have as much to lose as anyone.'

'Quite,' Cooper replied in a deadpan voice. 'Of course, we are not quite out of the woods yet.' He turned to Andreas. 'Did the woman give you the name of her handler at the SFO?'

Andreas nodded. 'His name is Sean Carter. We've checked him out – he used to be a DI at London Bridge.'

'I think perhaps you ought to deal with him.'

'No,' Andreas shook his head. 'Without the information he has nothing, and it's far better to know who you are dealing with than to dispose of him and have him replaced by an unknown quantity.'

Cooper nodded his head. 'You might be right,' he conceded. 'Is it possible that you could find our little hooligan, or has she gone completely off the radar?'

'Anything is possible, for a price.'

'And what would that price be?'

Andreas eyed up his clients. 'Five hundred thousand.'

Tunney spluttered. 'Don't be ridiculous! That's an outrageous sum.'

The man shrugged. 'It's your decision, of course.'

'I wonder, Andreas,' Sir Ainsley stepped between the two of them, 'if you and your friend might just give us a moment.' Andreas nodded politely and the two foreign men left the room. Cooper brought up a chair and sat close – uncomfortably close – to Tunney. 'Listen to me, Morgan,' he practically whispered. 'It will only take that locket falling into the hands of a reasonably intelligent person for the game to be up. If anyone discovers that I have been illegally involved with arms dealers, or that you have been instrumental in laundering the sums of money that we are talking about, we will both be looking at severe prison sentences. Under the circumstances, five hundred thousand pounds seems like rather a good deal, does it not?'

'You're not suggesting, I hope, that I assume this expense.'

'That is precisely what I'm suggesting, Morgan. You got us into this situation, so you can get us out of it.'

The two men stared at each other. Finally Tunney bowed his head in defeat. 'How do you know we can trust these people? I know next to nothing about them.'

'Andreas is the best there is. I've used him numerous times in the past, and he has never let me down.' Cooper stood up and went to the door to let the men back in. 'Five hundred thousand it is,' he told Andreas once the door was shut.

'Half now, half when we deliver the girl.'

'And the locket.'

'Of course. We will get all the information we need from her.' He smiled blandly.

'How –' Tunney began to ask, but Cooper interrupted him.

'Mr Tunney agrees to your terms,' he said in a tone of voice that would accept no refusal. 'Do you have any leads to go on?'

Andreas shrugged. 'The SFO have asked the police to track the girl down. We have people on the inside who will keep us informed of their progress. We will get to her before they do.'

'You'd better,' Tunney muttered, but Andreas ignored him and continued the conversation with Cooper.

'And what do you want us to do with the woman from the bank?'

Cooper turned back to look out of the window yet again. 'Do whatever you must,' he said in a quiet voice. 'Just make it discreet.'

Chapter Seven

'Same again?'

The girl shook her head. 'No, I shouldn't. I've got a report to write . . .' They had been there since midday, and apart from a few lunchtime drinkers they'd practically had the place to themselves, with the exception of an old man propping up the bar, nursing pints of dark bitter and smoking a pipe of pungent cherry tobacco.

He shrugged as he drained his pint, gazing at her over the rim of his glass with a twinkle in his eyes. 'Have you ever been down to the houseboats?' he asked out of the blue as he placed his glass down on the table.

'No,' she shook her head.

'Fancy a look?' He stared straight into her eyes.

She looked coyly down at the floor. 'No. It's freezing out there.'

'C'mon,' he persisted, his voice low and cajoling. 'Half of them are empty. We can just have a peek.' But the look in his eyes made it clear that peeking was the last thing on his mind. He grabbed their coats, took her by the hand and pulled her from the pub. She squealed, but she did not put up any resistance.

Outside the pub he put his arm around her shoulders and she snuggled up to him as they approached the small jetty leading down to the houseboats. A metal chain ran across it, which they climbed over with a quick, guilty look. The jetty was still slightly slippery from the icy night before, so they walked down as carefully as their merriness would allow, reeling occasionally as they lost their footing and clinging to each other a little more tightly than they perhaps needed to.

It was quiet among the houseboats, and the couple stood in silence for a few moments, listening to the water lapping against the wooden slats. A hazy mist was falling, blurring the other side of the river, shrouding them in a blanket of seeming solitude. She lifted her face up to his and they kissed, their eyes closed.

As they drew away from each other, they smiled sheepishly. 'Come on,' he said, pointing at a derelict-looking boat further down the jetty. 'No one's ever there.'

'I suppose this is where you bring all your women,' she suggested archly.

He put his hand to his chest. 'You're the only one. Hand on heart,' he told her.

'I don't believe you,' she replied as they climbed onto the boat. They clambered over the roof to the other side, where they could stand on the narrow deck out of the way of anyone else who might happen to be around. He stood with his back to the boat's railings as she approached him, kissed him once more and then rested her head on his shoulders.

And then she screamed.

'What is it?' he asked, shocked by the sound, but she was too hysterical to answer him. He spun round and looked out. In the water, banging gently against the side of the boat, was a body. The bullet wound on the head had rendered it an almost unrecognizable mess, but the longish hair splayed out in the water and the clothes that she still wore indicated that it was the body of a middle-aged woman. A magpie, braving the chilly waters in search of something to eat, sat on her head, pecking harshly at the pale wounded flesh.

The young man ran to the end of the boat, leaving his companion screaming with horror, grabbed the railings and vomited over the side.

The bird on the body flew away at the sound of his retching.

It had been a slow news day. Come to think of it, it had been a slow couple of weeks. Andy Summers, crime reporter on a national tabloid, had had quite enough of dredging up old stories that weren't really stories in the first place, of hanging round the courts hoping for a nugget of something printable. He was frustrated; more importantly, his editor was pissed off – he'd already received a bollocking in conference that morning, and he couldn't face another one tomorrow. This was the sort of run of bad luck that led to reporters being fired, and he knew it.

He had just finished making another fruitless round of calls to the same contacts in the Met and beyond, and they had all given him the same answer – 'Nothing you'd be interested in, mate. Sorry.' Andy had a finely honed journalist's instinct and he knew when these people were fobbing him off – today they weren't. He was sitting at his desk fiddling with his pencil, only vaguely aware of the hubbub around him as his colleagues rushed about in an attempt to finalize the following day's paper, when his phone rang. It was Janet at reception, as bubbly sounding but as to-the-point as ever. 'Hi, Andy, member of the public on the phone. Says he's got a story for you.'

Andy groaned inwardly. In his considerable experience, the average punter couldn't tell a story if it fell on them; but today he needed all the help he could get, so he took the call. 'Andy Summers, crime desk.'

There was a pause at the other end of the line. 'How much do you pay for a story?' His voice had a thick East End accent.

It was always the first question they asked, and the rules of engagement were that Andy never gave a proper answer. 'Depends on the story, mate. What have you got?'

'But you do pay?' His caller was obviously a rookie at this sort of thing.

'Yeah,' Andy replied nonchalantly. 'If we use it, we'll come to some sort of arrangement.'

The caller hesitated again. 'All right,' he said finally. 'You know that girl in the paper, the one caught running from the scene of the murder?'

It wasn't much of a description, but it had been such a quiet couple of days that Andy knew exactly who he meant. 'Yes, I know the one.'

'I can tell you who she is.'

Andy sat up a bit straighter – it sounded like this could be something after all. He'd better start turning on the charm. 'Thanks for coming to me with this, er . . .'

'Mike,' the caller said, audibly relaxing at Andy's change of tone. 'I run the local pub in a village down in Surrey. You get to hear all the gossip.'

'You don't sound like a Surrey boy,' Andy noted, his voice slipping into a mock Cockney accent as it often did when he was talking to people like this. His colleagues took the mickey when he did it, but it worked for him.

'No, I moved down here a few years ago. Better class of customer, if you know what I mean.'

'Of course. So who is it, then?'

'Her name is Francesca Mills. She ran away from home about four years ago. Everyone thought she was dead, to be honest. Terrible business.'

Andy allowed the conversation a respectful silence before continuing. 'So this girl's parents still live in the village, do they?' he asked.

'The mother does. Father died years ago – before my time. She's remarried now, local Old Bill. Nice enough couple. Keep themselves to themselves a bit, especially since the girl ran off.'

Andy thought about what he was being told. 'You realize that we need to go to the police with this, don't you?'

'The police know,' Mike told him. 'Apparently they've been round already.'

'OK,' Andy said, jotting notes in a little pad. 'Good. Tell me a bit more about the mother.'

'Well, like I say, I don't see her much in here. Not short of a bob or two, though – nice big house, couple of cars.'

'Sounds a bit grand on a copper's salary. What is he, chief commissioner?'

Mike laughed. 'Nothing like,' he confided. 'Word is, the first husband was worth a fair whack. Something in the city, don't know what. When he died all their insurances paid off. Course, it might all be rumours . . .' His voice trailed off a bit.

'Of course.' Andy was not averse to the occasional rumour if it helped flesh things out. He continued to make notes, the cogs in his newshound's brain working overtime. The story in his head was taking shape already: nice girl, well-to-do family, mother a housewife, step-father a copper, she goes off the rails and ends up the prime suspect in a murder investigation. On the right day it could even be a splash. 'Tell you what, Mike,' he told his informant, 'I might come down and see you. Maybe you can show me the house.'

'When were you thinking of?'

'Well,' replied the reporter, looking at his watch. 'What are you doing in about an hour's time?'

It took Andy and his photographer a bit longer than he had predicted to struggle through London and start following the directions Mike had given him, but he found his way to the pub soon enough. The Running Horses was a pretty place, with its thatched roof, old timber frame and limed walls, sitting serenely on one side of the village green opposite the church. The journalists ducked their heads as they walked through the low door into the small lounge bar. It was totally empty apart from a matronly woman behind the bar. 'What can I get you, lads?'

'Actually, we're here to see Mike.' Andy gave her his most winning smile as he sat on a stool.

The woman nodded. 'Mike!' she shouted over her shoulder. 'Someone to see you.'

The landlord was everything Andy had expected from talking to him on the phone. A large, thickset man, despite the cold weather he wore a T-shirt that revealed the faded pale blue tattoos up his arm. 'Hello, Mike.' Andy proffered his hand across the bar. 'This is Glenn, the photographer.'

'All right, fellas,' Mike replied in his rough voice. 'What can I get you, on the house?'

'Nothing, really,' answered the reporter, eager to get the pleasantries out of the way. 'Why don't we get on? Is the house far from here?'

'Not at all,' he said, disappearing behind the bar and returning with a heavy coat. 'I'll show you.'

As they trudged along the country lane, Andy started to ask his contact a few more questions. 'So tell me how you found out about all this.'

'Friend of Mrs Johnson's,' Mike replied shortly. He seemed to be less forthcoming than he'd been on the phone – a bit ashamed of what he was doing, perhaps. Andy decided that now was the time to spur him on a little.

'I spoke to my editor,' he said. 'Could be six grand in it for you, if the story hits the front page.'

Mike nodded his head slowly as they walked. 'She comes in the pub quite often – the friend, I mean,' he continued. 'Anyway, I overheard her telling someone that Mrs Johnson had told her all about it.' He chuckled to himself. 'She's a bit of a gossip, old Sally. Anyway, here we are.' They stopped by a driveway. The large wooden gate was open and there was a small two-door convertible parked by the front door of the big house. There were a few lights on, suggesting somebody was in.

'OK, Mike. Thanks very much. I'll take it from here and I'll be in touch.' He shook the landlord's hand.

'You'll let me know, won't you? About the money, I mean.'

'Course I will, Mike.' He smiled at him again.

Moments later Mike was walking back. 'You're a sly fucker, do you know that?' Glenn said to his colleague.

'Six grand!' He shook his head. 'Six hundred quid more like.'

'You never know,' Andy replied, smiling. 'We might turn up something amazing. Can you get a decent shot from here of whoever answers the door?'

'Should be fine, just so long as you stand to one side.'

'No problem.' He fished out of his pocket the small Dictaphone that he always carried with him, and moments later he was knocking on the heavy door to the house. There was no answer at first, but then he heard footsteps coming down the stairs. The door opened slightly and a woman's face appeared in the crack.

Andy was used to the people he was doorstepping looking pretty awful – in his line of work he was more often than not interviewing people who had gone through something dreadful. This woman's eyes were raw from crying and had deep bags underneath them – a sure sign that she had not been sleeping. She wore an unflattering, baggy tracksuit and her hair was a mess. She looked at him rather blankly, as if unsure whether she was supposed to recognize him or not. 'Mrs Johnson?' he asked gently.

The woman nodded her head.

'My name's Andy Summers. I'm a reporter. I wonder if I could just ask you a few questions.'

Harriet looked at him in horror. 'N-no . . .' she stammered. 'No, I don't want to talk to the press.' She slammed the door in his face. Andy was used to this happening. He knocked on the door once more. When there was no reply he knocked again. 'Go away, please,' Harriet's voice pleaded from inside.

'Look, Mrs Johnson,' Andy persisted. 'If you don't talk

to me now, I'm only going to stand on your doorstep until you do. This is your chance to tell your side of the story.' He tried to say it as sympathetically as possible, but it just sounded false.

There was no reply.

'Honestly, all I want is five minutes of your time.' He did his best to make his voice sound reasonable.

'My husband is a policeman,' Harriet told him, her voice wavering. 'If you don't leave my property, I'll call him.'

'Have you heard from Francesca, Mrs Johnson?' Andy ignored her threat.

'No, no, I haven't. Look, I really don't want to talk about this.' Tears started to well up in her eyes.

'I understand this must be very difficult for you, Mrs Johnson.' His voice was sympathetic now. 'Is there any message you'd like to give to her if you could speak to her? We're a national newspaper – she's bound to read it.'

'No. I mean, yes. I . . . I don't care what anyone says she's done, I just want her to come home.'

Andy could sense her loss, but he needed a picture to go with his story. He had to get her to open the door a little. 'What I really want to know, Mrs Johnson,' he asked her, 'is if this is the sort of thing you would ever have suspected Francesca of being capable of.'

The door swung open again, and Harriet looked at him in utter contempt. 'Of course not,' she whispered. 'She's my daughter. Now get off my property.' She slammed the door in his face.

Andy raised an eyebrow and cocked his head to one side before turning round and walking back down the driveway. 'Did you get her?' he asked.

Glenn gave him a thumbs-up. 'Piece of piss.'

'Good. We just need some shots of the house now – try and make it look as big as possible.' He pulled his phone out of his pocket and dialled a number. 'Janet, love, it's Andy. Put me through to the news desk, will you?' He waited for a moment, watching Glenn kneel down and shoot several pictures of the house. Then the news desk came on the line. 'Yeah, it's Andy. Put me on to Phil – I think I've got a story for him.'

Frankie poured the loose change that had accumulated in her polystyrene coffee cup into the palm of her hand and counted it out. One pound thirty-eight pence. There was a pound coin in there, donated by a studenty-looking guy who seemed as if he could use a few good meals himself, but the rest was a collection of coppers.

The light was beginning to fail. She had been moved on twice already today – once from in front of the Abbey and once from Bridge Street. Even in this cold weather, tourists had flocked to Bath to see the ancient Roman Baths and grand architecture for which the town was so famous, but also to see the street entertainers – Frankie remembered her mother telling her how this was the British capital for street performers, who came here from all over the world. Clearly the council wanted to avoid beggars hassling the lucrative tourists, which was why Frankie found herself unable to stay in one place for too long. Now she found herself on the high street, sitting by the cash machine outside a bank, hoping that the punters removing their twenty-pound notes would be moved by guilt if not by sympathy to give her a few coins. So far she hadn't had much success – the truth was that people avoid the cash machines if there is someone begging close by.

'You looking for something?'

Frankie glanced up to see who was talking to her. Two women, about her own age, were towering above her. They were both wearing the hotchpotch of clothes that Frankie recognized instantly as being the garb of the homeless, and each of them had a number of piercings on her face. 'What do you mean?' she asked, even though she knew exactly what they meant.

The two girls looked at each other with a vague grin. 'A fix,' one of them answered, speaking the words clearly as though Frankie were old and deaf. 'You looking for a fix?'

Frankie shook her head. In the four years she had been homeless, she had managed to stay off the junk – not an easy task when everyone around you had some habit or other. She'd lost count of the number of fleeting acquaintances who had succumbed to the pleasures of the needle or the pipe, and she didn't blame them – they offered a way out, a momentary escape from the drudgery, boredom and poverty. Frankie found occasional solace in a bottle of cheap booze, but she had managed to steer clear of the smack and the crack that soon became second nature to kids on the street. Suddenly she remembered the image of Mary, the skin around her nose raw from glue-sniffing. She hoped she was all right, but she knew that unless something drastic happened, her future would be a hopeless mess of addiction, her highs peddled by girls like these. 'No,' she told them. 'I don't need a fix.' She dropped the change back into her cup in preparation to leave, knowing the way this conversation was likely to go, then stood up and stared defiantly into the two girls' eyes. Their pupils were dilated and their expressions strangely vacant – it was a look she recognized only too well. The two girls took a short step closer and started to jostle Frankie. 'You shouldn't be round here, bitch,' the talkative one told her. 'It's our turf. Fuck off out of it.'

Frankie eyeballed them impassively. In London, a week ago, there would have been only one thing she could have done: stand up to them. Show anyone a weakness in a position like this and they would lay into you before you had time to run. If it meant a fight, so be it: she'd been in plenty of fights before and had survived, for better or worse. But today she couldn't risk a fight – couldn't risk a situation where the police might become involved. In any case her hand, still weeping into its now dirty bandage, was constantly throbbing from Strut's knife wound and she'd run out of painkillers yesterday. 'OK,' she told them reluctantly. 'I'm leaving.' She pushed past them and started to walk down the street.

'Hey!'

One of the girls caught her by the shoulder. Frankie turned and gave her a fierce look. 'What?' she snapped.

'I told you, it's our turf.' She looked meaningfully at the cup in Frankie's hand. 'We'll take that.'

Frankie looked at the meagre collection of coins in her cup. It wasn't much, but it meant the difference between a meal and going hungry. A man who had been at the cash machine when the girls had approached her hurried past, and Frankie became suddenly aware that all the passers-by were giving them a wide berth – it was clear to everyone that this was a potentially explosive situation that could go off at any time. If these girls were desperate enough – and every indication suggested that they were – they would do anything to get their hands on her afternoon's earnings. The three of them stared at each other, like animals defending their territory. One of the girls opened a flick knife and held it under her jacket so only Frankie could see it.

They stayed like that for a few moments, before Frankie threw her cup at their feet; the coins spilled out onto the ground, and a couple of them rolled a few metres down the road. Then she turned and walked away. She knew there was no need to run – the two of them would be on their knees by now, scrabbling around for the money. They needed it as much as she did – probably more if the drug-addled look in their eyes was anything to go by. She reached the end of the street and looked back; the girls were still there, but they had forgotten about her and were eagerly counting out the coins they had stolen.

The familiar hunger pangs were starting up again – it had been a long time since breakfast. She knew there was little chance of a meal tonight. Maybe she could scrounge enough to be able to eat tomorrow, but until she got the measure of this town she knew it was going to be difficult. She eyed up the shops – the usual parade of high-street names – but shook her head as she put thoughts of thieving from her mind.

Her hands were cold, so she put them in the pocket of her jeans to warm up. Her fingers touched the locket, and she pulled it out, gazing at it with renewed interest. It felt quite heavy, heavier than she had noticed before. The letters 'RG' had been engraved in swirling script on the front, and to one side there was a small clasp. Frankie pressed it in sharply, but nothing happened – clearly the mechanism was broken, or maybe the clasp was just ornamental and the locket was not supposed to open. She felt a momentary relief that she would not be forced to look at a cute little picture of someone's grandchild, but it didn't take long for her to brush aside any bogus feelings of guilt at her actions. She had done what she had to do. That was all.

And now perhaps the locket could help her. It could be solid silver – it was heavy enough. It was still not too late in the day to find herself a pawn shop where she could trade it in. She'd get less than a quarter of its value, of course, but that didn't matter – the money was more valuable to her.

It didn't take long for her to find the three gold-plated balls that indicated a pawnbroker's. The shop window was full of antique jewellery, watches and other valuable trinkets, and the wooden shop door was etched with the sign PA ALLEN – PAWNBROKERS OF FINE ANTIQUES. A little bell rang as she opened the door, making her jump slightly as she stepped inside. The shop was empty, and there was a long wooden counter dividing the customer area from a hidden section that was screened off by frosted glass. She stood there for a few moments before a plump woman in her late fifties appeared. 'Can I help you?' she asked in a bored tone of voice, her face sullen and full of suspicion as she looked over her half-moon glasses.

Frankie reached into her jeans, pulled out the locket and placed it on the counter. 'What will you give me for this?'

The woman picked up the locket and held it to the

light. Her face was unimpressed, but Frankie expected that – she was hardly going to let on that she thought it was valuable. 'Wait there,' the woman told her before disappearing behind the frosted glass. Frankie saw the silhouette of another person sitting down inspecting the locket. She could hear them whispering.

As Frankie paced nervously she noticed the camera in the top left-hand corner of the shop above the front door. It made her nervous, but she needed the money. She knew the woman was going to try and rip her off, that she would have to haggle her up, even if it was just a few pounds; but she was hardly in a strong bartering position, and the woman knew that. Nobody who found their way into these places ever was.

Finally the woman returned, her face expressionless. She put the locket down on the counter and shook her head. 'Tin,' she said. 'Worthless.' She pushed it towards Frankie.

Frankie felt her stomach lurch. It had to be worth something – anything. 'Please,' she whispered to the stony-faced woman, 'just a few pounds. It's all I have.'

The woman shook her head.

'What about the chain? That could be worth something.' But the woman was already eyeing the door meaningfully, and Frankie got the hint. She couldn't start making a scene. She bowed her head, took the necklace and left.

Outside, Frankie felt anger welling up inside her. She wasn't one for self-pity, but the events of the last few days were weighing heavily on her. She walked quickly away from the pawnbroker's, tears of frustration blinding her eyes, oblivious to everyone around her, and headed towards the river. She had always sought out the water when things got rough in London. It soothed her – a little patch of nature in the heart of the unkind city – and if ever she needed soothing, now was the time. The route had clearly been imprinted on her subconscious from her couple of days of wandering, and she found herself on North Parade Bridge in no time at all. The rush hour was starting, and the traffic was beeping aggressively. She leaned over the side and gritted her teeth as she did her best not to succumb to her tears. Start now and she'd never stop.

The locket was still clasped in her hand. Now it seemed the focus of all her anger and frustration – she should just get rid of it, throw it into the river. If she could divest herself of anything to do with what had happened in London, perhaps she could put it from her mind, move on. She prepared to hurl it over the bridge.

Just then, the engraving on the front caught her eye. 'RG'. The image of the terrified woman on Chelsea Bridge flooded into her head. Who was she? What was she doing now? Was she 'RG'? Did this cheap pendant mean something to her – some sort of sentimental value even if it was worthless in terms of money? Frankie had not stopped to think of the rights and wrongs of her actions. There had been no time, and she knew, in any case, that put in the same situation again there was nothing she would do differently. There was no room in her life for equivocation or sentimentality. But deep inside she felt a little twinge of regret. She was sorry for the woman she had attacked. There was no rhyme or reason for her being dragged into the mess of Frankie's life – she'd just been in the wrong place at the wrong time.

Suddenly it seemed churlish to throw away something that might once have been important to someone.

And then she thought of the little box of jewellery in her bedroom at home. Frankie had loved those trinkets, and often thought of them in her darkest hours. This locket was attractive enough in its way – a little too chunky perhaps, too brash for her taste – but for the first time in four years she had in her hand something pretty.

She put the chain over her head and tucked the locket under her jumper. You never know, she thought to herself with a rueful smile. It might just bring me luck one day.

Carter was at his desk staring at the CCTV photo of Francesca Mills that had been taken a few nights before at the cash machine. It was blurred and indistinct, but it was definitely the same person as the one fleeing the scene of the crime at Newington Park in the photo Taylor had shown him. There was a look of desperation in her eyes that almost made him feel sorry for her. He had passed this image on to Taylor, but neither of them had managed to do anything with it. The inquiries that had been conducted around the area made it clear that nobody noticed just another girl on the street.

He'd been in turmoil all day, unable to track Rosemary down and knowing that the one lead he had – the phone – had been a wild goose chase. There had been nothing he could do all day but wait and hope.

He had spent the morning reading desperately through the company profile of Lenham, Borwick and Hargreaves. It was frustrating work, especially when all he really wanted to be doing was finding the Mills girl. But every avenue led to a dead end – no driving licence, no criminal record to speak of. Not even a claim for any government benefits. Nothing that could track her down.

The phone rang. He picked it up instantly. 'Carter,' he said automatically.

'Sean, it's Yvonne.'

'Yvonne.' Carter's voice was drained. 'Are you OK? You sound pissed off.'

'No, I'm fine. Just one of those days. You know you asked me to put out a search yesterday afternoon?'

'Rosemary Gibson. That's right.' His voice picked up. 'Have you found her?'

'Sean, was she a friend of yours?'

Carter closed his eyes – he knew what was coming. 'An acquaintance . . . a contact . . . why, what's happened?'

'She was fished out of the river two hours ago.'

He muttered under his breath before answering. 'Where is she now?'

'She's undergoing a post-mortem at Charing Cross Hospital on Fulham Palace Road.' Carter was silent for a few moments. 'I'm sorry, Sean.'

'Are you sure it's her, Yvonne?' Maybe there had been a mistake.

'Yes. The fingerprint match has just come in.'

'How did you have her fingerprints?'

'She was burgled three years ago. Presumably her prints were taken then just to eliminate her.'

'OK,' he sighed. 'Thanks for letting me know. I'll go to the hospital now – do me a favour and ring ahead to tell them I'm coming. I'll be in touch.'

It took at least an hour to struggle through the evening traffic to Hammersmith, and Carter grew increasingly infuriated as the time passed, slamming his hand on the steering wheel every time he got cut up, and beeping his horn at any sluggish driver who crossed his path. Eventually, though, he screamed into the small car park and found one of the few spaces available. Minutes later he was being escorted down a sterile corridor to the post-mortem room. The hospital porter stopped outside a door. 'This is it,' he said.

Carter nodded his thanks and knocked on the door. A woman dressed in white opened it. 'Sean Carter, Serious Fraud Office. I believe you're expecting me.'

'Come in, Sean,' the woman told him soberly. 'You'd better put this on.' She handed him a surgical mask.

He walked into the room. A large white curtain cordoned off half of it, and there was one other person in there, a man standing at the sink washing his hands with a thick antiseptic gel – clearly the pathologist. 'I'll be with you in just one moment, Mr Carter,' he said over his shoulder. He finished washing his hands, dried them and then turned to Sean. 'Unpleasant, I'm afraid,' he said shortly.

'What happened to her, Doctor?'

The pathologist glanced at the curtain. 'How comfortable are you with dead bodies, Detective?'

'It's fine, Doctor. There's not much I haven't seen.'

The pathologist nodded, then threw open the curtain.

The naked female body lying on the table was unrecognizable. An incision, roughly sewn up, had been made from either shoulder, around her grey breasts and down the length of her abdomen; her pale, grey head was a mess. 'Jesus, Rosemary.' He turned to the pathologist. 'What happened to her?'

'Cause of death: bullet wound to the head.' He pointed

to the swollen hole in her forehead. 'Exit wound here on the forehead, entry wound at the back of the head. She was shot from behind at point-blank range. See here.' He pointed to the markings around the entry wound. 'Resin marks. The gun was no more than three inches away.'

'Time of death?'

'Difficult to say. We can usually estimate from the decrease in body temperature, but I suspect she'd been in the water for over three hours. At a guess I would say she's been dead eight to ten hours. Once I get the water temperature back, I'll have a closer idea.'

Carter pointed at the arms lying crookedly by her side. 'Why are her arms like that?'

'They were tied behind her back when she came in. I had to snap them to her side due to the onset of rigor mortis.' He pointed at the black marks around her swollen wrists. 'Severe bruising here indicates to me that she was tied up for some considerable period of time, and the ropes were tight when she came in. These three fingers here have been broken, and there's severe bruising along both sides of her abdomen, which caused internal bleeding – it would have killed her anyway if she hadn't died from the gun wound. But why they did that to her before they shot her, I can only speculate.'

But Carter knew. 'She's been tortured,' he muttered.

The pathologist nodded. 'That would seem the most probable cause. Stomach was practically empty, so she hadn't eaten for at least twenty-four hours before she died. Blood samples have been taken, but it's obvious she was under considerable duress just before death.'

Carter knew from experience that the blood samples would show traces of endorphins – the levels would indicate just how frightened she was before her death, but they both knew she had died in extreme pain. By the looks of what they'd done, she was most probably grateful for the bullet. 'Thank you, Doctor,' he said grimly. 'I've seen everything I need to.'

Outside the room, he stood leaning against the wall, knocked his head back and drew a deep breath. He was shaking, not from the horror of seeing the body – he was hardened to sights like that – but out of rage and frustration. Who the hell had done this to her? He knew that the information they had found was important, but he never imagined anyone would go to these kinds of lengths to stop it falling into unwelcome hands. And poor Rosemary. What kind of ordeal had she undergone? She was a middle-aged accountant, for Christ's sake. She had a neat little house and an elderly mother who relied on her. How could someone so unassuming – so *worthy*, damn it – end up like that? 'I'm sorry,' he whispered to the dead woman, hoping that she would hear him in a heaven he didn't believe in. 'I promise I'll find these people.'

But to do that he needed the evidence that Rosemary had died for, and only one person knew its whereabouts. Her name was Francesca Mills, and God only knew where she was now.

Chapter Eight

The next day dawned bright and cold. The people of Bath almost had a spring in their step as they made their chilly way to work, warmly wrapped in hats and scarves. The unseasonable early snow had held off for the past two days, and the dirty sludge had disappeared from the streets. The early Christmas decorations did not seem quite so out of place in Bath as they did in London, nor did the strains of carols coming out of the shops seem so premature.

But Frankie felt far from Christmassy. She had spent another night in a shop doorway and was cold, stiff, tired and hungry. In theory she was looking again for somewhere to beg – somewhere she wouldn't be moved on by police or junkies – but in reality she was walking aimlessly, just trying to keep moving as a buffer against the cold. Occasionally she would stand in the doorway of the department stores, feeling the waft of warm air blow against her as customers came in and out, but she would move on as soon as she saw a manager or security guard inside the shop walking towards her with a purposeful look on their face. By midday, the hunger pangs were as bad as ever, and her pockets were still empty of loose change.

She walked down a quaint little street that she hadn't been down before, full of tiny shops selling fancy goods – paintings, fabrics, jewellery. As Frankie wandered down, wondering if this might be a good place to stop and beg, she found herself outside a tiny flower shop. She gazed at it, suddenly captivated by the display outside. Small zinc-coloured buckets adorned the frontage, filled with flowers that could survive the winter chill, and there were little pots filled with delicate snowdrops and fragrant narcissi. She brushed her fingers against the soft, velvety blooms, caressing them with a subtlety that felt unnatural to her cold-bitten, calloused, sore hands. There had always been winter narcissi in her mother's garden. As a child she had learned how to recognize them – the six tiny petals with a small cup nestled in the centre – along with so many other flowers. Her mother was an avid gardener, and by the time Frankie was ten she could reel off the names of all the plants in the garden. She held a small narcissus flower between two fingers; she hadn't thought of this little bloom for years.

Another plant caught her eye. It was not much to look at – a green shrub in a large pot, with vibrant, glowing orange berries – but for Frankie it was like bumping into an old acquaintance she had not seen for many years. Her eyes wide open, a flicker of a smile played across her face as she remembered its name: Stinking Iris. And it did stink, too, if you squeezed the berries between your fingers. She leaned over to have a closer look.

But as she did so, she became aware of a figure in the doorway. She looked up guiltily, immediately conscious of how she must look – a woman clearly with no money handling all these precious plants. She stopped in her tracks. 'I'm sorry,' she muttered, the wind suddenly gone from her billowing sails. Her eyes flickered between the plant and the woman. She appeared to be in her early sixties, and was small but impossibly neat in a clean white apron. Her face was lined, and her mouth unsmiling – but there was a wary laughter behind her eyes that startled Frankie somewhat. She wasn't used to strangers looking at her like that. The woman glanced down at the plant that had caught Frankie's eye. '*Iris foetidissima*,' she said in a gentle southern accent.

Frankie was so surprised that she had not been asked to move on that she didn't know what to say for a few moments. Finally, though, she found her tongue. 'My mother always called it Stinking Iris. It used to make me laugh.'

'I prefer to use its common name,' the woman said, a little prim but not unfriendly. 'Gladwyn Iris. Though some people *do* call it Stinking Iris, and I must admit,' she lowered her voice conspiratorially, 'that they can get a bit fragrant if you're not careful with them.'

A smile danced across her face, and Frankie smiled back. 'Now then, young lady,' she continued in her soft, lilting voice. 'Will you be buying any flowers off me today?'

Frankie lowered her eyes, suddenly embarrassed by the question. 'N-no . . .' she stammered. 'No, I don't have any money. I'm sorry.' She turned to leave.

As she walked away she heard the woman's voice behind her. 'Excuse me, dearie,' she called. Frankie stopped and looked back at her. 'It's perishing cold. You look as if you could use a hot drink. Why don't you come in and have a cup of tea?'

Frankie was momentarily stunned. It was the first time she could remember anyone outside of the soup kitchens offering her a gesture of kindness – the first time, in fact, that anyone had offered her anything without wanting something in return. Her instinct was to walk away, to keep the hard, defensive shell around her that she had developed in order to survive; but something in the woman's look softened her. She seemed kind and trustworthy. 'Thank you,' she replied simply, and walked back up to the shop.

'It's not very often that you find a youngster like yourself who can identify *Iris foetidissima*,' the woman said brightly as they walked inside. 'Not that I have it in very often. It's not that popular, to be honest. But most of my customers wouldn't know a daffodil from a dandelion – they just want a bunch of something pretty to brighten up the house or to give to their wives to say sorry. Oh but I mustn't be so cynical!' She smiled to herself and turned to look at Frankie, who was gazing round the shop in wonder. It was a fairly ordinary florist's shop, if the truth were to be told, but she had not been in such a place for so long that to her it was a genuine riot of colour. She breathed in deeply, closing her eyes as the heady scent of the pollen hit her senses. 'Have a seat, dearie.' The woman indicated two wicker chairs with well-worn cream cushions in front of a small glass table, and Frankie sat down as the woman walked behind the little counter that had nothing but a till, a roll of Sellotape, several coloured ribbons on roll-holders screwed to the wall, some scissors and a neat pile of wrapping paper. Behind the counter was a small table with a kettle and some tea-making things. The woman switched the kettle on and then came to sit down.

Frankie felt suddenly uncomfortable. The woman's kindly face and the clear look of pity in her eyes made her feel awkward – she didn't want pity, and she responded poorly to it. She tried to break the silence, to think of something to say, but her mind was blank, confused; she felt she wanted to stand up, give her apologies and walk out.

'My name's June,' the woman said in an attempt to break the difficult silence.

'Frankie,' she replied quietly.

'Pleased to make your acquaintance,' said June, with impeccable manners. 'Now tell me, Frankie, what on earth happened to your hand?'

Frankie looked down at the bandage. 'I fell,' she said. 'There was some broken glass on the floor and I cut my hand.'

'You should take it to the hospital, young lady.'

'I did,' Frankie lied as June got up to make the tea. 'But I could do with another bandage.'

'Sugar?' June asked, seemingly ignoring Frankie's request.

'Yes,' replied Frankie. 'I mean, yes, please,' she added quietly.

'How many? Oh I'll tell you what, I'll just put it on the table and you can help yourself. Now I have a first-aid kit back here somewhere.' June placed the tea things on the table before walking into a room beyond the main shop and coming back a minute later with a large Tupperware box. 'I'm forever cutting myself on thorns and the like,' she said cheerfully as she sat down and indicated that Frankie should give her her hand. Before she knew it the older woman was untying the clumsy knot and unwrapping the dirty cloth. 'My mother was a nurse,' June chatted away. 'When we were children and we used to play doctors and nurses with our dollies, she would never let us get away with bandaging them up badly. She was a stickler for . . . oh, my!'

Frankie looked at the palm of her hand. The wound was dreadful still, deep and suppurating, and the filth of the street had seeped in.

'You fell over, you say?' June raised an eyebrow. Frankie didn't reply, so the older woman removed a bottle of antiseptic lotion and a wodge of cotton wool that she soaked and then dabbed on the hand. She worked as carefully as she could, but the stinging still brought tears to Frankie's eyes. When it was clean, June took a piece of surgical gauze from the box, laid it on the wound, then wrapped a clean bandage gently but firmly round the hand and tied it with a good knot. Her hands looked frail, but they were surprisingly strong. 'There we go, dearie,' she said as she packed up her first-aid kit.

'Thank you.' Frankie avoided her gaze, embarrassed that she had accepted help from this kind lady.

'So did your mother teach you a lot about flowers?'

Frankie nodded. 'As much as she could. It seems a long time ago now.'

'She sounds like a fine woman.' June spoke the words lightly and did not notice the tightening around Frankie's eyes as she did so. The younger woman didn't reply. 'Does she live here in Bath?'

Frankie shook her head. 'No,' she said shortly. She didn't want to continue this conversation. How could she possibly explain the truth about her mother to this sweet lady? 'I haven't seen my mother for a while,' she said in a tone of voice that she hoped would end the matter. 'I . . . I'm living here with friends . . .' She wasn't sure how convincing she sounded. 'Look, I don't want to sound rude, but why are you doing this?'

'What?'

'Don't tell me you invite all your customers in for tea.'

'You're not a customer,' June said pointedly. She picked up her cup of tea and looked at Frankie as she sipped it slowly. Her wrinkled brow was slightly furrowed, almost as if she was deciding whether to ask something or not. Finally she spoke. 'I could do with some help about the shop.' She looked around a bit apologetically. 'Oh I know it doesn't seem very busy, but I'm not as young as I was, and an extra pair of hands would be very useful – even if one of them is bandaged up!'

Frankie looked at her, her eyes wide.

'I was just about to put this sign in the window.' She showed Frankie a small card: SHOP HELP REQUIRED: APPLY WITHIN. 'I wouldn't be able to pay you much, mind. Just pocket money, really. But you know about flowers, and . . .' Her voice trailed off. 'Of course, you don't have to decide now.' She seemed somehow deflated, as if Frankie's silence was a tacit rejection.

'No,' the younger woman said quickly. 'It's very kind, it's just . . .' Suddenly she wanted to say so many things. That she had nowhere to live. That she had done terrible things. That she was wanted by the police. That she was grateful for the older lady's kindness. But she could not find the words.

Then an image of the two girls she had met on the street yesterday flashed into her head. Pocket money, June had said. Well, whatever it was, however much it seemed like pocket money to her, to Frankie it could mean the difference between dignity and destitution. And besides, she felt a warmth in this woman – something she thought she might never again experience in her life.

She smiled, and the smile lit up her face. 'Thank you,' she said, almost demurely. 'I'd love to.'

June looked delighted. 'Oh splendid!' she exclaimed. 'Now then, I'm sure I have some chocolate biscuits about here somewhere. A cup of tea is nothing without a chocolate biscuit, don't you think?'

Sean Carter knocked on the heavy oak door of the Johnsons' Surrey house. There was no answer, so he knocked again. He didn't quite know what he hoped to achieve here, but speaking to Francesca Mills's mother and stepfather was the only lead he had. His chances of finding the girl were tiny, but he had to try. To find her, he needed to know where she was likely to go; and to do that, he needed to know something about her.

When there was still no reply, he took a step back and peered through the letter box to look for signs of anyone at home. There were lights on, and he could just make out the sound of a radio playing in a distant room.

'What do you think you're doing?' A woman's voice called behind him. Carter stood up quickly and spun round.

'Mrs Johnson?' The woman in front of him was holding a pair of secateurs and a large bunch of herbs.

'Who are you?' She edged back.

Carter pulled his identification out of his wallet and approached her. 'DI Sean Carter, Serious Fraud Office. I'd like to ask you a few questions.'

'What about?' Harriet's face was etched with concern.

'It's about Francesca.'

She brushed past him on the way to the door. 'I've already spoken to the police,' she said brusquely. 'I've told them everything I can.'

'I work for the SFO, Mrs Johnson. Please, it will only take a few minutes of your time, and it's very important. I think Francesca could be in trouble.'

Harriet raised an eyebrow at him. 'I think, Mr Carter, that that is something of an understatement.' She wiped her feet. 'I suppose you'd better come in.' Carter followed her lead by wiping his own feet before she led him through to the kitchen. 'Sit down,' she offered as she placed the herbs and secateurs on the table. 'I find gardening helps me take my mind off recent events, but there's little to do at this time of year – just preparation for spring.' She sounded slightly apologetic as she looked out to her garden.

Carter took a seat and Harriet sat opposite. 'Mrs Johnson, I'm sure you've been through this already with the police, but I have to ask you again. Can you think of *anywhere* Francesca might be? Somewhere that meant something to her as a child. Friends. Family. Anything.'

Harriet put her head in her hands for a few moments and then looked back up at Carter. 'Francesca disappeared four years ago, Mr Carter. Since then, I have thought about her every single day. Every day I have wondered where she could be. Do you really think I haven't thought about this?'

'I'm sorry,' Carter replied, humbled slightly. 'I can't imagine how difficult this must be for you. But I do have to ask these questions, and you must think carefully about them.'

Harriet nodded gently.

'Can you think of any reason at all why Francesca might have run away?'

'No,' she said meekly. Carter was looking directly at her when she said it, and she appeared to be avoiding his eyes. He sensed there was something she wasn't telling him, but there was a look of frailty around her face that hinted that if he probed too far she was likely to crack.

'Mrs Johnson,' he said mildly, 'I wonder if there's anyone else I can speak to.'

'Well, there's my husband,' she said uncertainly, 'but he's at work. I'm not sure there's anything –'

'I mean someone outside the family,' Carter interrupted. 'Someone Francesca might have confided in. A close friend, perhaps.'

Harriet shook her head. 'She was always quite a solitary girl,' she explained. 'Hard-working; she didn't have many friends.'

'What about teachers, then? Did she go to school in the village?'

She nodded.

'And?'

'You'll have to ask them.' Suddenly it seemed as if she had clammed shut. Carter furrowed his brow at her quizzically, as if to ask her to expand on what she had just said, but Harriet was looking down at her hands resting on her lap. Everything about her body language suggested she had said as much as she was prepared to say. But he felt she was hiding something.

He decided to try a different tack. 'Has Francesca's room changed much since she left?'

Harriet shook her head mutely.

'Do you mind if I take a look?'

She took him upstairs and opened the door. The bedroom was neat and tidy, everything in its place. Teddy bears were piled at the end of the bed, and even her study books were neatly stacked against the large hi-fi, which had probably been top of the range four years ago, but now looked rather old-fashioned. Carter looked at the photos above the bed. 'Was that your husband?' he asked as sensitively as he could.

'Yes.'

'And are there any pictures of Mr Johnson in here?'

Harriet shook her head, to be met by an inquiring look from Carter. 'They never got on,' she told him in a quiet voice. 'She thought I married too soon after her father's death.' She turned to look out of the window. 'I only wanted her to be happy,' she said in a voice full of emotion. She began to sob.

Carter realized he had reached the end of the line here – for today at least. This woman needed to be left alone with her sorrow. 'Thank you for your time, Mrs Johnson,' he said. 'You've been very helpful. I'll show myself out.'

Carter was pensive as his car trundled down the driveway. What wasn't she telling him? Something about the whole situation made no sense at all. Why would a young girl run away from such a nice home? Her mother seemed like a decent enough woman, despite her reticence – but why would she hold something back? Maybe she just didn't want the police to catch up with her daughter. Maybe she was scared of the consequences. Maybe. But somehow he didn't think so.

He parked the car outside the pub and walked in. A burly barman with tattooed arms was sitting behind the bar reading the paper. He looked up as Carter walked in. 'What'll you have, squire?'

'Actually, mate, I was wondering if you could tell me where the local secondary school is.'

'Right out the pub, first on your left. You can't miss it.'

'Thank you,' Carter replied. He looked around the pub. It was full of memorabilia – old pictures of nearby landmarks, press cuttings of village events. If ever there was a locals' pub, this was it. 'Actually, mate,' he said as an afterthought, 'maybe you can help me a bit more. Do you know the Johnson family at all?'

The barman shrugged. 'A bit,' he said warily. 'Why?'

'Do you know anything about their daughter, Francesca?'

The barman was looking more hostile now. 'Who's asking?' he mumbled.

'DI Carter, Serious Fraud Office.'

The barman's face twitched slightly. 'Right. You a copper?'

'Yes.'

'Well, I don't know anything. She ran away from home a few years ago. Hasn't been heard of. Now are you buying a drink or not?'

Carter took the hint. 'No, you're OK, thanks.' He turned and left.

What was his problem? Why was everyone being so damn secretive?

The playground to the school was empty as he walked across it to the main entrance. A neat little sign directed all visitors to the reception, so he followed the directions and soon arrived at the door, which was painted an institutional grey colour, and knocked. A couple of minutes later he was being led down an echoing hallway to the headmaster's office. The smell of the place – that curious mixture of overcooked school dinners and freshly polished wooden floors – brought back memories of his own schooldays, and he smiled as he passed a noticeboard with a list of rules and regulations. No doubt they seemed impossibly severe to the young pupils in this place – God knows he'd been inspired to flout his own school rules in his time. A couple of kids ran down the corridor, screeching to a more sensible pace at the sight of grown-ups. Sean felt their curious eyes on him as they passed, but avoided meeting their gaze. It was weird: he'd been in the same room as some of the most dangerous criminals in London without batting an eyelid, but kids always made him feel uncomfortable. Just not used to them, he supposed.

The headmaster was a rotund little man, red-faced and slightly balding; he had a fairly jolly air to him. 'Peter McGill,' he introduced himself. 'Do sit down, Mr . . .'

'Carter,' Sean replied. 'DI Carter, Serious Fraud Office.'

The little man looked worried – people often did when he introduced himself like that. He assumed they were worried he might have caught up with them about some dodgy expenses on an old tax return. 'Don't worry,' he reassured the head. 'I just need to ask you a few questions about a former pupil at this school. How long have you been headmaster here?'

'About ten years. Often seems like longer.' He chuckled slightly at his own joke.

'Do you remember a pupil by the name of Francesca Mills?'

A shadow fell across Mr McGill's face. 'Yes, of course.

Poor Francesca. A lovely girl. Polite, hard-working. It was all terribly sad.'

Carter nodded in sympathy. He had taken an instant liking to this man – everything about him said that he took the care of his young charges very seriously indeed. 'Mr McGill, I'm going to be very frank with you if you don't mind.'

'Please . . .'

'I need to find Francesca Mills very urgently.'

'Inspector Carter, I'm sorry – I thought even the police had assumed that, well, that she was dead.'

'I have good reason to believe that's not the case.'

The headmaster nodded soberly, then picked up the phone. 'Hi, could you get Brenda for me, please?' He replaced the receiver and looked back at Carter. 'If you don't mind,' he continued, 'I'd like to ask another teacher to join us. Mrs Phillips – Brenda Phillips. She was Francesca's form teacher, and – well, I'll let her explain . . .'

He stood up and left the room. Five minutes later he returned with a youngish woman in her middle to late thirties, fair-haired and bespectacled with an open, honest face. 'Brenda Phillips, this is DI Carter from the Serious Fraud Office. He wants to ask you some questions about Francesca Mills.' Mrs Phillips nodded her head and took a seat.

'Mrs Phillips, do you have any idea why Francesca ran away?'

'Yes,' the teacher replied. 'I believe I do.'

Carter gestured at her to continue.

'A few months before she disappeared, I found Francesca alone in a classroom. She was sitting at a desk crying her eyes out. I asked her what was wrong. It was very unlike her – she was a happy little soul, although I had noticed her retreating into herself for a little while beforehand. She said nothing was wrong, and was very reluctant to continue the conversation, so I told her that if she ever wanted to tell me something in complete confidence, she only had to say. Then I left her alone.

'A week later she came to see me. I asked her what was wrong and . . .' Mrs Phillips suddenly looked uncomfortable, and turned to the headmaster for reassurance.

'Go on, Brenda,' he said. 'It's OK.'

She took a deep breath. 'She told me that she was being sexually abused by her stepfather.'

Carter closed his eyes. Suddenly so many things made sense.

'She didn't use those words, of course. She said that he came into her room at night and "touched" her. I alerted Mr McGill and we contacted social services.'

'And?'

McGill took up the story. 'Social services interviewed Mr Johnson and decided that he had no case to answer.'

Carter looked puzzled. 'Why?'

'Well, he claimed that Francesca had never really accepted him and, in her childlike way, was always trying to undermine his relationship with her mother. According to him this was just another in a long line of lies she had told to try and get him into trouble.'

'And Mrs Johnson?'

'Stood by him. Claimed she knew nothing of what Francesca was alleging and that she would be astonished if it was true.'

The three of them sat in silence. A bell rang in the

corridor indicating the end of a lesson, and there was a sound from all around of chairs being scraped.

Carter looked at the two teachers in turn. 'You don't believe Mr Johnson, do you?'

They eyed each other awkwardly. 'Mr Johnson was cleared of any wrongdoing by social services and by an internal police investigation,' Mr McGill said a bit stiffly. 'You're aware that he's in the police force, I presume.'

Carter nodded and was about to say something when Mrs Phillips interrupted.

'Francesca Mills was not the kind of girl to tell a lie like that. I spoke to her. I held her when she was so tearful she couldn't speak. There is no doubt in my mind that that girl was being abused. I don't know how long for, or to what extent, but I've always believed that is why she ran away. After Mr Johnson was cleared, it was made perfectly plain to me by the authorities that I should not tell anyone about the claims. Francesca barely spoke to me again. I imagine she thought I'd let her down. That everyone had let her down. And to be honest, I wouldn't blame her. We all thought she was dead – I can't tell you how relieved I am to hear that she's not. I always blamed myself for betraying her confidence, and not helping more.'

Her face was severe, her voice trembling. There was no doubting her conviction.

'Thank you for your frankness, Mrs Phillips,' Carter said sincerely. 'You've been most helpful.'

Chapter Nine

Frankie arrived for work early. It was a strange concept for her – arriving for work – and she felt rather odd as she walked the streets of Bath towards the flower shop. She had chosen somewhere to sleep that was a good distance away, as she didn't want June to know she was sleeping rough, but she had waited a good three-quarters of an hour outside the shop before June came down from her flat above and opened up.

'You must be freezing!' she exclaimed when she saw Frankie standing outside the door shivering. 'How long have you been standing there?'

'Not long,' Frankie lied. 'I just got here.'

'I don't believe you for a minute. Look at you – your lips are blue.' She practically pulled Frankie into the shop. 'Now, you can put your coat in the back room,' June told her as she pulled her newspaper in from the letter box, placed it down on the table and switched the shop lights on. The strip bulbs flickered slightly before illuminating the room. 'And if you've brought any sandwiches you can pop them in the fridge.' She looked at Frankie's empty hands. 'Ah well, not to worry,' she said lightly. 'I'm sure I can rustle something up for the both of us at lunchtime.'

Frankie stood awkwardly in the centre of the shop. 'What would you like me to do?' she asked nervously.

'Oh first things first,' June said in her light southern accent. 'It's far too cold to start working without a hot drink inside us. Sit down and I'll make us a nice cup of tea. Then we can get the displays out.'

Frankie sat down in the same seat she had occupied the previous afternoon and stole a glance at the newspaper while June put the kettle on.

Her heart stopped. She was on the front page – the same picture that she'd seen in the other newspaper, only twice as big this time.

She quickly put the paper face down on the table and glanced back at June. She was happily babbling away to herself about something or other – Frankie wasn't listening – and then she went into the back room. Frankie picked the paper up again and started to read.

PLEASE COME HOME! A MOTHER'S PLEA

Well-to-do Harriet Johnson, 51, made this impassioned plea when it was revealed that her daughter, Francesca Mills, was wanted by police in connection with the murder of a known criminal in London earlier this week. Francesca, 19, has not been in contact with her mother and stepfather, a local policeman, for 4 years.

Speaking from her comfortable home in leafy Surrey, a tearful Mrs Johnson could offer no insight into why her daughter should have gone off the rails in such a spectacular fashion. When asked whether her daughter was capable of such an action, she replied simply, 'Of course not.'

The murdered man has been named as Robert Strut, a known pimp and drug dealer. It is thought that his killer may have been working for him at the time.

Her eyes drifted away from the words. In the corner of the page was a picture of her mother, standing looking haggard at the door. It had been so long since Frankie had seen her, she'd almost forgotten how to conjure the image of her in her head. Now it all came flooding back in a maelstrom of emotions that she could not identify.

She quickly put the paper down again as June placed a cup of tea on the table for her and sat down. She reached for the paper. 'What's wrong with you, dearie?' she asked, looking at Frankie with concern. 'You look as if you've seen a ghost.'

Frankie said nothing. She just shook her head, stood up and turned her back on June, walking up to the tea things and spooning some sugar into her cup. She knew she looked different enough to the picture in the paper – to the casual eye at least – but surely someone sitting right opposite her would notice the similarity. She heard the rustling of the paper behind her, and then a silence. She dared not look round. 'I have something I have to ask you,' June said in a clear voice after a few moments.

Frankie turned to look at her, not knowing what she would do if she was challenged by this sweet lady who had been so kind to her.

'Are you good at crosswords?'

Frankie blinked. June had opened the paper in the middle, then folded it back on itself so that a page of crosswords and puzzles was displayed. 'I'm not bad myself, but they're so much more fun with two, don't you think? It's the only reason I buy a paper,' she confided. 'I much prefer to listen to the radio. So, are you any good?'

The younger woman shook her head. 'No,' she said shortly. 'No, I don't really do them very often.'

'Ah well, I'm sure you're better than you think.' June sipped at her tea and peered down at the crossword.

'Look,' said Frankie, wanting to keep moving so that her companion did not have a chance to browse through the newspaper with her sitting right opposite, 'why don't I start putting things out? I think you should have more flowers on display outside than you did yesterday. People like to see a bit of colour when it's so grey and miserable outside, and they should be OK in the cold, as long as it doesn't freeze.' She looked around and started grabbing pots of colourful blooms and green foliage, which she carried out and began to arrange on the empty metal shelving outside the shop.

June watched her, her face inscrutable. Finally she sighed. 'Very well,' she said as Frankie came back in to fetch more display material. 'I can see I'm going to have to keep on my toes when you're about, young lady.'

Frankie stopped. 'I'm sorry,' she said. 'I didn't mean to be bossy.'

June waved her arm dismissively. 'No, no, you're right. Let's get to work.'

'And June.' Frankie put her hand lightly on the older woman's arm. 'Thank you. You don't know how much I appreciate what you've done for me.'

Mark Taylor picked up his phone. 'Sean Carter here to see you, sir.'

Taylor sighed. 'OK, show him up.'

Once again Taylor didn't bother with the pretence of a greeting, he just indicated with a wave of his hand and not much enthusiasm that Carter should take a seat. Sean did so, then dumped a copy of a newspaper on the desk. 'Your handiwork?' he asked lightly.

'What's it got to do with you?'

'Oh come on, Mark. You *know* the commissioner's given me permission to use the Met's resources. Why do you have to make this so difficult?'

Taylor turned his attention back to what he was doing. 'And I suppose the commissioner is delighted that you got me to send four members of armed response to arrest an out-of-work builder who was just settling down to have a cup of tea in front of the telly. I'm just filling in the paperwork now – you know how much I love paperwork. And for your information,' he nodded at the newspaper, 'that's got nothing to do with me. In any case, why are you getting so worked up? She was in the paper two days ago. Some hack's been sniffing around and came up with the girl's identity about the same time as we did – the press office just confirmed what he already knew. We probably would have released her details to the press as we've got nothing else to go on, but he saved us a job. Got a problem with it?'

Carter shrugged. 'I just want her not to go further underground.'

Taylor shook his head. 'It's not likely. Her prints are on file, so if she gets into some sort of trouble – likely, knowing the kind of people she was hanging around with – then we'll be able to bring her in. Apart from that, our only hope is if she gets in touch with the parents.' He flicked the newspaper. 'Which means *this* could actually help.'

Carter shook his head. 'She won't be getting in touch with her mother.'

'Really? Well, you'll forgive me, Sean, if I take your hunch with a pinch of salt this time.'

Carter looked at his old friend. It had always been this

way. Sometimes he felt he understood his anger; at other times it was inexplicable to him. Today he was in two minds. But what he wished more than anything at this moment was that he could talk to Taylor the way they used to. Get his help. It was a lonely business doing what he did, and while he could handle loneliness elsewhere in his life, on the job sometimes you just needed a friendly ear. 'It's more than a hunch, Mark,' he told him. 'I've done some snooping.'

Taylor smiled briefly. 'Investigating, you mean.'

'Whatever. I asked around and talked to one of the girl's former teachers. It seems that just before she disappeared, Francesca Mills accused her stepfather of abusing her.'

Taylor looked at him with distaste. 'But he's on the force . . .'

'I know. Social services decided he didn't have a case to answer, and apparently there was an internal inquiry that cleared him. Reading between the lines, it looks like the mother believed him too. Francesca ran off soon after.'

'How do you know she was telling the truth? Kids lie about stuff like that all the time. Not that that's exactly your area of expertise.' It was an unkind joke, but somehow Sean knew it was not meant to be as unkind as it sounded.

'I don't,' Carter admitted. 'But the teacher was convinced. It all kind of figures – if the stepfather's on the force, he'll have seen situations like this before now. He'd know what to say to get social services on his side. And the mother was definitely hiding something.'

'Bastard,' Taylor muttered under his breath. It was one thing they could agree on. 'I spoke to him only a few days ago. He said he'd do anything to help us bring her in.'

'Of course he did,' Carter stated flatly. 'He's probably spent the last few years thinking his stepdaughter was dead. Suddenly she pops up again and he's nervous. If he can help get her a conviction for manslaughter at the very least, it makes her story even less convincing and him even more upstanding.'

'That's a pretty big accusation, Sean. A serving officer trying to get his stepdaughter convicted for manslaughter to save his own skin.'

Carter nodded grimly.

'But how come the papers didn't pick up on this?' Taylor asked quizzically.

'It seems the teacher was very discreet. And they can't just print wild speculation, even if they did find out,' Carter explained. 'And remember, there were no charges. So we can't let him know that we're on to him.'

'Why the hell not?'

'Because he's being helpful. At the moment, the family are the only link we have to Francesca Mills. We might need them in the future, and we don't want to scare this guy off.'

Taylor laid his pen on the desk. 'You don't have a daughter, Sean.'

He shook his head. 'You know I don't.'

'Well, let me tell you how it is. If someone did something like that to Samantha, I'd kill him. Without a second thought.'

'I know, Mark. But you've seen this happen before, and you'll see it again. We both know that.'

The two men sat in silence at the thought.

'Well, it doesn't really change anything,' Taylor said abruptly, suddenly uncomfortable with the vague sense of camaraderie the news had engendered between the two of them. 'She's still missing, and we still don't know how to find her. If she's got any sense, she'll keep her head down and make sure it stays that way.' He went back to his paperwork.

'I know,' said Carter, as he prepared to leave. 'That's what I'm afraid of.'

But Taylor wasn't listening.

Back at the office, Carter did his best to ignore the frustration building up inside him. A few days ago he had been in control, ready to bag the biggest conviction of his career; now he was flailing around, desperately trying to follow up a barely existent lead. This sort of detective work, he knew, was all about your gut feeling. Evidence could wait till later; all he needed to do now was trust his instincts. And his instincts told him that if Francesca Mills had managed to stay hidden from the ones who loved her all this time, she wasn't going to crawl out of the woodwork for him. He slammed the door to his office shut, took his phone off the hook and looked with loathing at the pile of files on his desk. There were other cases he had to attend to, but he knew he would not be able to concentrate on any of them while the image of Rosemary's grotesque corpse remained unexorcized in his mind.

He had to get his hands on that information, and he knew his chances of locating the locket were almost non-existent. Up until now, he had been reluctant to seek a warrant to search the bank's computer systems – it would just alert them to his suspicions, and in any case they had probably removed any trace of the transactions he was after once they knew that Rosemary was on to them. But now he didn't seem to have any other choice. With his boss, Andrew Meeken, at a training seminar for the rest of the week, he strode out of the office and went to find the secretary of the director of the SFO.

Minutes later he was being ushered into the director's office. Alistair Baker was a small man with a full head of suspiciously black hair that belied the fact that he was only a year or so from retirement. He wasn't an unfriendly man, from the few encounters Carter had had with him, just a bit distant.

'Come in, Carter.' Baker smiled, and the creases on his face became more pronounced. 'How are you?'

Carter shrugged. He wasn't really in the mood for small talk. 'Not too bad,' he replied blandly.

'Good. What can I do for you?'

'I need a Section 2.' This was a special power that the SFO had in order to question people or obtain documents in a hurry – especially when they believed documents or computer files may be destroyed in order to hide evidence.

'To do what?'

'Search the records of Lenham, Borwick and Hargreaves.'

Baker nodded impassively. 'Yes,' he said. 'Andrew Meeken informed me that you were investigating them. What do you hope to find?'

'Details of a high-level fraud,' he explained, 'possibly involving a government minister.'

'And what evidence do you have?'

Carter winced involuntarily – he hadn't been looking forward to answering that question. 'An employee of the

179

bank approached me. She noticed irregularities in the accounting.'

'I see.' Baker sat a bit further back in his chair. 'I think I'm right in saying that you have been investigating this case to the exclusion of everything else – including the others in your team. Am I right?'

Carter shifted in his seat.

'It's not good enough. We need to see more convictions from you if I'm to justify your presence at the SFO. Our resources are limited, as you know. We work in teams here, and there isn't room for people who aren't prepared to do that.' Carter looked away. He had to admit that he wasn't good at working with his team, the accountants – or number-crunchers as he preferred to call them – and the lawyers and IT professionals who combined to make up any normal investigation. He had been dealing with the Lenham, Borwick and Hargreaves file alone, and the director clearly didn't approve. 'I don't believe this investigation will lead anywhere, so I would like you to start concentrating on your other cases.'

Carter couldn't believe what he was hearing. 'This could be the most important conviction your agency has ever made,' he told his boss.

Baker smiled indulgently. 'I've heard that so many times before –' he started to say, but he was interrupted by Carter, whose thin patience had now given way to angry frustration.

'Look,' he fumed, raising his voice a little so that the director appeared rather taken aback. 'I have pictures of the Secretary of State for Defence meeting with the head of this bank.'

'So what?' Baker replied, angry now. 'There's no law against that.'

'Perhaps not. But there is a law against people being shot in the head. The person who located evidence of the fraud and downloaded it onto a storage device is now dead; the evidence itself has been stolen. You *need* to let me find it. If you close the case now, these people will get away with fraud *and* murder.'

As he spoke, though, he saw Baker's face remain unemotional. The director was silent for a few moments, allowing Carter's accusations to hang in the air while he considered how to respond. Then he spoke quietly. 'The last time I looked, *I* was the director of the SFO, and *I* will decide what I *need* to do. Does what you're telling me really sound very likely? I've been in this job a lot longer than you have, and I've seen this happen before.'

'Seen *what* happen?'

'Officers become so eager to tie up a case that they will start clutching at straws. We don't have the time or resources to allow you to keep chasing shadows like this.'

'But someone has died –' Carter started to say, but Baker interrupted him by firmly raising his right hand.

'You're not with the Met now,' he said firmly, his voice uncharacteristically loud. 'If there's a murder investigation to be made, let them make it. No doubt they will ask you for your input.'

'But I can't prove who did it –'

'Exactly. That is why I'm not granting the Section 2,' Baker said, interrupting him for a second time, before composing himself somewhat. 'I'd like you to take a holiday. When you come back – refreshed and with a clear head, I hope – the case will be closed and you will continue the other investigations within your team.'

Carter went to open his mouth to protest but Baker got there before anything came out. 'That is my final word on the matter.' He looked sternly at him.

As Carter got up to leave Baker was already buzzing through to his secretary. 'Show DI Carter out, would you?' he asked politely.

Before Sean knew it, he was walking down the corridor, avoiding the glances of the people he passed, not wanting to be caught in conversation. How the hell had he just allowed that to happen? Surely the director of the SFO, if he had given the investigation any scrutiny at all, would know how important it was? Carter stormed into his office and stood staring out of the window and into the drab office on the other side of the road. A few more flurries of snow had started to fall, and his mood felt as wintry as the weather.

Maybe he did need a holiday. There was always something about the approach to Christmas that made him feel a bit gloomy. The prospect of another festive season with his well-meaning parents and siblings alike asking him when he was going to 'settle down'. They had this notion of him as a carefree womanizer, and he didn't have the heart or the inclination to tell them the truth – that his romantic interludes were few and far between and that when they did occur they were short and not particularly sweet. None of the women in his life seemed to understand that in his line of work you couldn't just let everything drop because you had to go to the cinema. He would try to explain it but, the older he got, the more he found his explanations fell on deaf ears. The result? A succession of evenings in a bachelor pad that contained everything he could possibly want except the one thing he craved above all else: companionship. Sometimes he dreaded going home.

He thought of Mark Taylor. Maybe he had it right. Get the job done, then home to the wife and kid as quickly as possible. Satisfaction of a sort, but then Taylor didn't seem to be thriving on it.

Damn it, though – this was all smoke and mirrors. What was Baker thinking? It was a big case. An important case. Why was he being pulled from it without a more convincing explanation? There had to be more to it than the director was telling him. 'Politics,' he muttered to himself as though it were a forbidden word, before grabbing his coat from the back of his chair and walking out of the office, slamming the door behind him.

Frankie and June shut up shop at six o'clock on the nose. The older lady pottered a bit ineffectually while Frankie brought the stock in from outside and arranged it neatly on shelves in the shop. It had been a busy day, according to June; to Frankie it had seemed frantic – a far cry from the mind-numbing boredom of wandering the streets – and once she had used the front two pages of the newspaper to wrap up and discard some leaf trimmings, she had enjoyed every minute of it. She had even forgotten to worry about where she was going to sleep that night. But as her new employer flipped the sign in the window from OPEN to CLOSED, the events of the day suddenly seemed little more than a mirage.

When everything was cleared up, June went to the till and removed three slightly crumpled ten-pound notes.

She flattened them out in her hand before giving them to Frankie. 'There you go, dearie,' she said with a smile. 'I'm sorry it's not more.'

Frankie shook her head mutely. 'Thank you,' was all she could think of to say, but it seemed so inadequate.

'Now then,' June continued, 'before you go on your way, I want to have another look at that hand of yours.'

The wound looked so much better today, mainly because it was clean, and June kept uncharacteristically quiet as she dabbed at it once more with antiseptic, and replaced the bandage with a clean one. Only as she was finishing did the gentle babble of her voice start up again. 'So what will you be doing tonight, my dear?' she asked lightly.

Frankie was stumped. She couldn't tell the truth, obviously, but what could she say that would sound convincing? What did normal people do in the evening when they had time off and a bit of money in their back pockets? 'Go to the pub,' she ventured unconfidently.

'Meeting a young man, I'll be bound,' she suggested archly.

Frankie blushed even as she shook her head. Young men weren't something that were picked up on her radar – not in the way that June meant. They were something to be avoided, more often than not. Even if she felt differently now, she knew that they would be put off by her gaunt face and greasy hair, by the bags under her eyes and her dirty skin. And it would all be a pipe dream, anyway . . .

June watched Frankie closely as a look of confusion crossed the young woman's face. 'Well, if you're not meeting anyone in particular,' she said self-deprecatingly, 'perhaps I could come along myself.'

Frankie looked at her in surprise. 'Of course, June.' She smiled. 'I'd like that.'

'Oh splendid!' June clapped her hands in a strangely childlike way. 'Why don't we go upstairs to the flat and have something to eat?'

June's flat was neat and homely, the food she cooked warm and comforting. She watched Frankie pensively as the young woman wolfed the food down as if she hadn't eaten in a month, too intent to say a word, while she herself picked demurely at her own plate. 'You were hungry,' she noted with understatement as her companion finished off.

Frankie nodded.

'Ah well, I don't seem to have much of an appetite myself tonight. Shall we go?' She stood up and grabbed her coat from a peg, pretending not to notice the look Frankie gave the plate of uneaten food she had left. 'Come along then, dearie,' she said brightly. 'I don't want to be late tonight, not like you young things, out till I don't know what hour.'

As this unlikely couple walked into the nearest pub, Frankie breathed in the dense, beery fug. She felt nervous. Normally she would be asked to leave any pub she set foot inside, but tonight was different. The pale blue headscarf and clean jumper made her look less like a down-and-out, and the fact that she was with such a respectable-looking lady meant that nobody gave her a second glance. 'Now then, you find a seat,' June said in an orderly tone of voice that made it clear she was as much a stranger here as Frankie, 'and I'll get us both a drink. What would you like?'

'Vodka,' Frankie replied almost automatically as she looked round for a table.

June gave her an odd look. 'Vodka and what?' But her companion had already walked off to sit down.

A few minutes later she joined her, carrying a glass of wine and one of vodka, ice and lemon, with a separate mixer bottle of tonic. Frankie looked uncomfortably at the drink in front of her, unsure quite what to do, then poured a splash of tonic into the glass and drank the vodka down in two gulps, before June had even taken a sip of her wine. 'You're a fast drinker,' the older woman noted.

Frankie looked embarrassed. 'I'm sorry,' she muttered, before adding weakly, 'I was just thirsty.'

June took a sip of her drink. 'Tell me where you're staying again,' she asked, as if making light conversation.

'With friends.' Frankie knew she sounded sullen, but she didn't want to be drawn into this conversation again.

'I see.' There was an awkward silence. 'Don't you think you should call them to say you're going to be home a bit later?'

'No, it's OK,' Frankie stumbled on her words slightly. 'They won't be worried.'

'I see.' June did not sound convinced.

They sat in silence for a minute or two. Frankie drained the water that had melted from her ice, and June nursed her glass of wine unenthusiastically. Finally she spoke. 'You're not really staying with friends, are you, Frankie?'

'I am,' she replied. 'I just . . .'

June raised her hand to silence her. 'I think you're sleeping rough,' she said simply. 'Tell me the truth. I might be old but I'm not stupid.'

Frankie fiddled with her glass, unable to look her in the eye. If she told the truth, June might want nothing to do with her; but how long did she think she could keep this up? How long before June noticed her coming in to work every day in the same clothes that grew dirtier each time she wore them? How long before she got into a fight and came in with her face bruised and purple? How long before she simply let something slip? Slowly she nodded her head, then turned her wide eyes to look at June.

The older lady's face appeared almost relieved, as if this had been bothering her for a while and now everything was making sense. 'Why don't you go home? To your mother?' she asked softly.

For the first time since she ran away, Frankie considered telling someone, but something stopped her. How could June possibly understand what she had gone through? Some things are beyond other people's comprehension. And anyway, it was still too traumatic for her to talk about. She had done everything she could to put the past out of her head; speaking about it would just undo the good work she had done. 'I just can't,' she said a bit more forcefully than she intended. She instantly regretted her vigour as June lowered her eyes. 'I'm sorry, June,' she said quietly. 'I can't talk about it. Look, if you want me to stop working at your shop, I'll understand.'

June shook her head. 'No, dearie,' she declined. 'I don't want you to do that.' She took another sip of her drink. 'There's a spare room in the flat,' she said after a moment. 'It's not much to speak of, just a box room really, but there's a bed there. You'd be welcome to it, if you like.'

'June, you don't have to . . .'

But she was holding up her hand to silence her again. 'I had a daughter,' she said. 'She was about your age when she died in a car accident.'

Frankie noticed June's jaw lock as she did her best to stop the emotion from showing in her face. 'I'm sorry –' she started to say, but was cut short again.

'You remind me of her in so many ways.' June took Frankie's chin in her hand. 'People aren't meant to be on the street, Frankie. And they aren't meant to be alone. Please – you'll be doing me a favour. You can move out to your own place when you get yourself sorted.'

Frankie remained silent. She wasn't used to such charity, and didn't know how to react to it.

'Come on.' June spoke for her as she pushed her glass of wine away. 'Let's go home.' The two women stood up and left the pub.

They walked in silence as they followed the route back to the flower shop and, although it wasn't far, it took them a while to get there because June walked slowly. The shop was in sight when they heard voices shouting behind them. Frankie turned to see two girls running towards her. Why were they calling them? What did they want? She felt her hackles rising. It wasn't until they were close that she realized who they were: the junkies who had stolen her begging money a couple of days ago. They stopped a couple of metres away from her and June, their breath steaming in the air, their eyes alive and hungry. 'We told you to fuck off out of it,' one of them said, her voice tense with what sounded like excitement. She eyed June with a sneer.

Frankie took a step forward so that June was protected in the background. 'Fuck off,' she hissed. 'I'm not in the mood tonight.'

The girl moved cockily forward, glancing over Frankie's shoulder to look at the bag June was carrying.

The last time they had met, Frankie had been too distracted to notice much about her, but now, in the yellow light of a street lamp, she saw that her lips were covered in cold sores, and her nose was raw with infection from her piercings. She had an almost sarcastic look on her face as she glared at Frankie: this girl had chickened out of a confrontation once before, it seemed to say. She was bound to do so again. Her companion held back, looking up and down the street for signs of trouble.

Frankie stood her ground until the girl was no more than half a metre from her. She could vaguely hear June chattering in the background, telling her to move, to come home and leave them alone. But Frankie knew from experience that it had gone too far for that. There was a moment of silence, the calm before the storm, and then the girl pounced at her. She grabbed Frankie's hair in a vicious clump and twisted it round sharply so that she gasped with pain. Frankie fell to one knee, and the girl put her face up close. 'You, get out of here like I told you. The old lady's mine.'

Even though she couldn't see June, Frankie was aware of her backing away from the scene in terror. The girl twisted her hair harder; as she did so, Frankie clawed her right hand in front of her face and grabbed at the rings piercing the girl's nose. She pulled as hard as she could. The girl screamed and let go of her hair. Frankie fell back and looked in her hand: two small rings lay in her palm, smeared in a little puddle of blood. The girl was on her knees, her face in her hands and blood seeping through her fingers; her friend took one look and ran away down the street.

Frankie flicked the nose rings down onto the ground,

a look of disgust on her face, then wiped her hand on her coat. She took June, who was standing in shock at what had happened, by the arm. 'Come on,' she said urgently. 'Let's get off the street.'

'But . . . the police . . .' June stuttered. She appeared horrified by what had happened in front of her. 'How could you do that to that poor girl?'

'It was her or me,' Frankie snapped. She took one look at the pitiful sight of her assailant on the ground, put her hand in her pocket and fished out one of the ten-pound notes June had given her. Bending down to the weeping girl she pressed it into her bloody hand. Then she turned back to the older woman. 'And the police won't be interested,' she muttered. 'Come on.'

Chapter Ten

Christmas was always a time of mixed emotions for Frankie. In some respects it was easier than other times of the year – the punters were a bit more generous with their loose change, and the charitable organizations would open up more redundant buildings to supply extra shelter and food to see the homeless through the festive period. Of course, there was never any sign of them come January, but no matter: at least they made December a bit more bearable. At the same time, though, Christmas could be harsh. The glut of decorations and advertising everywhere you turned seemed to taunt you, to make it impossible to forget what you did not have. It was an unspoken thing, but Frankie knew that at this time of year everyone on the street was thinking of whatever home they had once known.

But this Christmas was different. Frankie was different. She had been working in the flower shop for four weeks now, and the transformation in her had been astonishing. June had watched with pleasure as the nervous young girl with suspicion in her eyes had gained confidence – not the aggressive confidence she had seen that first night after they had gone to the pub, more like a self-assuredness, self-esteem almost. It suited her.

It wasn't just her persona that had changed; she looked different too. Before, her face had been gaunt and white, worn thin by poor food and not enough of it; but a few weeks of eating properly meant that she had filled out and colour had returned to her cheeks. Now that she could wash properly every day, the blemishes on her once dirty skin had faded, and her hair – which she kept short and *would* insist on dying black, much to June's disapproval – had a lustre that was missing before. Her fingernails, once broken and dirty, were beginning to grow back. One evening June had caught her filing them down. Frankie had tried to hide the nail file as if it were some illicit object, clearly embarrassed that she was doing something to take care of her appearance after so many years. She had spent some of the money she earned in the shop on new clothes – not brand new, June suspected, but cast-offs from charity shops. Her taste was for simplicity – jeans and plain jumpers – and she always wore the same simple blue headscarf that exaggerated the blue of her eyes.

On occasions June would tell her companion how pretty she was that day; Frankie would look uncomfortable and change the subject. But despite the fact that there was a gap between them, a social divide that June could never cross, she thought she understood why. In some respects Frankie had had to grow up very quickly – too quickly. But in others she was still the little girl who ran away when she was fifteen. She had been unable to grow gradually into womanhood like a young girl should. Starved of love, she had grown like a plant starved of light; but now she was blossoming like the flowers she sold so effectively to the customers in the little shop.

Since she started, business had picked up. June had never made much money out of the place – that wasn't why she did it. But since Frankie had arrived, custom had been swift. June didn't know what was attracting them. Maybe it was the increasingly colourful displays in the front that Frankie took such pleasure in creating; maybe it was Frankie herself. The older lady had noticed certain customers coming in on a more regular basis, entranced, perhaps, by this new employee with her occasional shy smiles, her scrupulously neat apron and the headscarf worn so artlessly. It was clear to her eyes that had seen so much that Frankie had her admirers, but the young woman seemed so immersed in her new life that she was oblivious to it. Sometimes June would suggest that Frankie should go out, try and meet people, have fun; but Frankie would just smile and say she was happy to stay at home.

A couple of weeks before Christmas, Frankie persuaded June to stock Christmas trees and blood-red poinsettias. She had never bothered with Christmas trees before – it seemed like too much bother, and in any case she would never have been able to move them in and out of the shop. But Frankie was persistent, and sure enough they sold well. By Christmas Eve they had only four or five left.

The two women were going to spend Christmas quietly together, and both were looking forward to it. They had grown close in the last month, and felt easy in each other's company. Often they said nothing for long periods of time, but it was a comfortable silence. June did her best not to pry into Frankie's past, knowing that she would open up when the time was right, and her young friend appreciated not being faced with a barrage of constant questions. June had no family to speak of, and was glad of the company. As they set up shop on Christmas Eve, though, Frankie thought that June seemed distant some-how, not her usual self. She had been perfectly chirpy the night before, chattering away about the meal she was going to cook on Christmas Day. Would the turkey be cooked through? Did Frankie like sprouts? Frankie had smiled indulgently and assured her that everything would be fine. But now the sparkly June of the previous night had been replaced. 'Are you all right?' Frankie asked as she handed her a cup of tea.

'I'm sorry, dearie?' June seemed miles away. 'Oh yes, fine. Just a bit of a headache. I might have a little sit down while you set up, if you don't mind.'

'OK,' Frankie said brightly, and went about the business of dragging the remaining Christmas trees out to the front, and arranging the rest of the flowers on their metal shelves. As the day wore on, though, June seemed more and more out of sorts. Frankie did her best to cheer her up, but she seemed to be in a world of her own, leaving her young assistant to deal almost entirely with the running of the shop while she sat down and stared vacantly into space.

By five o'clock, Frankie was exhausted. Most of their stock had been sold to customers wanting to take a bunch of flowers to wherever they were going for Christmas, and now they were down to a single, small tree. She was just about to shut the shop when a young man came in, somewhat flustered, and looked around in a way that Frankie had grown to recognize – the look of a man wanting to buy something, but not knowing where to start.

'Can I help you?' she asked him in her quiet voice.

He was wearing a heavy coat and scarf, and his longish hair was tousled and windswept. She had a feeling that he was one of those who would quiz her in some depth about whatever they had on display. June always gave her an amused look when she answered these questions as earnestly and as fully as she could – she didn't know why.

'I need a Christmas tree,' he said with a confidence most men didn't seem to be able to muster in a florist's shop.

'We've one more outside,' she told him. 'I'll show you.'

As Frankie led him outside, the man started questioning her. 'My mum's coming to Bath to stay with me for Christmas. What can I get her? What do you think she'll like?'

'Poinsettias are nice at Christmas,' she suggested.

'Are they the ones with the red leaves? This is fine, by the way.' He tapped the Christmas tree and they started to walk back inside. Suddenly he stopped. 'Oh my God,' he breathed.

'What is it?' Frankie asked, pushing past, but instantly she saw for herself. June, who had been sitting at the little coffee table, was slumped over in the chair. Frankie ran towards her and straightened her up in her seat. Her eyes were open, but glazed, and she showed no signs of responsiveness when Frankie spoke to her, first in a quiet, comforting voice, and then loudly and in a state of panic. 'She needs an ambulance,' the man said, calmly taking control of the situation and dialling a number on the mobile phone he had pulled out of his jacket. Before Frankie knew it, he had called 999 and was then by her side, comforting June with constant, reassuring words.

Suddenly everything was a blur. When she looked back on the events of the evening, she could remember only disjointed fragments: holding June's hand as they waited for the ambulance; shouting at the man in the shop to do something, even though there was nothing he could do; the anxious look on the face of the paramedic placing an oxygen mask over June as she lay on the stretcher in the ambulance; the seemingly interminable wait at the hospital; the journey back to the flat, alone in the cab; how empty the place seemed without the gentle babble of June's chattering.

She'd had a stroke, the doctor whose face she forgot as soon as she left the hospital had told her. A bad one. She was lucky to be alive. It would be some time before they could assess the extent of the damage; they would have to keep her in for several days. Was Frankie the next of kin? 'No,' she told them sharply, not wanting to sign her name on any piece of paper. 'I'm just a friend. She doesn't have any family.'

And so the turkey remained uncooked, the sprouts uneaten. Frankie didn't care. She had missed out on enough Christmases – one more made no difference. All she wanted to do was make sure that the lady who had taken her in, shown her more kindness than anyone ever had, who was more maternal towards her than her own mother had ever been, came home.

It was going to be a quiet Christmas at The Stables – Harriet did not feel like celebrating. The press interest had gradually died down, the police had stopped calling. It was just the two of them. But something had changed in William since the picture of Francesca had come to light. It was nothing she could put her finger on, nothing she could pinpoint to criticize in him, but he had seemed detached, unwilling to help her through this traumatic time in the way he had when her daughter had first disappeared. She needed him now more than ever, and he just didn't seem to be there. He was always working late, finding one excuse or another, and on his days off he would take himself out of the house and she wouldn't see him for hours on end. When they did occasionally spend time together, he seemed monosyllabic and distant.

He had time off over Christmas. Maybe she could talk to him, get him to open up a bit. She had made an extra effort that day, decorating the tree and cooking a meal – making sure the whole house seemed festive for their Christmas Eve together. But as the time for him to get back from work came and went, and the dinner spoiled in the oven, Harriet realized that tonight was going to be just like all the others. She poured herself another glass of wine, not knowing whether to weep or to throw the drink against the wall in fury.

It was half past nine when he returned. Harriet could not smell the alcohol on his breath because she had been drinking too. 'Where have you been?' she questioned him aggressively. William didn't answer. He just walked past her into the front room where he poured himself a whisky. 'Where have you been?' she repeated. 'It's Christmas Eve.'

'Working,' he said shortly.

Harriet knew he was lying. Normally she wouldn't have the confidence to confront him, but the wine had loosened her tongue. 'No, you haven't,' she accused. 'I've been cooking all day for you. It's ruined.'

'Look, Harriet,' he said dismissively. 'Things don't stop just because you've been cooking. We'll call for a takeaway.'

'I don't *want* a takeaway,' Harriet screamed at him. 'I want dinner with my husband. On Christmas Eve!' She drunkenly threw her glass in his direction. It missed, but the wine soaked his face as it flew past.

'What the hell's wrong with you?' he shouted as he wiped the alcohol from his cheek.

'What do you mean, what's wrong with me? What's wrong with *you*?' Harriet was uncontrollable now, yelling like she had not yelled since the dark days after Francesca's disappearance. 'You've hardly spoken to me for weeks, ever since we saw the picture of Francesca. You're never here. It's like I don't have a husband any more. Like I don't have anyone.'

'Don't be so stupid,' William blustered, his eyes flashing. He was doing his best not to raise his voice, but he couldn't prevent it.

'Don't tell me not to be stupid! What am I supposed to think?' She glared at him, fighting the urge to say what she wanted, but it overcame her. 'Half of me thinks Francesca was right,' she hissed. 'Half of me thinks you *were* interfering with her.'

William stood perfectly still. 'Don't say that, Harriet,' he whispered. 'You know it's not true.'

'Well, sometimes I wonder.'

It happened in a flash. William strode across the room and thumped his screaming wife across the side of her face with the back of his hand. She stumbled backwards onto the sofa in shock, touching her fingers to her stinging cheek and gazing up at her husband with a mixture of fear and apology. William stood above her, red-faced and shaking. He raised his hand as if to strike again, then closed his eyes, took a deep breath and let his arm fall to his side. 'You forced me to do that,' he told his terrified wife in a threatening voice. 'Don't ever do it again.' He turned and left the room. Harriet sat there, too shocked even to move, as she listened to the front door open and then slam shut.

She walked about the house in a daze. This had never happened before – she had never seen him like this. He was tired, she told herself. He had been working hard, and she shouldn't have riled him like that. It had been the wine talking – she poured the remainder of the bottle down the sink in an act of defiance. She had the presence of mind to turn off the oven, but she left the food inside – something she had never done before – and walked upstairs to bed. Looking at herself in the bathroom mirror she saw a patch of purple bruising gradually appearing on her face. She touched it lightly and winced at its tenderness before removing her clothes and creeping into bed. As she lay there, part of her wondered if he would ever do this again, and what she would do if he did.

It was past midnight when she heard the door opening again. William stumbled up the stairs and into the bedroom. He dropped his clothes on the floor and fell into bed beside her. Harriet could smell the alcohol now, but whether that was because she had sobered up or he was more drunk, she couldn't tell. She turned to face him in the darkness. 'I'm sorry, William,' she whispered softly, her voice trembling slightly. 'I didn't mean to say what I did.'

But William didn't hear. He was already fast asleep.

Frankie spent as much of Christmas Day by June's bedside as visiting hours would allow. She seemed terribly weak: one side of her face had drooped and she had no control over it, which made her speech slurred and indistinct. Frankie did her best to be upbeat, telling her that the doctors were pleased with how she was getting on and that she would be home before she knew it; but both women knew the road to recovery would be a long one.

It was New Year before June was allowed home. Frankie had kept the flower shop shut all that time, preferring to visit June in hospital whenever she could, even though it meant spending more time on the bus than actually by her bedside. But once she was back, she insisted that the shop be opened up. Frankie argued. 'I need to be looking after you,' she complained. 'In any case, I can't run the shop on my own. There's too much I don't know how to do.'

'You'll be fine,' June replied, slowly and clumsily. It broke Frankie's heart to hear her speaking like that. 'And so will I. I can rest up here, and if I need anything, I'll let you know. You can always pop up and ask me anything you need to know.'

And so, reluctantly, a few days into January Frankie opened up the shop by herself for the first time. It was strange not having June there to chat to, and she found herself feeling lonely again for the first time in weeks. The post-Christmas custom was slow, and she was thankful for the fact that there was so much else to do – stock-taking, ordering, tending the plants. It all went some way to keeping her mind off the fact that June wasn't there. And in the background she kept the radio on. It was a comforting sound – it reminded her of June, and of her mother before that.

Frankie was just about to shut up shop on that first day when the little bell rang to indicate the door was opening. She looked up to see a man walk in, but it wasn't until he had approached the counter that she recognized him as the one who had helped the night June had had her stroke. He smiled at her. 'Hello,' he said brightly. 'I don't know if you remember me . . .'

'Of course I remember you.' Frankie smiled at him. 'Thank you for your help the other night.'

'Is the lady OK?'

'Fine, thanks,' Frankie informed him. 'A bit weak, but the doctors think she'll make a full recovery over time.'

The man looked genuinely relieved. 'And you didn't even get round to selling me that poinsettia.'

'Did you find something for your mother in the end?'

The man looked momentarily confused before realizing what she was talking about. 'No,' he said with a smile. 'I just regaled her with the story of my heroic actions and she let me off the hook.'

Frankie laughed. She had not had the chance to look at him properly before, but now she did she saw how nice-looking he was. His face was boyish, his brown eyes wide and trusting. His hair was still tousled and he had a slightly apologetic smile that seemed to Frankie to speak volumes. 'My name's Keith, by the way. Keith Osbourne.' He held out his hand. It was cold to the touch, but she suddenly felt a different kind of warmth as it enveloped hers.

'I'm Frankie,' she said simply.

'Frankie . . . ?' he asked.

'Just Frankie.' She smiled at him again and withdrew her hand. As she did so, she saw him notice the scar across her palm. It had almost healed now, thanks to June's care and attention, but there would always be an angry red mark there. Keith's face was a little puzzled, and he seemed to be on the point of asking her about it, so she quickly put her hand behind her back and looked away. 'We're closing in a minute,' she said. 'Did you want anything?' It sounded more unfriendly than she meant it to.

Keith glanced at her with a mixture of amusement and confusion. He turned round and picked the first bunch of flowers that came to hand – a bunch of forced tulips that had seen better days – and paid for them without speaking. Frankie blushed, feeling slightly ashamed of herself as he handed over his money. She smiled at him again, and he inclined his head lightly before leaving the shop.

Frankie was quiet that night, quieter than usual, not even apologizing for the food she cooked June. She wasn't much of a chef, and always found the need to comment on what had gone wrong with a meal before she served it. June would sit up in bed and tell her it was delicious, while Frankie sat on a chair by the bedside, a plate of food on her lap, keeping the older lady company as they ate. Tonight she hardly spoke, and although June eyed her questioningly, she knew better than to pry with Frankie. She was a closed book when she wanted to be. The meal passed silently, and once she had seen that June was comfortable, Frankie went to bed early.

That night, she dreamed again. The nightmares had become less frequent after she moved in with June, but since the stroke they had started again, as confused and as horrifying as ever. Every night she was revisited by Bob Strut; every night in her mind's eye the broken glass would be protruding from his neck, seeping blood that ran down his clothes. He would walk towards her, his face contorted into a warped grin; as he walked, he never seemed to get any nearer, and yet he seemed impossibly close – too close for Frankie to be able to get away. She wanted to turn and run, but she knew there were policemen behind her. And then, just as her panic was becoming unbearable, his face would change. She would see her mother, her face swollen as it had been in the picture she had seen in the newspaper; she would see little Mary, her red hair straggling over her ghostly white face; she would see her stepfather, his flat eyes dead and his jaw set; and she would sometimes see June, one side of her face drooping horrifically, her body bent double, but those sharp eyes still appearing to see right through her . . .

And then she would wake up suddenly, nervous and sweating, wondering where she was. In the weeks since she had been with June, she still hadn't grown used to the sensation of waking up in a bed, of feeling clean cotton next to her skin. She would feel disorientated and perplexed for a few moments, before putting her head back down on the pillow and lying there in the darkness, listening to the silence. Darkness and silence: two things you never experienced when you were sleeping rough.

That night she lay awake until dawn, unable to shake off the uncomfortable feeling the dream had given her. Things always seemed worse at night – she couldn't help wondering what the hell she was doing there in June's flat. She was a street kid, nothing more; she didn't belong here. The police were bound to catch up with her sooner or later. Just because her face was no longer in the papers, it didn't mean nobody would ever recognize her. And when they did, when the police finally came knocking, she would lose all of this. When she had been on the streets, the relative security of a prison cell had not seemed so distressing; but now this little flat, with its warmth and comfort, was the centre of her world. It would break her heart to leave it behind. And what would happen to poor June if she was discovered hiding a wanted criminal? So often Frankie had considered telling her everything, but deep down she knew she could never tell her anything about her past: if June remained in ignorance, she would be protected when the inevitable moment came.

As the blackness of the night turned to the cold grey of early morning, Frankie crept out of bed, pulled on some warm clothes and walked towards the kitchen. Passing June's room, she heard the soft sound of the radio, so she knocked quietly and put her head round the door. June was sitting up in bed, perfectly still, her head turned towards the curtains, a framed photograph in her hands. She didn't move as Frankie looked in, so the younger woman coughed gently. June turned to look at her and did her best to smile, but it turned to more of a grimace on her stroke-shocked face. 'Good morning, dearie,' she said quietly. 'How are you today?'

'I'm fine, June.' Frankie was always struck by her ability to ask after the health of others when she was in this state. 'And you?'

June gazed down at the photograph in her hand. 'I was thinking about Madeline.'

She seldom spoke of her daughter. All Frankie knew was that she had died in a car crash when she was nineteen years of age. June's husband had passed away a year later, ostensibly from angina, although she insisted his heart was broken. 'It would have been her birthday today,' she continued. 'Her thirty-first.' She smiled sadly. 'It's hard to think of her as a thirty-one-year-old. One of the advantages of dying young, I suppose.'

Frankie stepped in softly and went to sit at June's bed-side. She gently rested one hand on hers, but said nothing. Words of comfort did not come easily to her. The girl in the picture was pretty, laughing at some long-forgotten joke with the photographer, and something about the eyes made it obvious that she was related to June.

'You're like her in so many ways,' June told her. 'She was impulsive, secretive. When I heard about the accident, I was devastated. Of course I was. But you know some-thing? I wasn't surprised, Lord help me. Some people seem destined to come unstuck. Do you think that's a terrible thing for me to say about my own daughter?'

'I don't know, June,' Frankie replied in all honesty, but June didn't seem to hear her.

'She had been to a party with some friends. They said she hadn't had anything to drink, but who knows if that was the truth? On her way home a van driver ignored a red light and hit her from the side. She was killed instantly.' Tears started to fill her tired eyes. 'A parent should never have to bury their own child – somehow it seems wrong that I'm here and she isn't. Not a day has gone by that I haven't wished I was in that car instead of her.' She looked straight at Frankie. 'But I don't expect you to understand that, dearie.'

Frankie didn't know what to say. In a way it was true – self-preservation was the only thing that had mattered to her in all the years she was on the street. But as she sat there by June's bed, she remembered little Mary, wide-eyed and terrified, and what she had done to protect her; she looked at the older lady, and realized with a slightly uncomfortable sensation that the duty of care she felt towards her was stronger than she could have previously thought possible. 'I think I understand,' she said quietly.

June nodded. 'Maybe you do at that,' she conceded. Then she looked directly into Frankie's eyes. 'You can't run for your whole life, Frankie,' she said piercingly before looking back at the picture in her hand. 'One of these days you just have to let yourself be happy. After all, you never know what could be just around the corner. And it would break my heart if you were to end up the same way as poor Madeline. Ah, but I'm embarrassing you.' She smiled again. 'Do you know, I think I might like to come down and sit with you for a while today.'

'I don't think that's a very good idea, June,' Frankie protested. 'You need to rest a little longer.'

'Ah well, it won't be for long. And I *will* be resting – just sitting there is all.' She smiled her half smile again. 'Don't worry, dearie, I won't be getting in your way.' Her eyes twinkled, and Frankie knew she wouldn't be argued with.

She wouldn't have admitted it, but it was nice to have June back in the shop. As was so often the case, they spoke infrequently, but each took comfort in the other's silence, and June stayed there all day, a thick blanket on her legs and a battered paperback by her side, which she dipped into occasionally. There were few customers, and Frankie had her back turned when the door opened just before closing time. 'Hello, Frankie,' a voice said behind her.

Frankie wasn't used to hearing her name on anyone's lips other than June's – and even she called her 'dearie' more often than not. Her heart suddenly in her mouth, she spun round. 'Keith!' she said with undisguised relief when she saw him standing awkwardly at the counter. 'You made me jump.'

'I don't look that bad, do I?' He assumed a look of mock self-pity.

Frankie flashed him a smile. 'What can I do for you this evening?'

Keith looked round the shop and saw June sitting there. 'I'm glad to see you looking better,' he said politely. June looked bewildered. 'I was here the night you fell ill,' he explained.

'Ah!' June nodded her head. Frankie could have sworn there was a look of mischief in her eyes. 'You must be the young man Frankie has told me so much about.'

Frankie blushed and shot June a meaningful glare which Keith did his best to pretend he hadn't noticed. 'What's the most beautiful bunch of flowers you have?' he asked her, kindly changing the subject.

'For your mother?' Frankie asked delicately.

'No, actually. They're for someone I'm taking out to dinner tonight.'

It wasn't a response Frankie was expecting, and for some reason it flustered her slightly. Avoiding his eyes, she came out from behind the counter, took a large bunch of long-stemmed white lilies from a bucket, and arranged them with some glossy green foliage. 'I think she'll like these,' she said.

'Thank you,' Keith replied simply as she started wrapping them for him. He glanced over at June, who was watching him with an amused look in her eye, then handed some money over to Frankie, before taking his flowers and change. He looked straight into her eyes, then handed the lilies back to her.

Frankie felt a sudden urge to throw the flowers down and run into the back room, but something kept her there, her fists clutching the flowers tightly and her eyes betraying the worrying sensation she was feeling. 'So *will* you?' Keith asked.

'What?' She had no idea what he was talking about.

'Have dinner with me.'

'No.' She said the word hastily, too loudly, and instantly regretted it. 'I mean, no, thank you. I'd love to, but I can't.' She looked over at June. 'I can't leave June by —'

But June interrupted before she could finish her sentence. 'I'll be fine, dearie. You go out and have a nice evening. It's about time you did.'

'But . . .'

June held up her hand in that way of hers. It always stopped Frankie short. 'I'll be fine,' she repeated simply.

Frankie looked at the flowers — so delicate. And then she looked back up at Keith. 'Thank you,' she smiled almost girlishly at him. 'I'd love to.'

Frankie had not been in a restaurant for years. The occasional cafe, maybe, but nothing like this. The closest she had been was rifling through their bins in the streets of Soho in the small hours of the morning after the kitchens had cleared out, doing her best to hide if she found a morsel worth eating — there was always someone hungrier and more desperate than yourself to steal it away. She drank the red wine from the glass that Keith had poured her in big, nervous gulps as she looked at the menu without really taking in what it said. The restaurant itself was not busy — just a few couples murmuring quietly to each other — but it did not stop Frankie feeling out of place, as if everyone was looking at her and wondering what this woman was doing here when she so obviously didn't belong. She tried to tell herself that those were thoughts from her past.

June had seemed more excited than Frankie about Keith's invitation – but Frankie was very good at keeping her emotions under wraps. The older lady hadn't been in a position to flap around as she might otherwise have done, but she made firm suggestions about what Frankie should wear, and while other young women might have been annoyed by such interfering, Frankie was grateful. She had no experience of these things. At June's suggestion she removed her headscarf, and at the last minute she took the locket she kept in her bedside table and allowed it to peek out from the top of her plain white blouse. 'You look beautiful,' June had told her as she left, and Frankie had believed her.

Now, though, she just felt gawky. She didn't know how to act in front of this man whose kind self-confidence was so alien to her. Most of the men she had ever met were people to be avoided, people who wanted something from her that she wasn't prepared to give. But Keith seemed different. Polite. In control. She was grateful to him for the way he had taken charge when June had her stroke, but it was more than that. She felt she could trust him, and that wasn't an emotion that came easily to her.

Keith was studying the menu a little too intently, clearly unsure how to react to Frankie's awkward silence. 'What would you like?' he asked brightly.

Frankie glanced at the menu. It meant nothing to her. 'I don't know,' she told him honestly. 'I'm afraid I don't come to restaurants very often.'

'I'll order for you, then.' He caught the waiter's eye and ordered plates of pasta for them both.

Frankie finished her wine with another gulp, and he refilled her glass, politely pouring a dribble into his own to mask the fact that it was practically untouched. She felt the alcohol start to take effect, but it did not relax her; somehow it just made her feel more jumpy. She suddenly became acutely aware of the fact that she had hardly spoken. 'So,' she asked to break the silence, 'where do you live, Keith?'

'Just outside Bath. But I work in the centre, for a firm of accountants.' He looked apologetic. 'Not very exciting, I'm afraid. How long have you worked in the florist's?'

'Not long. Just a few weeks.'

'And before that?'

'I lived in London.'

Keith's eyes lit up. 'Why did you move here from London? Surely it's much more exciting up there.'

'No,' Frankie said flatly. 'It isn't.' She looked away.

'Do you have family there?'

Frankie shook her head.

'Friends?'

'No,' she almost snapped. 'Look, I'd rather not talk about London, OK?' She had already said more than she had intended to.

Keith looked curiously at her, a smile flickering across his face. 'OK,' he replied tactfully. 'I'm sorry. Small talk's not really your thing, is it?' Frankie made to respond, but he held up his hand to stop her. 'It's all right,' he said, smiling a bit more now. 'I can't stand it myself, to be honest.' He gave her a half wink then placed his hand over his mouth. 'My lips are sealed,' he mumbled, the words sounding comically muffled. A few of the diners around the restaurant gave him odd looks, but he ignored them and stubbornly kept his hand ostentatiously in front of his mouth.

Frankie felt a blush rising in her cheeks. 'Keith!' she whispered, half amused, half embarrassed. 'Stop it!' She leaned across the table and grabbed his arm, pulling his hand away from his mouth. Keith made some play of resisting her, and in the mock tussle that followed their hands became joined. Slowly Keith pulled her hand down onto the table, and for a few moments they sat like that, hand in hand, before Frankie awkwardly pulled hers away. She refused to look Keith in the face, but she knew he was still looking at her with those amused eyes.

'I'm just a very private person,' Frankie said quietly, as if to apologize for her previous outburst.

'That sounds very exciting,' Keith replied with the incessant playfulness that seemed to have grabbed hold of him. 'I like a bit of mystery. Am I going to find out that you're not a florist at all? Maybe you're a Russian spy, deep undercover . . .'

'Stop it, Keith.'

'Or a terrifying femme fatale . . .'

'*Keith!*'

'I've got it! You're a murderer, on the run from the police, always one step ahead and never knowing from day to day when your past is going to catch up with you.' He raised his glass in a toast to his own wild imagination, a big grin on his face. His triumphant look became a little crestfallen when he heard the aggressiveness in Frankie's voice.

'Shut up, Keith.' His words had suddenly brought home

to her the madness of her being there. As her eyes started to dart around a bit more, she still couldn't shake off the sensation that everyone was looking at her. She began to panic. What if she was recognized? What if June needed her back at home? What if Keith carried on asking her questions that she couldn't answer, for his own safety as well as hers? She liked him – she really did – but how could she possibly have kidded herself that this was a good idea? 'Look, I'm sorry, Keith,' she heard herself saying. 'I really am. It's nothing to do with you, you're very sweet, but I really shouldn't be here.' She felt her voice wavering as she stood up, fighting back the tears. She walked away from the table and left the restaurant.

Keith sat there for a few moments, his brow crumpled as he did his best to ignore the prying stares of his fellow diners. Suddenly he stood up, laid a few notes on the table, put on his coat and grabbed Frankie's, which she had left on the back of the chair. Then he chased after her.

She was already halfway up the street, walking quickly and purposefully away. He ran towards her, only calling out her name when he was a few metres away. She turned in surprise. Her arms were hugging her body to protect herself from the cold, and the light coating of mascara that June had persuaded her to wear had smeared around her eyes. 'What the hell are you doing?' he asked, his good manners giving way to embarrassment. 'You can't just walk away like that.'

'Don't tell me what I can and can't do, Keith.'

They stood in silence for a moment, before Keith muttered an expletive under his breath and walked away.

But he hadn't got far before Frankie called him back. 'I'm sorry,' she said quietly.

Keith stopped and then stood still, as if wondering what to do, as if wondering whether this strange, wild girl was worth the attention he was giving her. Finally he returned, holding out her coat for her and she put it on gratefully. Rather timidly, he put his arm lightly around her shoulders, but her body shrank away from his touch and he instantly removed his arm. 'Can I at least walk you home?' he asked. Frankie nodded.

It took ten minutes to get back to the flower shop and they did not say a word to each other all that time. There didn't seem to be much to say. As they stood at the door to the florist's, Frankie looked at him. His soft, brown eyes seemed riddled with emotions: annoyance, confusion, embarrassment, kindness – or maybe she was reading too much into it. She knew she had behaved strangely, but it had all been too much for her. 'Good night, mystery woman,' he said. They stood awkwardly together, and Frankie smiled apologetically, clutching her hands together in front of her. Keith leaned over to kiss her on the cheek. 'You'd better go in,' he told her. 'It's cold.'

But Frankie didn't go in. Instead she moved imperceptibly closer to him and, as she did so, he gingerly put one arm around her shoulders again. He felt her body go tense, but this time she didn't pull away. He moved his face in front of hers and she could feel his trembling breath warm against her skin.

As he kissed her lips, she wrapped her arms around him, holding him tightly, like a lost girl in desperate need of love.

PART THREE

Chapter Eleven

Eighteen Months Later

Morgan Tunney felt his shirt stick to his body, clammy and sweating in the June heat. It had been a relief to get into his car with its comfortable seats and air conditioning, but you wouldn't have known it to look at him. His face remained red and bothered, and he mopped his brow occasionally as his driver wove his way through the back-streets of Belgravia towards Piccadilly. 'Get a move on,' Tunney said more than once, only to hear a cautious 'Of course, sir' in reply. He was late, and he didn't want to give Sir Ainsley the opportunity to start the meeting without him. There were things he wanted to say.

As he approached the room, he knew Andreas had already arrived – his cropped-haired companion was standing outside, silent and steely as always. Tunney nodded at him as he opened the door and walked inside. As he did so, he could immediately sense a tension in the air. Cooper and Andreas were standing at either end of the room. Both men were extremely good at remaining expressionless, no matter what they were thinking, but the lack of any small talk was clearly significant: there may have been nothing being said, but there was clearly plenty left unsaid. 'I'm sorry I'm late,' Tunney said gruffly. He squinted slightly as he walked into a stream of light that was flooding through one of the large windows, illuminating little scraps of dust floating in the air. He stepped out of the way of the sun.

'Please, Morgan,' Cooper almost purred, 'don't mention it. Take a seat, won't you?'

Tunney shook his head. 'I'd rather stand, thank you.' Cooper was the consummate politician, but the banker had no intention of being lulled by his impeccable manners. 'What have you discussed?'

Cooper looked over at Andreas. 'Nothing, yet. Andreas quite rightly suggested we wait for you.'

'Good.' Tunney turned to the blond man. 'I want my money back.'

Cooper and Andreas exchanged a glance. 'I'm afraid that won't be possible, Mr Tunney,' Andreas stated quite firmly.

'Listen to me.' Tunney looked at both men with all the authority he could muster. 'I paid two hundred and fifty thousand pounds over a year ago for you to find some runaway girl. A straightforward operation for someone of your reputation, I would have thought.' He pointed at Andreas. 'You haven't come up with anything, so I want my money back.'

'Morgan,' Cooper started to say. 'I really think –'

But he was interrupted by Andreas. 'Sir Ainsley, I'll deal with this.' He turned to Tunney, who had started to sweat again, more profusely this time. 'It is true, Mr Tunney, that you have paid me two hundred and fifty thousand pounds, and it is true that I have not yet located the girl in question. It is also, crucially, the case that nobody else has found her. It may be that she is dead. If so, I will be very sorry – not, you understand, out of misplaced sympathy, but because if she is you will not end up paying me the remainder of my money. And I really want that money, Mr Tunney. You have my personal guarantee that the moment she surfaces, I will find her – and the information that she is carrying.'

The three men stood in silence. Andreas appeared to be gauging their reactions. He continued talking in a slightly quieter tone of voice. 'In any case,' he said, 'it would be unwise of you to take your funds back.'

'Why?' Tunney appeared wrong-footed by Andreas's reaction.

'I would hate to be placed in a situation whereby I am forced to make use of this information for my own ends when the girl does come to light.'

'Are you blackmailing me?' Tunney spluttered. Cooper remained perfectly still.

Andreas smiled. 'Simply making you aware of the realities of the situation. Now, if that is all, I hope you will excuse me. I am a busy man.'

'Not yet.' Tunney removed a handkerchief from his pocket and wiped away a trickle of sweat that was falling down the side of his face. This was not going as he had expected. In his world, the possibility of losing money was enough to make people do almost anything. Andreas had responded far too coolly for his liking – indeed he had slickly turned the tables on him. Now he had only one place to go, one final card to play that he hoped would gee the bloody awful man into action. He doubted he would ever follow through on the threat, but he calculated that they wouldn't want to take the risk . . .

Tunney spoke nervously, like a child facing up to his bullies. 'As we're all being so honest with each other, I've a few things to make clear myself. If this girl is not found soon, I'll have no option but to go to the police myself.'

'Don't be a fool,' Cooper exploded. 'You'll incriminate yourself along with the rest of us.'

'I don't think so,' Tunney retorted. 'If I give them information leading to the arrest of a cabinet minister, I suspect they will deal with me rather leniently.'

Cooper looked furious, and for once he seemed lost for words; Andreas, on the other hand, was quite unflustered. 'You will do what you see fit, of course,' he said calmly as he walked towards the door. Something seemed to pass between him and Cooper – a look of inquiry from the blond man, and a gentle nod from the politician. Andreas inclined his head towards them. 'Gentlemen,' he intoned politely, then walked out.

'Just find her!' Tunney shouted after him as the door clicked shut.

Sean Carter looked tired. More than that, he looked bored. Since Rosemary's death his team had captured four embezzlers and nine fraudsters, with a total fraud of £19 million. His arrest sheet was good, but to his dismay four cases had collapsed at court; only three had ended up with convictions, and even they totalled only four years in a minimum-security prison. He was getting tired of white-collar workers with their greed and arrogance, and he didn't think he could stomach them falling through his fingers any more. The files on his desk were piling up, unread and unattended to, and although when he came in that morning he had been all fired up to do something about it, his enthusiasm was waning once again. The days all seemed to merge into one: shuffling papers in the office, then back home to his empty flat for takeaway and TV. He wasn't feeling good on it. At times he had even thought of signing up with a dating agency.

He had been so close to bagging a major conviction with the Rosemary Gibson case, but it had been well over a year ago that the previous director had closed the file, and since then he had felt trapped in an accountant's nightmare, buried under spreadsheets and financial reports that meant next to nothing to him. When he had joined the SFO, it had been a big move for him, but now it seemed like it was dragging him down. It all went back to Rosemary's death, which had affected him more than he'd have admitted at the time: it was he who had persuaded her to go through with the whole operation, and even though nobody could have predicted what would happen next, he felt responsible. The police inquiries into the killing had drawn a blank, and Francesca Mills – his only lead – seemed to have vanished. Mark Taylor had said she would most likely be dead in a year, and he was probably right. And now Carter felt next to helpless, stuck in that featureless office on Elm Street. He half wished he was back with the Met.

There was a knock on his door, and Andrew Meeken, recently promoted to director of the SFO, just as everyone knew he would be, stuck his head round the corner. 'Sean,' he said, his voice as understated but as friendly as ever, 'could I have a word?'

'Yes, sir.' Carter didn't stand up, but he gestured that Meeken should take a seat opposite him.

'I've been bringing myself up to speed on the Lenham, Borwick and Hargreaves file you asked me to look at.' He laid a file on Carter's desk. 'It seems to me,' Meeken continued, 'that there's more to this case than is in the file. Would that be an accurate analysis?'

Carter nodded. 'Would you care to enlighten me?' Meeken asked.

Carter took a deep breath and in a slow, measured voice told Meeken everything. How Rosemary had come to him with her suspicions that something untoward was happening at the bank. The locket, the girl who had stolen it, Rosemary being fished out of the Thames. A grim look passed over Meeken's honest face. 'So why was the case closed?' he asked quietly.

'I drew a blank. The previous director decided my resources were better used elsewhere.'

'But you disagree?' Now it was Meeken's time to be perceptive.

Carter nodded. 'Look, Andrew,' he said, 'I can't back up what I'm about to say.'

Meeken indicated that he should continue.

'Rosemary Gibson was close to the chairman of the bank, Morgan Tunney. When she was in his office one day, she saw paperwork relating to a company called Rankin Systems. They were not a client of the bank, and she knew that place inside out. But she noticed large funds coming into the bank and then being siphoned off.'

'Who are Rankin Systems?'

'They're an arms company. And a year before all this happened they had been awarded a major contract by the Ministry of Defence. But there was an outcry when Rankin Systems went over budget on the order to the tune of £250 million. The overspend was personally approved by the Secretary of State for Defence.'

'And you think Rosemary Gibson stumbled across

something to suggest that the arms company, the bank and the secretary of state were involved in some kind of fraud? It's pretty thin, Sean.'

'That's what I thought. So I had the chairman followed.' He picked up the file, flicked through it and pulled out a couple of A4 photographs. They showed two men getting out of a black London cab. 'Morgan Tunney and Sir Ainsley Cooper,' he said simply.

Meeken's eyes narrowed. 'The head of the bank and the secretary of state. You think they were involved in a £250 million fraud . . .'

Carter nodded. 'I'm convinced Tunney was laundering the money through his bank and passing it on to Cooper. But without the information Rosemary Gibson appropriated, I can't prove a thing. For her to turn up dead, though, she must have been on to something.'

Meeken was silent for a moment. 'Why didn't you get a Section 2?'

'I tried to, but it was declined through lack of evidence.'

'But even if you find this information again, won't it be inadmissible in court?'

'Not if we get witnesses to back up the claims and follow the paper trails to the other accounts. I know it's untoward, but I really think we were on to something major.'

'So why did my predecessor close the file?'

Carter didn't answer for a moment. He'd had a long time to think about that, to mull things over. The theory that he had come up with convinced him, but he didn't know how Meeken would take it. 'At a guess,' he said finally, 'I'd say he was scared.'

'Scared of what?'

'Think about it.' Carter was becoming more animated now. 'He's less than two years from retirement and a comfortable pension. Out of the blue I give him circumstantial evidence that the secretary of state is involved in one of the biggest financial and political scandals in recent years. Who knows if other cabinet members are implicated; maybe the PM's involved, maybe not. Whatever the truth is, the government will do everything they can to make sure this stuff doesn't reach the light of day.'

Carter leaned back in his chair. The two men sat there in silence for nearly a minute before Meeken spoke. 'Thank you for telling me this, Sean. Here's what we're going to do. From now on, I want you to consider this case reopened.'

Carter started to protest, but Meeken cut him short.

'Direct all your resources onto it, Sean. If there's an ounce of truth in your suppositions, I want to know. Let me know what you need to get the job done, and it's yours. This is too important to be relegated to an inactive file, gathering dust. And Sean –'

'Yes, Andrew.'

'Good work. Keep it up.'

'Are you sure you'll be OK, June?'

Ever since the stroke more than eighteen months ago, Frankie had been almost stiflingly overprotective of her friend, concerned that she shouldn't overexert herself in any way, even though six months after it happened June had almost recovered. The slur in her voice was hardly noticeable any more, and the droop down the left-hand side of her face was gradually rectifying itself thanks to the gentle exercise routine imposed with regular visits from the community nurse. She still seemed to get tired more easily than she used to, but perhaps that was to be expected – she was in her sixties, after all, even if her sprightly conversation sometimes made you forget that fact.

'I'll be fine,' June chided lightly. 'I used to run this shop by myself, you know, and you're only going to be away for a day. I'm much more worried about you – are you sure you can manage the train journey with Jasper?'

Frankie walked across the shop to where her tiny son was sleeping soundly in his carrycot. She had already had this conversation with Keith that morning – and every morning before that for the last week – but she was determined to take her little boy with her. It wasn't that Keith wasn't perfectly able to look after him, or that his mother wouldn't love a bit of time with her grandson; it was just that Frankie couldn't bear to be away from him. Keith was understanding. She knew he found it difficult letting her go back to work at the flower shop every day, but she had dug her heels in – she'd really taken only a couple of weeks off after Jasper had been born, and even then she had insisted that he drove her over to see June as often as possible, just to make sure that she was coping. Now he dropped her and Jasper off on his way to work every morning, and the two women would take turns in looking after him while the other dealt with customers. It couldn't last like this, they all realized that. Before they knew it, Jasper would be toddling about, and other arrangements would have to be made. But for the time being, Frankie just wanted to be with him every moment of every day.

He looked so beautiful when he was asleep. So like

Keith. All he needed was the tousled mop of brown hair and they'd be almost indistinguishable. She smiled to herself at the thought as June came over and stood by her. 'It's an awfully long way to Plymouth,' she persisted. 'Can't Keith drive you there instead?'

Frankie shook her head. 'He can't take the time off work,' she told her, although that was not strictly true. He *had* offered – several times – but she had declined. In fact, they had argued about it every night for the past week. 'For crying out loud, Frankie,' Keith had asked her last night in a whispered shout so as not to wake the baby, 'why do you have to have everything your own way?' He had stormed out, slamming the door behind him, only to return an hour or two later with beer on his breath, calmer, but far from mollified. At times like that, when Keith's normally mild temper got the better of him, she wished more than anything that she had someone to talk to, a friend other than June. But the friends they had were all Keith's.

The fact remained that this trip was just one of those things she wanted to do. She loved Keith desperately, just as she loved June, but she was still not comfortable relying on them. After so many years of doing things her way, it took some getting used to being part of a family again. Maybe that was why she wanted to take Jasper up to the flower show, just the two of them – so that she could give herself the feeling of being needed. 'He's picking me up during his lunch hour and taking me to the station,' she told June.

June knew better than to argue with her: when Frankie was in a mood like this, nothing would change her mind. 'Whatever you say, dearie,' she backed down.

Frankie gave her a grateful smile and looked back down at Jasper. His eyes were open now – it always marvelled her how he could go from being fast asleep to wide awake and full of life almost instantaneously – so she leaned down to give him a smile. He reached out and grabbed her hair. 'Ow!' she said playfully, unwrapping his hand from around the locks that she had allowed to grow long again, even if she did still insist on dyeing them black. Keith didn't understand why she was so adamant about it; he had just learned that it was one of those things he shouldn't talk to her about. Like her family. Like her past. Like marriage.

It was unfair on him, of course it was, and she had grown to recognize that look in his eyes when he would gaze at her, mystified, confused. She knew he was wondering what secrets she was hiding, what her past had to say about her; and she knew he had probably guessed more than she dared imagine. At first it had made him suspicious that she refused to have a bank account – living cash in hand from day to day – or sign her name on any official documents. He was frustrated that she refused to apply for a passport so that they could go away on holiday – she insisted it was because she didn't want to go abroad or leave June, but he wasn't so sure. But as they had grown closer, he had learned to dismiss these little foibles, or at least to ignore them. Her paranoia was part of her charm, he would tell her. Now when his mother gave him a hard time about Frankie's occasional abrasiveness, or the fact that she didn't want him to meet her family, or why they couldn't get married if only for Jasper's sake, he stood up for her, even though he had asked the same questions himself a hundred times. When she finished every last scrap of a plate of food, leaving it so clean it looked as though it didn't need to be washed, he gave her an amused and indulgent smile. She would get frustrated if she had to throw food away but Keith would dismiss it with a sarcastic comment that always made her so cross. And when she quietly wept to herself after they made love, as she so often did, he would hold her in his arms, not asking the questions he wanted to ask but which he knew she didn't want to hear.

One day she would tell him. Tell him everything. But not yet.

The morning passed quickly. There were arrangements to design and orders to make. Frankie busied herself around the shop while June sat with Jasper, feeding him from a bottle and looking for all the world like a proud grandmother. As the radio announced the one o'clock news, Keith walked in. He kissed Frankie on the lips, June on the cheek, then lifted his son from the cot and held him up to his face. Jasper smiled and gurgled at the sight of his father. Keith looked over his shoulder to Frankie. 'Come on, then, intrepid explorer. Ready to go?'

Frankie nodded. Her suitcase was already in the car but the small overnight bag she had packed for Jasper was behind the counter, so she went and picked that up before embracing June. 'Are you *sure* you'll be OK?' she asked for the third time that day.

'I'll be fine, Frankie,' June assured her. 'You just have a nice time and I'll see you the day after tomorrow.' She brushed Jasper's cheek with the back of her finger and made a clucking sound, then took her place at the stool behind the counter. 'Go safely,' she told her friend.

It wasn't far to the station, but Frankie was glad of the

lift. As they sat in traffic, Frankie put her hand on Keith's knee. It had taken a long time for her to be able to share these little gestures of affection, and she still couldn't bear to be touched by anyone other than her family; every time she gave one of these little caresses, Keith would stroke her hand in return. He knew how difficult she found it, and he wanted her to know that it was appreciated. 'Thank you for letting me do this,' she said above the sound of Jasper's gurgling. 'It means a lot.'

Keith shrugged, but not in a dismissive way. 'Just as long as you're both all right. Call me when you get there. Do you have change for phone calls?'

'Yes.' Frankie had refused to let Keith buy her a mobile phone, despite his protests. She found herself uncomfortable with such technology; and even more uncomfortable with the idea that someone could use a phone to track her down.

'And enough money for cabs?' Keith insisted.

Frankie nodded. Suddenly she was feeling nervous. She hadn't been away from both Keith and June since they had all met, and she was going to find it difficult, frightening almost. But it was a fear that she had to face. She looked straight into Keith's eyes. 'I know you've had to be very patient with me,' she said meekly. 'When I get back, we'll sit down and I'll tell you a few things.'

Keith looked serious. 'Not before time,' he chided.

Frankie nodded. 'I know. I love you.' She squeezed his leg a little harder.

'I love you too. Hurry back.'

It was only nine o'clock in the evening, but June found that she became tired very easily these days. She would never mention it to Frankie, of course, as she worried about her quite enough as it was; but although she had missed her friend since she moved in with Keith, it did at least give her the opportunity to have the surreptitious early nights that she had started to crave more frequently. She poured the hot milk she had heated in a small pan into her mug, then went to bed.

Although she was tired, June seldom slept that well. As soon as her head rested on the pillow, her mind started filling with the familiar old worries. How long would she be able to live alone like this? What would have happened if Frankie hadn't been around when she had her stroke? She always did her best to hide her concerns from everyone around her, but alone in bed at night they were all too clear in her head. To keep her mind occupied on other things, she always had her bedside radio playing quietly in the background. It didn't really matter whether she was interested in the programme or not – the gentle murmur of voices kept her distracted from other thoughts. More often than not she would drift in and out of sleep until she was, ironically, woken by the lethargic music that indicated Radio 4 was shutting down. Then she would switch it off, turn out her bedside light and hopefully sleep until morning.

Tonight, though, she didn't sleep, and she didn't even hear the words of the radio announcers as they chattered their way into the small hours. It was only a matter of time, she knew, before she needed looking after properly. She had no doubt that Frankie and Keith would take her in, but their house on the outskirts of Bath was small enough as it was, and now there was a child – there was no room there for an elderly lady. And besides, God only knew what kind of past she had had to endure – Frankie was a secretive soul, and she had seen both sides to her – but at the very least she deserved a chance of a decent future. June couldn't see how that could possibly involve her.

She chided herself for starting to think in such a way: once her thoughts took that path, she knew there would be no respite until morning. She would allow herself to keep the radio on. Perhaps it would distract her enough to start sleeping. But she would turn the light out, and close her eyes.

An hour later she was only half asleep, but her eyes sprang open when she heard a noise downstairs. It was difficult to make out above the sound of the radio, so she leaned over and switched it off.

Nothing.

She closed her eyes, cursing her overactive imagination. And then she heard it again. It sounded like the tinkling of shattered glass and the muffled noise of male voices talking. She lay perfectly still, listening in horror to the unmistakable sound of people in her shop. The door leading up to the flat was locked but flimsy – Frankie had been on at her for ages to get someone in to make it more secure, but it was just another thing she hadn't got round to doing. Like installing a grille over the front window of the shop. June insisted that no one would want to break into a flower shop when there were electrical stores nearby, but Frankie had given her an almost withering look and told her she'd be surprised what desperate people would do for money. Now June had to suppose that she'd been right, but still – a flower shop. There was no money in the till, and she couldn't imagine there was a big market for stolen lilies.

There was no telephone in her bedroom, and she was too frightened to risk getting up and moving to the kitchen where it was kept, in case she alerted the intruders. She could do nothing but lie there and listen: to the sound below and to the thumping of her heart. She jumped when she heard one of the intruders try the handle on the door leading to the flat. They rattled it hard, as if not wanting to believe it was locked, and then it fell silent. June lay there, straining her ears to hear what was going on, but suddenly she could hear nothing. Had they left? She didn't know.

Tentatively she got out of bed. The room was dark, but she didn't dare turn on the light in case she drew attention to herself. She felt her way round the bed and, groping in the blackness, approached the door. Her dressing gown was hanging on a hook; she pulled it over her nightdress before slowly opening the door and walking out onto the landing. She put her ear against the front door and listened hard. Silence – all she could hear was the sound of her own breathing, heavy but faltering. In darkness, she felt her way along the corridor into the kitchen. She still did not dare turn on the light, so she fumbled around the work surfaces trying to find her cordless phone; she knocked over a teacup that had been left out – the silence around her seemed to amplify the noise a hundredfold, and June only made it worse as she clumsily tried to silence it.

Finally she found the phone and used the tips of her fingers to locate the buttons and dial 999. 'I think someone's just broken into my property,' she whispered to the woman operator who answered.

'Are you by yourself?'

'Yes.' June's voice was full of fear, but it came out as impatience.

'Are the intruders still there?'

'No . . . I don't know . . . I don't think so . . .'

'Stay where you are. I'll have someone with you as quickly as possible.'

June gave the operator her address, then took a seat at the table. Everything seemed deafeningly quiet all of a sudden, and what with the silence and the darkness, she found it difficult to tell how much time was passing. It could have been ten minutes or an hour later that she was brought out of her reverie by a banging on the door. 'Police!' she heard a man's voice shout. She shot up, fumbled for the light switch and hurried downstairs as fast as her frailty would allow.

The officer who was waiting for her at the door was tall and uniformed. He held a flashlight in his hand and gave June a reassuring look as she let him in. And then her knees gave way as she found herself overwhelmed and exhausted by the night's events. The policeman grabbed her as she fell, then helped her up the stairs and back into the kitchen.

Soon she was sitting at the kitchen table with a cup of sweet tea in front of her. There were two police officers there now – the man she had opened the door to, and a woman, who had fetched a rug from June's bedroom and draped it over her shoulders. She sat opposite her, talking to her in that slow, overly solicitous voice she had noticed the younger generation used with her more and more these days. 'It looks as if it was just some local kids breaking in to see what they could get out of the till. They used a brick to smash the window and tried to force the till open – they didn't manage it, though.'

'There's nothing in there anyway,' June said as her trembling hands raised the cup of tea to her lips. 'I empty the till every night and bring the money up here.'

'That's very sensible. We've got someone checking the shop for fingerprints at the moment – it's procedural more than anything. He'll need to take your prints just so that we can eliminate them, and he might ask you a few questions about anyone else's prints we can expect to find here. We'll have an officer posted outside until the twenty-four-hour glaziers arrive to board up the window. In the meantime is there somewhere else you can go? Somewhere you might feel more comfortable?'

June shook her head. 'I'd really rather stay here, officer. I'm feeling a little shaken up.' She didn't mention that she had nowhere else to go. She had thought of calling Keith, but she didn't like to be an intrusion. In any case, she had guessed enough about Frankie's past to know that she would probably not welcome the police going round to her house, so she kept quiet.

The policewoman nodded sympathetically. 'If you're sure,' she said. 'It will take us an hour or so to finish up downstairs. Victim support will come round and talk to you in the next few days. If you need anything in the meantime, you can call me or talk to the officer outside.' She removed her notepad from her top pocket, wrote down the station number and handed it to June.

'I will. Thank you for all your help.'

The two officers left, leaving June in her kitchen, alone, shaken and still very frightened. Her only comfort was the officer waiting outside until the glaziers arrived.

The ugly, seventies frontage of Bath police station seemed less severe in the half-light of dawn, the harsh concrete lines, which were supposed to mingle gently with the ashlar facades of the period buildings around, were softened slightly by the sunrise. The road outside was practically empty, and the stillness of the fading night was interrupted only by the dawn chorus, almost deafeningly loud and strangely beautiful in the middle of the city.

In the basement, Rob Elliott was looking forward to the end of another night shift. He looked at his watch a quarter to six. Fifteen minutes and he'd be out of here, and not before time. It had been a particularly slow shift. He picked up a green file – a scene of crime officer's report that had been dropped in an hour or so ago – and pulled out a sheet of fingerprint markings. The system in front of him was logged on to the NAFIS – the National Automated Fingerprint Identification System. It contained a database of nearly six million prints, and Rob felt as if he'd seen practically every single one of them since he started in the job a couple of months ago. If the computer came up with a match, he'd inform the SOCOs involved and they would pass it on to the officer in charge; and that would be that as far as he was concerned. His friends teased him that he was a budding Sherlock Holmes; if only they knew the monotonous truth. The title of Fingerprint Officer might sound grand, but the reality was hours on end stuck in the basement feeding bits of paper into machines. Rob inserted the sheet into the slot and waited for it to do its business. Get this one done, he thought, and I'll go home.

Suddenly the computer beeped. Rob furrowed his brow and looked at it – normally it didn't make a sound. A small window had appeared on the screen. He grabbed his glasses from the table and studied it: CLASSIFIED FINGERPRINT MATCH. The words flashed slowly on the screen, and below was an instruction to call a London number immediately. Rob had never seen anything like this before – not that he necessarily should have done – and for a moment he considered calling the duty sergeant down, just to double-check what he should do. Then he looked at his watch again. Ten to. Get any of that lot upstairs involved and he could be here all morning. He picked up the phone and dialled the number.

There was a ringing tone at the other end; it stopped for a moment, and then the tone started up again, slightly different this time as if the call had been diverted to another number. It took a while for it to be answered; when it was, the voice at the other end was curt and unfriendly.

'Yes?'

'This is Rob Elliott at Bath Police Station. I've just fed some fingerprints into the NAFIS database and I got a message to call this number.'

The voice at the other end softened slightly. 'Thanks for calling, Rob. This is a branch of Scotland Yard. Can you give me the details of the case?' Rob didn't bother to ask which branch, knowing the number to be secure as it was already on the database.

'Just a minute.' Rob opened the file and scanned

through the scene of crime report. 'Break-in at a commercial premises in Bath.' He read out the address.

'What time did the incident take place?'

'It was phoned in at 01:08. Officers attended the scene ten minutes later, but there was no sign of the suspects. Owner was still there – she lives in a flat above the shop.'

'Does the file give any indication of whether the fingerprints are likely to be the suspects'?'

Rob took another look at the file. 'I'm sorry, I can't tell. I've never had to do this before.' He sounded a bit flustered.

'Don't worry,' the voice said soothingly. 'Take your time.'

He read the report again, more slowly this time. 'The scene of crime officers seem to think so.' He carried on reading. 'But they were found all over the shop. They don't match those of the owner, but it seems a bit unlikely to me that the burglars would have left such a trail.'

The voice at the other end of the phone ignored Rob's suppositions. 'Is there anything else?'

'Hang on.' He read a bit further. 'Yeah, apparently there's a girl who helps out sometimes in the shop, but we haven't identified her prints yet.'

'Do you have a name?'

'The owner says her name is Frankie Gibbs.'

'Right. Let me just check I have that address written down correctly, and I'll need the crime number,' he said. Rob read it out again. 'OK, good,' said the voice. 'Thank you for calling us so promptly.'

There was a click at the other end of the line as the voice hung up.

Chapter Twelve

Morgan Tunney's Belgravia house was grand but anonymous. A black metal railing protected the pavement from
the sheer drop leading down to the basement – passers-by
could never help glancing down to ogle the ultra-modern
kitchen it housed, which was a stark difference to the
Georgian elegance of the building itself. The square in
which it stood was quiet, off the rat run of the London
rush hour that would soon start up, and the leafy gardens
at the centre were peaceful and empty.

On the roof opposite Tunney's house a blond-haired
man was lying down in the sniper position, looking
through the lens of an SSG-3000 high-powered sniper
rifle. It was resting on its tripod, with the front of the
attached long-barrelled silencer barely visible through the
parapet of the Georgian building.

Andreas had been there since dawn. He knew Tunney's
schedule, and he knew that he often left early in the
morning. Today was different, for some reason: he was
late. Andreas didn't know why, but he didn't let it bother
him. Tunney was in there, he was sure of that. He'd be
out soon enough, and when he was . . .

He massaged his right shoulder slightly: he didn't want
to become stiff when the time came. Military training and
years of experience had taught him that. It was a light
enough weapon, although the reflex-sight attachment
added to its weight, but the whole thing had started to

feel heavy after over an hour of being pointed in the direction of the front door. It was worth it, though: the fibre-optic device created a red dot in the middle of the scope, visible only to the shooter and not to the target. Andreas seldom missed, but it was good to have this insurance. Attached to his ear was a Bluetooth mobile phone attachment; but the phone had been switched to silent mode since he arrived, and his attention remained firmly focused on the house.

There had been movement inside for a while now. He had seen the lights switch on and curtains pulled open; and a wodge of letters that a postman had left half sticking out of the letter box had been pulled inside. It was only a matter of time before Tunney's car arrived and he stepped out of the house. Andreas was already going to have to eliminate the driver, and he hoped that there would not be any unfortunate pedestrians walking along in the wrong place at the wrong time.

Andreas didn't like Tunney. He was a greedy little man out of his depth, with little respect for the blond man's professionalism. Of course he would never let his personal likes and dislikes get in the way of his work, but under different circumstances he would have been happy to eliminate the fat little banker and his unpleasant attitude. As it happened, though, he thought this was a mistake. Why bring attention to the situation by leaving a dead body on the streets of central London? There was no way Tunney was going to squeal – he didn't have the guts. Andreas knew his type.

But this wasn't his call. He had his orders, and deep down he knew everyone was being jumpy with good reason: they had failed to find the girl.

Andreas clocked the black Bentley as it pulled into the square and parked outside the house. The heavy red front door opened, and Andreas trained his sights on it. He wanted to wait until the door was shut and his target was on the street before he fired – that way he would have a few extra moments to make his escape before the wife realized what had happened. Two figures appeared at the door: Mr and Mrs Tunney, kissing each other goodbye in a scene that was no doubt being replayed across the whole country. The front door swung shut and Tunney walked down the steps to the pavement, oblivious to the fact that a small red dot was trained expertly on his forehead.

And then Andreas's phone rang – not a ring tone, but a vibration in his jacket pocket. He cursed under his breath in a foreign language, slipped his hand into his pocket and pressed a button, keeping his gun firmly directed at Tunney's head as he waited impatiently for his driver to get out of the car and open the door for him. Andreas wanted to wait until the two men were next to each other before he fired. 'Yes?' he whispered under his breath.

'The girl Francesca Mills. We've found her.'

Andreas blinked heavily. The two men were together now. If he was going to take them out, this was the time. Tunney was just starting to duck down in order to climb into the car. His finger twitched on the trigger.

And then he let the gun down.

He watched in silence as the two men got into the car and drove slowly away. He hadn't noticed it, but a thin film of sweat had collected on his upper lip.

'Andreas, are you there?'

'Yes,' the blond man replied quietly. 'I'm here. Are you

240

sure it's her?' He was already dismantling his gun and packing it into a metal case by his side, ready for the next time.

'Definite. We have a positive fingerprint match.'

Andreas stood up and walked down the fire escape. 'Good,' he said. His bleak face did not indicate that he was pleased. 'Where is she?'

Keith put his key in the front door and was surprised to find it unlocked. He shook his head and chastised himself slightly – he must have forgotten to lock it that morning. Hardly surprising, he supposed. He'd slept badly, what with Frankie and Jasper being away for the first time since his son had been born. He'd been worrying about them. Frankie had told him on the phone last night not to be silly, that they were fine, but it was a father's prerogative to worry about his family, and he'd told her so, saying it as a joke but in fact he was perfectly serious. Keith was looking forward to having her back.

And then there was June. She had called this morning to tell him about the break-in, and although she was doing her best to be calm, to play it down, he could recognize the note of stress as she spoke. She had insisted that she was OK, that the police had looked after her well and that someone had come to repair the damaged window, and Keith had promised that he would bring Frankie round the moment she got back. 'Don't worry about it,' she had told him, but Keith was adamant. Truth be told, he was a bit frustrated that he wouldn't be able to spend the evening alone with his family, but he knew that Frankie would insist on going round when she heard the news. Maybe they would argue about it, maybe they wouldn't.

So with everything going on in his head, it was no wonder that he was distracted enough to forget about locking the door.

He walked into the house and put his keys on the table in the hall as he always did, then went into the kitchen. He had scrawled a note to himself on a piece of paper on the kitchen table: 'J/F, collect 6.55.' He looked at his watch. Twenty-five past six. Frankie's train was due into the station in thirty minutes, so there was time for him to have a quick shower and to get into some clean clothes. He walked up the stairs, undoing his tie as he did so.

Moments later he was dropping his clothes onto the bedroom floor. It made Frankie mad when he did that – she was almost obsessively tidy – and he smiled slightly at the image of her picking up his clothes with a silence that said more than any argument could hope to. He walked naked down the hallway to the bathroom, where he switched on the shower and waited for the hot water to come through before getting in and soaping himself down.

Once he had finished, he grabbed a towel and started to dry his hair as he tottered, dripping wet, along the hallway and back into the bedroom, leaving a trail of damp footprints on the carpet behind him. He stepped into the bedroom, dried himself and walked over to the other side of the bed to collect his clothes.

Then he heard the door shut softly behind him.

He jumped at the unexpected noise and turned round, his skin tingling with the momentary shock. Standing at the door was a tanned, thickset man with blond hair and blue eyes. He was holding a small black gun, and it was pointed directly at Keith. 'Are you familiar with this gun?' he asked in a steady, threatening voice.

Keith froze, too shocked even to shake his head.

'It's a .44 Magnum, one of the most powerful handguns in the world. If I shoot you now, the bullet will pass straight through your body and into the wall behind you.' He smiled a humourless smile. 'It goes without saying, then, that you will do precisely what I say. If you try anything foolish, I will kill you without a second thought. Do you understand?'

'What do you want?' Keith demanded, suddenly shaking from cold and fear in equal measure. The man opened the door and stepped backwards. He stood at the top of the stairs and gestured with a flick of his gun that Keith should walk down. 'I need to get dressed,' he told him – the words came out jabbering and indistinct. The blond man shook his head and flicked his gun again impatiently.

Keith walked reluctantly to the door and headed down the stairs. 'Go into the kitchen,' he heard him say firmly. Despite the fact that there was a man with a gun behind him, he still felt embarrassed by his situation and held his hands modestly over himself to hide his nakedness as he turned left at the bottom of the stairs and went into the kitchen. It wasn't a big room, but there was enough space for a small dining table and chairs.

'Pull out a chair and sit in the middle of the room,' the man said.

Keith did as he was told. The blond man pulled a roll of gaffer tape from his pocket and wrapped it in thick swathes over Keith's midriff and round the back of the chair. Keith struggled, but his arms were taped to his sides and he couldn't move them. The chair rattled a little as he jerked his body around, so the man took his gun and rapped him fiercely around the side of the face. Keith shouted in pain, then sat still while his legs were taped to the chair.

Once he was secured, the man seemed more relaxed. 'You're making a mistake,' Keith breathed at him. 'I don't know what you want, but you've got the wrong person.' He was too scared now to be embarrassed, aware that whoever this man was, he wouldn't hesitate to hurt him badly.

'Shut up,' the man replied. He looked around the kitchen and opened a few drawers, rifling through the cooking implements before finding what he was looking for. He walked back to Keith holding a small, black, kitchen blowtorch. He pulled a lighter from his pocket, lit the blowtorch and held it close to Keith's face. 'Where is she?' he asked directly.

'I don't know what you're talking about.' Keith stared straight at him, hoping that the lie did not show in his eyes. Somehow it made sense that this man was after Frankie. Somehow the mystery seemed complete.

The blond man nodded his head slowly. He moved the blowtorch away from Keith's face, then pushed it hard against his shoulder. Keith screamed as the flame burned into his flesh. As the man pulled the blowtorch away, his victim started retching – from the fear, from the pain, and from the smell of his burning skin that had suddenly filled the room. It didn't seem to worry his torturer – he waited until the retching had stopped before punching the burn wound and then inflicting another one on the opposite shoulder. Keith shouted less loudly this time – he was unable to catch his breath enough to do so, and his voice sounded hoarse and strangulated. 'Please . . .' he begged.

'Let's try again,' the blond man insisted grimly. 'Where is she?'

'I told you, I don't know what you're talking about.'

Instantly the man placed the burning blowtorch against Keith's skin and listened impassively as he screamed again. Then he unlocked the safety catch and pointed his gun directly at Keith's forehead. 'I will kill you if you don't tell me where Francesca Mills is.'

A huge sob escaped Keith's mouth and his head drooped onto his chest. 'Gibbs,' he whispered. 'Not Mills. You've got the wrong person.'

'Where is she?' The blond man's voice was implacable.

'She's not here.'

'I didn't ask you where she's not. I asked you where she is.'

Briefly, involuntarily, Keith glanced at the piece of paper on the table with the train time written on it, then scrunched up his eyes, waiting for the inevitable. But with the skilled observation of the trained interrogator, the blond man noticed his subtle movement. He picked up the piece of paper, then nodded in satisfaction. 'I suggest we wait for her,' he said blankly. 'Where does the woman keep her jewellery?'

Keith gazed at him in shock. 'Is that all you want?'

Suddenly Andreas swiped him again across the side of his face with the butt of the gun. 'I don't like repeating my questions. Where does she keep her jewellery?'

'She doesn't have any,' Keith spat. 'Not here. Look, if it's money you want, my wallet is upstairs. Take it . . .'

'Shut up,' Andreas told him in a level voice. 'Francesca Mills seems to have a habit of surrounding herself with tiresome people. The lady in the flower shop, for example.'

Keith looked daggers at him. 'What have you done to June, you bastard?'

'Nothing, yet. She has been lucky. I could have killed her when she refused to tell me where you live but, fortunately for her, her address book was close at hand. I promise you, though, that I will put a bullet in her skull if I don't get what I want, just like I will put one in yours. Now, you are lying about her jewellery. She has a silver engraved locket. Where is it?'

Keith looked at him in utter confusion. 'She's wearing it. She always does. Why –'

But his question was interrupted by the sudden ringing of the phone. The two men stared at the cordless handset as it sat on the kitchen table, a little red light blinking in time with the ring. It sounded four or five times before Keith spoke. 'Let me answer it,' he demanded through gritted teeth.

'I don't think so,' the blond man replied almost to himself. 'We'll let her think that you are out and make her own way here. It will be easier for us that way.'

Frankie hung up the phone. Where the hell was Keith? He had promised to pick her up. She tried his mobile number, but it rang out and went to voicemail. 'Keith, it's me. Where are you? Jasper's tired. If you're not here soon I'll have to make my own way back.'

All around her the station was buzzing – it was rush hour and the concourse was a sea of activity. She had one foot hooked around a wheel of Jasper's pram, and had been keeping an eye on him as she called Keith. Her son was asleep, blithely unaware of all the bustle around him.

She stood for a moment in the open booth. This wasn't

like Keith – normally he couldn't wait to see his little boy and he had been so adamant on the phone last night that he would be there to pick them both up. There must be some explanation, she told herself as she hitched her rucksack further up her shoulder, then pushed the pram towards the exit and the bus station opposite. Caught up at work, maybe, although it was out of character.

There was a long queue for her bus, and she took her place at the end of it with a sigh. The woman in front of her smiled affectionately at Jasper, who was still asleep. 'He's beautiful,' she said to Frankie, who smiled back – she never knew quite how to respond when people said that to her out of the blue. She always wanted to agree with them, but it seemed somehow arrogant. He *was* beautiful, though. Just looking at him seemed to dispel her frustration and tiredness.

Although it took only five or ten minutes by car, it was a slow bus ride home – not because of the traffic but because it was a circuitous route back to the suburb of Bath where Keith and Frankie lived, made more tortuous by the fact that plenty of people embarked and disembarked at each stop. No one actually made any comments about the amount of space Frankie and her pram were taking up, but the barbed looks and impatient sighs all around her were enough to indicate that at least some people considered it an imposition. But Frankie was oblivious to them: she was used to it, and she knew she and Jasper had as much right as anyone else to be there. She was far more bothered by a man who had been in the queue behind her and who just sat there looking stony-faced while an elderly lady stood right next to him, gripping the handles as firmly as her frail hands would allow. Frankie wanted to say something, but found herself reticent. There was a time when she would have thought nothing of a confrontation, but months of keeping a low profile had cured her of that – apart from when it came to Jasper, of course.

As if woken by that thought, her son suddenly started crying, which only evoked more annoyance among some of the regular commuters. Must be hungry, she realized, and she bent down over the pram and gently stroked his cheek. It always felt so soft against her rough, calloused hand. 'Shhhh . . .' she comforted him. 'We'll be home soon.'

Eventually the bus arrived at Frankie's stop. She struggled to push the pram through the little crowd of people around the exit, then awkwardly bumped it down onto the pavement. It was a complicated route that took her into the heart of the quiet residential area where they lived. She remembered the first time she had taken the bus from the shop to Keith's house, smothered with apprehension and unsure whether she really wanted to take the step in their relationship that her arrival alone at his place would undoubtedly initiate. On that occasion she had had to write down Keith's bewildering directions on a scrap of brown paper; now, though, she could find her way blindfolded, she had walked it that often.

It took ten minutes to reach the house. Frankie left the pram in the driveway as she always did – Keith would bring it in later for her – and lifted Jasper out. The walk had settled him a bit, and his crying had changed to the gentle cooing that she always found so adorable. She held him close to her body and hurried up to the door. She pulled her keys from her pocket and opened up.

It was strangely quiet inside. Frankie slung her rucksack onto the floor in the hallway as she wondered why there was no music playing in the house. Keith was always playing music. She called out to him. 'We're home!' Jasper gurgled as if in confirmation, and she stepped towards the kitchen, absent-mindedly tickling her son under his chin as she went.

She would never forget the sight that met her in that kitchen for as long as she lived. Every detail etched itself on her consciousness in a moment: Keith, naked and bruised, taped to the kitchen chair; horrific wounds on his shoulders weeping blood down his arms; the look of dejected panic on his face as he stared at her, his mind clearly even more tortured than his body; the smell in the room, a strange odour of burning that she could not place; and the man standing behind Keith, blond-haired and grim-faced, one hand over his captive's mouth to stop him from shouting out, another aiming a gun directly at the back of his head. 'Sit down,' he told Frankie curtly as he removed his hand from Keith's mouth.

She shook her head and took a step backwards, her arms instinctively wrapping themselves tighter around Jasper.

'I will kill this man without a second thought if you do not do what I tell you.' The blond man spoke quickly but concisely – he obviously didn't want her to get away. But Frankie took another step backwards, her every instinct screaming at her to do what she could to protect her son.

'Very well,' the man continued. He moved the gun away from Keith's head and pointed it towards Frankie. His hand was perfectly still. 'If you do not sit down like I told you, I will kill Jasper immediately. The bullet will kill you too.'

Suddenly Keith shouted out. 'You bastard!' he yelled, and tried in vain to struggle out of the chair.

'Shut up,' the man spat. He moved the gun away from Jasper for a moment to bring its butt down hard on Keith's head; but Keith was too inured to the pain now for it to affect him. As heavily as he could, he used the weight of his body to rock the chair forwards and then sharply back. The blond man collapsed roughly underneath him, and swore violently in a foreign language as he did so.

'Frankie,' Keith shouted breathlessly. 'Run! Now!' And then, as Frankie turned and sprinted back down the corridor with Jasper still in her arms, she heard him shout again. 'I love you,' he called, but more quietly this time.

Frankie stopped momentarily and looked back over her shoulder. She could hear scuffling in the kitchen and she wanted to go back, to help Keith overpower this intruder in her house. But as instantly as she stopped, she started moving again: she had Jasper to think about. He was her first priority, and she knew Keith would feel the same. She had to make sure her son was safe. She fumbled with the latch of the front door before opening it and running outside. She hurtled through the gate and away from the house.

And then she heard it.

It wasn't as loud as she expected a gunshot to be, but there was no mistaking it. At first she thought that she and Jasper had been fired at; but she soon realized that it was not as close as that. Even though it had not been directed at her, Frankie felt the impact of that bullet thud through her very being. Her body screamed at her to go back and hold Keith in her arms, but her legs kept running as she clutched her son tightly. She knew what she had to do.

She turned back and saw she was being chased by a different man from the one who had killed Keith. She tore furiously down the street and round the corner – there was no way she could outrun anybody, carrying Jasper at the same time, so her only chance was to hide herself in the confusing maze of streets that she knew well but which she could only hope would confuse and lose her pursuer. She ran blindly, turning left here, right there, not thinking where she was headed but desperately trying to get as far away from home as possible. As she ran, the image of Keith, broken and beaten, filled her head. She screwed up her eyes, expecting tears to come, but for some reason they did not. They seemed inadequate – the desperation that Frankie felt was more profound than that, more gut-wrenching and hopeless. She had no idea who that man was, but she knew, without quite knowing how, that he was there for her and not Keith. Keith had known that too: she had seen it in his eyes. It was all too terrible to bear. The man who had held her in the dark and promised to look after her and her child had done just that; the man who had given her back her life and her dignity had sacrificed himself to protect her.

Jasper started screaming, howling in the way that Frankie felt she wanted to. It was almost as if he knew his father was dead.

Chapter Thirteen

Frankie didn't know how long she ran, with Jasper wailing piteously and a silent scream in her own heart if not in her mouth. The horror of what had just happened had barely had time to sink in, but now that she had caught her breath her whole body became saturated with a thousand different emotions. Self-loathing – the terrible thing that had just befallen Keith was her fault, she was sure of it. Why else would anyone want to do such things to him? Fear – for herself, certainly, but mostly for the small child in her arms. Disbelief – this could not have just happened. But above all, sorrow – great pounding waves of it threatened to make her whole body collapse. Her Keith. Her darling Keith, one of the only people in her life who had ever cared for her, accepted her for what she was and loved her. She would never see him again, and it was too much to bear. She felt strangely unable to cry, but the pain she was feeling was coursing through her body like hot metal in her veins.

She had been running without thinking, and had no idea where she was, but now, looking around to take in her surroundings, she saw that she was outside her local supermarket. It was fairly crowded, somewhere she could lose herself – even though she thought she had shaken off the men, she still felt a desperate need for anonymity, a few quiet moments to allow her to compose herself, to come to terms with the terror of what had happened. She shifted Jasper onto one arm, picked up a shopping basket and walked in.

When she was running, she hadn't noticed the stares from concerned passers-by; now, though, she couldn't ignore the looks she was getting. Her face was damp with sweat, as was the lightweight denim jacket she was wearing; her eyes were raw and she was sniffing heavily; and Jasper was complaining as loudly as he could. Although she might have wanted anonymity, in fact she was a spectacle, cutting a swathe through the crowd of shoppers who eyed her with interest, but did not want to get too close to this traumatized-looking woman and her bawling child.

The first thing she had to do was to comfort Jasper, so she marched purposefully down the aisles of the super-market looking for the baby items, then grabbed a carton of formula milk, a bottle and some teats. She then strode to the checkout and waited in line to pay with one of the few notes she had remaining in the back pocket of her corduroy trousers. A woman in front let her go first – whether out of compassion or irritation at Jasper's screaming Frankie was too preoccupied to notice – and when she had paid for everything and stuffed the change back in her pocket, she made her way to the cafe area at the front of the supermarket. It had closed down for the evening, but there were tables and chairs there, out of the way of everyone else. She prepared a bottle for Jasper, who drank his milk gratefully and hungrily.

As she held her feeding child, she could feel her arms shaking, and gradually the trembling started to take over her whole body. She stared at Jasper without seeing him – the image of Keith strapped in that chair with a look of abject fear was all she could focus on. She just couldn't believe what had happened. Who were these men? Random thieves? She didn't think so. But why Keith? Why her? She had always half expected the police to catch up with her, but not this. Maybe they were associates of Bob Strut, the man she had killed. It was the only thing that made sense. And yet, if they were, how had they tracked her down?

At the thought of Strut, her shaking became more pronounced. It was all her fault. And now, Keith's life had been taken in exchange for Strut's – it hardly seemed a fair trade.

Jasper finished feeding, and Frankie knew she had to snap out of it. She also knew precisely what Keith would say if he had been here: look after Jasper, Frankie. Look after our son. She held the now contented baby up to her shoulder and started patting him gently on the back; with dreadful clarity, she saw the impossible predicament she was now in. She was already wanted by the police for murder, a fugitive from justice. Supposing the men who had killed her innocent partner covered their tracks successfully – it would not take the police long to work out that it was she who had fled the scene of the crime so quickly. So there was no way she could go to them: they would never believe her. She wasn't thinking about herself, but about Jasper. His father dead, his mother in custody, he would be taken into care, ripped away from the one person in the world who loved him more than life itself. She held him a little bit tighter and vowed, in a silent promise to herself and to Keith, that that would never happen . . .

There was only one person who could help her. Frankie

could not even begin to imagine what June's reaction would be when she told her what had happened, but she was the only person in the world the distraught young woman could turn to. She would have to tell her everything, of course, but she knew June would do whatever she could to make things right. Frankie stood up gently so as not to wake Jasper, who was now sleeping soundly on her shoulder. She put the empty bottle into her pocket, then walked over to the public payphone that was only a few metres away. Using her free hand she awkwardly fished some change out of her pocket and dialled June's number.

It took a while to answer, but that was nothing new – June always took an age trying to find her cordless phone. But Frankie was not prepared for what happened when the ringing stopped. Instead of her friend's gentle southern voice, she heard nothing. 'June?' she asked timidly. 'June, is that you?'

To her astonishment, a man answered. 'Francesca Mills?' he asked, very precisely.

Frankie gave a sharp intake of breath, but didn't answer. 'Is that Francesca Mills?' the voice repeated implacably.

'How do you know my name?' she whispered. 'Who is this?'

For a moment there was no reply, just the brief clatter of movement as the phone was passed elsewhere. Then she heard June's voice. It was wavering and terrified. 'Frankie, I don't know what's going on. There are men here, they've tied me up . . .'

But the phone was moved away before she could finish and the male voice came back on the line. 'Be here within half an hour, otherwise she dies.'

Frankie listened to the heavy breathing at the other end of the line, and the silence was suddenly broken by the sound of June in the background. 'Don't come here, Frankie!' she shouted. 'Get away!' There was a scuffling, and then she heard June scream. It was a terrible thing to hear a woman of her age shout in what was clearly a mixture of pain and fear, and Frankie couldn't stand listening to it. She slammed the phone down on its cradle, but clutched on to the receiver as if it was her only way of maintaining contact with her friend.

She couldn't let this happen. Keith had died because of her, and it would haunt her for the rest of her life. There was no way she could let the same thing happen to June. She picked up the phone and dialled 999. 'You need to send a police car,' she said urgently to the operator who answered. 'There's an elderly lady being held at gunpoint, and she will be killed if you don't arrive as soon as possible.'

'How do you know this?' The operator's question was calm but firm.

'I can't tell you. You just have to get there.' She told the operator June's address. 'Please,' she continued, tears in her voice, 'just hurry.' She hung up.

A small queue of people had materialized behind Frankie – women, mostly, with trolleys full of heavy shopping, waiting to call taxis to take them home. They tutted under their breath and raised their eyes skyward when she picked up the receiver for a third time and falteringly dialled a taxi number that was pinned on a noticeboard in front of her. 'I need a cab,' she said curtly, 'to take me into Bath.'

'Five minutes,' the voice at the other end replied.

Ten minutes later she was still waiting outside. She had taken her jacket off and swaddled Jasper in it: it was midsummer, but dusk had brought with it a faint chill. The little hairs on her bare arms were standing on end. Finally a cab arrived. She stepped forward towards it, but a young man in a hooded top suddenly barged in front of her and made as if to open the back door for himself. 'Hey!' Frankie called. 'That's my cab.'

'Fuck off.' He turned to look at her, and Frankie saw that even though there was aggression on his face, he was just a teenager. She walked up to him and drew herself to her full height, then pushed him away and opened the door. '*You* fuck off.'

Her voice was as calm as she could make it, but the teenager must have seen the anger in her eyes. 'All right, take it easy,' the boy whined as she climbed in, holding Jasper protectively to her chest.

'Parade Gardens,' she instructed the driver. She didn't want to pull up right in front of the flower shop, so she asked to be dropped nearby and would then walk surreptitiously the rest of the way. 'Please drive quickly, I'm in a hurry.'

The cab driver laughed gently as he drove away. 'Everyone's always in a hurry,' he said in a slow Caribbean accent. 'Where you say you going, darling?'

'Parade Gardens,' Frankie repeated. 'And please hurry.'

The driver looked in his rear-view mirror at this girl whose voice dripped with desperation. He looked as though he was about to say something, but then thought better of it. He nodded his head slowly, then upped the speed.

Fifteen minutes later, Frankie carried Jasper out and

handed the driver a ten-pound note. There was no change. Jasper was still sleeping, so she held him gently but firmly against her shoulder and headed off towards the flower shop. She whispered a prayer to herself as she hurried along a convoluted route to the road where June lived. Please, let the police be there. Let June be OK.

There was no way she could just walk down the road and knock on June's door, so she made her way to the end of the street and stood round the corner with her back against the wall for a minute, catching her breath and preparing for what was to come. Then, gingerly, she put her head round the corner.

The scene that met her eyes made her catch her breath in horror, as though she had been punched hard in the stomach. The street was illuminated by the flashing lights of two police cars. The area around the shop was cordoned off by blue and white police tape and five or six police officers were standing around – a couple were taking statements from passers-by. And as she watched, as if in slow motion, a private black ambulance, just like the one that had taken her father away after his death, drove past her and stopped outside the flower shop.

Frankie looked on in stunned silence. Then she hid herself back round the corner of the street and slid slowly down the wall, too overwhelmed even to cry. A deathly chill had overcome her body, and as she held on even more tightly to her sleeping child – the only source of warmth she had – she heard a cry. It sounded alien, divorced from her body, but in fact the hoarse, desperate shout came from her own lips.

'*No! Please, God. No!*'

*

Andreas found himself walking briskly over Pulteney Bridge, away from the flower shop. His associates had all left in different directions, losing themselves among the theatre-goers and diners in the centre of Bath. They would meet up later to discuss their options, and Andreas knew he had to have a plan by then. He wasn't one for dwelling on past mistakes, but he couldn't help cursing himself for allowing the girl to escape the house. Everything that followed had been a natural consequence of that, and although it was far from ideal leaving a trail of two dead bodies, he was sure he had covered his tracks well.

He felt his mobile phone vibrate in his pocket and he put it to his ear without even checking who the caller was. 'Yes?' he asked curtly without stopping.

'It's Cooper. This line is secure, I take it.'

'Sir Ainsley,' he acknowledged. 'We can talk freely.'

'I hope you have some good news for me, Andreas. Do you have the locket?'

'Not yet,' Andreas answered curtly.

There was an uncomfortable pause. 'What do you mean, not yet?' Cooper asked in a threatening tone of voice. 'I thought you had located the girl. How long do you need?'

'We had to abort. The police arrived.'

'What?' Cooper whispered, incredulous. 'We're not paying you all this money for you to allow a slip of a girl to pass through your fingertips.'

'I have made arrangements, Sir Ainsley,' Andreas told him a bit stiffly.

'I should bloody well hope you have. What the hell's been going on?'

'It's best you don't know.'

Cooper sounded furious. 'Don't treat me like a child,' he said waspishly. 'You're not talking to Tunney now. Tell me what you have in mind before I put someone more competent on the case.'

Andreas's eyes narrowed – he wasn't used to being spoken to in this way, but he knew Cooper was a man to follow through with his threats, so he briefly explained the events of the past few hours.

'I see,' Cooper said when he had finished, his voice strained. 'And this is your idea of making arrangements, is it? It sounds like a total bloody mess to me.'

'On the contrary,' Andreas replied, his voice level. 'The girl is wanted for murder. There is nothing to link me or my associates to the house or the flower shop, so the police will naturally assume that she is implicated. She will be the prime suspect for three murders – she won't be able to hide for long, and they will put all their resources into finding her. And I have already demonstrated that I can get to her before the police.'

'Are you sure she has the locket?'

'Positive. Her partner confirmed it before he died. She wears it all the time.'

'Did you get any indication that she knows what it is?'

'None whatsoever. You can rest assured that she doesn't have an idea.'

'I can rest assured,' Cooper snapped, 'when you deliver that locket to me. Find it. Now.' He slammed the phone down.

Andreas held the handset while he gazed out over the River Avon. The image of Francesca Mills's horrified face flickered in his mind.

He knew he had to find her. His reputation depended on it.

Half a mile away, Frankie was wandering blindly. She had nowhere to go, no one to turn to, and she walked as if in a dream. Of all the nightmares she had experienced in her life, this was the worst. She almost refused to believe it was happening, but then the image of Keith's terrified face would rise in her mind, and she knew she wasn't imagining things. Her head was a jumble of confusion; she couldn't think straight.

She found herself outside the theatre. People were spilling out into the street, and a couple of policemen in luminous yellow coats were walking the beat. The sight of them suddenly brought her back to reality: what the hell was she doing? They would be looking for her, and she was an easily recognizable target – a lone woman wandering the streets of Bath with a baby and no obvious way of looking after him. She turned and walked away from them, looking around for somewhere to rest and collect her thoughts. Jasper might have been little, but he seemed to grow heavier with each step Frankie took.

She made her way towards North Parade Bridge: there was a park on the other side where she could sit down and tend to her son. He was still sleeping, but needed changing, so she called into a late-night shop to buy the smallest packet of nappies she could find, and some wipes. As she was browsing the shelves, she saw a little pair of nail scissors, which gave her a dreadful sense of déjà vu: the terrible night after she had killed Strut, when she had to change her appearance. It suddenly struck her that she was in a similar situation, only worse. Tonight she had run from the scene of two murders; and even though the blood was not on her hands, she couldn't risk being caught. No one would see in her a desperate mother, afraid for the life of her child and mourning the death of his father and her best friend. In the eyes of the police, she would just be the same street bum that had eluded them for so long. She took the scissors and what Jasper needed from the shelves, paid for them and left. Moments later she was over the bridge, sitting on a park bench changing Jasper's nappy; but her mind was elsewhere. For nearly two years she had tried to avoid thinking about Strut and the life she had led beforehand, but now it was all she could remember. That night she had unknowingly taken the first steps that got her off the streets. It hadn't seemed so at the time, but in a bizarre way she had been fortunate – if it hadn't been for Strut she would never have left London, never have met June, never have met Keith. She shook her head as tears started welling once more in her eyes at the thought. Poor Keith. Poor June. If Frankie had never come into their worlds they would still be alive. Everyone she touched seemed to come to harm. How could she possibly think she had been lucky? Luck was not for people like her.

And now she was back where she started, alone and desperate. Had it not been for Jasper she might have considered turning herself in, tried to persuade the police that the deaths of Keith and June were nothing to do with her. The worst she could expect was a prison cell, and under the circumstances that didn't seem so bad. But there was no way she would let anyone separate her from the only thing she had left in the entire world.

It was suddenly clear what she had to do. She had to

make her own chances, to do whatever it took to ensure her safety and that of her child.

She would have to return to the streets.

It was the only place she had a chance of never being found, the place she knew best, the place where she could become just another faceless vagrant, ignored by anyone who saw her; the only place Jasper would be safe and no one would try to take him from her; the only place she knew she could survive.

At least for a little while.

He was awake again now, but quiet, gazing up at his mother with his bright eyes, free from the worries that plagued her. Frankie let him lie there as she pulled the nail scissors she had bought from their wrapping and hacked off her long dyed-black hair in clumsy fistfuls, discarding the locks in a bin just next to the bench. It would take a while for her natural hair colour to come through, she knew – she could worry about that when it did. She put her hand in her pocket, pulled out what money she had left, and started to count it. Sixty-three pounds. Two years ago, on the street and with no one to care for, it would have seemed like a fortune. Now, with a small baby, it seemed a pittance.

As she sat there, a couple walked past arm in arm. Frankie stared at them wide-eyed: they seemed so happy, just enjoying each other's company as they strolled in silence. Forty-eight hours ago they could have been her and Keith. As they passed, the woman turned her head back to look at Frankie. There was an unmistakable look of disapproval on her face. What was she doing there, so late at night, with a baby lying on a bench wrapped in a denim jacket? What kind of mother was she? Frankie's eyes fell to the ground as she felt the hot flush of shame rise in her cheeks. She gathered Jasper up in her arms once more and started walking in the opposite direction, back towards the town.

She walked aimlessly with Jasper wrapped tightly against the night air. Had anyone looked at her, they might not have even noticed the baby pressed against her body – it just looked like a bundle of clothes, though why she should be carrying such a bundle would be a mystery. She attracted a few curious looks, but mostly she was ignored.

Frankie had no idea how late it was, but as she walked past a pub she saw people spilling out onto the street, suggesting it was some time past eleven. They were boisterous, as they often were after enjoying a night with friends, and she moved away when she saw a few of them jostling with each other. It was nothing more than drunken playfulness, but it was best to keep your distance – these things had a way of escalating, and the last thing she wanted was to put her child in danger, or draw attention to herself. She moved away, doing her best not to catch anyone's eye, but she had the uncanny sensation that she was being looked at. It was confirmed when she heard a voice behind her. 'Hey, darling, what's the hurry?'

She quickened her pace to walk further away from the crowd, but heard the clatter of footsteps behind her. They belonged to more than one person, she could tell from the sound, but it was only a single man who eventually swaggered up behind her, lurching slightly from his drunkenness. Frankie could smell the alcohol seeping from his pores, and it made her gag. Since moving in with

Keith she had managed to avoid it herself. Now the very thought of it churned her stomach. 'Leave me alone,' she told the man, not even turning to look at him. Her hackles were rising, and she knew she was in danger of losing it.

'Come on, gorgeous. We're going to a club – why don't you join us?' He slurred his words, but his voice was transparently cajoling, not aggressive. He put his arm around her and squeezed suggestively.

For Frankie it was the final straw. It had taken months for her to get used to Keith holding her in that way, months for her to overcome the natural revulsion she felt at the touch of a man; now she felt herself repelling this man who was forcing himself on her, however innocently. She stopped still. 'Get the hell off me!' She whispered the words viciously, but the man ignored her and seemed about to say something else, something to persuade her to go with him. 'Get off me!' She screamed the words this time, hysterically and with a fury in her eyes that made the man instantly move his arm and step away. Frankie looked around: there were four of them, including the one she had just shaken off. He was looking a bit shocked by her reaction, surprised that she had taken it so badly, and embarrassed too. His friends had smirks on their faces, clearly oblivious to the subtleties of the situation, all of them looking as if they might have a go themselves.

But then, wakened by the sound of his mother's voice, Jasper started to cry. The men looked in surprise at the bundle of denim in Frankie's arms – clearly they had not suspected it contained a baby. Their expressions changed from amusement to guilt and lack of interest and they melted silently away to find another target for their boisterous drunkenness.

Frankie stood there shaking, not knowing what to do to calm Jasper when she was in such a state herself. Tears streaming down her face, and a feeling of helplessness welling up inside her, she disappeared into the night, leaving just the memory of Jasper's wailing in the minds of the crowds of people who would most likely forget all about her the moment she left their sight.

DI James Cole of the Avon and Somerset Constabulary was having a long night. He had already attended the scene of one shooting, and now a second had been reported on the outskirts of town. Forensics and other SOCOs (Scene of Crime Officers) were already on their way.

It really wasn't the sort of thing you expected in Bath. Dead bodies might be two a penny up in London, but not down here, and he was still shaken up from the scene he had witnessed earlier that evening. It made you sick, the things some people would do. The woman had been tied to a chair using garden twine that she kept behind the counter of her little florist's shop. It had cut deeply into her thin wrists – the forensics officer had pointed out the little puddle of blood that had collected at the back of the chair. The bullet that had killed her had passed through one side of the head and out of the other – it hadn't taken long to find it on the other side of the room – but the wounds were surprisingly small. It had been the look on her face that had shocked him more than anything. Total fear. Total panic. He knew it would stay with him for a long time.

He pulled up outside the house where the second shooting had been reported. There were already police cars and an ambulance there, their lights flashing silently, and the area had been cordoned off. A few members of the public had congregated in a small crowd just outside the cordon, and a couple of members of the local press were being politely but firmly kept away by the officer guarding it.

Inside was devastation. A man had been taped naked to a chair, but, unlike the old woman, was lying on his side. His body had deep wounds on the shoulders, and the bullet wound in the head was identical to the one he had seen a few hours previously. 'What have you got, Simon?' he asked the same forensics officer who had been at the other crime scene.

Simon was kneeling down by the body. He glanced up, and when he saw it was James he got to his feet. 'The entry and exit wounds suggest this man was killed by the same type of gun that shot the old lady. The wounds on his shoulders indicate to me that he was tortured quite extensively before he was shot.'

'What with?'

Simon pointed to the work surface where a small kitchen blowtorch was lying on its side.

'Jesus,' James said under his breath. 'What kind of sick bastard does a thing like that?'

'The same kind that puts a bullet through a sixty-four-year-old woman's skull.' He turned back to his work. 'I'll give you more as and when I have it.'

Simon got back to work, while James continued to look around the room. It was immaculately tidy, with the exception of a few children's cloth books, with brightly coloured pictures on the fabric pages, lying on the table, and that morning's breakfast things – just one bowl and one cup, Cole noticed – stacked up by the sink. The walls were painted a subtle green colour, and they bore no pictures; but there were two photographs in silver frames on the side. One was of a small baby, probably no more than a couple of weeks old. The other was a young woman with long black hair and a sad, slightly enigmatic smile.

'Excuse me, sir.'

James looked round to see a young sergeant standing at the door.

'Yes, Pete. What is it?'

'Fingerprint report from the earlier scene, sir.'

'That was quick.'

The sergeant shook his head. 'It's from yesterday. Apparently the place was dusted for fingerprints after a burglary last night, and something's just come up.'

James rolled his eyes to the ceiling. 'So who was he?'

'It wasn't a he, sir.' He handed his boss two A4-sized photographs. 'It's a she.'

James looked at the photographs. One of them showed a young girl, no more than fourteen or fifteen, a cheerful family shot in full colour. The other was quite different. Although it was undoubtedly the same girl, she looked older and desperate. The photo was grainy and indistinct – he recognized it as a CCTV still – and she was clearly running from something. 'She's wanted by the Met in connection with a murder nearly two years ago. She's been on the run ever since.'

James looked at the picture, then looked back at the photograph on the side. There was no doubt about it:

though the images could not be more different in many ways, this was the same person. He felt a feeling of contempt welling up in him. This was the girl responsible for these despicable acts. It hardly seemed possible, but there it was – twenty years in the job had taught him that when all the evidence points towards somebody, there was generally little room for doubt. 'Get the fingerprint boys to sweep this place as soon as they can,' he told the sergeant. 'And first thing in the morning I'll get hold of the officer in charge of the case in London. Tell him we've found his killer.'

Chapter Fourteen

Mark Taylor was on his second cup of coffee when the call came through. Sergeant Steve Irvin was just going through a few things with him – yet more stuff to pile up on his desk, which made him even grumpier than he normally was at that time of the morning. 'Just a minute, Steve,' he told the younger man as he picked up the phone, quietly grateful for a gap in the proceedings. 'Taylor.'

'Good morning, DI Taylor. DI James Cole, Avon and Somerset.' His voice had a soft West Country lilt to it, which Taylor couldn't help thinking sounded a bit yokel-ish. 'I wonder if I could have a moment of your time.'

'Go ahead,' Taylor replied, rolling his eyes slightly at Irvin. 'What can I do for you?'

He listened as the officer filled him in about the two murders on his patch, before asking if he would send down the files relating to Francesca Mills. Cole was immaculately polite, but Taylor understood what he was saying between the lines: this is our case now, not yours. Stay out of it. And Taylor would: he had quite enough on his plate without the need to reopen the Francesca Mills case. 'That's fine,' he said shortly. 'Let me know if I can do anything to help.' He didn't sound particularly enthusiastic about the offer.

'Thanks. I'll be in touch if I need anything else.'

Taylor hung up the phone and indicated to Irvin that he should carry on, so the young sergeant continued the briefing. But his boss was distracted, and barely took anything in. As Irvin's voice droned on in the background, Taylor's mind was elsewhere. Everything about that call had been wrong. Francesca Mills had killed Bob Strut in self-defence, there was no doubt in his mind about that. OK, so it didn't make her whiter than white, but two shootings within an hour of each other? They didn't bear the hallmarks of a desperate street killing. And where would she get a gun from? He knew those vagrants – if they had a few quid in their pocket they'd be much more likely to spend them on cheap drink and drugs rather than firearms. Maybe she'd fallen in with some council estate gang. Maybe she'd been so desperate for her next hit of crack that she'd been prepared to do anything, and this was the result. But then again, maybe not.

Irvin had stopped talking, and was looking at the DI with an expectant look on his face. 'I'm sorry, Steve,' Taylor told him. 'We'll have to finish this later. I need to make a call.'

Irvin nodded, picked up his papers and left, while Taylor tapped a number into his phone. It was answered immediately. 'Sean Carter.'

'Taylor here.' Taylor sounded businesslike, even a trifle embarrassed, and determined to make this call as short as it could be.

'Mark. What a surprise. You must want something. I thought I was in your bad books.'

Taylor ignored the sarcasm. 'You are. But something's come up you should probably know about.'

'What?'

'Francesca Mills. She's cropped up in Bath, along with two dead bodies.'

Taylor heard rustling at the other end of the line as Carter grabbed a pen and paper. 'Go ahead,' he said, all traces of light-heartedness gone from his voice.

Taylor filled him in on the salient points of his conversation with DI Cole. 'I just thought you should know, that's all.' He sounded almost apologetic.

'Mark, listen to me. Francesca Mills is not guilty of those murders. I told you before that I thought she was in danger. I still think she is.'

Taylor paused a moment before answering. 'How can you be so sure? If I were in Cole's shoes, she'd be my prime suspect.' But he didn't sound so sure of himself.

'It doesn't matter how I know – surely you can see that this doesn't add up. You've got to speak to someone, get the investigation back under your jurisdiction. We'll work on it together, but it'll be your case, I promise. And we *will* find her.' Carter was cajoling now, almost desperate.

'Forget it, Sean.' Taylor spoke decisively, as if he'd known Carter would ask him this. 'You asked me to keep you abreast of things, and that's what I'm doing. There's no way I can take on a double murder from outside my area even if the suspect has killed before. You know that. Now if you don't mind, I've got work to do.' He slammed the phone down on its cradle, annoyed by Carter's pure desperation. Then he stood up, and stormed out of the office for a breath of air.

Carter's mind was racing. This had all been so sudden, and now he had to think fast. He knew Taylor was right. Half of him wanted to go straight to Meeken, get his orders from above, but he knew Meeken would just tell him to do what he thought was appropriate. That was the trouble with having a superior officer who trusted you implicitly – no guidance. In any case, he was too personally involved in the whole thing to let go of it like that. One thing was clear to him, though: he had to get to Francesca Mills, and he needed this DI Cole on his side.

It took him ten minutes to track the inspector down, and he didn't waste any time when he got him on the line. 'DI Sean Carter, Serious Fraud Office. I need to speak to you about Francesca Mills.'

'Go ahead.'

'I know she seems to be implicated in the two shootings you're investigating, but I have reason to believe that she's not the killer.'

'I see.' Cole's soft West Country accent sounded sceptical. 'It doesn't look that way from where I'm standing, DI Carter.'

'No, I understand that. But I need you to tell me what you've got. Have you identified the victims yet?'

'Yes. One of them was June Baird, sixty-four. Mills was an employee at her flower shop. The other was her partner, Keith Osbourne. It seems they had a child together. Both were tied up, probably tortured, then shot in the head.'

Carter closed his eyes as the image of Rosemary rose in his mind, her body broken and contorted, the small bruise-like wound of the bullet that had ended her life festering on her forehead; the bruising round her wrists that showed she had been tied painfully tight; the broken fingers and the torture injuries along the side of her body – the deaths sounded almost identical. Everything was slotting into place: whoever killed Rosemary Gibson killed these two people. He didn't even have to see the bodies to deduce that. It was how these people worked. And he knew one other thing beyond doubt: Francesca Mills had not killed Rosemary, and she was not responsible for these killings either; but he had no way of knowing whether she was now in the killers' possession or not. If she was, it was only a matter of time before she showed up dead; if she wasn't, they would be directing all their energies into finding her, and she would be on the run, frightened and panicking. They were bound to catch up with her sooner or later. Either way, the outlook was extremely bleak – both for her and for the case.

He knew how the police worked – he'd been part of the system for long enough. There was no way this DI was going to alter the course of his investigation on the say-so of a faceless call from the SFO. Why would he? If he wanted that to happen, Carter would need to go in above his head, but he wasn't sure that was the right call. The safest place for Francesca Mills, if she was still alive, was in police custody, and the best people for that were local boys with local knowledge; there was really nothing to be gained from getting permission to stomp all over their territory. He would do everything he could from his end, but at the moment he wasn't sure what that would or could be. He knew one thing for definite, though: he had to make sure he was first to hear if they caught up with her. 'I'm sure you'll do everything you need to,' he said reasonably. 'But could I ask that you let me know the moment you think you're near to an arrest? There's more riding on this than I can explain over the phone. These murders are too similar to one I've been investigating – one that I know Francesca Mills didn't commit. I won't tread on your toes, but I might be able to help you make the right conviction.'

'If you say so.' Cole still sounded dubious, but Carter had the impression he could trust him.

'What's your game plan?'

'We're going to release information to the press, try and get her face on the front page of every newspaper.'

'You know they'll be all over this like vultures over rotting meat. Are you sure that's what you want?'

'We've really no other way of finding her, and it seems unlikely that she's going to stick around in Bath – she has a small child, and that will just draw attention to her. She'll want to get away.'

Carter thought about that. 'I wouldn't be so sure,' he said. 'She's lived on the streets for years, and she's managed to elude both the police and –' how could he put it? – 'other parties for all this time. She's good at melting into the background, being anonymous. Sometimes it's easier to hide in the most obvious places, so it wouldn't surprise me at all to learn that she's still in Bath.'

'If you're right, and she's not responsible for these murders, I'd tend to agree with you,' Cole replied. 'Whoever she is, she's made a life here. I'm no psychologist, but I guess she probably wouldn't want to leave. But I have to be honest with you, DI Carter. I *don't* think you're right. I think Francesca Mills killed these two people in the most brutal way imaginable. All the evidence points to her and if I find her, I'm going to arrest her for murder. I don't know how it stands in London, maybe you're used to all this, but I can tell you that when word of this gets out, the community down here will be in shock – we have to be seen to be doing the right thing.'

'I understand that,' Carter replied, half to himself. 'But it just doesn't make sense that she would kill people she had been working and living with, people who protected her.'

'Sometimes people just flip. Pressures of life. Betrayal. Jealousy. You must have seen it happen before, just like I have. And we know what this woman is capable of – her past shows it.'

Carter felt frustration welling up in him once more, but he could sense that this was a good man, just doing what he thought was right. And he needed him onside. 'All I ask is that you keep me in the loop. Agreed?'

'Whatever you say, DI Carter. Now, if you'll excuse me, there's a lot to do.'

Andy Summers read the press release slowly, and then for a second time: he wanted to make sure he had understood it all correctly, but really there was little room for doubt. It was perfectly concise.

POLICE ARE APPEALING FOR INFORMATION FOLLOWING THE DEATHS OF A MAN AND A WOMAN LAST NIGHT. ONE OCCURRED IN CENTRAL BATH, THE OTHER IN THE ALEXANDRA PARK AREA ON THE WEST SIDE OF THE CITY. THE DEATHS ARE BEING TREATED AS SUSPICIOUS, AND IT IS THOUGHT THAT THEY MAY BE RELATED. POLICE ARE ANXIOUS TO SPEAK TO A YOUNG WOMAN BY THE NAME OF FRANCESCA MILLS, WHO IT IS THOUGHT MAY BE ABLE TO HELP THEM WITH THEIR INQUIRIES. THE PUBLIC ARE ADVISED NOT TO APPROACH HER IF THEY SEE HER, AS SHE IS BELIEVED TO BE ARMED AND EXTREMELY DANGEROUS.

A picture of the young woman in question was attached, and Andy recognized it instantly: he had plastered the girl all over the paper a couple of years ago. She looked different now, of course. In fact, she was startlingly different. The picture he had seen before showed a gaunt, frightened, malnourished waif; now her hair was darker, her face had filled out, her skin was less blemished, and although her large eyes still suggested a wariness, there was something softer about them. She looked beautiful.

Andy had been in the business long enough to know that it made the story all the more appealing.

All the papers would run with it, he knew that much. It had been a decent story before – now, with two more killings under her belt, the elusive Francesca Mills was on her way to becoming a serial killer. It was front-page news, and he wanted to make sure that he got the whole story. He knew he still had the mother's number some-where – a conversation with her would beef up his story no end – so he flicked through the little green notebook in which he scrawled down his contacts. It took a while for him to find the number he wanted – he couldn't remember the name after all this time, but he hoped it would just jump out at him when he saw it. Eventually it did, scrawled in his small, spidery writing at the bottom of a page: Harriet Johnson. He dialled the number.

It took a while to be answered, and when it was Andy was momentarily wrong-footed by the sound of a man's voice. 'William Johnson.'

'May I speak to Mrs Johnson, please?' Andy could sound terribly well-heeled when he wanted to.

'She's not here, I'm afraid. May I ask who's calling?' Johnson sounded businesslike, slightly suspicious.

'My name is Andy Summers. I'm a reporter – I spoke to Mrs Johnson some time ago now about your daughter, Francesca . . .'

'I see.'

'I'm sure you're aware of the recent developments.'

'We are.' Johnson was giving nothing away.

'I understand it is a very difficult time for you at the moment,' Andy continued smoothly, but I wonder if you are able to shed any light on what's happened.'

'We've told the police everything we know. No doubt if they want to release any of that information, they'll do so.'

Andy realized he was going to have to be more persuasive. 'I seem to remember that you're on the force yourself,' he said conversationally.

'That's right.'

'Then you know how it works. Within a few hours you are going to have every crime reporter in the country camped out on your doorstep. They won't leave you or your wife alone until you give them something. Why don't I come around now and you can give me your side of the story? Say what you have to say in your own words, and then we'll leave you alone. This way you control what's written, and you protect your wife from all this – it must be very hard on her at the moment.'

Johnson was silent for a while. Andy knew he was considering his options, so he decided to press him further.

'Mark my words,' he continued. 'At this moment there are eight or ten people just like me, trying to find out as much as they can about your stepdaughter. They'll be talking to her school, her old friends – anyone and everyone they can find.'

Andy left it at that, and gave Johnson the space to think. Finally he spoke. 'OK,' he said quietly. 'I'll meet you. Not with Harriet, and not here. And this is off the record – I don't want anyone to know I've spoken to you.'

'What?' asked Andy, confused. He could see his exclusive slipping away. 'If the rest of the press don't know you've spoken to me, they'll continue to hound you. And if it's a question of money, we can sort something out –'

'Don't be idiotic,' Johnson interrupted. 'I'm not interested in your money. And I don't care about the rest of the press. I'm doing this to keep you personally off our backs. As soon as I've spoken to you, I'm taking Harriet away somewhere until this has all blown over. So I repeat: this is off the record. Do you understand?'

'Perfectly,' said Andy, backing down. 'Where would you like to meet?'

An hour later, he found himself pulling into Clacket Lane service station, just past junction six of the M25. It wasn't so unusual for him to have meetings at places like this – people tended to think they were more conspicuous than was actually the case, so they often wanted to meet somewhere out of the way where they felt they wouldn't be recognized. Truth be told, they could probably have met in the village pub over a quiet pint and nobody would be any the wiser, but Andy was happy for Johnson to arrange the meet for wherever he felt most comfortable. He'd get more out of him that way. He got out of the car and made his way over to the service area.

Johnson was sitting in Burger King, as he said he would be, wearing an old brown leather jacket and a plain white shirt. He was a pretty unprepossessing-looking man, Andy thought, with his grey moustache and slightly dumpy body, nursing a polystyrene cup full of undrinkably hot coffee. Andy took a seat opposite and proffered his hand with a smile. 'Andy Summers,' he said in a friendly voice. 'Pleased to meet you.'

Johnson nodded briefly but did not shake Andy's hand. The journalist swiftly let it fall to his side, then carried on as if nothing had happened. 'Can I get you anything?' He gestured vaguely at the food counter.

'No, thank you.' He looked down at his cup of coffee.

'Fine,' replied Andy. 'Anyway, thank you for agreeing to meet me.'

'I'm only doing this to keep you away from my wife. She's been through enough as it is, and she's hysterical. But if my name appears anywhere in your article, I will deny ever having met you.'

'I understand completely where you're coming from, Mr Johnson. When did you learn this latest news about Francesca?'

'First thing this morning.'

'Who from?'

'Avon and Somerset Constabulary.'

'And you'll be helping them with their inquiries?'

'Of *course* I'll be helping them with their inquiries,' Johnson snapped. 'I'm a serving police officer, I'm not going to let . . .' He suddenly stopped himself and looked away, his brow slightly furrowed and his face cross. Had it not been such a difficult situation, Andy might have thought he was play-acting.

He knew he'd have to play this delicately. This guy was

under stress, and was clearly not good at concealing it. It was a fine line between getting him to open up and having him storm away and reveal nothing. 'Go on, Mr Johnson,' he said lightly.

Johnson stared at Andy. 'You have to understand that Francesca was always a difficult child,' he said.

'Difficult in what way?'

'Manipulative. Duplicitous. Even as a kid. She drove her mother and me to distraction with her lying and her deceitfulness. After she killed that man in London, you said she'd gone off the rails. The truth is, she'd gone off the rails a long time before that.'

Andy sat there making shorthand notes on a pad. He nodded his head in understanding, but secretly he was surprised at Johnson's frankness. He had manipulated enough people in his time to realize when he was being manipulated himself, and he had the distinct impression that was what was happening now – Johnson was speaking the words as if he had already rehearsed them well. But sometimes he didn't mind, especially if what he was being told was good stuff. 'Did the police give you any idea about who the latest killings were?'

The side of Johnson's face twitched slightly, and he hesitated before answering. 'A man she was living with, and a lady she worked for. Shot them in the head.' He looked away.

'Did she steal anything?'

'They didn't say.'

'You don't seem convinced, Mr Johnson,' Andy suggested quietly. 'What's your gut feeling about her motive?'

'Who knows why people do what they do, Mr Summers?' Johnson replied. 'I'm only telling you this because I don't want any more people to get hurt. Now, if you'll excuse me, I've said all I want to say. I trust you'll remember what I said about mentioning my name.' He stood up and nodded his head in a curt gesture of farewell.

Just as he was turning to leave, Andy spoke up again, determined to get one more question in. 'Mr Johnson, are you sure Francesca hasn't got in touch with you? Not once? In nearly six years?'

Johnson stared him down. 'Not once since she left. Trust me, we won't be hearing from her.'

'What makes you so sure?'

But Johnson didn't reply. He simply put his hand in his pocket, removed his car key and walked away, disappearing into the swarm of hungry people.

Andy tapped his pencil on the sticky table. All his journalist's instincts told him that there was more to this than Johnson was letting on, and he was intrigued to know what. Why was he implicating his stepdaughter even further? Why was he so adamant about keeping his own name out of this? Johnson's amateur deception had been perfectly transparent to an old pro like Andy Summers, and something told him he should be directing his investigative prowess towards the stepfather as well as the daughter.

And yet, the story he was constructing in his head was undeniably good. Francesca Mills, the tearaway child, goes on the run from the police after killing a man. She evades capture for nearly two years, then kills her partner and her employer in a murder spree that seems to elude explanation. Now she's on the run again – who knows when she'll strike next? A perfect story – one that could run for days if not weeks. No doubt there was more dirt to be dug by investigating the Johnsons' home life, but that would have to wait until he was further down the line.

He looked at his watch: two o'clock. If he left for the office now, he'd be back in time to file it for the early editions.

The night was coming to an end, finally.

The daytimes weren't so bad – at least they were warm and she didn't have to spend the whole time making sure Jasper was comfortable; and there was distraction on the streets in the form of the endless performers. It didn't take Frankie's mind off her situation, of course, but at least Jasper could be transfixed by the jugglers and other street entertainers – a few moments of contentment for him and respite for her. It was exhausting carrying both a baby and the two carrier bags in which she held everything she needed to feed and change him. But the two nights she had spent sleeping rough since the shootings had been the worst she had ever encountered. For most of the time Jasper had refused to settle, and who could blame him? He was used to a cot and warm blankets, not the scant comforts his mother could offer him now.

The previous night she had been up to her old tricks, stealing clothes from the bin liners left outside charity shops. Somewhere in the back of her mind she had been aware of the indignity of going back to this way of living, but she had to do what she could for herself and her son, and if that meant going back to stealing, so be it. She had found a couple of old jumpers for herself, but baby clothes were harder to come by. In the end she had torn an old sheet in half and used it to swaddle him and protect him from the night chill; but it was amazing how quickly the grime of the street had dirtied his clothes and his skin. Like his mother, Jasper had started to look uncared for and unkempt.

She had spent the nights away from the centre of town. During the day it was busy enough for her to be unseen, and somehow she was more comfortable there – she didn't allow herself to go past June's shop, but it felt good to know it was nearby. But at night, after the evening crowds had died away and the streets had emptied, she felt vulnerable. It wasn't just the occasional policeman that made her edgy, it was the other vagrants, winos and drug addicts who congregated there after dark. Two years ago she would have sought out their company, taking what comfort she could from the outcast, sometimes aggressive community. But that was a different lifetime, and she would do anything before she took Jasper into that arena.

And so she had hunted out an alleyway on the outskirts of town. An old sofa had been discarded there – it had a musty, rotting smell that suggested it had been there some time. In places the stuffing was gone, and the springs pushed through; but it was more comfortable than sitting on the pavement. At times, when Jasper's crying had got too loud, she'd had to move away, fearful of waking the occupants of the nearby houses; but for most of the night she sat there in the silent darkness, holding her son close, her emotions numb.

She hadn't slept for forty-eight hours. She hadn't eaten.

The small amount of money that remained in her pocket she had been rationing, spending it only on what Jasper needed and ignoring her own requirements. But that money was fast dwindling, and she had no way of replenishing it. Begging was certainly out of the question – if she was seen doing that, the police would recognize her immediately. That would be the end of it – she would probably never see Jasper again. As the sky grew brighter, so the realization grew in Frankie's brain that she couldn't go on like this. When the money ran out, how could she feed her son? How could she keep him clean? Even if she managed to keep him alive, what would the future hold? Suddenly, unbidden, she remembered Mary. Young and desperate. She had known next to nothing about her history, but she knew instinctively that she came from a damaged home, the product of parents who couldn't and wouldn't look after her. Frankie shuddered to think what had become of her.

Then, in a moment of sudden clarity, she realized that what she saw in Mary, others had surely seen in her. And now, history was on the verge of repeating itself. She looked down at her son, and touched his dirty cheek lightly. There was no way she was going to allow that to happen.

This couldn't continue. She knew what she had to do.

Gathering up her things, she swaddled the sleepy Jasper and walked out of the alleyway and into the street. There was only one other option now, one other place she could go where she knew Jasper would be safe and cared for. It wouldn't be for long, she promised herself; just long enough to get back up into London and sort out this situation the only way she knew how: by herself.

She turned and made her way towards the station, determined to leave Bath behind her for ever.

It held nothing for her now.

Chapter Fifteen

Frankie's train pulled into Croydon just after midday – she'd had to wait at Bath station for a couple of hours as she could only afford the cheap ticket with what was left of her money, and she had also had to wait half an hour at Reading to change trains. Now she was practically penniless, but it was OK: she knew the way from the station, having travelled it with Keith a number of times. It was devastating to be back here without him, but she tried to push that thought from her mind.

The leafy street of Victorian terraced houses in which Keith's mother lived was not far from the station, and Frankie was there ten minutes after she arrived. She had walked briskly, her head lowered as she tried not to be noticed or recognized; but once she was outside the house she simply stood there on the other side of the road, out of sight behind a large recycling bin, looking, scanning, making sure no one else was around. She could see the lounge curtains were drawn and she waited to check if there was anyone else in the house. There was no movement.

Although she'd had the conversation a hundred times in her head on the way up, she had no idea how she would be received here. Keith's mum had never been her greatest fan, and no doubt she would know her son was dead by now – she suspected she would not be greeted with open arms. She took a deep breath, walked across the road and up to the house, then knocked on the door.

Frankie hardly recognized Keith's mother: she was a tall woman, with dyed blonde hair and a proud face, but today she looked bedraggled and haggard, and her eyes showed the signs of constant weeping. Once the door was open, she looked at Frankie with a mixture of horror and contempt. Frankie just stood there, holding Jasper tightly and not knowing what to say. 'I'm so sorry, Elaine,' she finally managed to whisper hoarsely.

Elaine took a step backwards, saying nothing.

'I need your help, Elaine,' Frankie continued. 'Please. You must know I didn't have anything to do with Keith's death.' Her voice wavered as she spoke: it was the first time she had acknowledged out loud that he was dead, and the words cut into her like a shard of glass.

'What have you done, Frankie?' She was still recoiling from the young woman on her doorstep, but her eyes kept flickering towards the child in her arms.

'Please, can I come in? I need help with Jasper . . .'

Frankie stepped tentatively over the threshold, and was encouraged when Elaine didn't stop her. 'Close the door,' the older woman told her as she turned and walked down the mosaic tiles of the hallway into the sitting room.

Frankie followed. It was a small room, just as she remembered. The only difference was the mess – Elaine was normally impeccably tidy, but since her son's death two nights before, she had clearly let her standards drop. The only source of light came from the sun, which shone through a small gap in the drawn curtains. On the coffee table in front of the sofa was a pile of photograph albums, all of them sprawled open. Frankie caught her breath as she glanced down at them: they were pictures of Keith as a child. There was no mistaking those soft brown eyes or the way the smile danced around his lips even when he was a child. At the corner of one of the pages there was a photograph of him as a baby: had she not known better, Frankie might have mistaken it for Jasper.

Elaine took a seat on the sofa. She was still eyeing Frankie with a lack of trust, but her fear was overcome by a stronger emotion. 'May I hold Jasper, please?' she asked in a strained voice.

Gently, Frankie unwrapped her son from the sheet in which he was swaddled and handed him over to his grandmother. Normally Elaine's eyes would soften when she saw her grandson, but this time they filled with tears. She held him close to her breast. 'He's so like Keith,' was all she managed to say before she found herself overcome with sorrow.

'I didn't kill him,' Frankie repeated herself. 'You do believe me, don't you?'

'That's not what the police think.' She handed Frankie the newspaper that was lying next to her. Frankie took it and looked aghast at the front page. It was her – the picture Keith had taken the day she had found out she was pregnant. She didn't need to read the article, the headline said it all: KILLER ON THE RUN! 'You've been on every news bulletin for the last few hours,' Elaine told her. 'I'm surprised no one's recognized you yet.' She stared hard at her son's ex-partner. 'You can't blame me for not knowing what to think.'

'I know what it looks like, Elaine, but please believe me. I saw Keith moments before he was killed. If I hadn't run away when I did, the man who did it would have killed me and Jasper too.'

Elaine said nothing.

'He told me to run, Elaine,' she insisted, her voice now full of tears. 'It was the last thing he ever said.' She put her face in her hands and allowed the desperation that had been building up inside her to finally release itself. Huge sobs racked her body, punctuated only when she drew breath.

At the sound of his mother's tears, Jasper started crying too. Elaine stood up and removed him from the room, only returning when both mother and son had regained their composure. She stood framed in the doorway as she gently rocked her grandson in her arms. 'You're going to have to go to the police, Frankie,' she said shortly. 'You do realize that, don't you?'

Frankie shook her head dismissively. 'I can't,' she said as Elaine walked into the room and laid the gurgling Jasper on the sofa.

'Why not?'

'I just can't,' she said aggressively, before realizing she had overstepped the mark. Elaine's lips tightened and she looked away. 'I'm sorry, Elaine,' Frankie continued, more subdued now. 'I know it looks bad, but if I go to the police now, they will never believe that I am innocent. I *will* go to jail, and Jasper *will* be taken into care. I'll never see him again – and nor will you.'

The two women stood there in silence, gazing at the small child who lay there with no conception of what was going on around him.

'I think I know who did this, Elaine. I need to go to London to find them. To put a stop to this. Then I'll go to the police, I promise. It will only be for a few days, but if I take Jasper with me, they will kill us both.' Her eyes looked down to the floor. 'And if *they* don't, the way I have to live will.'

'What do you mean?'

Frankie hesitated. She had never told anyone in her new life about her past, not even Keith, and especially not his mother, who had never quite managed to approve of her. But she needed her help. She needed to explain why she couldn't take Jasper with her. 'Before I met Keith,' she said in a quiet, trembling voice, 'I lived on the streets.' Frankie glanced up at Elaine – a look of realization crossed the older woman's face as if things suddenly made a great deal more sense. 'While I was there, there was a fight. A man was forcing a young girl to do –' she winced slightly at the memory of it and glanced down at her son – 'things she didn't want to do. I intervened and the man died.'

Elaine gazed at her in shock. 'You killed him?' she whispered.

'If I hadn't, he would have killed us both,' Frankie stated firmly. 'I don't regret it for a minute, and I would do the same again. But the police know it was me – that's why I can't go to them.' Elaine could not disguise the look of contempt on her face. 'Don't judge me, Elaine.' Frankie's voice wavered dangerously. 'You don't know what it was like.'

The two women looked at each other, their eyes flashing in silent confrontation.

'I'm sorry, Elaine,' Frankie finally backed down. 'I know how difficult this is for you, especially now. But you have to understand: if you don't help me now, that's the world I will have to take Jasper back to.'

Elaine stared at Frankie as she considered the news she had just been told. 'I'm supposed to call the police the moment you try and get in touch,' she said quietly.

'Please, Elaine. Don't do that. You're the only person I could come to. I've nowhere else to go, and I need someone to look after Jasper, just for a little while, until I sort everything out.'

'What about your own parents? Keith told me you'd never even spoken to him about them. Are they dead?'

'My father is. My mother is still alive, but I can't go to her.'

'Why not?'

'I just can't. Please try and understand, Elaine.'

'I can't pretend that I do,' she replied flatly, then paused. 'But I'll do what I can, for Jasper if no one else.'

Frankie closed her eyes as relief crashed over her. 'Thank you, Elaine.'

'But it had better not be for long.' She looked down at the photographs on the table in front of her, and picked up an old black and white picture. It showed her as a much younger woman, sitting on a carpet with Keith and a small teddy bear. Her eyes lingered on it. 'A child shouldn't be without its mother.'

'I know, Elaine,' Frankie replied. 'Trust me, I know. I'm going to find the men who did this to Keith, deal with them, and then come back. I promise.'

Elaine nodded. The tension between the two was still there, but it was softening. 'Jasper needs a bath,' she said.

Frankie agreed. 'I know. It's been a while.'

'What if the police call?'

'Are you expecting them to?'

'No, but . . .' Elaine left it hanging.

Frankie turned to her son and picked him up. 'There's nothing else I can do,' she whispered to herself. 'I will be back, whatever happens.'

As she spoke, Jasper gazed up at her, his clear eyes seeming to pierce her very consciousness. She put his soft cheek against hers and whispered very gently in his ear, 'Mummy will be back soon. I promise.' Frankie knew that she was doing the right thing, but now that it came to it, she found it almost impossible to let him go. He felt so warm in her arms, so tiny, and the bond of love between them seemed impenetrable. But she knew she had to do this, to separate from each other for a while, no matter how brutally it ripped her apart to do so. 'I love you,' she whispered, then laid him back down on the sofa.

Frankie looked at her son one last time, then turned her back on him, her set jaw barely disguising her despair at what she was doing.

Elaine was fishing in her purse; she took out a few banknotes and handed them to her. 'It's all I have,' she said shortly. Frankie started to open her mouth, but Elaine interrupted her before she could speak. 'You can leave from the back,' she said urgently. 'You know how nosy people can be. The garden gate leads on to an alleyway that will take you round to the main road.'

Frankie nodded. She wanted to embrace Elaine, to thank her for what she was doing, but she knew it wouldn't be appropriate. Without looking back she moved quickly down the hallway towards the kitchen. The back door was open, so she strolled across the grass that covered the small garden and unbolted the large wooden gate at the bottom. She sprinted down the alleyway, stumbling occasionally but managing to keep to her feet, then peered round the corner when she reached the end. A couple of men were loitering on the other side of the road, but she was too far away to make out their faces, which meant they were too far away to see Frankie clearly, so she took a deep breath and walked swiftly in the other direction, holding her head low so as not to be recognized.

The further she walked from Elaine's house and the more distance she put between herself and Jasper, the more she thought her heart would burst. She could not afford to make an exhibition of herself, so she did her best to restrain her emotions, but she felt like a corked bottle ready to explode. It was the first time she had been without her son since he had been born, and it was as though she had left a little part of herself behind.

By evening, Frankie was back in London, her body aching for Jasper, just as it was aching for Keith.

The money Elaine had given her had been enough for a train ticket, some food and a pair of dark glasses, which she had bought in a shop in Croydon in an attempt to disguise herself from curious members of the public who might have seen her face in the papers. There was now only a handful of change left in her pocket as she sat on the edge of Waterloo Bridge, watching the setting sun turn the water a burning, vibrant red, waiting for night to fall.

Night-time was when the people she needed to speak to congregated. Strut's associates. The men she was going to have to face up to if she wanted her life back.

As the sun set and dusk fell, she removed her sunglasses, thinking that they were likely to bring attention to her rather than act as a disguise; but she didn't move from her position. After all, she had nowhere to go. Not yet. She just gazed at the skyline that she knew so well from tramping over the bridge day in, day out. How well she recognized it, and yet how alien it seemed, a stark reminder of those dark days of a previous lifetime.

Sitting there, absorbed in her thoughts, she suddenly became aware of something on the periphery of her vision. It was twenty metres or so away, towards the north side of the bridge, that a young couple were looking at her and whispering surreptitiously to themselves. Frankie remained absolutely still but continued to watch out of the corner of her eye. The man had a newspaper in his hand: the two of them looked at the front page, back at her, and then muttered something to themselves again.

Frankie knew in that instant that she had been recognized.

She had expected herself to panic if this happened, but instead a calmness descended upon her as she slowly pushed herself away from the side of the bridge and started walking south, away from the couple. Her pace was steady, measured – she didn't want them to know she had seen them – but she felt herself tense. Time seemed to happen in slow motion, but in fact she had walked only a few paces when she heard a voice behind her. 'Hey!' it shouted. 'Wait!'

'Shit,' Frankie muttered under her breath. She glanced over her shoulder and saw the man start running towards her, dodging the people who were walking the other way. All pretence of nonchalance dissolved as she started to flee, as quickly as her tired legs would allow.

Frankie was almost off the bridge when he caught up with her. She felt his hand on her shoulder as she stumbled to a stop then turned to face her pursuer. He was a young man, though his hair was thin, and he was stocky and strong-looking. Now that he had caught up with her, he didn't seem to know what to do; or perhaps he was just taken aback by the wildness in Frankie's eyes. In a matter of seconds her demeanour had changed from being thoughtful and quiet to that of a wild animal trapped in a corner. 'What do you want?' she hissed at him. 'Leave me alone.' Adrenaline was pumping through her body, not brought on by fear but by another emotion – raw desperation.

'It's you, isn't it?' the man said loudly so that passers-by could hear – though without exception they hurried past, not wanting to be part of this scene. 'The one the police want.'

Frankie shook her head without taking her steely blue eyes off his. His partner was by his side now. 'It's her,' she said, a certain excitement in her voice.

The man took a step forward, half in order to protect the girl, half to make his approach towards Frankie, but in his bravado he was scarcely prepared for what happened next. She stepped right up to him, so that he was only a hair's breadth away. Then she raised her knee as hard as she could and hit him sharply and viciously in the groin. The man bent double, gasping and crumpled over like an inflatable toy devoid of air, as his partner rushed to his aid.

Frankie ignored her. She knew from experience that she had to get away before the few people who had turned to come to the man's aid came at her mob-handed.

She flashed a malevolent glare at the woman, then ran again, disappearing from sight among the commuters heading down towards the station.

She cursed as she ran, a stream of expletives escaping her lips in a way that had not happened for years. The police would be called, there was no doubt about it – they'd be swarming the area within minutes if they thought she was still nearby. But she couldn't get away. She had to go to Newington Park, to revisit the scene of her crime, talk to people and find out where and when she could locate Strut's henchmen. She tore down Waterloo Road, ignoring the annoyed shouts of the people she occasionally bumped into, then hurtled across the busy roundabout of St George's Circus. Cars beeped furiously at her – one even had to swerve to miss her – but she kept running, desperately trying to put as much distance between the bridge and herself as she could, and in the shortest time possible. Once she reached the little park where the vagrants, the drunks and the junkies hung out, she would be anonymous once more.

There it was up ahead. Her chest ached with breathlessness and she was forced to slow down to a brisk walk. Just in time, because, as she did so, a police car came streaming past in the opposite direction, back towards Waterloo. She turned her head to check nobody was following her: there didn't seem to be anybody – she had got away. And then the familiar iron railings of the park were next to her.

She looked through, and couldn't believe what she saw.

Frankie stared into the park for a few moments, then took a deep breath and forced herself to run once more, up to the gate. It creaked open and she walked in, her glance darting quickly to all corners of the park, but there was no way her eyes were deceiving her. It was practically empty.

It had never occurred to her that this place would ever be cleaned up. The dustbin fires and hopeless vagrants were as much a part of the landscape as the very trees themselves. Stunned, she walked over to the corner of the park where she had fought with Strut. In her memory it had always been cold and claustrophobic; now it seemed open, spacious and, in the sympathetic half-light of dusk, even attractive. She closed her eyes and remembered the sight of Strut lying there, bleeding to death, with Mary whimpering nearby; when she opened them again, all she saw was grass, and a small patch of flowers.

In another corner of the park there was a figure, huddled over on a bench. As she walked towards him, Frankie could see that he was talking to himself – or to some imaginary companion. He had a grizzled, grey beard and wore an old woollen top with a hood that covered the top of his head, almost concealing his eyes. By the time she was a few metres away, Frankie could smell him: a pungent mixture of alcohol and neglect that she recognized so well but could no longer stomach – she resisted the impulse to gag as she stood there and watched him. The tramp looked up and noticed her; as he did, his incoherent mumbling became louder. His hands were shaking and his eyes rolling.

Frankie suppressed a feeling of fear that two years ago would not even have entered her head. She had to try and speak to him, to find out what had happened, where the vagrants who used the park had moved to, and to do that she needed to be in control. 'Where has everyone gone?' she asked in a clear voice. 'When did they clean this place up?'

The tramp fell silent.

'Where is everyone?' Frankie repeated her question.

Suddenly the tramp jumped up. As he did so, he roared – a strangely inhuman sound. Frankie was startled, but stood her ground, staring severely straight at him as he staggered towards her. His arms were flailing now, and the unidentifiable sounds he was making were peppered with curses. 'Fuck off . . .' She could barely make out the words. 'Fucking leave me alone . . . fuck off out of it.' As he approached, she could see his watery eyes, the whites red and bloodshot, the irises curiously uncoloured.

Still she stood her ground. Her look of contempt and distaste masked her pity, but he wasn't to know that. In an instant, perhaps realizing she wasn't to be frightened away, he stopped still, then turned and, muttering all the time, returned to the bench. He looked away and seemed to be ignoring her very presence.

Frankie knew his mind was shot, pickled by alcohol, poverty and fear. He probably didn't even know where *he* was, let alone anyone else. Just another casualty of the street. There was nothing she could do for him. More importantly, there was nothing he could do for her. Not in this state. Not now. Not ever.

She turned and left the park. Not once did she look back.

Sean Carter was deciding what to have for dinner when his mobile rang. It had been pizza last night – and the night before that, come to think of it: the staple fare of the hard-working bachelor. He was sifting through the bewildering array of takeaway menus that fell through the door of his ground-floor flat in south London when he heard the familiar jingle struggling to be heard in the front room over the sound of the television. For a moment he considered letting it ring, but not for long – you never know, it might be an invitation out, and he could do with a drink. He hurried into the front room and picked it up. 'Sean speaking.'

'DI Carter. This is James Cole, Avon and Somerset. We spoke yesterday.'

Carter strode over to the television and switched it off. 'What can I do for you, James?'

'More what I can do for you, really,' Cole replied. 'You wanted to know if there was any progress on the Francesca Mills case.'

'Have you found her?' He asked the question directly, urgently.

'No, we haven't. We've found another body. Same modus operandi.'

Carter felt a chill descend on him. 'Who is it?' he asked.

'Her name is Elaine Osbourne. She lives in Croydon. She's the mother of the guy Francesca Mills was living with – the one she killed.'

'Shit,' Carter swore under his breath. 'When did this happen?'

'Forensics are on the scene now – we'll know in an hour or so. But there's something else that doesn't make sense.'

'What?'

'The house was full of baby paraphernalia. Nappies, wipes – you know the kind of thing.'

Not really, Carter thought, but he was up to speed with what Cole was getting at. 'Francesca Mills?'

'Exactly.'

'Do you have any direct evidence that she had been in the house?'

'No. Nothing yet. Like I say, forensics are still working on it. But she had a child.'

'You think the child at Elaine Osbourne's was Mills's son?'

'That's our working hypothesis, but I haven't got much more to go on.' Cole's soft voice sounded tired. 'All I know is this: I've got a serial killer on my hands. If there's anything you can tell me that will help us find her, now would be the time.'

Carter remained silent. He knew Cole didn't believe Francesca Mills was innocent, and he didn't blame him. 'If I come up with anything,' he said finally, 'you'll be the first to know.'

'I'd appreciate that, Sean.' Cole rang off.

All thoughts of supper had disappeared from Carter's head. He paced up and down the flat, furiously trying to think of an explanation for what had happened. Things were looking increasingly bad for the Mills girl, and he could understand why Cole was so determined she was his killer. When Cole had said the words 'serial killer', somehow things had clicked into place. She fitted the profile: trauma at a young age, a history of abuse, a history of violence. But there were too many inconsistencies. He kept thinking of the look in her teacher's face when she had told him the terrible story of Francesca's past.

The baby was the key, he was sure of that. Everything

Francesca Mills was doing was designed to guarantee his safety. What if she had taken her son to his grandmother, believing it to be the only safe place he could be? He was sure that Francesca hadn't killed Elaine, which left two options. Either she had been there when Elaine's killers had arrived and had managed to escape with the child – unlikely, even given her remarkable capacity to disappear from these situations; or she had left the child with his grandmother. In that case, she didn't know Elaine was dead. And she didn't know her child was missing.

He dialled a number and put the phone to his ear again. 'Andrew Meeken.' The mild-mannered voice of his boss at the SFO came on the line.

'Andrew, it's Sean Carter. I need your help. It's urgent.'

'Tell me what you need.'

'A phone tap,' Carter replied. 'And that's just for starters . . .'

Frankie had never spent a night without Jasper since the day he had been born. It was the longest of her life.

She had found herself a shop doorway in a deserted part of town where neither the public, the police nor other vagrants would be likely to worry her – where it was she didn't know, as she had wandered aimlessly from Newington Park into the backstreets of south London that she only half remembered. Curled up in the doorway and overcome by tiredness, she had managed to grab an hour or two of fitful sleep, but her slumber was filled with the familiar old nightmares – only now they included her son. By the small hours she could bear it no more, so she got up and continued walking.

She felt directionless. When she had left Jasper, her plan had been to come to London and find out where Strut's associates were. What she was going to do when she found them she had no idea, but it hadn't occurred to her that the familiar faces that could have given her information would be gone, scattered across London. Now she was alone, without a plan and without her son. Every ounce of her wanted to rush back to Elaine's and pick him up, but she knew how dangerous that would be. Whatever happened, though, she had to speak to her, to check that Jasper was OK, and maybe hear him gurgle down the phone. She wandered for hours, waiting for day to come.

Frankie didn't know what time it was – five o'clock, maybe five-thirty, maybe six, even – when she decided she could wait no longer. Jasper would be awake by now, which meant that Elaine would be too, so even though she didn't know what she was going to say, she was determined to call. She found that she had gravitated – as she always did – towards the river, and along the south side of the Embankment. The imposing circular shape of the Millennium Wheel loomed above her as she headed south to the nearby main road where she found a phone booth and dialled Elaine's number.

It rang three times, then suddenly went silent. There was a click, and then another ring, after which it was answered immediately. Frankie's heart turned to ice when she realized the voice that answered was not that of Jasper's grandmother.

'Hello.' It was deep, and thickly accented. Frankie recognized it immediately – she had heard it only days ago.

'Who are you?' she whispered in horror. 'Where's Elaine? Where's Jasper?'

'Your son is well, for the moment,' the voice stated flatly. 'If you wish that to remain the case, you will do precisely what I say.'

It was a few moments before Frankie could speak. Her stomach was tied in knots, and an almost insufferable feeling of nausea threatened to overwhelm her. She gripped harder on the receiver, as if it had the power to steady her. 'What do you want?' was all she finally managed.

'At the end of this conversation, I will give you a telephone number. You will go to another telephone and call it. If I do not hear from you within ten minutes, you will never see your son again.'

Suddenly Frankie wanted to scream, to shout so many things at the faceless voice at the end of the phone; but her terror restrained her. 'Give it to me,' she said as she searched the floor for something to write with.

The man recited a number – it was easy to remember but Frankie wrote it on the palm of her hand anyway with a dirty old pen. 'I mean what I say,' he concluded. 'Ten minutes.' He spoke as if to end the conversation.

But Frankie could not leave it like that – every one of her motherly instincts had lit a fire in her heart that was smouldering malignantly. Whether he heard her or not she couldn't say, because she hung up the minute she had finished; but there was no way she could stop herself from speaking.

'If you harm my son,' she stated quite plainly, 'I *will* kill you.'

Chapter Sixteen

Frankie slammed the phone down and frantically looked around her. There were no other phone booths immediately in sight – should she continue down the road, or head up to the riverside walkway in order to find another one and make the call? Whatever, she had to stay focused; she had to push away the sense of desperation that was rising from the pit of her stomach; she had to stay calm. For Jasper's sake.

But then, as she was preparing to leave, something made her jump: the phone was ringing. Frankie stared at it, then looked around her. There was no one there, nobody who seemed to be waiting for a call. Tentatively she picked it up. 'Hello,' she said nervously.

'Francesca?' It was a man's voice again, but a different one this time, one Frankie did not recognize.

'Who's this?'

'You need to listen to me very carefully, Francesca.' The man spoke quickly, almost breathlessly. 'My name is Sean Carter. I'm a police officer. I was listening to the conversation you just had.'

Frankie shook her head, even though there was no one there to see her do it. 'I don't understand.'

'Elaine Osbourne is dead, Francesca.' She closed her eyes. Deep down, she had known that was the case. 'I think she was killed by the same person who murdered her son and your friend June Baird. My colleagues think that person is you.'

'I didn't kill them.' There was a plea in Frankie's voice.

'I know you didn't, Francesca. But I can only help you if you listen carefully to what I have to say. Do you understand?'

'Go on.' This was all happening too quickly for Frankie. As Carter had been speaking, her eyes had been darting all around her, catching the gaze of the early morning passers-by. Whenever someone returned her look, she felt an uncomfortable prickle of suspicion. Time was running out – all she wanted to do was hang up and find another phone to make her call, to check Jasper was still safe; but what this police officer was saying demanded to be heard.

'Calls to Elaine Osbourne's house are being diverted to the man you've just spoken to; but our technology allows us to listen in to any calls made to Elaine, and they know this. That's why he's given you a new number to call him at, a secure line that we won't be able to tap in to or trace.'

'But why do I need to call from a different phone myself?'

'Because they know we'll have traced this number and could listen in – if you use a different phone box, we won't be able to.'

'They've got my son,' Frankie said numbly, as if ignoring everything Carter had told her. 'I have to go and get him. I'm sorry.'

'Wait!' Carter spoke sharply. 'These men want something from you. As soon as they have it, they will kill you and your son. They've already killed four people that I know about. Trust me, they won't think twice about it.'

'Don't be stupid,' Frankie told him impatiently. 'I don't *have* anything.'

'Yes, you do, Francesca. Listen to me. Nineteen months ago you attacked a woman on Chelsea Bridge.'

Frankie remained silent.

'When that happened, you stole a small silver locket from around her neck.' He paused. 'Do you still have it?'

Frankie touched her hand to her neck: the locket was there against her skin, as it always was. But it was worthless, not even good for a few quid in a pawnbroker's shop. 'What are you talking about?' Francesca asked disparagingly.

'Have you still got it?' Carter was insistent.

'Yes.'

She heard the police officer exhale heavily. 'That's what they want. It's more than just a locket, Francesca. It's an electronic device that contains enough information to put some powerful people in prison for a very long time. They'll do anything to get it back. You have to help me make sure that never happens. Do you think you can do that for me, Francesca?'

Frankie's face was a picture of paranoid confusion. What was this guy talking about? None of it was even beginning to make sense, and she was overcome by her long-held mistrust of policemen. They'd never helped her before – why would they want to help her now? 'How do I know you're telling the truth?' she asked curtly.

'Take out the locket,' Carter urged her. 'Hold the clasp in for three seconds.'

Frankie did what she was told. The small USB storage device clicked out.

'Do you believe me now?'

Frankie gazed in astonishment at the locket and said nothing.

'Do you believe me, Francesca?' Carter repeated his question.

'It doesn't matter,' Frankie replied. 'They have my son. That's all I care about.'

'I told you,' Carter was sounding desperate now, 'they will kill you if you go to them.'

Frankie remained silent. 'What do you want me to do?' she asked after a while.

'Make the call. Find out where they want you to go, then call me back by dialling this number. Do you have a pen?'

'Yes.' Frankie found herself writing a second number onto the palm of her hand.

'I can arrange for armed officers to be on the scene within minutes.'

'What about my son?'

'We'll do everything we can to ensure that he's not harmed.'

Again Frankie shook her head. 'That's not good enough. I don't trust men with guns – the more there are, the more likely it is Jasper will get hurt. I won't do it.'

'Francesca, I promise. We can protect you and your son.'

'I don't think you can. I don't think you want to, either. How did these people find me in the first place?'

'Your fingerprints were discovered at the flower shop where you work.'

'Who by?'

Carter hesitated, almost as if he knew where Frankie was going with this. 'The police,' he replied grudgingly.

'Then if what you are saying is true, someone in the police must have passed this information on.'

'Francesca, I swear to you. The only people who know about this conversation are you and me.'

Frankie's mind was in turmoil. Half of her knew he was right – she had seen the look in the eyes of the man who had killed Keith. Grim and determined. The very thought of seeing him again filled her with fear, but there was really nothing else she could do. She slammed the phone down and ran off, looking for somewhere else to call her son's captor before time ran out.

'Francesca! Francesca, are you there?'

Carter held the phone to his ear, but there was no reply. She had hung up on him. 'Fuck!' he spat, before looking across the room at Mark Taylor and the team of three people at computers he was standing over. 'Was that long enough?' he asked. 'Did you get the trace?'

One of the men nodded. 'We got it. York Road, pay phone.'

'Is she going to play ball?' Taylor asked Carter abruptly.

The question hung in the air for a few moments, before Carter finally shook his head. 'No,' he said quietly. 'I don't think she is.'

'I'm on it, then.' Taylor spoke with sudden efficiency as he walked to the door. 'I'll get the nearest squad cars in the area to pick her up.'

As Taylor left, Carter slumped down in his chair. He sat there for several seconds before slamming his fist down hard on the table. 'Damn it,' he whispered under his breath, then jumped up and followed his colleague out of the door. 'Mark!' he called. 'Mark! Wait! It's too late – she'll be gone. If she sees squad cars coming after her, she'll never trust us . . .'

But he knew he'd had his chance. After the call from Cole the night before, he'd gone direct to Meeken, who explained the case to the Met commissioner and had it transferred back to London under Taylor, with input from Carter and the SFO. He had tried to talk her round, and she'd chosen not to help. Taylor wouldn't wait. He wouldn't have done so either, in his position.

Minutes later, four police cars screamed up to the phone booth Frankie had used, their blue lights flashing and sirens wailing. The officers jumped out, but there was nobody there. They looked up and down the road, still practically deserted because of the early hour, and saw nobody fitting the girl's description. One of them tapped a button on his radio, which hissed into life. 'No sign of her,' he said.

A pause, and then Taylor's voice came over the airwaves. 'Roger that.'

Frankie strode purposefully across the concourse of Waterloo Station and headed towards the row of public telephones. She glanced up at the enormous clock hanging from the ceiling: a quarter past six. No wonder the place was so empty. A few down-and-outs were sleeping in bundles in out-of-the-way corners, lucky not to have been moved on, but Frankie scarcely noticed them. Her brain churned over the conversation she had just had with the police officer, Sean Carter. She hated to admit it to herself, but there was something about him that she trusted – and trust wasn't something that came easily to Frankie. It had seemed to her that beneath everything there had been concern in his voice – what she didn't know was whether it was concern for her, or concern for something else. His own agenda. She couldn't say how dispensable he was going to find her – or her son.

None of the phones was being used. Frankie chose one at the end, inserted one of her few remaining coins and dialled the number. It was answered immediately. 'What took you so long?' It was the same thickly accented voice, but this time it sounded suspicious.

'You said ten minutes. I want to know that Jasper is OK.'

'You are not in a position to make demands, Miss Mills.'

Frankie snapped. 'Listen to me, you piece of shit,' she whispered down the phone line. 'If you don't give me some indication that my son is all right, I'm going straight to the police – I don't give a fuck what the consequences are for me.'

There was a pause. 'That would be most unwise of you,' the voice said flatly. 'But under the circumstances I will grant you this one concession. After that, you do precisely what I tell you to.' Frankie heard a rustling at the other end of the phone, and then the voice spoke again, slightly distant this time, as though he was talking to somebody else. 'Hit the child,' he said simply.

'No!' Frankie shouted down the phone, but it was too late. Instantly she heard the sound of Jasper's voice, wailing in sudden surprise and pain. 'Jasper!' she breathed. 'Sweetheart . . .'

But Jasper's voice was relegated to the distance again,

as the man's voice came back on the line. 'I will not tolerate any more delays. You of all people understand what I am prepared to do – have I made myself perfectly clear?'

Frankie said nothing. The words wouldn't come.

'As I told your partner minutes before I fired a bullet into his skull,' the man insisted impatiently, 'I do not like to repeat my questions. Have I made myself perfectly clear?'

'Yes,' Frankie replied in a small voice.

'Good. Where are you now?'

'Waterloo Station.'

'You will make your way to Aldgate East. Once there, turn down Commercial Road. Half a kilometre on your left you will see an Indian clothes shop with no name and a metal grille over the window. Next to it is a green door with three bells. It is unnumbered. You will ring the bottom bell five times and wait. Now, repeat those instructions to me.'

Frankie did as she was told, stutteringly repeating the salient points of the man's directions. In the background she could still hear Jasper's crying.

'Good,' the man sounded satisfied. His voice went distant again as he spoke to somebody else in the room. 'Shut the child up,' he said irritably. Frankie listened intently as Jasper's crying became quieter – it sounded as though he was being removed from the room. 'You will be watched as you leave Aldgate East. If anyone is following you, your son will be killed. If anyone else arrives at the address, your son will be killed. If you take longer than one hour from now, your son will be killed. Am I clear?'

'Yes, but . . .'

'No buts. Am I clear?'

'Yes.'

'Good. You have exactly one hour.' The line clicked as he hung up.

Frankie slammed the phone down in fury. Her body ached to hold Jasper in her arms, and she felt the hopelessness of her situation with the sharpness of a knife edge. That man, whoever he was, had mistreated her son, ordered his henchman to hit him without a second thought. He had killed Keith and his mother. He had killed June. Would he really shoot a small child? She had to get there. She had to do what she could to rescue him.

If only Keith were there. Then she wouldn't feel so helpless and alone.

Instantly the image of Keith, bound to the chair, with a look of uncontrollable fear in his eyes, sprang into her mind. She knew that whenever she thought of him, that horrific image would come to mind. Who was this man who reckoned he could do these things, give and take life like some malign god? Frankie had been running from people who wanted to interfere with her all her life – her stepfather, the pushers on the street, Bob Strut. Damn it, there was no way this lowlife was going to harm her child. There was no way she was going to let him be damaged in the way she had been for half her life.

Frankie had been backed into a corner; but as people had found out to their cost before now, that was when she was at her most dangerous.

She could do what the man said; or she could call the police. Or maybe there was a third option. Maybe she was not as helpless as everyone thought. An idea began to take shape in her head. It was risky, but not nearly so risky as doing nothing. Resolutely she picked up the phone, opened the palm of her left hand and dialled the number Carter had given her.

Frankie didn't have to wait – Carter sounded breathless when he picked up the phone. 'Francesca? Is that you?'

'I don't have long,' she replied in a deadpan voice.

'Have you spoken to him?'

'Yes.'

'Where is he?'

'I'm not going to tell you.'

'Francesca, you have to believe me – if you go and see him, you *will not* walk out of there alive.'

'It's a risk I'm prepared to take.'

'It's too much of a risk –' Carter sounded desperate.

'That's my decision,' Frankie interrupted him. 'But maybe we can help each other. I'm going to be perfectly frank with you – I don't like policemen. I don't trust them. What I'm about to do is for the sake of my son, but how do I know you're not going to take me into custody and put Jasper into care? How do I know I can trust you?'

There was a silence at the other end of the phone, almost as if Carter was deciding what to say. When he finally spoke, it was slowly and with precision. 'Francesca, listen to me. I know more about you than you think. I know why you ran away from home. I know about your stepfather. I know what he did to you.'

Frankie took a sharp intake of breath, and a hot flush of shame crept up from her neck; but her face remained expressionless. She said nothing.

'I believe you, Francesca,' Carter continued, quietly

persistent. 'I know you're not a murderer, and I know you've been through more than anyone should ever have to go through.'

'How did you find out?'

'I spoke to your teachers. They told me everything, and it all makes sense. I promise you, Francesca, I will do everything in my power to help you when this is all over. But you have to tell me where these men are, and you have to promise me that you will not take that locket to them.'

The locket. It was the cause of everything. Frankie gently put her fingers to it. She wanted to rip it off her neck and throw it away, but she knew it was the only bargaining tool she had.

'I'm not going to promise you anything.' She sounded almost businesslike, not wanting to allow the emotional advantage of this smooth-talking police officer to get to her. 'We're going to do this my way, or not at all. Do you understand?'

Carter hesitated. 'Go on,' he said tentatively.

'Before I hang up, I'm going to tell you where I am. Don't bother sending anyone to pick me up because I won't be here long enough for them to catch me. I'm meeting the men who have my son within the hour. After that, I'm going to persuade them to come back here with me. If you're on site, you can arrest them. I don't give a damn about your precious necklace. As far as I'm concerned, they can have it.'

'Francesca, there's no way they are going to come with you. They'll kill you, and I can't let that happen. You've been through too much to lose everything now. I want to help you, Francesca, I really do. We can sort everything

315

out but you have to trust me, this isn't the best way –'

'I've got something they want,' Frankie snapped, but her aggressiveness belied her true feelings. There was something about this man that she trusted. 'That puts me in control. It's *my* son, we'll do it *my* way. It's the only way I'm prepared to do this.'

The ultimatum hung in the air, before Carter replied. 'OK,' he said grudgingly. 'Where are you?'

Frankie breathed deeply before answering. 'Waterloo Station. Main concourse.' She put the phone down in its cradle.

When she turned round, she saw the station had filled up slightly. It was not busy by any means, but the tubes must have started up and a few early morning commuters were walking hurriedly across the previously empty expanse of the station concourse. Frankie pulled her dark glasses out of her pocket and put them on, not wanting to be recognized in the way she had been last night, and stepped purposefully away.

She knew she didn't have enough money to buy a tube ticket; she'd have to get some somehow – any way she could. A glance up at the station clock told her that it was twenty-five past six. Fifty minutes. She'd have to hurry.

But there was something else she needed to do first . . .

Sean Carter gently replaced the phone. Taylor was in the room with him, and had not taken his eyes off his face while he had been speaking to Francesca Mills. 'Well?' he asked the SFO officer.

'We need to move fast,' Carter told him.

'Where is she?'

316

'Waterloo Station. How quickly can armed officers get there?'

'Ten minutes, tops.'

'Good. We need every entrance covered, but make sure they stay out of sight. Issue all the shooters with the most recent picture of Francesca, but make sure they don't move in on her until whoever she's with is well inside the station. We don't want them making a run for it and escaping the perimeter.'

'And what about us?'

'We'll be on site, on the concourse. Hopefully we'll have the advantage – she doesn't know what we look like, but we should be able to recognize her and arrest whoever she's with before anything happens when she gets there.' He turned to leave the room.

'*If* she gets there,' Taylor muttered, following him out.

The huge clock read six-thirty as Frankie walked briskly out of the ladies' washrooms and up the steps to the station concourse. She had slicked her hair back with water, and still wore her dark glasses, though if she had worried about standing out she needn't have done: the whole place was buzzing much more than it had been when she had walked down to the ladies' five minutes previously and surrendered a twenty-pence piece to gain entry – it left only one more twenty-pence piece in her trouser pocket. The station announcer was booming a message over the tannoy system in huge, echoing tones, but Frankie didn't take in a word he said – the only sound she was aware of was that of her own heavy breathing as she walked across the concourse, not to the tube station but to the far end by the final overground train platform.

She had no money. There were only two ways she could make the tube journey: by trying to dodge her ticket, or by stealing the cash she needed. Both were risky, but there were no other options – there wasn't time to walk to where Jasper was being held, so she had to make the choice. She knew from her days on the streets that it was possible to get onto the tube without a ticket by jostling through the barriers with a fare-paying passenger. But a big station like this would be packed with attendants during the rush hour, all of them keeping a close eye on the barriers. Sometimes there were even teams of transport police hiding round corners, ready to check everyone's ticket. A half-hour delay with them could mean the difference between life and death for her son.

No, she told herself. Much better to go the other route. People never expected to be robbed first thing in the morning while hurrying to work, so their guard would be down. She could swipe a bag and lose herself before anyone even knew what was happening. At least, that was what she kept telling herself.

A small queue of commuters had formed at the two cash machines tucked away at the end of the station. They were men, mostly, all blending into one with their grey suits and almost identical briefcases, staring ahead and resolutely paying no attention to the hungry-looking tramp in his mid-forties who sat ever optimistically by the machine, mechanically asking each one to spare some change before they walked away tucking a wad of notes into their wallets.

As Frankie loitered, she eyed up her potential targets. She didn't have the time to be too fussy, but equally she would be foolish to choose someone who could overpower her easily. She decided on a man who was third in line. He was older than the rest, more slight of frame – Frankie hated herself for thinking it, but the kindly look on his face suggested that he would be an easier target than the others. Less suspecting. In an instant she thought of June. What would her friend think if she knew what Frankie was about to do? Would she judge her? Or would she understand that she was just doing what she had to? Frankie would never know.

The minutes passed interminably as she waited for the old man to take his turn – her eyes flickered between him and the huge clock face. She felt a strand of her slicked-back hair tumble onto her forehead, and she absent-mindedly flicked it back. Eventually he took his turn, removed the notes from the machine and walked away, placing his wallet in his right-hand coat pocket. Frankie fell in behind him as he walked away from the cash machines and towards a stall in the middle of the station. She stood behind him as he ordered a drink and then, as he removed the wallet from his pocket, she grabbed it. Before the man knew who had taken it, she had turned and was running towards the exit.

As she ran, she heard a voice behind her. 'Stop that woman!' it called. Frankie looked over her shoulder; the heavy frames of her dark glasses obscured her view some-what, but it seemed to her that there were no more than a couple of people in pursuit. They were still shouting, but the crowds didn't want to know – it was far easier not to get involved.

Frankie was a good way ahead of them as she tore through the main entrance of the station. At the top of the flight of stone steps that led down to the road, though, she stopped. Ripping off her shades and her jacket, she took up position by the wall, where she sat down, ruffled her hair forwards and put out the palms of her hands. There was nothing more anonymous than a beggar on the streets of London, and for once Frankie was glad to be able to use it to her advantage. Her pursuers ran straight past her – a younger man first, then the man she had robbed, trailing behind slightly – and down the steps to where two policemen in yellow jackets were standing. Frankie watched as the younger man talked animatedly to them – she couldn't hear what he was saying, but he was clearly explaining the nature of the attack – and pointed with a broad sweep of the arm in the direction away from the station.

Very slowly, and with an outward calm that belied her inner panic and thumping heart, Frankie stood up. Her jacket was in her arms, and underneath it she clutched the wallet firmly as she slipped unnoticed back into the station. Although every cell in her body screamed out to her to run, she maintained her slow pace as she walked across the concourse towards the escalators that led down to the tube station. As she did so, she glanced up at the clock.

Six-forty.

The escalators were only a few metres away, but it seemed as though it was taking an age to reach them. Frankie allowed herself to quicken her pace slightly and finally arrived at the top of the moving stairs.

She stepped onto them, and disappeared from sight.

Chapter Seventeen

Three minutes past seven.

Frankie emerged from Aldgate East station into the fringes of east London. The dark glasses had been replaced, the denim jacket put back on, and once she had removed the cash, the wallet had been surreptitiously discarded on the platform of Waterloo underground station. She felt bad for the old man, but there was nothing else she could have done.

A calm had descended upon her now, an unyielding sense of purpose. Sitting on the train she had ignored the strange looks her dark glasses and still-wet hair were attracting, instead just stared straight ahead, her body rocking in time with the movement of the train. And now, as she looked around her to get her bearings, she felt a similar sense of tranquillity. She *was* going to collect her son. She *was* going to make everything right again.

A glance at the local map in the tube station had told her where she had to walk – it wasn't an area she knew that well – and she had hurried up the steps to street level to be met by a roar of traffic that startled her for some reason. She had been up most of the night, in the relative quiet, and it was strange to see London transformed into its familiar, busy self. She crossed the road and headed in the direction she had been instructed, walking the opposite way to most of the other people on the pavement.

Frankie knew she was probably being followed – the

man on the phone had told her as much. It was a horrible feeling, and she felt that at the very least she wanted to know who her pursuers were. Out of the blue she stopped still, then moved to stand with her back to the nearest shop window, and looked carefully around. Almost nobody had taken any notice of her, but on the other side of the road she saw a man also standing still, making no pretence of the fact that he was staring directly at her. 'Why would he pretend?' Frankie muttered to herself. They wanted her to know that she was being followed. She looked left and right. Another man was there on the same side of the road as her, watching and waiting. She could see this guy's features more clearly: he looked commonplace in his jeans and a black T-shirt. He was wearing a Bluetooth mobile phone earpiece attachment and seemed to be talking quietly into it, but he was too far away for Frankie to be able to make out what he was saying. She returned his look with a stare filled with poison, then turned and continued on her way.

As Frankie made her way past the hotchpotch of run-down ethnic clothes stores, fast-food outlets and mini-marts that made up Commercial Road, she tried to keep her mind focused on the plan ahead. Eventually she found what she had come there for. The shop front was covered by a big metal grille, just as she had been told it would be, and unlike every other shop she had passed, it had no name. The grille was clamped down at the bottom by a series of sturdy-looking padlocks, and through the gaps Frankie could see a display of colourful saris and long rolls of cream-coloured silks. The men were still following her, but had stopped a short distance away when she had reached her destination, simply standing there watching her examine her surroundings. The one closest to her still appeared to be talking into his phone – clearly warning someone that she had arrived. She peered closer into the shop window. There were no lights on inside, no sign of occupancy, and the display itself, on closer examination, seemed to be covered in a layer of dust and neglect. Whoever was holding Jasper, she could tell, was not on the ground floor.

To her left, the green door she had been told about was old and dirty, its paint peeling off to reveal a grey undercoat that was itself blistered. None of the three bells along its side was marked with any name; Frankie allowed herself a few seconds to let her fingers linger over the bottom bell before she pressed.

One.

Two.

Three.

Four.

She paused, took a deep breath, and . . .

Five.

The final ring was longer than the others. Determined. She took her finger off the bell and waited.

For a full minute nothing happened. Frankie glanced nervously at the men watching her – they were busy looking around them, clearly checking that they hadn't missed anyone who might have been following her. She was just about to ring again when the door quietly clicked open. Frankie waited for it to be opened wide, but it remained ajar just a couple of inches so she gently pushed it.

Inside was a dark, narrow hallway leading to a flight of stairs. The light from outside flooded in, silhouetting

Frankie in the door frame; but the stairs themselves remained in darkness. Frankie peered up them, but it took a while for her eyes to adapt to the change in light, and it was only after a few moments that she realized there was a figure standing at the top. 'Close the door,' he said abruptly.

Frankie did as she was told and the entire hallway was plunged into darkness. She removed her sunglasses and put them in her pocket. As she stood there, she could still hear the morning rush-hour traffic outside, only muted now; and then her eyes blinked as a light was switched on. It was a bare bulb hanging from the ceiling by a long flex, and although it was dull, it momentarily stung Frankie's eyes. When she had got used to the light, she looked up the stairs again. The figure had disappeared, but at the top was an open door. Frankie felt her fists clenching – what good that would do she had no idea – and slowly she climbed the stairs, which creaked noisily beneath her feet.

The room into which she walked was sparsely furnished. Against the right-hand wall was a table with two modern-looking telephones attached by a jumble of wires to a grey metallic box. Next to them was a computer screen; Frankie glanced at it and saw a series of real-time images of the outside of the shop, as well as various points between there and the tube station and a black metal staircase that she assumed to be the back exit. A man sat in front of it, watching it closely – he didn't turn round to acknowledge Frankie's presence, he just stared at the screen.

In the far right-hand corner was another door, and just next to it an old brown sofa. On the floor was a threadbare rug covering the boards. Standing on the rug was the blond-haired man she had last seen in her kitchen, holding a gun to Keith's head. He was holding a gun now, too, only this time it was directed at her.

Frankie didn't want the emotion to show on her face, but she couldn't help it. She looked at the man with undisguised hate; he returned it with a cool, emotionless gaze. 'Where's my son?' Frankie spoke the words flatly.

The blond man shook his head. 'Not yet,' he told her. He turned his head to the man at the computer. 'Anything?'

'No, Andreas,' he replied. 'She wasn't followed.'

'Good.' He turned back to Frankie. 'You have something that doesn't belong to you. A necklace. Give it to me and I will let you have your child.'

Frankie stared straight into Andreas's piercing blue eyes. She lifted her chin boldly. This is it, she told herself. Take control now, or you'll never leave this place. 'I don't have it,' she stated firmly.

Andreas smiled, an unpleasant, patronizing smile, and he raised his gun so that it was pointing exactly at Frankie's head. 'You're lying,' he said. 'If you lie to me again, your son will live the last thirty seconds of his life as an orphan. Your partner told me that you wear this necklace all the time. Give it to me.'

'I told you, I don't have it,' she repeated, clearly and concisely.

Andreas nodded slowly, and he clicked the safety catch of his revolver.

'But I know where it is.'

Frankie heard her breath shaking as she stared at the gun barrel Andreas was pointing at her.

'What do you mean?' he breathed.

'I know what it is you want. I've known about the necklace ever since I first found it.' She hoped the lie did not register too plainly on her face, but Andreas was as inscrutable as ever, giving nothing away.

'I don't believe you.'

'Then you'd better kill me. But I've left a message with a friend explaining exactly where it is. If they don't hear from me within two hours, they will go straight to the police.' Her eyes tightened, and her voice dropped to a whisper. 'You don't think I'd be stupid enough to bring it here, do you?' she hissed.

Andreas remained perfectly still, but Frankie noticed a bead of sweat appearing on his forehead. 'Where is it?'

'I'm not telling you anything until I see Jasper.' The ultimatum crackled across the room, and for once Frankie saw a flicker of emotion pass across Andreas's face: anger and indecision. He clearly hadn't expected her to bite back. He lowered the gun and called to someone in the other room. 'Bring out the child.'

Frankie heard a chair scraping, and then another man came into the room. In his hands was a bundle, which he carried clumsily and inexpertly. He looked for guidance to Andreas, who nodded in Frankie's direction, then delivered Jasper into her arms.

The moment he did so, she let out a gasp of relief and walked quickly over to the sofa where she sat down with her sleeping son in her arms, then looked at his face: it was dirty and unkempt, and there was even what appeared to be the beginning of a bruise on the side of his face – she turned to Andreas, aghast, but he was expressionless once more. Gently Frankie unfolded the coarse brown blanket in which her son was wrapped to see that he was naked apart from a full nappy that had clearly not been changed for some time. His body was dirty, his eyes raw from crying. 'Oh my God,' she whispered hoarsely. 'What have you done to my child?' She desperately started to try and clean him up with an unsoiled corner of the blanket. As the rough cloth rubbed abrasively against his skin, he woke abruptly and started crying. Frankie recognized the sound immediately. 'He's hungry,' she said accusingly.

His gun still in his hand, Andreas walked up to them. He pressed the gun against Jasper's head. 'Where is it?' he repeated, speaking over the sound of Jasper's crying.

'Get me something clean to wrap my little boy in.'

Andreas shook his head. 'Not until you tell me where it is.'

'Waterloo Station.' She moved Jasper away from the gun.

'Where at Waterloo Station?'

'I'm not telling you until we're there. Now get me a clean blanket.'

Andreas gestured at his accomplice to do as she said, and he disappeared into another room. 'If you think you are leaving here before we have the necklace, you are very much mistaken, Miss Mills.'

The other man walked in with a blanket. Frankie took it, wrapped Jasper up and laid him on the sofa. Then she stood up, pulled herself to her full height and stepped inches away from Andreas. 'What do you think I've got to lose?' she asked him. 'I had three people in the whole world, and you killed two of them. I know perfectly well that if I wait here while you send somebody to retrieve the locket, I'll be dead before they return. I'm saying nothing until I'm in the middle of the station, with Jasper, in full view of everybody.' She sat down again and cuddled her little boy.

Andreas's breathing was heavy as he stood towering above the young woman and child in his custody. Frankie looked up at him to see an expression of indecision in his face, as though he were judging what to do with her. She remembered the sight of Keith's body, horribly wounded and tortured. Perhaps this man was deciding whether to deal with her in the same way. She did not know if she could withstand such pain in the way that Keith had done, but she couldn't give him the chance to find out. She returned his look with a gaze so steely and determined that it made Andreas's eyes momentarily flicker away. I won't crack, the unspoken conversation between them seemed to say. Whatever you do to me, I won't crack.

The man at the computer had turned away from the screen and was looking up at his boss. 'It's a trick, Andreas. Too dangerous.'

'Shut up,' Andreas snapped at him, suddenly overcome by his temper. 'You're supposed to be watching the cameras. Do your job.'

'There's no one following her, Andreas. Use your head. If you go to Waterloo with her, the police will be waiting.'

'I told you to shut up,' the blond man half screamed.

'Andreas –' The man started to argue, but in a flash Andreas had lifted his gun and fired it. It made a hushed thudding sound as he fired a bullet directly at the man's head. In an instant, one half of his face disintegrated and he was thrown backwards onto his screen, which tipped over as the man slumped slowly to the floor.

Frankie averted her eyes and held Jasper close to her.

'Jesus, Andreas, what the fuck do you think you're doing?' the man who had fetched Jasper's blanket asked.

'Shut up, Ryan, or you'll be next.' Andreas muttered the words under his breath. He turned back to Frankie. 'If this is a trap, and the police are waiting for us, you will both die before they have the chance to take me. Do you understand?'

'Why would the police be waiting for us?' Frankie still had her head turned away from the horrific sight of the dead body next to her, and she could feel her limbs trembling with the shock of what she had witnessed. 'What have they ever done for me? They think I'm a murderer – the moment they find me they'll chuck me in a cell and take my son away.' She turned to look at him; his face was a picture of cynicism. 'Look,' Frankie continued, trying to sound as dismissive as she could in the circumstances. 'I don't give a shit about your precious fucking locket. You can have it, as far as I'm concerned. I just want to make sure my son is safe, away from the police and away from bastards like you.' She spat the expletive as viciously as she could.

Andreas stared at her, as though trying to determine if she was telling the truth. Nobody spoke; it was an ominous, heavy silence, broken finally by the blond man. 'We will go there by car,' he said. 'Ryan, you will drive. You,' he waved his gun at Frankie, 'will sit next to him. I will sit in the back with the child. If there is any suggestion that we are being followed, I will kill him.'

'No,' Frankie replied. 'Jasper is not leaving my arms.'

Andreas bent down so that their faces were level. 'I'm beginning to have had enough of your demands. Ryan, take the child. If she speaks again, hit him, hard. If she speaks after that, kill him.'

'No!' Frankie shouted as Andreas turned away and Ryan started to tussle Jasper from her. He raised his fist and landed a heavy blow on the side of her face. Frankie felt the signet ring on his finger connect sharply with her cheekbone, and she momentarily lost her grip on her child. Before she knew it, he was in Ryan's arms, screaming. 'Give me my son!' she shouted, jumping up to grab him from Ryan; but she fell to the floor as Andreas brought his knee hard into her stomach, doubling her over in gasping pain. As she crouched on the floor, she felt the hard steel of Andreas's gun against the back of her head.

'Take the child to the car,' Andreas said to Ryan. 'Wait for us there. And for God's sake, shut him up.'

Ryan looked awkwardly at the child, then clumsily placed his hand over the baby's mouth. It didn't stop Jasper screaming, but it muted the sound somewhat and forced him to take quieter breaths through his nose. Ryan took the child into the back room, and Frankie heard a door click open and shut. Then silence.

Andreas bent down, grabbed a clump of her hair and pulled her up to her feet. Frankie gritted her teeth as he did so, unwilling to shout out and give him the satisfaction of knowing how much it hurt. He put the gun to her neck and whispered so close to her ear that she could feel his hot, heavy, cigarette breath on her. 'I want you to know that I like killing people,' he said, the accent in his voice strangely amplified by its quietness. 'I enjoyed killing your partner, and I enjoyed killing the two women. I'm deeply disappointed that I can't add you to the list.

But I will, if I get the vaguest impression that this is a set-up. I don't care if there are people around. Do you understand?'

Frankie nodded.

'Good. Walk slowly to the door.'

He removed the gun from Frankie's neck and prodded her in the back. She stumbled forward, regained her balance, then walked into the other room. It was a kitchen of sorts – a grimy stand-alone sink and a rickety old oven – with a back door on the far wall. Andreas grabbed a coat from the table and draped it over the gun that was still pointing in Frankie's direction. 'Go on,' he said.

Frankie opened the door and stepped out. She found herself at the top of the metal staircase she had seen on the computer monitor, and as she walked down it, her footsteps clattered and echoed from the high brick walls surrounding the courtyard it led to. Andreas nudged her towards a side alley leading out to the main road, then guided her down the street to where a rather nondescript estate car was waiting, its hazard warning lights flashing. The windows were darkly tinted, so it wasn't until Frankie had climbed inside to the passenger seat that she could be sure Jasper and Ryan were in there. Her son was quieter now, and Ryan looked straight ahead, with the occasional flicker of a glance in the rear-view mirror; he certainly made no attempt even to acknowledge Frankie's arrival in the car.

'Go,' Andreas told him as soon as they were all in, and Frankie heard the locks clunk shut.

It was rush hour and the car crawled interminably slowly through the traffic; Ryan seemed to be getting flustered by the stop-start journey, swearing under his breath and slamming his hands on the steering wheel; but if Andreas was frustrated, Frankie heard no sign of it from the seat behind her. Occasionally she would look over her shoulder to check on Jasper, but each time she felt the tap of the gun on the back of her head. 'Eyes forward,' Andreas would say. They were the only words he spoke until they reached Waterloo Bridge. As they did so, Andreas's mobile phone rang. 'Yes,' he answered, then was silent as he listened to whoever was at the other end. 'I'll have it in ten minutes.' He flipped the phone shut, and silence fell upon the car once more, broken only by Ryan's swearing and Jasper's whimpering.

As they pulled off the bridge, he spoke again. 'I think it's time you told me where it is.'

'Not until we're inside the station,' Frankie said through gritted teeth. 'I told you.'

She heard Andreas breathe deeply behind her. 'Ryan, park the car as near to the entrance as you can, somewhere you won't be moved on. Keep the engine running and wait for us.'

'For *you*,' Frankie corrected him. 'Jasper and I won't be coming back.'

Andreas said nothing.

Ryan had turned off Waterloo Road into one of the side streets that surrounded the station. He pulled up by the kerb. 'Stay where you are,' Andreas told Frankie. 'Don't get out of the car until I tell you to. Ryan, unlock the doors.' They clunked open again, and Andreas climbed out with Jasper. Frankie watched over her shoulder as the blond man walked round the back of the car, his gun still covered by the coat in his arms, then stood beside Frankie's door. 'Get out now,' he told her.

She opened her door and walked briskly to the pavement. 'Give me Jasper,' she told Andreas.

'No,' he shook his head. 'You get him when I get the necklace. Walk ahead of me and remember: my gun is aimed straight at the child. Don't make me nervous with any sudden movements.'

Frankie didn't reply; she just threw him a vicious look then began walking down the street. Behind her she could hear Jasper starting to cry again but she knew she had to keep her cool. It shouldn't be more than five minutes and she'd have him in her arms; and once that happened, she would never let go.

Within minutes she was walking up the steps to the station's main entrance and heading towards the centre of the concourse under the hanging clock. She turned round and looked for Andreas – he was trailing a few metres behind, his head not moving but his eyes darting in all directions. All around them, busy commuters were hurrying to and from trains, a sea of people crashing like waves into each other. Frankie looked nervously around.

Andreas approached her. 'Where is it?'

Frankie hesitated.

'I'm not going to ask you again.' The steely look in his eyes was determined, terrifying.

'I've hidden it in the ladies' toilets,' Frankie told him.

'Go and get it. Now.'

'Give me Jasper first.'

Andreas shook his head.

'I'm not doing anything until I've got my son.' Frankie tried to make herself sound uncompromising, but the words came out more shrilly than she had intended.

Andreas shrugged. He turned and started walking away,

333

and within seconds it was difficult to keep track of him with all the people criss-crossing between them. Frankie ran past the man holding her baby and stood in front of him. 'OK,' she told him. 'Wait here.'

Frankie turned her back on him and hurried towards the stairs that led down to the toilets. Before she descended, she looked behind her: Andreas was watching her intently. Their eyes locked for a moment, then she dragged her gaze away and rushed down the steps.

There was a short queue at the turnstile, and Frankie waited impatiently for the women in front of her to insert their twenty-pence pieces and make their way inside. It seemed to take for ever. Finally, though, it was her turn. She fished a coin out of her pocket, dropped it in the slot and pushed her way through. There were a number of women milling around, washing their hands or fixing their make-up. The cubicle where Frankie had hidden the locket, however, was in use, so she took up position at a sink where she could see it in the mirror, and started fiddling with her hair, damping it down with her hands, all the while keeping a keen eye on the cubicle door.

When it opened, there was a line of women waiting, but Frankie spun round quickly and barged in, knocking roughly into the shoulder of the woman who had just come out. 'Hey,' she complained, but Frankie ignored her as she slammed the door shut on herself and locked it firmly. There was no time now to gather her thoughts; she just had to get it all over with. And quickly.

She lifted the lid of the cistern. There, floating in the water, was a baby's bottle. And inside the bottle was the locket.

With trembling hands, Frankie fished it out and carefully took the locket out of the bottle, making sure no water got onto the device. Once it was safely in her hand, she pushed it into her pocket, then flushed the lavatory before opening the door and running out, to disparaging looks from the other women.

Frankie tore up the stairs and ran across the concourse to where she had left Andreas and Jasper. The one time she wanted to see the police, there was no sign of them. She had no choice but to trust this Sean Carter, and she knew that as soon as she had Jasper back in her arms the safest place she could be was in his custody. If he didn't show, she was going to have to trust that Andreas wouldn't dare shoot her with so many people around. She would demand Jasper from him, then throw the locket into the crowd – while he was trying to find it, she could make her escape. She had to have Jasper in her arms first, though.

But as she approached the spot, she stopped, a wave of nausea engulfing her.

They weren't there.

She looked around her in desperation. There was no sign. Maybe the police had arrived; maybe they had caught him. But there was nothing to suggest that was the case – the public were just milling around as they had been, with none of the shocked excitement that would have accompanied an arrest. Her eyes wide with horror, she started gasping irregularly, desperately trying to think what to do for the best.

And then she felt something against her back. She recognized it immediately. Andreas's gun. He was inches behind her. 'Start walking towards the exit. Now!' he whispered. Frankie stood still, then felt the gun dig further into her back. 'Walk!'

She stepped forward. Her eyes flickered left and right as she looked for any sign of a police presence, but there was nothing. Her mind was racing: it was all going wrong. Frankie cursed herself for thinking she could deal with this on her own, even though she knew deep down that there was no one else she could have trusted. She considered screaming, but with Jasper still held hostage she knew she couldn't risk it.

The entrance was getting nearer, and it seemed to Frankie as though the crowds were unfolding in front of her. She wished somebody would clumsily bump into her, give her an excuse to grab Jasper from the man behind her, but it didn't happen. Now she was at the top of the steps, ready to walk down; the moment she did so, she would be out of the station, and the police, if they were there at all, would have missed her. She hesitated. 'Walk!' Andreas told her again, only this time there seemed to be a note of restrained urgency in his voice.

And then, as she was taking her first pace down the steps, there was an eye-piercing flash of light.

Momentarily blinded, Frankie stumbled and felt herself tumble down the stone steps. It seemed to happen in slow motion. Her arm thudded excruciatingly against the corner of one of the steps, and then her head. As she fell, she could hear shouting all around her, adrenaline-filled voices. 'Don't move!' they were yelling. 'Everybody get down!'

There were screams. Frankie found herself at the bottom of the steps; she tried to push herself up using one arm, but a shot of pain crashed up it so she used the other one. People were running away from the stairs, and a group of five or six men had surrounded Andreas and the helplessly screaming Jasper. They wore black and grey riot gear, with thick bullet-proof vests and heavy metal helmets, and were carrying MP5K machine guns – all of them trained on Andreas. The blond man was backing away from them, looking around for a means of escape; but there was none and he clearly knew it. Frankie watched, her muscles frozen with shock, as Andreas allowed the coat covering the gun to fall slowly to the floor. The gun was pointing directly at the baby.

Nobody spoke. Nobody dared, it seemed. Andreas was the first to break the silence. 'Put your weapons down or I will kill the child,' he said clearly.

The police officers didn't move. They just kept their weapons pointing straight at him.

'I'm not messing around,' Andreas insisted. 'You have three seconds.'

Frankie looked directly at her son.

'Three,' Andreas counted down

'Do something!' she shouted at the men surrounding him, but still they stood their ground.

'Two.'

'Francesca!' She heard a voice off to her side and momentarily glanced in its direction to see a man in a leather jacket with several days' growth on his face. 'Stay where you are!'

'One.' For the first time Andreas's voice had a hint of desperation in it.

'Stop!' Frankie shouted, and with all the energy she could summon she threw herself up the stairs.

'Francesca!' The man behind her was calling again, but Frankie wasn't listening; all her attention was fixed on the man holding her child and the curl of his upper lip as he prepared to do the unthinkable. His eyes flickered in her direction as she ran towards him.

And then she heard the shot. It resounded through her like thunder.

She saw Jasper fall from Andreas's arms, naked, as the blanket around him unfurled. 'No!' she screamed, sounding scarcely human as she caught his tiny body before he hit the ground. 'Jasper!' she whimpered. 'Please, no!'

Above her there was movement. Andreas was falling, toppling down the stairs just as she had done only half a minute earlier. She glanced up in time to see a horrific exit wound on the front of his forehead before he fell face down by her side. Behind him a marksman had his gun pressed against his shoulder.

Frankie heard shouting. 'Get away! Get away!' But she didn't respond. Because in her arms, she realized, Jasper was still crying.

Unharmed.

Alive.

In his mother's arms.

It was finished. Francesca Mills doubled over in exhaustion and emotion, and wept as she had never wept before.

Sean Carter found himself frozen to the spot. Armed police were securing the area, shouting at passers-by to keep away and training their guns on the body sprawled down the steps; but even from the distance of a few metres he could see the river of blood flowing from the dead man's head – there was no possibility that he would be getting up again.

It took the firearms officers a little longer to come to the same conclusion, but eventually they lowered their weapons; elsewhere, snipers pulled their rifles away from the edges of the surrounding buildings and back out of sight. A cordon had been erected in seconds, and police vans were screaming up to the scene. One officer was trying to move the weeping girl holding the baby, but she was too distraught, too hysterical, even to listen. She just sat there, awkwardly holding her child – wrapped up in the jacket she had taken off – and burying her head against him. The other arm hung limply by her side. Carter ducked under the cordon and hurried up to talk to Francesca Mills.

'Francesca?'

There was no reply.

'Francesca, are you OK? Are you both OK?'

Nothing.

'Francesca, I'm Sean Carter. We spoke this morning. Please talk to me.'

Ever so slowly, Frankie raised her head to look at him. Carter was taken aback by her appearance. All he'd had to go on was the photograph found in her house, but she looked quite different now. The hair was shorter, of course, but there was a huge purple bruise across the side of her face and a haunted expression in her eyes that touched him. Pain, shock, and God knows whatever other emotion that was coursing through her. He put his hand on her shoulder. 'Francesca, listen to me. I want to get you and your child to hospital, check you're both all right.'

Frankie gazed numbly at him.

'Do you understand what I'm saying?'

She nodded.

'Good.' Carter shut his eyes briefly and took a deep breath. 'Francesca,' it seemed he could barely dare ask the question. 'Do you have the locket?'

Frankie appeared to consider the question for a moment. 'In my pocket,' she said weakly.

The relief on Carter's face was considerable. Frankie tried to fumble with her good hand into her pocket, but it was difficult because she was holding Jasper. 'Let me hold him for you,' Carter offered, but Frankie shook her head abruptly, eventually managing to pull the necklace out.

She dropped it into his hand. 'Take it,' she breathed. 'I never want to see it again.' She turned back to Jasper and held him close once more.

Carter considered questioning her further, but he could tell a traumatized witness when he saw one, and he knew it would be much better to wait until the shock of whatever hell she had just been through dissipated a little. He stood up and walked back down the stairs. On the other side of the cordon, his face a mystery, stood Mark Taylor. 'You get what you wanted?' he asked Carter shortly.

Sean nodded.

'Good,' Taylor continued. 'Then I suppose *I*'d better have a word with the elusive Francesca Mills.'

Carter put his hand gently on Taylor's arm. 'Not now, Mark. It's not the time.'

Taylor looked down at Carter's hand and brusquely pulled his arm away. 'Come on, Sean,' he said. 'I've got a job to do as well as you. She may not be guilty of your three murders, but she still has questions to answer for me.' He bent down under the cordon, then looked back at his colleague. Something unspoken passed between them, something that clearly made Taylor feel uncomfortable. He tore his gaze away from Carter and, with what looked like reluctance, walked up the steps towards Frankie.

'Francesca Mills?' His voice cracked slightly as he spoke, and Frankie raised her head to look at him. 'My name is DI Mark Taylor. I'm arresting you on suspicion of the manslaughter of Robert Alexander Strut. You do not have to say anything, but it may harm your defence if you do not mention when questioned something which you may later rely on in court. Anything you do say may be given in evidence.'

Frankie looked blankly at him, then turned her head to look directly at Carter, standing below her at the bottom of the stairs. Her face suddenly became etched with such hatred that Carter could not bear to see it.

The locket firmly in his grasp, he turned and walked away.

Chapter Eighteen

Ainsley Cooper sat behind his desk at the Ministry of Defence, somewhat distracted. The Chief of Defence Staff and the Under Secretary of State were briefing him on a range of matters, and Cooper was doing his best to absorb their information diligently. He didn't much like either man, and he knew the feeling of disregard was mutual, but they normally managed to maintain a cool civility. Today was different, though. Cooper was finding it difficult to keep his attention on what either man was telling him, and his lack of focus had not gone unnoticed; but he had been ignoring the irritated glances his two subordinates had been throwing at each other across the room. His mind was on other things.

He had last spoken to Andreas earlier that day, when he had been assured that everything was under control. Since then, nothing. He didn't dare phone him for fear of who might answer. Cooper might have been aggressive towards the man, but he did trust him to do his job well, and the fact that he had gone off the radar was deeply unnerving.

There was a knock on the door. Cooper raised an apologetic hand towards the Chief of Defence, who stopped in mid-sentence. 'Come!' he called.

The door clicked open, and his private secretary walked discreetly in. He whispered something to Cooper, then stood waiting for his instructions. 'They'll have to wait,' he said dismissively.

'They say it's urgent,' the private secretary replied, casting an uncomfortable glance at the two other men in the room.

Cooper's lips twitched as he tried to decide what to do. 'You'll have to excuse me, gentlemen,' he said finally. 'Perhaps you could wait for me next door. This shouldn't take long.'

The two men nodded soberly, stood up and left the room, with the private secretary following quietly behind them. Cooper remained seated at his desk, his face perfectly expressionless – the result of a career spent giving nothing away; but had anyone been there to notice, they would have observed that he was absent-mindedly scraping away at the cuticle of his right thumb, always a sure sign that he was on edge.

A minute or two later the door opened and his secretary ushered in two more men. One of them, smart and suited, he recognized, although he couldn't quite put a name to the face – it often happened in his line of work – but the other man, scruffy and unshaven, he had never seen before.

'Good afternoon, Sir Ainsley,' the man in the suit politely broke the ice. 'Andrew Meeken, Director of the Serious Fraud Office. This is Detective Inspector Sean Carter.'

'I hope this is important, Mr Meeken,' Cooper said, ignoring Carter and without any words of welcome. 'You're interrupting government business.'

'I wouldn't be here in person unless it was, Sir Ainsley, as I'm sure you are aware. I'll let DI Carter explain.'

Cooper nodded his head slowly and looked directly at Sean. 'Go ahead, Detective Inspector. But make it quick.'

'This won't take long, Sir Ainsley,' Carter told him. 'Over the past couple of years I have been investigating certain irregularities at Lenham, Borwick and Hargreaves. You are aware of them, I presume?'

'Vaguely.' Cooper didn't take his eyes off Carter.

'That's what I thought. We have photographs of you meeting with their chairman, Morgan Tunney.'

'I meet a lot of people in my line of work, Detective Inspector,' Cooper said impatiently.

'I'm sure. But certain information has come to light,' Sean continued delicately, 'in respect of which we believe you might be able to help us with our inquiries. We'd like you to accompany us to Scotland Yard.'

There was a meaningful silence, before Cooper turned back to Meeken. 'I am the Secretary of State for Defence,' he said quietly. 'I am more than happy to do anything I can to help the Serious Fraud Office, but I will do so here, and at a time convenient to myself. Have I made myself perfectly clear?'

Meeken smiled. 'Perfectly clear, Sir Ainsley.'

'Good.'

'Unfortunately it was DI Carter who was not completely clear in his explanation. What I believe he was trying to say was that you have a choice. Either you accompany us to Scotland Yard willingly, or DI Carter has the authority from the commissioner to arrest you on suspicion of fraud.'

'You're insane. I'm going to call security and have you removed.'

'Your security officers already have instructions to restrain you if you try to leave the building without my express permission, Sir Ainsley.' Meeken stood up and walked to one of the windows of the second-floor office. 'There are usually a few journalists milling around here, aren't there? A picture of the Secretary of State for Defence being bundled handcuffed into a police van would make fine front-page news for tomorrow's paper, don't you think?'

'Are you trying to blackmail me, Mr Meeken?'

'Not at all, Sir Ainsley. Just making sure you are aware of all the options open to you. You may be interested to know that Morgan Tunney was taken into custody about two hours ago. He's already begging for a plea bargain – I understand he actually broke down in tears in the police car.'

Cooper's eyes narrowed as a look of contempt crossed his face. 'You realize, I hope, that the Prime Minister is a close personal friend of mine?'

'Indeed,' Meeken replied calmly. 'The Prime Minister is being apprised of the situation as we speak. Now, are you going to let DI Carter accompany you to Scotland Yard?'

Cooper looked at the two men, who returned his gaze implacably. 'You wouldn't dare arrest me,' he whispered. 'It would be more than your jobs are worth. Go to hell.'

Meeken gave a regretful little shrug, then nodded at Carter. Sean approached Cooper. 'I'm arresting you on suspicion of fraud. You do not have to say anything, but it may harm your defence if you do not mention when questioned something which you may later rely on in court. Anything you do say may be given in evidence.'

He pulled a set of handcuffs out of his jacket pocket and approached the minister. 'Put these on, please.'

As he tried to close them round his wrists, Cooper pushed him away with surprising force. 'Don't be idiotic,' he snapped. 'You can't handcuff me, don't you know who I . . .'

But before he could finish, his voice trailed off. Carter had turned his back on him and was walking to the door. He nodded at someone outside, then held the door open for two security officers who came in and stood perfectly still, awaiting his instruction. He gave the handcuffs to one of them. 'Take the minister to the front reception,' he ordered. 'There are some police officers waiting there to escort him to Scotland Yard. He's under arrest. Make sure he doesn't leave your sight.'

'You seem quiet, Sean.' Meeken was in the passenger seat as they were driving in the evening traffic along the Embankment behind the police van that was transferring Ainsley Cooper to the Yard.

'Just tired,' Carter told him. 'It's been quite a couple of days. And I've been working on this for a long time.'

'You've done well,' Meeken acknowledged. 'But you know it's not finished yet. Cooper will pull all the strings he can to get himself off.'

'We're ready for him. By all accounts Morgan Tunney is squealing like a pig to slaughter – he's ready to admit his part in the fraud, and to give us details of the money his bank has passed Cooper's way, and how he did it.'

'And how did he do it?'

'Well, we're still deciphering the evidence Rosemary Gibson discovered. It's a pretty complicated paper trail, but from what we've managed to learn from Tunney so far, the arms company Rankin Systems were depositing some of the money they overcharged the British government at the bank. Tunney was then surreptitiously authorizing transfers of large sums into companies of which Cooper is either a major shareholder or on the board of directors. He's covered his tracks well, but if we're diligent we'll be able to trace the money through the company accounts back to him, I'm sure of it. It might take a bit of time, but the fraud charges will stick; and if Tunney wants to cut a deal he's going to have to help us nail the accessory to murder charges too. It's going to be a long few months for the minister.'

'Just don't underestimate how much the government will want to cover this up, Sean. It's political now – we might have had difficulty getting this far, but our problems are only just beginning, believe me. Have you arranged everything with regard to Francesca Mills?'

'Yeah, it's all sorted – at least, it will be by the morning.'

'What about Mark Taylor?'

'He's onside – I'd never have thought it of him, but I actually think he feels bad about arresting her. Not that there was much else he could have done, I suppose, but he seems to want to make things right. And his eyes lit up at the thought of a change of scene. There won't be any problem transferring him to the SFO, will there?'

'No, it's all in hand.'

'Good. I don't think you'll regret it. He's a bit rough around the edges, but he's decent enough. We were friends once. Who knows? Maybe we will be again. You sure you're happy for me to proceed with our plans for the Mills girl?'

Meeken nodded. 'The commissioner's received the authority he needs and has given the go-ahead. He wants to see this put to bed as much as we do – a glorious collaboration between the Met and the SFO. Won't do his career any harm at all.'

'Or yours,' Carter observed slyly.

Meeken smiled. 'Especially if we nail them with the accessory to murder charges as well as fraud. But it will be a tough call to get a jury to believe a street girl like her above a cabinet minister. We don't really have a choice about what to do with her if we're going to see this thing through.'

They drove in silence for a few moments before Meeken spoke again.

'And besides,' he said, 'it's the least we can do. If anyone needs a break, it's her.'

The hospital room in which Frankie lay was stark and white. Jasper lay beside her in a Perspex cot, asleep, as he had been for most of the past twenty-four hours. Sleep was the best thing for him, the doctor had said – he had undergone extreme trauma over the past couple of days, and this was the best way for him to recuperate. He had winked at her reassuringly. 'They're a lot tougher than they look,' he had said. 'He'll be fine. It's that arm of yours I'm more worried about.' Somehow that had made Frankie feel a little better.

She glanced, grim-faced, through the small pane of frosted glass in the door; the telltale silhouette of the policeman guarding her room was still there, wandering slowly back and forth. On first arriving here in the police van, her only thought had been to escape, but it soon became apparent to her that she was too exhausted even to sit up, let alone to run, and the cast around her arm made it difficult to hold Jasper. Yesterday had all been something of a blur, an endless stream of doctors and nurses, but she had slept well and deeply since then, made drowsy by the painkillers, the warm hospital room and the clean linen. But now her mind was racing again. She was in as much trouble as she'd ever been. How could she stop Jasper from being taken away? What could she do? With the police officer standing outside the room, not much. And she had to be honest with herself – maybe this was the best place for him, at least for the moment.

There was a knock on the door. Frankie didn't bother to answer, knowing that whoever it was would walk in anyway. But she was surprised to see who entered: Sean Carter. The past twenty-four hours had taken their toll on the officer – black rings under his eyes and a haggard look on his face, which was covered in even more stubble than before. He carried a newspaper in his hand. 'Good morning, Francesca.' He spoke almost sheepishly.

Frankie turned away, ignoring the man who had failed to keep his promise to help her.

Carter stood over the sleeping Jasper for a few seconds, before pulling up a chair to the side of Frankie's bed. 'How is he?' he asked.

'How does he look?' She still refused to look at him.

Carter accepted the reproach with a silent bow of his head. 'And you? How's that arm of yours?'

'Sprained. But they say it will fix.'

'I thought you'd like to see something.' Carter unfolded the paper and placed it on Frankie's bed. She read it without much interest: DEFENCE SECRETARY ARRESTED. A picture of a tall man with receding hair took up most of the front page. Frankie didn't know who it was, and she didn't care. 'That's all thanks to you,' Carter explained. 'The information we retrieved from that locket will put him and a lot of other people in prison for a very long time indeed.'

'I look forward to seeing them there,' Frankie replied bitterly, passing the newspaper back to him. Their eyes met. 'You said on the phone that you'd help me – well, you've got a weird way of doing it.'

'And I'm still going to, Francesca –' he started to say.

'Don't give me that bullshit,' Frankie snapped. 'My son could have been killed.'

'No, Francesca,' Carter had suddenly raised his voice. 'Your son is alive because of us. Don't forget that.'

Jasper stirred slightly, and they both looked at him. Somehow the sight of his sleeping face eased the tension between them and they sat in silence for a while. 'There's someone here to see you,' Carter said finally.

'I don't think so,' Frankie replied automatically. 'Everyone I know is dead, remember?'

'Not everyone. Francesca, it's your mother. She's downstairs. Your stepfather got wind of your arrest and she got in touch with DI Taylor immediately. You don't have to see her, of course, but . . .'

'But what?'

'Well, who knows when you'll see her again? Maybe you should say hello, for her sake if not for yours.'

'What do you know about it?' Frankie muttered.

'More than you think. I meant what I said on the phone – I know about your stepfather, and I believe you. But

I've spoken to your mother, and I really don't think she knew anything about it.'

Frankie couldn't find the words. She shook her head. 'It's in the past,' she told Carter, her voice unfriendly. 'I've moved on.'

Carter opened his mouth to argue, but clearly thought better of it. 'It's your decision. I'll ask your mother to leave.' He stood up and walked to the door.

'Wait.' Frankie stopped him before he left. 'Let her come in. I want her to see what she's done.'

Carter narrowed his eyes. 'OK,' he said finally. 'If that's what you want.'

Frankie felt the uncomfortable sensation of apprehension rising in her stomach as she waited for her mother to arrive. When she did, it was like one of the many dreams she had dreamed since leaving home – unreal, but with a horrifying sense of inevitability. The two policemen walked in first – Carter and Taylor – and stood on either side of the door as Harriet entered. As the years had passed, Frankie had found it difficult to bring a vision of her mother's face into her head, but now that she was in front of her, the sight overwhelmed her with memories. She looked older than Frankie remembered, and there was a sadness in her eyes that she did not recall. Along the side of her face there were the remnants of a bruise.

'Francesca,' she whispered.

Frankie didn't answer.

Harriet turned to look at the policemen on either side. 'Would you excuse us?' she asked in a wavering voice. Carter threw an inquiring glance at Frankie, who nodded her head almost imperceptibly, then the two of them walked out, closing the door softly behind them. Harriet stepped towards her daughter, her eyes flickering occasionally towards the baby asleep in the cot beside her. When she was barely a metre away, she stopped, then hurled herself forward and flung her arms around Francesca's neck. 'My Francesca,' she wailed. 'I thought you were dead.'

Frankie tried to pull away, but her mother was holding on to her too tightly for that. When she did let go, she finally allowed herself to take in the sight of Jasper. 'Is this my grandson?' she asked in a small voice. She stretched out her hand to touch the sleeping child on his cheek, but just as she was about to do so, her daughter spoke.

'Don't touch him.'

How often Frankie had imagined this moment. How often she had practised the lines in her head, rehearsed exactly what she wanted to say in minute detail, silently explaining to her mother just what had been brought about by her refusal to believe her daughter. But now that it came to it, she felt differently. More detached. Less inclined to share the truth of her life with this woman who had long since given up any right to be part of it.

Harriet looked at her with a confused expression. 'What do you mean?'

'He's not your grandson, because you're not my mother. Not any more. You haven't been part of my life for years, and I don't want you to be part of his.'

Harriet's eyes widened. 'You don't mean that, Francesca. You're exhausted. You're in shock. It's understandable . . .'

'Shut up!' Frankie hissed. 'Don't you dare pretend you understand me. You've no idea.'

'No,' Harriet snapped. 'No, I don't. What's happened to you, Francesca? How could you do these things?'

'If you'd listened to me about William, none of this would have happened.'

'Francesca, you're not still blaming William? Maybe he can help you now. He has contacts . . .'

'Oh Mum.' Frankie felt a curious mixture of contempt and pity. 'How can you be so blind? Tell me, where did you get that bruise on your face?'

Harriet touched her hand lightly to her cheek. 'It's nothing –' she started to say.

'He did it,' Frankie interrupted. 'Didn't he?'

'No.' She said the word firmly, but she refused to look at her daughter as she did so.

'I know what he's like, Mum. Believe me, I know better than anyone else. Get out of there while you can.'

Harriet turned her gaze back to her daughter; it was a scared, haunted look. 'I can't,' she whispered.

Frankie appeared unmoved. 'You have to. And you have to leave us alone. Jasper and me.'

'But you're my daughter. My little girl.'

'I *was* your daughter. But I'm a different person now – you said it yourself. Not the same little girl that ran scared all those years ago.'

Tears were streaming down Harriet's face now, but Frankie looked on severely. 'I'm sorry, Francesca,' her mother begged. 'Give me another chance. I can't bear losing you again.'

She made as if to hug her daughter again, but this time Frankie held up her good hand and warned her away. 'No.'

Shocked, her mother remained perfectly still, clearly

unsure how serious Frankie was being. 'You can always come home,' she whispered. 'I mean, if they . . .' She looked almost involuntarily at the door that the police officers were guarding.

'No,' Frankie said firmly. 'I can't. I don't have a home any more.'

They stared at each other, mother and daughter, the silence between them saying more than any words. Slowly, Frankie felt along the wall by her bed until her hand came in contact with a small switch. She pressed it briefly, and a few seconds later the door was opened slightly by Sean Carter. He looked inquiringly at her. 'Could you come in?' she asked him. 'Both of you. You all need to hear what I have to say.'

Carter and Taylor entered. They stood with uncharacteristic solemnity by the door while Frankie composed herself. 'Are you OK?' Carter asked.

'No,' she replied. She looked back at her mother, her mouth half open as though she was deciding whether or not to speak. 'What would happen if I gave you proof about my stepfather?' she asked finally.

'Francesca –' Her mother started to speak, but Taylor interrupted her.

'What do you mean?'

'Proof that he was abusing me.'

There was a shocked pause before Taylor replied, 'We'd arrest him. Immediately.'

'And what would happen then?'

'If he's found guilty he'd go to prison. And believe me, that's the last place a nonce wants to be.'

'Francesca,' her mother insisted. 'Think about what you're saying.'

'I have thought about it, Mum,' she replied, her voice deadpan. 'I've thought about it for a very long time.'

Her mother stood in silence as Frankie took a deep breath. And then she spoke. As she did so, her voice sounded monotone, emotionless, as if she was just reciting something that had been etched in her memory for years, revisited so often that the words now seemed devoid of meaning to her. She opened her eyes and turned to look at the two police officers. 'When my stepfather was abusing me, he used to take pictures. He would let me see them, and said that if I ever told anybody, he would show them to my friends. He kept them in a box in the attic, along with other photographs of other children.' Frankie gestured towards her mother; the blood had drained from Harriet's face as she stood there horrified. 'She knew nothing about it. If you search the attic, you'll find them there, unless he's destroyed them. But I doubt he has.'

Harriet's breathing became shaky and uncontrolled as she put her arm against the wall to support her suddenly frail-seeming body. 'Nobody believed me,' Frankie continued. 'Not even my own mother.' Her jaw was set, but as she looked directly at her mother once more, she could not avoid a tear from forming in her eyes. Slowly she wiped it away.

'You never told me about this.' Harriet seemed to have difficulty forming the words.

'I tried to!' Frankie snapped. 'You just weren't prepared to listen. You were *never* prepared to listen.'

Harriet took a faltering step towards her. 'I'm sorry, Francesca,' she whispered hoarsely. 'I'm so sorry. Let me prove it to you.'

'No. It's too late for that. You have to leave now.'

355

'Please don't send me away, Francesca.' Harriet's voice dripped with desperation.

But Frankie was shaking her head. 'Now, Mum,' she repeated firmly.

'Will I ever see you again?'

'I don't know.' Frankie spoke softly. 'One day, perhaps. But not for a very long time.'

Taylor walked up to Harriet and took her gently by the arm. 'We'll have to investigate this,' he said quietly. 'Someone will take you to the police station – you'll need to wait there for a while to give us time to search the attic. You won't be able to call your husband, I'm afraid.' He started to escort her from the room.

As Harriet approached the door, she stopped and fished in her handbag, pulling out a big bunch of keys. She rifled through them before locating the smallest one there was and handing it to Taylor. 'This is the key to the attic,' she told him. 'Make sure you find what you're looking for.' She turned back to look at her daughter. 'I want to help you, Francesca. Please let me.'

But Frankie was staring resolutely in the other direction.

And then her mother was gone.

Taylor re-entered the room immediately. 'I've called for someone to escort her back to the station,' he muttered to Carter, before turning back to Frankie and standing there in awkward silence. 'Why did you never tell anyone?' he asked finally.

'Because I was ashamed,' Frankie defended herself robustly. 'I still am. I didn't know where he kept the photos until the night I ran away and stumbled across them when I got the old coat from the attic. But by then it was too late – no one believed me.' She glanced over at the door. 'I hate my mother for what she's done, but I don't want her going back to him. Not that it's anything to you.'

The two men looked uncomfortable, clearly unsure what to say.

'In any case,' Frankie continued, 'if I'm going to go to prison, I don't see any reason why he shouldn't do too.'

Taylor and Carter looked at each other. 'Do you need any more convincing, Mark?' Sean asked him.

Taylor looked troubled as he replied, not to Carter but to Frankie. 'Look, Francesca, I know you don't give a shit about the fact that I've just been doing my job, but here's the bottom line. I know you killed Bob Strut in self-defence, and frankly I'm glad he's dead – he was a scumbag and the world's a better place without him. The CPS will no doubt come to the same conclusion, but these things take time, and with your history there will be no chance of bail. Your son will be taken into care, and even after you're acquitted there's no guarantee that you'll get custody of him. I'm sorry.'

'Spare it –' Frankie started to say, but she was interrupted by Carter.

'Just a minute,' he said, more than a little irritably. 'You're being discharged today, Francesca. Into custody. After that, you're likely to be put into a witness protection scheme. But it's not infallible. The people you've incriminated have already shown they have moles on the inside. It won't be hard for them to discover your location, and they may come after you. For revenge, if nothing else.'

Frankie was silent.

'What if you were given a second chance?' Carter asked her.

'What are you talking about?'

357

'Do you think you could start from scratch, just you and Jasper? Like you did before?'

Frankie looked at each man in turn. 'I don't understand.'

'Just answer the question, Francesca. Do you think you can do it? Think carefully – it's important.'

But Frankie didn't need to think. She had lived on the streets and on the run. She had learned how to cope, how to depend on herself and nobody else. She knew she could do it. Mutely, but with a serious, wide-eyed expression, she nodded her head.

Carter opened the briefcase he was carrying and pulled out a brown padded envelope. He handed it to Frankie. 'In here you'll find a passport, birth certificates and all the documents you need for you and Jasper to start a new life with new identities.'

Frankie looked at him in astonishment. 'How?' she asked.

Carter shrugged. 'Ways and means. But there's more. The fraud we uncovered with your help involved an arms company and a merchant bank. In circumstances like this, it's not unheard of for them to make a reward to our informants. They pass it on to us, so the informants can stay anonymous. In there you'll find a bank book with twenty thousand pounds deposited in your new name.'

Frankie was finding it difficult to believe what she was hearing. 'That's all there is to it?'

'Not quite,' Carter told her. 'Permission for these documents comes from the highest authority; the same authority has ordered that all evidence of their issue be destroyed. The same goes for all your past records, even your fingerprints. Everything has been destroyed,

Francesca – anything that can lead people to you. To all intents and purposes, Francesca Mills doesn't exist any more, and apart from the three of us, only a handful of people – trustworthy people – know about it. It's the only way to keep you safe. But now you have to disappear.' He smiled. 'But then, you're good at that, aren't you?'

Frankie looked at them both as it gradually became clear to her what they were saying. She nodded her head.

Carter took a deep breath. 'OK, Francesca,' he said. 'If you're prepared to take the risks, here's what we're going to do.'

Ten minutes later, Carter and Taylor were outside the room, talking to the police officer on guard. 'She's being transferred,' Carter told him. 'Holloway.'

The officer raised an inquiring eyebrow.

'The commissioner wants her under high security.'

Carter waved a document under the policeman's nose, but he didn't examine it thoroughly – it was enough for him that he was receiving orders from a superior. 'OK, sir,' he said respectfully.

Carter knocked on the door, then he and Taylor walked back into the room where Frankie was now fully dressed, her arm in a sling over her jacket. 'Are you ready?'

Frankie nodded. She picked Jasper out of the cot, then handed him to Carter. Taylor took her good arm, then clipped some handcuffs around the wrist, attaching the other link to his own. 'Let's go,' he said.

The three of them walked through the busy corridors of the hospital, a curious-looking trio. Carter was aware of Frankie staring straight ahead, ignoring the stares of doctors and patients alike who had noticed the fact that she was handcuffed to a man who, although not in uniform, clearly had the demeanour of a police officer. He had to hand it to her – she seemed to be keeping it together despite everything.

Carter blinked as they walked out of the hospital into the bright sunlight, and he felt Jasper move his head away from the glare as he did so. Amazing kid, he thought to himself. Good as gold, considering what he'd been through. He felt good about what he was about to do.

They approached the car. Wordlessly, Taylor removed his key fob from his pocket and clicked the central-locking system open. Then he undid the handcuffs and opened up the back door for Frankie. She climbed in, and Carter handed Jasper gently over to her. 'Thank you,' she said, and even allowed herself to smile nervously at him. Carter returned the smile with encouragement, then shut the door and walked round to take his place in the passenger seat next to Taylor. Within seconds the door had been locked again and they were driving off.

As they pulled out of the car park and onto Lambeth Palace Road, Carter looked over his shoulder to the back seat. 'Do you have everything?' he asked Frankie.

She nodded, and patted the inside pocket of her jacket where she had stashed all the documents.

'Good. Remember to lay low for a while. It's unlikely the Met will put too many resources into finding you, but if you crop up doing anything out of the ordinary, they'll have no choice but to follow it up. So no mugging defenceless women and stealing their jewellery, OK?' He winked at her.

Frankie looked a bit sheepish. 'OK,' she replied. Her face turned serious again. 'What about my stepfather?'

'If what you say is true,' Taylor answered her question, 'he'll be in custody before the end of the day. I'll see to it personally.'

Frankie slowly nodded her head, her face a picture of mixed emotions, but she said nothing as the car made its way over Westminster Bridge. She looked out of the window and saw the grand sight of the Houses of Parliament. The sun sparkled and danced on the water of the Thames flowing in front of it, and Frankie drank in the sight that she knew she wouldn't see again for a very long time, if at all.

The car pulled up at a set of traffic lights by the side of St James's Park. Around them were crowds of people – tourists, mostly, with their cameras and rucksacks, there to experience the postcard delights of London. The traffic was busy, and she heard the occasional beep from drivers frustrated by the increasingly oppressive heat of the day. 'OK, Francesca,' Carter said, looking straight ahead. 'Now!'

In the vanity mirror he saw Frankie gently moving Jasper off her lap and into the seat next to her. She pulled out her dark glasses, put them on, took a deep breath, then sharply jerked her good elbow, protected by the sleeve of her jacket, against the window.

Nothing happened.

She did it again.

And again. This time the glass shattered, some of it falling onto her sleeve, but most tinkling in shards onto the road. Frankie put her arm out and opened the door from the outside, shook the glass from her sleeve, then gently picked up Jasper and eased out of the car. She didn't say a word.

'Good luck,' Carter said under his breath, but by that time Frankie was already pacing purposefully away. She didn't look back as she headed west along the side of the park.

Taylor switched his police radio on and it crackled into life. 'DI Taylor,' he said urgently into the radio. 'Request assistance. Suspect escaped, woman, early twenties, short dark hair, carrying a small child.'

'Copy that,' the operator crackled back. 'Suspect last seen headed in which direction?'

Taylor and Carter looked at each other. Sean nodded at him encouragingly. 'Suspect last seen headed east. We are in pursuit now.' He switched his siren on, pulled the car out, and did a U-turn across the width of the road.

They screamed off in the opposite direction, and as they did so Carter looked back over his shoulder through the rear windscreen. He thought he could just make her out, taller than most people around her, head held high and a confident stride in her step that made her stand out from the summer crowd.

Then she turned a corner, and was gone from sight.

Epilogue

A Year Later

Sean Carter was eating chocolate and glancing through a sheaf of photographs when the door opened and Mark Taylor burst in. 'It's customary to knock,' he said mildly.

'It's customary to share the bloody chocolate.' Taylor's face showed no sign of humour; Carter smiled anyway. Gradually, tentatively, the old friendship had started to return. And although Taylor had been his grumpy old self ever since moving to the SFO, bloody rude to him on an almost daily basis, Sean had known him for long enough to spot the telltale signs that the world felt a little less heavy on his shoulders. Taylor had never said thank you to Sean for his part in getting him moved to the SFO, but you couldn't expect miracles. He was content with the odd offer of a pint, the occasional reminiscence about old times. And to be fair to Taylor, he had blossomed in his job. Meeken seemed genuinely pleased with his new appointment, and Carter had been glad to have the company of somebody a bit more on his wavelength, especially during the rigorous process of preparing the Ainsley Cooper case for trial. But now it looked as if the government were hanging Cooper out to dry – he and Morgan Tunney were both facing the rest of their lives behind bars, and the SFO were smelling of roses. Deep down, Carter knew that Taylor enjoyed being part of that.

'You wanted to see me?' Taylor asked cursorily. 'I'm about to leave – I don't keep your hours.'

'Heard any news about William Johnson?' Carter asked conversationally, breaking off another piece of chocolate and popping it into his mouth before offering a piece to his friend.

'Sentenced last week to eight years.'

'Where?'

'Transferred from Maidstone to the Scrubs upon sentence.'

The Scrubs was the name all police gave to one of the hardest prisons in the country: Wormwood Scrubs.

Carter winced. 'Nasty.'

'My heart bleeds for him.'

'What about the wife?'

Taylor shrugged. 'Not my business. Is that all you dragged me down the corridor to ask?'

'No, actually. I thought you might like to see these.' He handed the photographs he had been flicking through to his colleague, then sat back in his chair and watched Taylor's face as he looked at the images. He was expressionless, but his lack of acerbic commentary told Carter a great deal. Wordlessly Taylor handed the pictures back.

'Bit risky, isn't it? Having her watched, I mean.'

'It's OK, Mark. I was very discreet, and I just wanted to keep an eye on her. She's settling in nicely, don't you think? Looks like the Mediterranean sunshine agrees with her.' Carter sounded almost proud of himself as he looked through the photographs once again. Francesca Mills looked a lot different to how she had a year ago. Her short black hair had grown long again, and had been allowed to revert to its original blonde colour. Some of the grainy surveillance pictures showed her pottering around in the little flower shop Carter knew she owned in the square of a picturesque village hidden deep in the hills of Provence, in the south of France; others showed her playing with a delightful little boy and a small crowd of other children. There was a look on her face that Carter couldn't quite identify. Not happiness, exactly, but . . . serenity. That was it. She looked serene.

'So are you going to carry on stalking her,' Taylor interrupted his thoughts, 'or are you just going to let her be?'

The two policemen looked at each other for a moment. 'I think I'm just going to let her be, Mark,' Carter said finally. 'I don't think she needs anything else from us, do you?'

And without waiting for an answer, he stood up and walked to the side of the room where a small document shredder sat on a table next to a fax machine. He switched the shredder on and, one by one, passed the photographs through its grinding teeth. Then he turned back to his colleague and smiled.

'Time to go home, I think.'

If you enjoyed *Frankie*, look out for Kevin Lewis'
first novel,

Kaitlyn

Read on for a taster . . .

Chapter One

April 1976

'How much longer?'

There was an unmistakable note of panic and desperation in Peter Connelly's voice as he shouted to be heard above the noise of the wailing siren.

'Ten minutes tops,' came the reply.

'Blood pressure's dropping,' said Peter. 'Better give the hospital a call.'

In the front of the ambulance Diana Jameson jerked the heavy steering wheel hard to the right, narrowly missing a blue Mini Cooper that seemed to have come out of nowhere, then reached for the radio. 'Control, can you put me through to ST.'

She was doing nearly 60mph now, weaving her way through the late-night London traffic, her eyes tightly focused on the road ahead. A series of clicks followed by a short buzz and then a muffled cough told her she had got through to the dispatcher at St Thomas's.

'What have you got, Diana?'

'We're coming in hot. Male, eighteen months, major multiple chest trauma. Looks like a collapsed lung and torn windpipe. Pete says his BP's falling fast.'

'What's your ETA?'

'Seven minutes.'

'OK. Bring him in on bay number two. We'll be ready.'

Peter Connelly took his eyes off his patient for a fraction of a second to look at the woman and young girl – the boy's mother and sister – sitting on the red bench opposite him in the back of the swaying ambulance. Both had blank, shell-shocked faces. He was just about to say something to reassure them when the steady beep of the heart monitor suddenly changed to a single, terrifying, BEEEEEEEEEEEEEEEEEEEEEEEEEEEP.

'Shit.'

'You need me to pull over?' Diana shouted.

Peter didn't answer. The blue, pursed lips, the twitching chest muscles and the rapidly dilating pupils told him he had only seconds to act. He inserted a second IV needle into the little boy's arm, hooked it up to a bag of plasma, then ripped open a resuscitation kit.

A quick glance at the heart monitor: 36. The alarm had sounded when the boy's pulse had fallen below 40. If it dropped below 25 his heart would stop for certain and the chances of getting it started again would be almost zero. Out of the corner of his eye Peter could see silent tears running down the little girl's face as he started to prise open the boy's mouth, ready to insert the tube. It's hard enough to get it right in a hospital and almost impossible in a fast-moving ambulance when the patient already has a torn windpipe. Peter peered into the boy's mouth, deep into the shadow of the hole past his vocal cords, and shot the tube forward.

Two pumps on the air bag and the machine came back to life, pushing out a series of steady beeps. Peter gently stroked the boy's arm. 'How we doing, Diana?'

'Just coming up to Waterloo. We'll be there in less than a minute.'

Directly outside the sliding doors of bay number two a small group of nurses in short-sleeved shirts were shuffling about and rubbing the bare skin of their arms to keep warm. A moment later Dr Nathan Bishop, the lead paediatric trauma surgeon, arrived. 'Heads up, ladies, I've got a feeling this is going to be an all-nighter,' he said softly.

Pale-blue flashes lit up the night sky and the wail of the sirens grew from faint to deafeningly loud as the ambulance pulled into view. The team shifted into their final positions. There was no need for words – they all knew what they had to do and that they had to make every second count.

The back doors flew open even before the tyres had screeched to a halt. 'He almost arrested twice on the way over but I think I've managed to stabilise him. Left lung's collapsed and there's extensive trauma,' Peter explained breathlessly as he clambered out. 'I could only get the tube halfway in because the windpipe's torn.' The expanding legs of the trolley bed clattered on to the tarmac and moments later the patient came into view.

He was tiny, curled up in the foetal position and naked apart from a soiled nappy wrapped round his crotch. According to the log, Christopher Wilson was eighteen months old but at that moment he looked so frail and undernourished that he could easily have passed for half that age.

Bishop gasped – virtually every inch of the boy's body was covered with purple bruises. In twenty years on the job it was one of the worst things he had ever seen. The original 999 call said the boy had fallen down a flight of stairs but it took only a quick glance for Bishop to know that simply wasn't true. He could see the impressions left by the fingers that had been fixed round the child's throat, the deep red stains under the skin where veins had been ruptured; the circular impact marks left by the ring that whoever punched him had been wearing.

They were running through the brightly lit corridors now, Bishop barking out instructions as his fingers danced gently over the boy's body and the fluorescent tubes flashed by overhead. 'We need to get the laryngoscope in there right away. Hook up the ECG and administer epinephrine followed by an atropine drip. Come on, people, let's go.'

By the time the trolley had smashed through the

heavy rubber-edged double doors into the sterile environment of Theatre One, Dr Bishop was in the adjacent sink room scrubbing up. 'Where are the parents?' he asked the senior nurse.

'The mother, she's the one who called it in, is being taken to the family room. Daughter's going there too.'

Dr Bishop thought for a moment while using a small brush to scrub his nails vigorously.

'How old is the daughter?'

The nurse shrugged. 'Dunno. Young. Five, maybe six.'

Dr Bishop nodded thoughtfully as he inspected his fingers for any remaining traces of dirt. 'OK. I need to get into the theatre so do me a favour, ID the mum to reception so that everyone knows who she is and what she looks like. And get someone to keep an eye on her to make sure nothing happens to the other kid.'

'And then what?'

'Then call the police.'